D0475525

DATE DUE 22

THE GHOSTS OF ELKHORN

THE GHOSTS OF ELKHORN

KERRY NEWCOMB
AND
FRANK SCHAEFER

THE VIKING PRESS / NEW YORK

LIBRARY OF CONGRESS CATALOGING IN PUBLICATION DATA

Newcomb, Kerry.
The ghosts of Elkhorn.
I. Schaefer, Frank, joint author.   II. Title.
PS3564.E875G47   813′54   81-51890
ISBN 0-670-33819-2   AACR2

Printed in the United States of America
Set in Caledonia

For Ann and Paul Newcomb

*

For Frankie

*

Special thanks to Aaron Priest, agent and friend

THE GHOSTS OF ELKHORN

1

The wind spilled down the mountain, kicked up the dust on Main Street, slid through the broken front door of the funeral parlor, and woke the Wind River Kid. Dreams faded before the reality of creaking joints, tired muscles, cells that refused to regenerate, and veins that creaked with blood. He smacked his lips and groaned, worked a kink out of his left shoulder. He groaned again and scratched his belly. He rubbed the grit out of his eyes and stretched carefully. It was a full five minutes before he lay still again, sighed, and ruefully admitted to himself that damn and by damn he was awake.

Outside, patched with a mid-September frost, the town of Elkhorn, population one, waited. The wind returned and stirred the dried leaves pressed against the walls of the defunct funeral parlor. They sounded somewhat like the rattle of chains in a ghost house, Wind River thought, then reconsidered, and decided more like the clatter of loose false teeth. There was a certain comfort to be gained in knowing one was beset by choppers rather than the spirits of the dead. Lying soft and warm under the covers, he thought about that for a while, too, and finally concluded that he was blessed with the best of both possible worlds, if best was the word. On that note, he sat up and looked around for the ghost of Aden Creed.

Wind River's frown, as sour as the taste in his mouth, faded when he saw he was alone. The morning grew a little brighter with the knowledge he'd be able to wash in peace and quiet. Cheered, he swiveled sideways and, careful not to touch the floor, pulled on the socks he'd put under his pillow the night before. Warm feet on cold boards made a big difference. So did the new sun that bounced a yellow beam of light off the water in the basin and turned his hair as gold as it had been when he was a child. Suddenly pensive, he glanced back over the seventy-one years and tried to remember what it had been like to be a child, what it had been like being born, to be so close to a woman that he was inside her, to be loved like that. He had no idea of what his mother looked like, but he hoped her face wasn't as ugly and gnarled as his reflection made him out to be.

The taste in his mouth was back. Wind River scooped up a handful of water, held it in his mouth until it was warm enough not to hurt his teeth, and then swished it around a minute before spitting it into the hole in the corner. Hell. He wasn't all that bad off, he thought, moving to the mirror he'd lugged up from Widow Guthrie's dress shop. He'd had his share of ladies in a youth that had stretched from then until now. He walked straight and steady, and his belly was still flat. He had his hair, long, white curls that caught at his shirt collar, which was more than could be said for Aden Creed, and he did not drool like Lode Benedict down in Mountain City.

A shingle flapped on the roof. Wind River glanced around to see if Creed had entered, but he was still alone. Muttering thanks, he crossed to the stove to build up the fire. That was another part of the morning he liked, especially when fall was in the air. He poked ashes down the grate, blew on the coals until they glowed red. He dropped in a handful of dried pine needles and twigs. When red flames followed the sweet smell of smoke, he added split wood, closed the lid, and slid the coffeepot into place.

Different paths had brought the Wind River Kid and Aden Creed to the town of Elkhorn. Creed had been carried there in 1868 after getting caught in a slide that nearly tore off his left leg. By the time the leg mended, he and Angelina at the Victorian Palace were thick. He had forsaken his mountains to stay with her in Elkhorn. A year later in the winter of 1869, when a skinny, bedraggled, half-frozen and near-starved thirteen-year-old boy staggered into the rough and roaring mining town, Creed and Angelina took him in, fed him, and nursed him back to health.

The runaway had had no parents and no place to go, so it was only natural he should stay. Creed, the gimp-legged mountain man who had always wanted a son, took the boy under his wing. He taught him mountain lore: where to sleep in a storm, how to hunt without sound, build a fire without smoke, walk without leaving tracks. He taught him the taste of strong coffee and thin mountain air, the red smell of beaver blood, and how to wait through the lonely vigil of the hunt and pass the test of stinging snow. But Angelina was there, and she was another kind of teacher who preferred steak served on fine china and knew the difference between good wine and bad. She instructed Wind River in the sophisticated ways of men who wore silk vests and sent cards dancing from manicured fingers and always won at the gaming tables.

Creed had argued, remonstrated, berated, and derided, but to no avail. There were the mountains, and there were the wild and sinful ways of men, and the boy chose the latter with scarce an apology or word of thanks. A man of eighteen, he put on his suit, packed his carpetbag, saddled one of Creed's pack mules, and rode out of Elkhorn for Mountain City, Denver, and points east and south, into a world of gaiety and light, a world of luck and the men who ruled it, a world of sweet soiled doves who cooed and dipped their low-cut bodices and gazed in open avariciousness at the stacks of chips and showered their lusty treasures on the winners, only the winners. They called him Kid then. He was good with the women and better with the cards. He learned the easy shuffle and the Dakota slide and the palmed queen and the left-hand cut and a dozen other deals. The cards danced for him as did the women in the night.

As a man will discover a natural talent previously untried, he became a shootist quite by accident. A poor loser in a tiny settlement called Wind River, Montana, disputed the three fours that Kid held. Seconds later, the cowboy lay dead, slain by a hand that was swift with cards and as quick with the gun worn more as an ornament until that single moment when it appeared in Kid's hand like an extension of fate. Before too long and too many more poor losers, the Wind River Kid had built a reputation as a man who was plain downright authoritative when it came to staying alive.

It had been as simple as that.

Luck had ridden with the Wind River Kid, had sat at his side at a thousand poker tables, and had given him everything he asked for and some things he didn't, like enemies. For eighteen years, he had shrugged off the enemies, turned his back and contemptuously walked away from them, or simply shot them. And then one day his luck, and his nerve, had run out. Paunch Pepperdine dead at his feet, Butch and Dupree Pepperdine riding to avenge the death of their father, Wind River tucked his tail between his legs and ran.

The year had been 1892, the Wind River Kid a lean thirty-six, no longer a kid but stuck with the name because that was the way everyone remembered him. His nerves as frayed as his shirt collar, he had headed for Elkhorn, sanctuary of his early days, there to find Aden Creed for the second time. Wiry, a tattered fossil too damned stubborn to lie down and quit, the ex-mountain man had become an eccentric, drunk old coot who eked out a living working the tailings of a silver mine and running a string of traps that seldom caught anything. At seventy, long since kicked out of Angelina's heart and her Victorian Palace, Creed still had his principles. When he and Wind River met in Wind River's room at the Great Northern Hotel, Creed didn't like what he saw, and said so. Wind River told him to go to hell, but Creed wasn't inclined right then because there was work to be done—work requiring a mountain man with cougar courage, a keen eye to sight along the steel barrel of a Hawken rifle, and a willingness to die in a coward's place.

Memories of long ago drifted and died in the short walk from basin to stove and back again. The sun had moved on and restored Wind River's hair to its present and rightful white, which was fine with him. He'd stared at his past too many times to want to again that morning, and gratefully plunged his head into the water, scrubbed and snorted and blew like an old bear in a mountain stream. "Whee-unhh!" he said, shaking his head and shivering, then reaching quickly for the whiskey bottle behind the washstand. Red flannel long johns spotted with ice-cold water, he leaned back and took a swallow of pure hell. "Whee-heohhh!" he croaked, still testing his voice, "and one to grow on." He wiped his hand across his mouth, looked about to see if Creed had snuck in, then drank again. Fire coursed through his veins and his throat burned. "That's got her started," he wheezed. "Now to finish the job."

The fire in the stove was roaring, the coffee steaming. He added a handful of fresh grounds to the sludge at the bottom of the pot, emptied in a quart bottle of water, moved the morning coffee to the edge of the firebox so it wouldn't boil too fast. The initial heat generated by the whiskey was fading, and Wind River became conscious of the cold. Moving quickly, he grabbed for his clothes. The elbows of his Sears, Roebuck plaid flannel shirt were frayed, but elbows were the least important parts of shirts, so long as long johns were whole. His dungarees were patched, but like his bones were basically sound and had a good deal of life left in them yet. As for his boots, it was true that the soles were thin and had started to work loose, but he had leather and awl and thick waxed string, and would repair them some time before the first real snow. The one thing he didn't dare forget was the thick, padded plaid cap with the earflaps tied up.

The coffeepot was singing. Wind River decanted a cup of the steaming black acidic brew and moved outside into the sunlight. The year before, the day after he'd moved out of the Horned Owl Saloon and into Muenster's Funeral Parlor, he'd rolled his sitting log up the street. Now he checked the sky and sat and stared at the morning, taking his time because that's what it was, his time, and Elkhorn's.

Outside of winter, spring, summer, and fall, time wasn't worth much for a seventy-one-year-old man. Hadn't been for Wind River for over a quarter of a century. As far as he was concerned, he was alive and that was all that counted. He simply didn't care that the year was 1927, for example. He neither knew nor cared that Rif rebels had been bloodily

suppressed in Morocco, that transatlantic commercial tele-
phone service had been opened between New York and
London, that Trotsky had been expelled from the Com-
munist Party, that Germany had repudiated any responsibil-
ity for World War I. He had not read *The Great Gatsby* or
Elmer Gantry or *Winnie the Pooh*. He had not heard of
Picasso, Kafka, or cosmic rays. It did not matter to him that
Darwin's theory of evolution had been banned in Tennessee
or that Lucky Lindy had flown the Atlantic nonstop, so long
as all named parties stayed out of Elkhorn and left him in
peace.

The sun was what mattered. The sun and the fresh air and
the private, empty sky. Wind River set his cup on the log
and stomped around, flapped his arms to work a little life
into his muscles. He picked up his cup and drank, set it
down again, and stretched. He stared down Main Street.
Burnished gold by the sun, the gray-washed buildings
hinted at earlier, precarious days of grand fortune. To the
east, visible through the empty lot where Doc Bufker's
house used to sit, he could see the Rampage Valley, long and
wide and green. To the south was Damnation Hill, obscuring Fremont Valley and the road to Mountain City. To the
west and north, granite slopes, gray slabs of rock poking
through thick clusters of pine and evergreen, rose to
windswept peaks. The trees had been stripped from the
north slope years earlier, and a puckered wound marred its
upper face where men had dug and died for silver. The town
itself was still in moderately good shape because Wind River
had a habit of repairing a walkway or floor plank whenever
he fell through. If civic improvement now and then kept him
from breaking a leg, it was well worth the effort.

The Wind River Kid knew the valleys and the mountains
as well as he knew Elkhorn. He knew every gulley and
ravine. He knew Elkhorn Creek from where it sprang out of
the rocks a mile and a half north of town at Silvertip Spring.
He knew the first ankle-deep yards that ran through a
polished cleft of granite. He knew the aspens, the wild
flowers, the mosses that bordered it as it grew to a singing
brook. It was said that the men who panned Elkhorn Creek
for gold in the old days had to keep a hand free to flip the

trout out of the way, so teeming were the waters. Wind River was sure the story was true because the fish had come back during the last ten years, and it was no trouble at all to scoop out a lunker when bacon ran low. He knew the deer trail that funneled cautious bucks and dainty-eyed does out of the aspens, guided them through the tumbled boulders and past Silvertip Falls all the way to where the Elkhorn joined Oak Creek above Mountain City. He knew Silvertip Falls and the pristine glen at its base better than he wanted to. There Elkhorn Creek fell twenty feet into a cold, icy pond. Blackfeet and Crow, Cheyenne and Nez Percé had bathed in that holy glade. The wild creatures had drunk there since time immemorial and did still. Wind River avoided the glade. Aden Creed derided him about his aversion, but he didn't care. At least three men had died there. Three the Kid knew of. But that was a black thought, best forgotten. Easily forgotten, most days in the routine born of years of silence and loneliness.

A wolf will urinate a boundary around his domain. Wind River pissed in the alleys. Years might have rusted his vitality but never tarnished the image of himself as a gambler and a gentleman, and gentlemen did not wet the street. This morning, Wind River peed belly-high on the barbershop from three feet away, flipped it dry, and stuffed it back with a satisfied smile. "Seventy-one by God," he crackled, crossing the open space between the barbershop and the Great Northern Hotel and stopping under the porch to check the sky again. Twice before he'd looked, but it never hurt to check again. A man couldn't be too careful. The goddamn falcon had showed up a year earlier, taken a dislike to Wind River, and swooped down on him whenever it had the chance. Wind River sometimes suspected Creed of conspiring with the bird, but he couldn't be sure and hadn't accused him. Shrugging his relief, he headed back into the street to finish his coffee.

Mornings were a clock of sorts, one with actions instead of hands. The waking and scratching, the rising and rinsing, the fire and the coffee, the water and the whiskey. Likewise, each morning, he surveyed Elkhorn and made note of the myriad changes that had occurred overnight. The changes were minute, not even recognizable to someone who hadn't watched so closely for thirty-five years. A crack widened a hair's breadth here, a knothole fallen out there. Here a beam had shifted, there a spot of rust had peeled off a nail. In truth, the town looked much the same as it had since the turn of the century, except that only the main street was left, the eight houses that had been the residential section having fallen in the slide of '03, when the eastern slope gave way and slipped into Rampage Valley. As it stood on this golden morning in 1927, Elkhorn was a hotel, a boardinghouse, a barbershop, a funeral parlor, a general store, a dress shop, a bank, a restaurant, a newspaper office, an assay office, a stable, a sheriff's office, five saloons, the Victorian Palace, and a whorehouse that still smelled like women when the wind and humidity were right.

Each of the other buildings smelled of memories, too; some sweet, some sour. This morning, Wind River stood for a moment in front of what had once been a whitewashed cottage, where columbine bloomed wild in the spring. Doc Bufker, Elkhorn's one and only doctor, had lived and practiced there. A singular and vainglorious physician, Bufker was a stalwart believer that pain had medicinal as well as religious attributes, and once had cured a miner's headache by stomping on the surprised fellow's toe. The cure, once discovered, became a frightening panacea. Many a lad left Doc Bufker's limping, rubbing a bruised arm, massaging a kicked buttock, and unable to remember exactly what ailment had led him to the doctor. Bufker had come to Elkhorn in 1887 after being expelled from the medical profession in Gettysburg, Pennsylvania, the year before. Two years later, he had married a whore named Mon Cher, who took a vow of respectability before God and the doctor, but forgot to make a similar pronouncement to the rest of mankind.

The doc's troubles started in '93, one evening in June when he was called out to repair the busted wing of the town marshal, Deke Long. Managing to clean the wound and bind it without complication, he returned to his house, eased himself wearily through the white picket gate that Mon Cher had added for a homey touch, and paused to take a leak in the garden. There, watering the downy phlox and fairy bells that would later revert to a wild state, he beheld, through the bedroom window, his wife giggling in her altogether in the arms of not one but two miners. Bufker did the only manly thing he could have. He dug into his battered black satchel for the derringer nestled between his surgical tools and a decanter of Foxworth's Black Strap for the Jitters and Croup, Soothes Diarrhea. He waited for the miners to leave — he couldn't blame them, after all — reached over the windowsill, steadied his arm, and fired a small caliber bullet with surgical precision into the forehead of his beloved.

If he'd shot the miners, or Mon Cher, in the act, he would have gotten off scot-free for an act of passion any man in his right mind could have understood. It was the waiting until the miners left that did him in. Doc Bufker stood trial and was trundled off to prison in Denver, where he found a thriving vocation ministering to the aches and agues of outrageous patients. The house itself became a landmark when the drama it had contained found its way into the San Francisco *Police Gazette* under the title "Princess of Passion Slain." The issue made its way to Elkhorn, and for a while people walked about with their chins lifted in civic pride, and their egos bloated with self-importance, because Elkhorn was by damn on the map!

Unlike the present, with events taking place in splendid isolation, one thing followed another back in 1893, when Elkhorn was still alive and thriving. Three weeks after the *Gazette* brought notoriety to town, the Reverend Phillips, whose church languished for a roof and doors, burned the Bufker house to the ground in a fit of sanctimonious despair. Phillips left Elkhorn the next night. A broken man, he moved to Mountain City, where he lost his religion, became a baker's apprentice, and later a baker more concerned with men's stomachs, he was proud of saying, than with their souls. He died of a stroke in 1912, when Doc Bufker, his debt to society if not to Mon Cher paid, returned to Elkhorn, found the town abandoned, and set up shop in Mountain City. At sixty-eight, Phillips had thought he had forgotten, but hadn't. Hastily repentant, he died cursing the blasphemous bunch in Elkhorn who had never shown him anything but the slow side of lethargy when it came to building the house of God, yet made a temple of notoriety out of the house where Satan had lived and basked in scurrilous glory.

Wind River headed down the street. To his right was the barbershop, to his left the sheriff's office and jail, still intact but fifty feet down the slope created by the slide, followed by the general store and the Widow Guthrie's dress shop. The Great Northern Hotel sat on the west side across, naturally, from the Great Northern Bank. A side street separated the bank from the south and seedy end of town. To the west, the Horned Owl Saloon sagged dangerously, mirroring the Jo-Letty Restaurant across the street. Lorine's Boardinghouse and the Silver Lode Saloon faced the Twin .45 Saloon that balanced precariously on the edge of the slide, its rear hanging over empty space. Why the Elkhorn *Chronicle* sat at that end of town was a mystery that no one had solved, but rumor had had it that Endicott Norman, the owner, once had been more than friends with Angelina, who ran the Victorian Palace next door. The last two buildings on the east were the Texas Saloon and the Gold Nugget Saloon. Sometimes, when he wanted to feel horny, Wind River wandered into the Gold Nugget for a look at the naked blonde over the bar. Faded though she was by years and weather, everything was still there. This morning he passed by, dug his bootheels into the dry dirt street in front of Lucie Pleasant's whorehouse and bath, the last building on Main Street, and turned to survey his town. Everything was intact, as whole as it would ever be. Up by the livery, a cloud of dust exploded and disappeared, a phantom on the breeze that funneled down from the granite peaks. Somewhere to his left a jay scolded. He could hear the wind in the pines behind him. All was well with the world. Wind River gazed with contentment on Elkhorn, in all its pristine shabbiness.

A fart echoed like a drumroll, followed by the raw rasp of a knife blade cutting through wood. Wind River's shoulders tensed as his eyes roamed up and down the street searching out the direction. Ghosts always announce themselves. Some come with chains to fill the night with rattling dread, some with moans crimson with horror and promising gore, some in anguish or mad glee, some sobbing for murdered lovers, some with shrieking pleas for release from their curious imprisonment. A fart and a whittle announced Creed's earthly materialization.

Wind River spotted him on the front porch of Lorine's Boardinghouse. Curled slivers of wood covered his moccasins and his egg-smooth skull was shiny in the morning sun. Creed glanced up as Wind River approached. "Morning, younker," he said lazily.

"Morning," Wind River said, liking the sound of the old talk and glad, in spite of himself, to see the old mountain man. "You're at it early."

"Yup." His blade never missed a stroke as it bit into the wood with a *flick flick flick.*

Wind River knotted his fists, dug them into the small of his back, and stretched. "What're you makin'?"

"Same as always." Creed spit on his knife, honed it on his boot before starting on the antlers. He never whittled anything but deer. "Better set and soak the warmth. Can't tell when there'll be more, this time of year."

"Up and about is better. Gets the blood movin'," Wind River said, looking around as if he'd misplaced something. "Mite early for too much settin'."

"Our age, it's never too early for settin'," Creed answered, watching him. "It's back there on your log."

"What?"

"Where you left your coffee," the mountain man's ghost explained.

Wind River grimaced. The morning had been going fine, and then Creed had to trample all over his thoughts. "Thanks," he said sarcastically, his mellow mood gone.

"No call for that," Creed said. "I was just tryin' to help."

"The hell you say." Wind River was getting cantankerous. "I didn't ask for help."

"You gonna be that way..." Creed stood. If seventy years of prodigious eating hadn't filled him out, neither had an extra thirty-five of wandering about without earthly sustenance thinned him down. His long arms and legs fit his six-foot-plus frame just right. "Well, good day for a walk. Maybe I'll check my traps."

"You ain't got no traps," Wind River unkindly reminded him, trying to get even.

Creed rammed his knife into its sheath. "I'll check any-way, if it's all the same with you. The memories are sweet. Besides, there might be one I missed."

"Be nothing but rust, now," Wind River said, rubbing it in.

"Maybe I'll check yours then," Creed snapped.

Wind River's hands bunched into fists and his shoulders hunched menacingly. "You leave my damn traps alone, you hear?"

Creed chortled like he always did when he got Wind River's goat. "Sure, Kid. Whatever you say."

"And I ain't no kid!"

"So you ain't." Creed's eyes danced merrily. "I forgot," he said, farting explosively.

Wind River wrinkled his nose. "Cut that out."

"Wasn't me."

"Hell it wasn't. Who else is there?"

"Wolves." Creed arched one eyebrow, spat into the dust as he stepped off the porch. "You stayed in the hills like you was supposed to, you would of known that's what wolves sound like when winter's comin'." He chuckled, began to amble toward the trees, and paused. "Oh, yeah. You better get my old Hawken down and clean it up."

Wind River frowned suspiciously. "Why?"

"Might need it." Creed pointed toward the graveyard on the slope below the old mine at the north end of town. "Scar came down last night. Heard his footfalls. Woke me. Damn red eye and yellow teeth. Not a calming thing to see in the night. I called out to him in Injun."

"I don't suppose," Wind River snorted derisively, "he said what he wanted, did he?"

"Might have, but I never learned to speak bear." Creed looked as if he was going to fart, but didn't. "He was pawing at the graves, though. A bad sign in any tongue. Change coming, Kid. Even here. Even to Elkhorn."

"I guess a man who believes a bear could be damned near sixty years old can believe anything else he's a mind to," Wind River said with a smirk.

Creed scratched his jaw and picked a scab of dust from his drooping beak of a nose. "Laugh if you like," he warned. "All the same, you best watch out for Ol' Scar. When I took his eye, I left him with a bad temper. He ain't content to watch no more. Ol' Scar's up to mischief."

Wind River watched the mountain man saunter into the emerald line of evergreens and head north and east. That meant the old bastard would be following the trail to Silvertip Falls and the glen. For a second, Wind River was tempted to follow, to prove, to Creed and himself . Well, to prove that he could.

But what for? To listen to more nonsense about bears that should be dead and God knew what else? Grumbling, he walked back up Main Street to get his cup and, like a prize fool, didn't listen and, like even more of a prize fool, failed to hear the whistle of wings arced back in a perfect, single-minded dive. Only when it was too late, when there wasn't time for more than a flit of imagination, did he suspect, and then WHAP! and he was rolling in the dirt. He came to his feet with a stone in his hand.

"Goddamn!" Wind River shouted, chunking the stone at the rising falcon and missing by a country mile. "Bird!" he shouted, shaking with fury. "Goddamn beady-eyed bird!"

The falcon's screech, a pulsing, piercing call of joyous victory, echoed high and taunting on the frail mountain air, and then he was gone, swooping deep into Rampage Valley.

That did it. Wind River gingerly felt the lump rising on the back of his skull. He picked up his hat, retrieved his cup, and stomped into Muenster's Funeral Parlor. If he had any sense, he thought, he'd leave. Saddle up and ride out. He'd threatened to a hundred times before, but this time he really would. Let the damn bird, Creed, and his imaginary bear have the whole bitching town. That was the answer, by God, and that's exactly what he'd do. Right that minute, while Creed was checking his rusted beaver traps and the goddamn beady-eyed bird had meat, not meddling, on his mind. Leave and never come back.

The coffee was cold, the fire down to a pile of coals. "Determination," Wind River said, adding wood. That's all it needed. A blaze sprang up and he put the lid back, shoved the pot over to heat up. Hell, he had determination by the yard, by the acre. His stomach growled, and he reconsidered. Better to have breakfast and then leave. Travel on a full stomach.

Humming a cracked tune, he poked a finger in the coffee. It was still cold, which got him thinking again. With all he had to do to get ready, it would be noon before he could ride. Better to take his time and leave in the morning. That way, if he took the shorter, steeper, cut off trail, he'd have to spend only one night on the ground before he got to Mountain City.

Wind River perked up, began to feel good again. Like he was only fifty, maybe. Where would he go? It didn't matter. Luck would lead him. Always had. Brought him to Elkhorn, took him away, and brought him back. And now away again. "Damn and by damn," he said aloud, anticipating all the people he'd meet, all the sights he'd see. He grabbed the whiskey bottle and toasted his new freedom. "Whee-unhh!" he said, his eyes glistening with excitement. Damn and by damn, but he was going to have himself a time!

He was leaving. This time for good.

2

Silent lay the markers, wood and stone. Some, faithful in their vigil of the years, waited resurrection whole. Others, broken by snow and ice and insects, lay crumbled in the dust.

DEL STUDER 1842– OCTOBER 17, 1869
A GOOD FRIEND AND HONEST
BUT NOT TOO SMART OF A HUNTER
KILLED AND PART ET BY A GRIZZ

Wind River squinted at the marker as the sun angled down toward the western peaks and sliced the clearing into streaks of shadow and painfully bright light. Right next to Del's grave was another weathered plank with the letters and date burned into it.

OCTOBER 19, 1869
THE GRIZZ
FOUND DEAD ABOUT HALF A MILE FROM DEL

Grizzlies and men were an age-old combination. Only one king to every mountain, all that time and space allowed. Wind River sauntered on, hoping to give the impression he

was just out for a stroll and not looking to see for himself if
Scar had come down during the night.

LUCIE JEAN MARCKHAM
JUNE 1, 1890 – DEC. 16, 1893
A LOSS BORNE BY US ALL

Wind River remembered Lucie Jean. He remembered
her stiff and dead in a pink, frilly dress in a white satin-lined
coffin made by the blacksmith and his twelve-year-old son.
He could not remember the blacksmith's name. Lucie had
been three years old, the youngest child left in a town that
was itself dying. A month after she died her father had closed
the store and departed with his wife and two sons, leaving a
total of five less in Elkhorn. Wind River had given Lucie a
card once. The queen of hearts from his last deck, as he
recalled. Enraptured, squealing with delight and scraped
knee forgotten, she had scurried back to her father's general
store. Six months later winter killed her, a winter that
brought fever and pneumonia to chill and fill the lungs of a
little girl and whisper a lullaby of dreamless sleep.

Great claw marks had ripped the ground covering Lucie.
"Son-of-a-bitch!" Wind River muttered, anger contorting
his face. "Son-of-a-bitch grizzly!"

A breeze sifted through the tall pines. How long was a
mountain grizzly supposed to live? Hard to say. Twenty-five
years, maybe? Not as long as Scar. Hell, Creed had shot the
damned thing in what? Eighty-eight or something?

"Eighty-seven. October. And he weren't no cub then."

Wind River squawked and spun around so quickly he lost
his footing and tripped over a splintered marker.

Creed was sitting on his own gravestone, a piece of shined
granite paid for by Wind River. The letters were cut deep
and said:

ADEN CREED. MOUNTAIN MAN
1822 – JULY 17, 1892
KILLED BY OWL HOOTS

"Easy, Kid, " Creed said, tapping his pipe on the stone. "It's a long way downhill with a broken leg."

There was more than a hint of truth in that, Wind River thought with a shudder. He picked himself up and dusted his Levi's. "Damn, Aden, but you give a man a death, sneakin' up like that."

"Can't be helped," Creed replied, innocence looking out of place on his face, like a smile on a wolf. "I'm past makin' a ruckus. Quiet sort of comes natural to a fellow in my condition."

"Okay, okay," Wind River snapped. "I don't want to hear about it." He pointed to the claw marks on Lucie's grave. "What was he doing here?"

"Scar?"

"What else has claws like that? An eight-foot beaver? Hell yes, Scar. What was he doing to her grave?"

Creed peered at Lucie's grave as if he hadn't noticed anything out of the way before. "Offhand, I'd say digging. But you can see that for yourself."

"Why?"

"Grizzly business, I reckon." The mountain man chuckled, amused by his pun.

"You bastard."

Aden leaned forward. His mud-brown eyes drilled into the Wind River Kid's. "You never in your life cared about anyone or anything except yourself. So why this sudden, self-righteous concern? Spare us. Spare me."

"You don't know," Wind River said, sniffing defensively. "If that bear comes to Elkhorn, I'll kill it."

"He is here already. He has come for our memories." Creed looked dreamy, as if, having seen so much of the past, he had learned how to look into the future. "Scar ain't like me. He still has his claws. He'll dig up those graves and he'll tear down Elkhorn board by board. That old rogue won't die until the mountain is pure again."

"You never did talk sense." The words sounded empty.

"Weren't no point to it. You never would listen." Creed tucked his thumbs inside his belt. The bright beads strung by a long-dead Cheyenne squaw brightened his soiled buckskin shirt and breeches. "Be that as it may," he said, standing and looking around. "These graves are getting me depressed."

Wind River glanced upslope where the mountainside receded into concealing shadows. He thought there had been a movement in the underbrush, but could not be certain and decided against checking. Let claws rip, let snout dig, let jaws snap the whole town to battered, shredded wood. What the hell, when it came right down to it. He was leaving. What happened to Elkhorn was its own business. Still, he couldn't help being apprehensive. Creed had been around a long time and knew things most living men had never thought of. Wind River stared at the underbrush. Had it moved again? What breathed there out of sight? What waited, certain as sin, patient as fate? A hungry grizzly named Scar? "If you've come for my memories, you one-eyed bastard," the Wind River Kid said in a voice as soft as the shadows, "you can have them. And good riddance. To you both."

Creed led the way down the hill toward town. With the angle of the sinking sun just right, occasional patches of amber-colored light danced through the mountain man's body. Just like him, Wind River thought sourly. About the time he thought the old man was real, Creed took to appearing and disappearing, or worse, that tricky in-between state. Trouble was, who could tell the difference anymore? Real bear or ghost? Probably looked alike and sounded alike. Probably even smelled alike, to judge from Creed's farts. One good thing about the falcon, Wind River thought, rubbing his noggin as he picked his way across a stony place, that bird was for sure real.

He wouldn't have to put up with it much longer, though. Only one more night. Wind River pushed into the nearly dark livery to check on his horse, a hammerhead Appaloosa with a penchant for viewing the world as a wholly unremarkable place. The horse begrudged a gallop and, come boot, quirt, or curse, stuck to a firm and steady gait that more properly might be called a plod. The Wind River Kid would have complained bitterly in years gone by, but no longer. With age settling in the small of his spine, he was content to

let the beast set his own pace. Wind River peered through
the gloom. He liked the livery, the smell of hay and dust and
horse. Not very many places in town were warmer either,
when it came right down to it. Relaxed, he pulled the last
bag of oats out of the old tin lard can he kept it in, walked out
the back door and poured half of what was left into the trough
tacked to the rear of the barn. Sure enough, the Appaloosa
perked up his ears at the sound and plodded toward his
beneficiary and master, and his oats.

The Appaloosa was one horse that couldn't have cared less
about the struggle between men and mountains. Or bears,
for that matter, so long as they left him alone. An appetite
appeased, a roll in the grass, a cinch drawn none too tightly,
and an occasional pail of oats or corn were all he asked of life.
Wind River watched him dip his muzzle into the trough and
then, talking softly, checked his legs and hooves, feeling the
tendons and looking closely at each shoe. "Well, you're fit, I
guess," he finally said, slapping the horse's rump. "Kind of a
waste, puttin' up all that hay, but what the hell. Let Creed
eat it, if he wants."

It was that time of day. Wind River left the Appaloosa and
climbed the fence to sit on the top rung. Daydreaming, he
fished a cigar from his pocket, dug out a match, and filled his
lungs with the acrid, pungent smoke. Charlie Russell might
have sketched him then. Still part of the Old West, the old
ways, Wind River rested his elbows on his knees and
watched the shadows fill Rampage Valley and creep up the
eastern hills. In the distance, the sun was still bright on
Diamond Peak, his favorite. Years ago, Creed had taken him
there and shown him the outcropping that was so thick
with mica that it reflected light like a mirror. Wind River
still enjoyed watching it sparkle at sundown, and pretending it was real diamonds just waiting for him to go and pick
them up.

A hush was on the hills and the town. Somewhere an owl
hooted softly, calling to the wind that soughed through the
trees. Darkness would fall fast when the light left Diamond
Peak, but Wind River didn't care. After thirty-five uninter-
rupted years in Elkhorn, he could have found his way
blindfolded. The chill worked its way through his flannel

shirt and long johns, attacked his skin. The Appaloosa finished and came to him, butted his head against Wind River's calf, and then stood silently as gnarled, calloused fingers scratched behind his ear. Too bad he was leaving, in a way, Wind River thought lazily. A man could travel a far piece before he'd find a view to compare. Oh, he'd seen the sights in his day. Places with taller trees and steeper mountains and wilder rivers. Richer places and poorer places. Towns to the south where there were more wildflowers than a man could count, towns to the north where the aurora streaked the night sky and stole a man's breath. But never quite the same combination of peace and tranquillity, never quite the easy days and star-song nights, never where the dusk fell quite so slow and soft, where the earth seemed to sing itself to sleep with a lullaby more sweet than any sung by woman.

A fart broke through his thoughts. Wind River's hand froze and his head twisted back and forth looking for Creed before he realized the sound had come from the Appaloosa.

"Don't you start on me now, horse," he said, giving the animal a final scratch, then shoving him away with his foot. At the same time, the last bit of light on Diamond Peak faded. With it, Wind River's spirits fell. Another dark night alone faced him. Christ, but it was all too much. A bear, a falcon, and the ghost of a mountain man all picking at him. Beauty be damned; he was glad he was leaving.

Glad, hell. He was ecstatic. Another few days and he'd be among people again. Bright lights and music. Action. That was what he yearned for. He flexed his fingers, tried to imagine what it would feel like to have a new deck of cards in his hands. Oh, he'd take 'em, all right. They'd never suspect an old geezer like him. They'd let him sit in, wink, and plan on taking all his money. He'd show 'em, every man jack of 'em. Eyes slitted, he could see the cards falling, could hear the soft whisper as they slid across green felt tables. In his mind's eye, he counted the deck. He'd know who held what, who was bluffing, who playing straight. Wouldn't be luck, either. His memory was razor keen.

Hot water baths. Perfumed soap. Steaming towels wrapped around his face in barbershops where the talk was quiet under the clean sound of clicking scissors and razors being stropped. Steaks and potatoes and fresh vegetables. Clean napkins and shining silverware and gilt-edged plates that sparkled in candlelight. Waiters moving silent as cats and never having to be told twice. Coffee with sugar and real cream, and fruit and brandy and cheese. Women with golden hair and low-cut bodices who smelled like lavender and roses and Paris itself. Women with soft hands and sweet breaths, women who smiled and laughed gaily and held on to a man's arm when he won, even if he was old enough to be their grandfather, women who could leech the years from dry bones. He wondered if there were any women like that left.

"Ooo-weee!" he shouted suddenly, unable to contain the excitement. More alive than he'd felt in years, he pitched away the glowing stub of his cigar and climbed down from the fence.

"Oh, come, you painted beauties," he sang. "Enfold me in your arms."

By God, but he'd celebrate. Eat at the hotel, right in the dining room.

"Hug me and kiss me, and whisper of your charms."

Wear his finest. It was his last meal in Elkhorn, after all.

"If you love a winner, well, that's what you've found."

Invite Creed, even! No point in doing something half-assed.

"I'm a wild-eyed stallion who's pawin' the ground."

The Wind River Kid was breaking loose!

3

Wind River kept his good clothes in a huge, carved cedar wardrobe in the President's Suite at the Great Northern Hotel. Mason Nederly, president of the Northern Mining Corporation, wouldn't mind. He had died before the mine played out in 1891.

Nederly died, then the mine, then the town.

A neat progression, Wind River thought, stripping off his shirt. His boots and pants followed, a dingy pile in the corner, before he pulled his single white shirt off the hanger and shook it. A little billow of dust puffed into the room. Wind River sneezed, pulled on the shirt and buttoned it with care, making sure the ruffles stood out as they should. A string bow tie, clumsily handled because it had been so long since the last time he'd bothered to dress formally, followed. Pop! Black trousers snapped like a whip and spawned another cloud. Wind River pulled them on and buttoned them up, then carefully threaded the thick, worked-leather belt with the silver buckle through the loops. His vest was black with deep red trim, fancy but understated. The buttons were mother-of-pearl, and stood out like a vertical row of eyes. Stooping, he hauled his boot bag out of the bottom of the wardrobe, catching, in the process, a velvet wrap that fell open and spilled its contents onto the floor.

What lay there gleamed dully in the dim light. Black grain

leather brushed soft from years of careful oiling and service. Blue metal remarkably free of rust. Worn bone grips, almost black in the coiled-snake carving. There was only one, a .44-caliber Colt revolver converted by an expert gunsmith from cap and ball, holstered to be worn forward of his left hipbone, butt forward in the cross draw favored by gamblers. A man didn't have to stand but could clear leather while sitting at the poker table. Wind River squatted and stared at the gun without touching it as he slipped backward through time. He heard a soft oath, a cry of anger. His muscles remembered the fluid movements so long engrained they were automatic and always led to twin explosions thumbed so quickly they sounded as one. He saw days of slumber, nights of sweet women, the run of Lady Luck, and the thrill of accepting a challenge and never backing down. Never. Of living on the raw edge of nerve.

"Strap it on, Kid," Aden Creed said from the dimly lighted doorway.

"Goddamn you," Wind River said, looking up guiltily.

"Not very friendly words for one who was as close to you as a father," Creed sniffed.

"I never knew my father. I don't think my mother did either."

"Put it on."

"Leave me alone. You were invited for dinner. Not to watch me dress, or to butt in where you're not wanted."

"A hostile tongue is a busy tongue."

"You ought to know. Yours is as busy a one as I've ever heard. Especially for a dead man," Wind River said. He rewrapped the gun and shoved it beneath a pile of moth-eaten linen on the wardrobe floor. Where he was going, he wouldn't need a gun. Not a man-killing gun, anyway. That part of his life was far behind him and there was no sense in trying to regain it.

Creed sighed. "Out of sight, out of mind. Just as well, I guess. Little too late to do anything else. Oh, well. You can right some of the wrongs all of the time and all of the wrongs some of the time, but you can't right all of the wrongs all of the time."

Wind River stared at him, a pained expression on his face.

The mountain man coughed, shrugged. "Proverbs. A person in . . . uh . . . my condition ought to have a command of wise sayings."

"You make more sense when you pass gas," Wind River replied sarcastically. He pulled out his coat, shook it and put it on. The silvering on the mirror had flaked off during the years, making him look like a ghost himself. He shifted from side to side in order to get the whole picture, adjusted his tie, and checked his hair. Satisfied, he picked up the oil lamp and walked out of the bedroom.

Creed stepped aside, then followed. A breeze gusted in his wake, disturbing the thin layer of dust that had settled on the worn burgundy comforter on the bed in the corner. The fringed canopy overhead fluttered and more dust drifted down like pollen, unseen in the sudden darkness. In the hall, a chromolithograph of Andrew Jackson, framed in the disrespect of wormy wood, tilted askew as the wall vibrated to Wind River's footsteps. A hanging scrap of wallpaper cast a swiftly moving shadow as the lamp passed.

Wind River set the lamp on a table in the hall in order to make a grand entrance into the dining room he'd spent an hour arranging. A half dozen oil lamps with flames dancing lightly inside globes of milky glass lit the scene. The tablecloths, once white, cast a glow like old gold. Silver gleamed at the twenty places set. Wind River strolled casually to his table in front of the fireplace, sat, and lit a cigar, pretending that no one was watching him. When the cigar had burned halfway down, he sighed, rose, and headed for the lobby.

That was the trouble with daydreaming, he thought, spinning the dial on the combination lock. Just about the time everything was going right, reality intruded, and a man was forced to fix his own supper. The door to the safe swung open. Wind River checked the last couple of pounds of bacon, found they were still good. He'd take them with him for the trail in the morning. He removed a bag of dried chili peppers, sugar, flour, and the coffee he kept at the hotel for just such occasions. Whistling a tune he'd heard in Daisy's parlor down in Mountain City, he shut the safe, spun the dial, and hurried to the kitchen.

The rabbit he'd trapped the day before and had thrown in

the oven to roast prior to dressing smelled like ambrosia. The beans he'd put on to soak that morning were already boiling. Wasting no time, Wind River dumped out the sourdough he'd carried down from Muenster's, fashioned biscuits, and dumped the rest of the dough back into the clay crock for a starter. Sliding the biscuits in to cook, he pulled out the rabbit. The drippings were meager, but enough for gravy. He transferred the rabbit to another pan and slid it back into the oven. To the first pan, a black iron skillet that had been left behind when the hotel was vacated, he added water, a palmful of flour, a three-fingered pinch of salt, and a double shake of pepper. When the gravy began to boil, he moved it back from the fire so it could simmer safely. The coffee water was boiling by that time, so he dumped in new grounds and a dab of salt. If he'd had an egg, he thought, he could have used it in the biscuits and added the shell to the coffee. That would come soon enough, though, he promised himself. Another two days and he'd be in Mountain City and have all the eggs he wanted. A cloud of steam billowed from the bean pot when he removed the top. Wind River tasted, crushed a dried chili pepper into the brown liquid, stirred, took another taste, and smacked his lips. Pausing to check the rabbit and move it toward the side of the oven to hasten the cooking, he scooped two ladles of lard from a tin, dropped it into a skillet, and set it on to heat. By the time he'd peeled and sliced three potatoes, the grease was smoking. He pulled the skillet off the hot part of the stove and, humming "The Girl from San Antone," arranged the wet potatoes in the hot grease. By heavens, but he'd have a meal to travel on!

Everything was ready, all calculated to be cooked to a turn by the time he'd had a drink. Wind River wandered back into the once plush dining room of the Great Northern Hotel. Hurrying into the circle of warmth that held the night chill at bay, he poured himself a drink and eased into an armchair taken months earlier from the lounge.

"Smells good," Creed said wistfully, from a nearby lounge chair. "Fresh game and thick gravy," he added.

Wind River sipped his drink. On nights when the wind howled, longing and lost, he was grateful for company.

"There's enough for two," he said, tilting his glass in the mountain man's direction, feeling generous on the advent of departure.

Creed chuckled, nodded toward the Hawken rifle hanging over the fireplace.

"What?" Wind River asked, immediately regretting his question.

"Joe Walker."

Wind River wanted to sit and stare into the fire, not listen to an old man's ramblings. "Oh, yeah. Him," he said, hoping he'd get away with it.

"Had a squaw we all called Paddle Face. Wasn't too kindly of us, but what did we know then? Me, I was a young 'un. Figured I could whip any two of anything that came my way. Anyway, Paddle Face had dug a Sioux arrowhead out of Joe's hide a year or so earlier, and Joe loved her as much as any man could, I reckon, with that plain-as-mud face she had. Why she loved him was a mystery, but I always figured it was because he was as ugly as she was. Wouldn't nobody else have nothin' to do with either of 'em when it came to romance.

"Be that as it may, one night when a bunch of us had been lookin' at the bottom of a few jugs from the inside, we got to thinkin' how much fun it would be to sew her up in a blanket and hang her from a tree branch. We were lit as swamp fire and that's all there was to it. And the more we talked about it, the more determined we got to dangle Joe's woman in front of their tepee. The reason why was we'd had us a shootin' match that day and Joe had gone and filed the sights off our Hawkens the night before and won him a twenty-dollar gold piece. We figured to get his squaw so mad he'd have to spend it all on her just to have some peace and quiet. Well, before you could say Snohomish Pass without chokin', me and Fred Nabors and Eli Just had snuck up on her and set to work."

Creed snorted and choked until tears came to his eyes. His drink forgotten, Kid leaned forward, hopelessly caught.

"Paddle Face was worse than a she grizzly defending her cubs," Creed went on at last. "That Cheyenne woman lit into us tooth and holler, fist and claw."

"And?" Wind River prompted, when Creed, chuckling, dissolved in another fit of laughter.

"She whupped us. Cleaner'n first wash up in the spring. The three of us. Nigh busted Nabors' head with the leg bone of a moose, cracked Just's arm with one swing, broke my nose, as you can still plainly see. Trussed us together and tied us to the very same tree. That's the way Joe found us when he come home from drinkin' and whorin' up the whole of that twenty dollars. When Paddle Face found out he was broke, she laid into him with that selfsame moose bone and tied him to the three of us, then packed that tepee to the back of Joe's sloe-eyed mule and left. Lucky for us some Paiutes that had been in town come upon the camp the next day and after havin' themselves a good laugh cut us loose or we might have been there until we was bones." Creed leaned back and closed his eyes. "I learned one thing out of that, Kid."

"Which was?"

"To keep a civil tongue in my head when it comes to Injun women." He tapped his pipe in the palm of his hand. "Least-aways, Injun women with moose bones handy." The fire crackled. A log settled, sent sparks roaring up the chimney. Creed sucked on his empty pipe. Air rasped through the hand-carved mouthpiece, sounding asthmatic. "How long since you first seen me after you came back, Kid?"

Wind River swirled his drink, shook his head. "Long time. Don't recall exactly. Sometime after Daisy's brother run off to join that Roosevelt fellow and get himself killed by the malaria in Cuba. What's that? Twenty-five, -seven years?"

"And this is the first time I told that story?"

"As I recall."

"I don't like repeatin' myself. I wintered with a rough-cut Irishman in Crow Valley once. Old red-headed bucko knew one story, just one. Like to wore my ears numb with the telling."

"Seems I've heard more than one tall tale told again myself," Wind River said, amused. His right eye began to twitch and he rubbed it angrily. A nervous tic made him feel older.

"Me?" Creed asked, looking hurt. He seemed to sag deeper into the chair. "I suppose. Don't seem fair. Ain't bad enough I wind up dead, I got to lose my memory besides."

"Happens to the best of us, " Wind River said, starting for the kitchen as an excuse to change the subject.

A roar and a crash of wood stopped him in his tracks. Reluctant to leave the friendly hold of the lamplight, the festive brightness of the dining room, Wind River paused midway to the kitchen, at last turned and trotted through the lobby to the front door. No sooner had he stuck his head out than the roar came again, followed by a terrific crash. The silver hairs on the back of his neck standing on end, Wind River ducked back inside and slammed the door.

"Scar," he heard whispered close to his ear, but when he turned around, Creed was still sitting by the fireplace, his face, bald head, and hands crimson in the light from the dancing flames.

"It can't be," Wind River said, running back into the dining room. "No bear lives that long."

The repeated roar reverberated along the street, rattled what few windows remained, and beat against the walls. Somewhere at the north of town, a building was being demolished, board by board. "You brought him here, bastard."

Creed didn't move. "A bullet from my Hawken marked him," he said hollowly. "Scar doesn't forget. No one leads him. No man, least of all me."

"A Hawken marked him, a Hawken can kill him," the Wind River Kid said, hurrying to the fireplace. He grabbed the ancient rifle off its rack over the mantel, took powder, patch, and shot from the bag hanging there. Quickly he tamped a charge of gunpowder, rammed in a .50-caliber lead ball wrapped in a cloth patch. He grabbed a dusty box of caps lying next to a broken candelabrum, extracted one, and fitted it over the nipple beneath the hammer. Ready, he strode purposefully toward the front door.

The darkness outside was full of raw, primeval anger, full of fang and claw and, baleful in the night, a single, glowing eye, red as bloodlust. Wind River hesitated, shrank back into the shadows. His knees seemed made of jelly, his stomach of ice. A voice in his head hammered, "Go away, go away."

As if in miraculous response, the commotion ceased. At first, there was terror in the silence, but as it lengthened, Wind River relaxed. The eye was gone. The air smelled clean. Whatever had been there had retreated to the mountains and the trees. Still weak, Wind River let himself back into the Great Northern Hotel, walked as casually as possible to the dining room, pried his bloodless fingers from the barrel of the muzzzle-loader, and returned the Hawken to its rack.

"Piece by piece," Creed said from his chair. "Grizzlies have an unforgiving nature. Saw an old silvertip take a slug to the heart once and come on to tree me and maim the one who shot him before he realized he was dead. Scar's no different. He'll be back. He's claiming his valley. Piece by piece."

"Oh, shut up," Wind River yelled, and then, nose twitching, sniffed wildly. "Damn!" he whispered faintly. "Oh, shit!"

The bear forgotten, he raced into the kitchen to find smoke pouring from the oven and the top of the stove. A dense cloud obscured the ceiling. The gravy looked like sun-dried mud, caked and cracked, the potatoes like curled shingles. Choking, he pulled the fry pans off the stove, then grabbed a rag, jerked open the oven door, and stepped back from the billowing smoke that momentarily engulfed him. His eyes teared. Knowing it was too late, Wind River reached in the oven anyway and pulled out his dinner. The rabbit looked like a small, wizened log with legs. The sourdough biscuits were black lumps of coal. Wind River stared at them, shook his head. Some feast, he thought. Some triumphant departure. Resigned, he fried bacon, piled a plate high with beans, splashed coffee into a cup, and returned to the table in front of the fireplace.

"Bacon good?" Creed asked from his chair.

Wind River chewed, swallowed automatically. "Bacon is bacon."

"It won't work, your leaving."

Kid almost choked, and silently cursed the mountain man

for coming into his thoughts again. "We'll see," he said, forcing all expression from his face, making the words flat and emotionless. "We'll see."

When he glanced up, Creed was gone.

4

Morning light left nothing to the imagination. The barbershop had been mangled. Half the front wall had been knocked out. Inside, the marble counter and sink had been overturned and lay broken on the floor. The horsehide chair had been slashed to ribbons. Worse, as he discovered soon after, part of the graveyard had been dug up and rooted in as if it had been no more than a turnip patch.

Wind River tugged his hat firmly down around his head and hunkered inside his worn sheepskin-lined coat. He stuffed his whiskey bottle into his pocket and, without looking back, walked out of Muenster's Funeral Parlor. The Appaloosa waited patiently. Wind River went through everything once more just to make sure he hadn't forgotten anything. His clothes were all packed, his bale of skins, bedroll, and provisions all loaded. Everything else would be left behind. He checked the pieced-together combination wagon and travois that trailed behind the Appaloosa. The wheels, taken from the front of an old and stove-up wagon at the livery, were a bit shaky but would make this last trip, he decided. It was time to move out. Face as grim as the clouds, he swung aboard the Appaloosa and gave it a kick in the ribs.

The Appaloosa plodded down Main Street. Wind River looked straight ahead. Whatever doubts he'd had no longer existed. In one night, the barbershop had been reduced to a ruin and bones were visible in the graveyard. Maybe it had been Scar, maybe it hadn't. It no longer mattered who or what. Wind River was leaving, giving Elkhorn back. Forever.

A board creaked. The wind whistled through a knothole. Elkhorn was saying goodbye. Wind River hadn't seen Creed since the night before, and a twinge of guilt gnawed in his craw. He reined in on top of Damnation Hill and twisted in the saddle for a final look. A tinkling piano, the hint of a melody, beckoned from Lucie Pleasant's Sporting House. Lucie's lilting, flirtatious laugh, a song as beckoning as any siren's, a wondrous invitation to the wanderer weary of a world with too little warmth, floated above the valley.

"The wind," Wind River said, his voice soft and sad, reluctant in his throat. "C'mon, horse," he added to the Appaloosa stallion, and turned his face south, down the mountain. Behind him, Damnation Hill rose and blotted Elkhorn from view.

5

The children in the Mountain City schoolyard ran to the fenced end of the lot to watch Mayor Alexander Martin Grant's Buick rumble down the dirt road on its way to City Hall. Two dozen dirt-smudged faces winced in unison as the huge black car backfired and belched a cloud of smoke. Four dozen admiring eyes swiveled on a single pivot until the automobile had rolled past and out of sight. When the boys returned to the field, several mimicked the car, steering imaginary wheels and careening down the base paths to their positions. The girls, starry-eyed, fashioned daydreams of marrying rich mayors or ranchers or fat old businessmen in Denver who would buy them beautiful cars.

The girls were leading 17–12 in the eighth inning. Giggling, the power hitter of their team, a big-boned girl of twelve, took her place at home plate. The first two strikes sailed past her before she could clear her mind of all the fantasized delights of city life. The third, a slow, high, looping pitch, she stroked into left field, much to the embarrassment of the ten-year-old pitcher whose ears had been red from the first inning of play. As the girl raced to third with a standing triple, the boy stood on the mound, head lowered, enduring the scornful appraisal of his peers and wishing he could just go home after the game instead of having to sit through an afternoon of classes and the slings and arrows of his outraged playmates. If only they wouldn't stare. It wasn't his fault.

He glanced up at the hills that bordered the rear of the school property and glimpsed the old man on the Appaloosa. The horse was dragging an improbable wagon and moving with a slow, shuffling gait. They had obviously come down the path that wound over the bluff, through the hills, and into the mountains, although the pitcher had never ventured that far. He knew the man. Everyone who had lived in Mountain City for very long knew the man. He was the hermit who lived in the old town high up the mountain. The boy had heard his father talking. Twice a year, spring and fall, the old man came to town for supplies. In between times, the kids made up stories about him. "Hey! The spook's here! Look!" the pitcher shouted, grateful for the opportunity to shift the attention from himself. Their righteous anger quickly forgotten, his teammates turned.

The girls, the younger ones at least, screamed and ran toward the schoolhouse. The boys hurried from the field, shouting, "Spook, spook," falling over themselves to be the first to the fence. This was even better than the mayor's Buick. Some of the boys moaned like the wind and grabbed and tickled anyone standing close. Others climbed to the middle strand of wire and called out to him.

Wind River ignored them all. He'd spent a day and a half on the trail and was in no mood for a bunch of brats. He fought the desire to nudge the Appaloosa into a trot and, to keep from losing face, pretended he was riding at precisely the speed he wished. The muscles in his neck tightened and he hunched his shoulders inside his shirt and coat. At last, as he left the schoolyard behind, the chorus of merry, youthful voices that meant no actual harm faded.

Three wagons were being loaded in front of Lewis Weldon's General Store. Wind River recognized none of the men hard at work loading rolls of wire and bundles of hoes and rakes and other assorted implements on the wagons. He dismounted, tethered the Appaloosa, and unhooked his buggy. The ropes holding his bale of skins in the undersize wagon bed were tight and it took him a minute to loosen them. By the time he finished, he realized the men loading the wagon were staring at him. Ignoring them, Wind River slung the small bale of skins over his shoulder and walked out of the dirt street and into the store.

Weldon's was a large, dingy cavern of a room filled with textures and smells, and piled and hung with more goods than any one person could use in a lifetime. The left wall of the store was given over to toiletries, hats, and knickknacks for dresses and sewing. The right wall was covered with racks of denim pants and wool shirts and suspenders and work gloves and long johns for men. In between, stacked and hung and crated, was everything from cast-iron stoves to wheels of hard cheese and barrels of crackers arranged according to a logic only Lewis Weldon understood. To the left of the door, where the farm equipment was kept, the wall was bare. Wind River looked around and discovered other empty spaces and bare patches of floor. A quick inspection revealed other discrepancies. The harness and tack section was roped off. The hardware section, hinges and hasps and tools and enough nails to build Elkhorn a hundred times over, had been picked bare. A layer of dust muted the mother-of-pearl finish on the rack of hair combs. Business, Wind River thought with a worried look, was bad.

Lewis Weldon was bent over a ledger at the rear of the shop. He scribbled a few last notations and gave a listless teenager at his side a clipboard filled with paper. "Have Mr. Bascomb sign this before he moves them wagons. All three papers for each load, mind you."

"I know. I know," the teenage boy whined, and trotted through a side door.

Wind River approached, slung his hides onto the counter, and waited. Weldon looked up, shifted the wad of tobacco in his cheek. "Well, I swan if it isn't the Wind River Kid. My palms have been itching all day long. Now I know why."

"Afternoon, Lewis. Thought I'd stock up."

"Gettin' set for winter, eh? Looks like you made it just in time. Snow coming soon. Might not be able to get out again this year."

"You're right about the snow," Wind River said noncommittally. That he wasn't going back to Elkhorn was none of Weldon's business. "Still buyin' skins for Sears?"

Weldon took time to spit in the old peach tin that accompanied him everywhere, scratched his head, poked at the bale. "Well, seeing as it's you," he said, not looking too happy. "What you got?"

"Sixteen squirrel, five foxes, three lynx, a bobcat, a catamount, rabbits, and eight beaver."

The storeowner slit the leather thong holding them together and separated the small pile. Squirrel and rabbit weren't worth much and nobody had use for beaver but the cat skins were prime and would bring a good penny. He said as much.

"Don't need a lot," Wind River said. "Mostly staples. Beans, flour, bacon, coffee, some molasses, sugar, and cornmeal. Cigars, of course. Lard, too, come to think of it, and some matches. Them hides cover it all?"

"Oh, sure." Weldon scribbled a tally, ran a column, and added it up. "Won't be able to get it from me, though. Much as it hurts, I'll have to give you cash."

Wind River stared uncomprehendingly at Weldon, looked around the store. "What the hell you talking about?" he finally asked.

"Just sold it all at auction. None of the stuff you see there belongs to me anymore."

"What?"

"Yup. Business crumbling into dust, just like Elkhorn." He scratched an ample paunch and ran a few fingers through the white fringe of hair trimmed close to his scalp. "You recollect that little Jew fellow I hired couple, three years ago to clerk for me?"

"I think," Wind River said haltingly.

Weldon led the old man to a nearby window and pointed. A block toward the center of town, near the Mountain City Hall and Civic Auditorium, was a new brick building with a massive sign that read PIGGLY WIGGLY.

"What the hell is that?" Wind River said.

"The future. The goddamn future." In disgust, he squirted a stream of tobacco juice into the can. "Young Ritz saw it coming and saved his money. Directly, he talked Langdon over at the bank into loaning him some more, and then ran off to Dever and bought himself a franchise with one of those chain-store outfits. Next thing I knew, he'd bought out Gregory's Palladium and there was a bunch of city carpenters out here helping him fix it up. Didn't take a week before three trucks drove up, erected that there sign, and filled his store with food." Weldon shook his head as if he still couldn't believe it. "I'll tell you, it makes a man's head swim."

Wind River clucked in sympathy. "Well, hell, Lewis, you still got your store. Way it looks like Mountain City is growin', there's room for two."

Lewis Weldon snorted and turned away from the window. "You been out in them mountains too long, Wind River. He's stocked with nothing but food, sells cash and carry, doesn't make deliveries, lets people wait on themselves, and runs the place by himself. He even puts advertisements in the *Star*. Hell, he's underselling me and everybody like me."

"I'll be damned," Wind River muttered, dubious. He followed Lewis back to the counter. "Just food?"

"Well, tobacco and such, but that doesn't really count." Weldon beat his fist on the counter in frustration. "I don't mind a boy with get-up-and-go, mind you. I just wish he'd gotten up and gone somewhere else."

Wind River was confused. From what he'd seen in the years he'd been coming to Mountain City, no more than ten percent of Weldon's business could have been in groceries. "You still have all that other stuff," he said with a wave of his hand.

"Had, not have. Lulie Harskell's selling ladies' apparel over on Elm Street. Ol' Bert Brown been running a Western shop cross the road from Ritz. Folks are talking about Kresge or Woolworth moving in with one of them nickel-and-dime stores. Way I see it, I've got to specialize to keep afloat." He pointed to one roped-off section. "That's why I got all them tires and such. Before the month's out, my gas pumps'll be put in, too."

"Can't eat tires, can't drink gas," Wind River said, his face looking as if he'd chewed into an apple and come up with half a worm.

Weldon rolled his eyes and gave up. The Wind River Kid

was just out of touch. Mountain City was growing, now numbered over a thousand souls according to Mayor Grant. Already, nine people in town owned cars. Before the year was out, Weldon's General Store would be an auto parts store, garage, and maybe even a Ford or Chevrolet dealership. There was no sense in trying to explain that to a hermit, though. "Don't have to," he said. "I'll buy my food at the Piggly Wiggly like everybody else."

"If he's still there, six months from now," Wind River said, anxious to get his money and be gone.

"He will be, prices he sells things for. Besides, he contributes to all the churches. Even gave a flag to the Boy Scouts. You want your money now?"

"Yeah," Wind River said, trying to puzzle out what Boy Scouts were. Young Indians? Little boys in cavalry blue? Didn't make any sense.

Weldon went to the cash drawer and started counting out bills. He looked up when his wife walked out from the rear of the store. "Look who's here, Penelope. It's old Wind River himself."

Penelope stared through Wind River. "Oh," she said, and turned and walked back out.

"She hasn't been the same since Lulie opened that ladies' apparel store," Weldon said, shaking his head. He counted out a small stack of bills and eight dimes, laid the money on the counter. "Yep, specializing is the coming thing."

Wind River recounted the bills and change, and stuffed them into a small bag hung on his belt. "Looks like the coming thing is a fellow walking his legs off trotting from one specialty store to another." He snorted in disgust.

"The future belongs to the farsighted," Weldon said.

"Glad to hear," Wind River said, heading for the door, "it belongs to somebody."

Wind River stood on the wooden sidewalk and looked down Silverado Street. He'd been gone too long, as he could plainly see. Oh, he'd come to town, of course, but always just to buy his supplies, stock up on hooch, and, when he felt up to it or she'd have him, make a little visit to Daisy. He'd never cared, never taken the time to find out, what else was happening. Now it was important, and Wind River viewed the scene from a different viewpoint. Mountain City might not be much, but it was a harbinger of things to come. If he planned to go on to bigger and better, he'd better scout the situation with a keen eye.

Everything had grown, to begin with. When he'd started coming to town for supplies back in '95, less than half the buildings he now saw had been there. It bothered him that he hadn't even noticed them going up. Back in '95, he knew lots of folks. He hadn't paid attention to where they'd gone over the years. Now there were few he recognized. He tried to remember when someone had told him the lead smelter down the road had gone in, but couldn't. A year earlier? Two? Three? However many, the difference was disconcerting.

The Appaloosa nickered and Wind River roused himself. Hell, he was longing for city lights, wasn't he? That's why he'd left Elkhorn. If he thought Mountain City had changed, God only knew what the big cities were like. Taking a deep breath, he rubbed his palms together and decided he'd best get moving.

The Western shop wasn't all that bad. Kind of classy, compared to Weldon's, as a matter of fact. Smelled of leather and new cloth. A rack of fancy new Stetsons caught his eye. A glass case held worked-silver belt buckles. A counter that ran the length of the store was full of sheepskin-lined gloves, mufflers, thick wool socks. Winter coats filled one rack built right into the wall, and there were mirrors everywhere, even a low one for the boot section, which ran all the way across the back of the store.

"Well, the Wind River Kid," a voice said. Wind River turned to see Bert Brown glowing in the front door. "Good to see you. First time in here, ain't it? What do you think?"

Wind River hadn't seen anything like it since the last time he'd been through Denver, which had been in '89, but he wasn't about to admit his ignorance. "I think," he said, pointing to a pair of knobby-looking leather boots, "that anybody who pays seventy dollars for a pair of boots is a damned fool."

"That's prime ostrich leather is why." Bert's smile was warm. "Used to live pretty high on the hog yourself, Wind

River," he said, recalling with a twinge of nostalgia how the Wind River Kid had once been a legend for the children of Mountain City. He sneaked a look at the old man's boots. "Mark 'em down right smart, being as it's you. They aren't as tough as prime bull hide, but they're a durn sight prettier. Last a long time, you take care of them."

He'd bought his last pair of boots eight years earlier. Those on his feet had seen three sets of soles and double that many heels. The tops sagged like winter-worn long johns. If he was going to the big city... "How much?" he asked, unable to take his eyes from them.

Bert looked at the old man, remembering the first time he'd seen him. Bert had been a boy of twelve, the year 1892, when the rumors ran through Mountain City that the Wind River Kid had arrived. Every kid in town found an excuse to get down to Silverado Street. And sure enough, there he'd been, coming out of the Elephant Saloon. His clothes were black and elegantly cut, his walk modest but with a hint of a swagger, no doubt for the audience he knew was watching. He was trim and lean and exuded an aura of danger. Just for the kids, he let his coat fall open far enough for them to glimpse the slanted holster and the dark, well-used grip of the gun that had made him famous.

They hadn't known then that he was running, of course. They were children, too young to recognize the look of a hunted man. The Wind River Kid was the Wind River Kid. Handlebar mustache, hat tilted just so, boots so bright you could see your face in them; he was their hero. "Thirty-five dollars," Bert said with a gulp, hoping his wife never found out. "Half price."

Wind River looked quizzically at him.

"You wouldn't believe the mark up on these things," Bert lied, fearing his long-ago idol might suspect charity. "Don't worry. I won't make anything, but I won't lose anything, either."

They were light brown, the color of half-parched coffee beans, made of inch and a half squares of tough leather, each with a puckered spot where, Wind River supposed, a feather had been. "You take gold?" he asked.

"Nothing faster."

"Need a dozen pair of new socks, too. And gloves."

"Two ounces of dust and you carry them out with you," Bert said.

A few minutes later, his feet warm in brand-new woolen socks, Wind River's face broke into a cracked smile as he looked in the special mirror and beheld his feet. Watch out, Denver, he thought, wriggling his toes and deciding he felt better than he had in years. "They'll do," he said aloud. "Let's see your scales."

6

The clock on the Presbyterian church said two o'clock when Wind River walked out of the hardware store with a new ground cloth and the few pieces of tack he'd needed for the Appaloosa. The afternoon street was quiet. Almost lazily, Wind River mulled over whether he'd buy his grub or go see Daisy next. Three years had gone by since he'd had his ashes hauled, and Daisy had been on his mind more and more over the past months. The last time had been in the spring of '24, and from then on things had gone from bad to worse. In the fall of '24 he'd had to buy a new saddle and the purchase had left him broke. When he went to town in '25, he was told Daisy was in Denver for a cure in the spring, and she was shut down in the fall because of the new preacher. In the spring of '26, her prices had gone up, a fact he hadn't known until he'd bought everything else and ended up at her place short a dollar and she wouldn't give him any on credit. In the fall, she was closed for remodeling. He wasn't sure what had happened that spring. He'd sold his pelts and bought his grub, and then mentioned to Lewis that he was going over to Daisy's. Lewis had offered him a drink to get himself ready. One led to another, and before Wind River knew what was happening, it was morning, he had a hangover, and he was three miles out of town on his way back to Elkhorn. Now fall had come, and Wind River was one determined man. Horny as a mountain goat in rutting season, he wasn't going to let anyone or anything get in his way. He had almost a hundred dollars in cash saved, plus another nine ounces of gold in his poke. Daisy or one of her girls was going to be his that night, and more than once, by God. Without interruption, too.

Which meant business before pleasure, Wind River decided. Ready to brave the Piggly Wiggly, he led the Appaloosa down Silverado and tied him in front of the store. Nothing in his life before then had prepared him for what followed.

First off, the door didn't even have a handle. Wind River puzzled about how to get in, finally saw the sign that said EXIT ONLY. USE NEXT DOOR FOR ENTRANCE. A hand pointed the way. "Well, damn." Wind River grumbled, following a set of green, painted footsteps to the correct door. "What the hell kind of fool. . . ."

His mouth agape, Wind River stopped just inside the door. WELCOME TO PIGGLY WIGGLY! a sign in big red letters said. *Please feel free to use our courtesy baskets!*

Wind River looked around, spied a row of heavy wire baskets on small wheels. Experimenting, he touched one, moved it around until he got the hang of it. A sign saying ENTER was stuck on a post with arms sticking out of it. "Just push on through," a cheerful voice called. Wind River peered around a corner to see Aaron Ritz standing behind a counter. "Good to see you, Mr. River," the pleasant-faced dark-haired young man said. "How do you like my new store?"

The turnstile creaked as it turned. Wind River jumped when the following paddle swatted his rear. He was pleased that Ritz remembered him, but wasn't about to acknowledge it. "Let you know when I'm through," he said.

He'd never seen the like. Electric lights blazed even though it was the middle of the day. The floor was swept and immaculate, the walls above the shelves painted a clean white. Signs hung all over urging him to buy everything from soup to soap. Three women, two of whom were dressed in what looked like their Sunday best, moved confidently through the store, casually filling their baskets. Feeling shabby, awkward, and out of place, Wind River pushed his basket down the aisle.

Aaron Ritz stocked more groceries in his store than Lewis Weldon ever had. Shelf upon shelf jammed with merchandise greeted Wind River. Boxes and bags of salt. Baking soda. Spices. Row after row of canned vegetables, all piled neatly on top of one another and out where a man could get at them instead of rooting around in the boxes like at Weldon's. Boxes of crackers, tins of sardines, jars of mustard and pickles. Flour and sugar and cornmeal in bags all the way from five pounds to fifty, although why anyone would bother with a five-pound bag of any of them was a mystery. Same way with lard, Wind River thought, suspiciously inspecting a tiny one-pound package before adding two eight-pound tins to the supplies already piling up in his basket.

The aisles guided him, dictated his path past luxuries beyond number. Six kinds of coffee, three of tea. Peanut butter. Jams and preserves, jars of honey and molasses and cane syrup. Sauces and condiments he'd never heard of, and more tinned fruits to make a man's mouth water than he could count. Bins of potatoes and carrots and onions and turnips. Bag upon bag of beans. Wind River was wide-eyed and weak-kneed. Never had he seen so much food in one place except in restaurants back when his wandering path took him through the big cities, and that was different. By the time he arrived at the counter, his basket was full. "Yes, sir, Mr. River. Good to see you again," Ritz repeated, waving toward the window at a well-dressed gentleman walking past. Ritz started pulling boxes and bags out of the basket. "Beautiful weather we're having, isn't it?"

"Didn't see no sides of bacon," Wind River responded. "Didn't see no liniment."

Ritz's fingers played a merry tune on the cash register. "Yes, sir. Sorry. I've got sliced bacon by the pound, but for sides, you'll have to go to the butcher. As for liniment, the pharmacy carries it." He flipped a tin of peaches, the last item in the basket, deftly caught it, and dropped it in a nearly full cardboard box. "That be all, then? Sure I can't interest you in some marmalade? Taste mighty nice of a winter morning."

Wind River looked nervously at the pile he'd already bought. "How much I owe you so far?" he asked.

The cash register chimed and four numbers jumped up. "Thirty-seven twenty-four," Ritz said, beaming.

A sinking feeling hit Wind River's stomach. Stunned, he looked at Ritz, at the box of expensive groceries he'd bought, and back at the rest of the store. He'd been taken. Sucked in by pretty signs and bright lights. Just like a pilgrim, a country boy come to town for the first time. A pair of con artists trapping a novice between them and dealing from the bottom of the deck couldn't have done a neater job. The marvel was, none of the other shoppers looked even vaguely worried. Their faces bland, they dropped cans and packages into their baskets without a backward glance. One, dressed in a severe gray suit, approached the counter and eyed him impatiently. "I reckon I got enough," Wind River said hurriedly, wishing he hadn't succumbed to the lure of dill pickles and peanut butter and strawberry jam. Weakly, embarrassed to ask Ritz to take back what he didn't need, he undid his purse from his belt and counted out the money.

Ritz didn't even help him carry it all out. Not that Wind River needed help, of course, he grumbled to himself as he dropped a twenty-five-pound sack of beans on his wagon. It was the principle. You could say what you wanted about Lewis Weldon, but at least he gave a hand to a customer. "You've hauled worse," Wind River growled when the Appaloosa balked. Wind River led him down the street to the butcher's, left him untied while he bought a slab of bacon, then to the pharmacy while he bought liniment and, in a fit of forgetfulness, a rope of licorice he didn't need any more than the dill pickles. Back outside, he stared at the full wagon, wondered what had possessed him. "Well, horse," he finally said, shaking his head, "I guess we can go wherever we want. If Denver looks bad, we can keep right on going. Eat our way across the whole damn country," he added sourly.

He took the reins and led the Appaloosa away from the

center of town, away from the Piggly Wiggly sign and toward Daisy's. Now and then he thought he recognized some of the townspeople, but no one acknowledged his nod. The idea depressed him. New people, new stores, a whole new way of life. Hell, nothing looked the same or felt the same. What he wouldn't give for the old days. What he wouldn't give . . .

An orison to turn back the clock, a supplication useless as a spit in a windstorm. Wind River kept his eyes on the dirt in front of him, on alternating left and right toes of new boots. He didn't want to look at the new people and their homes and the world they were building. Memories of older, sweeter times rubbed salt in the open wound of his brain. Leaving Elkhorn was going to be harder than he had thought. There was a comfort in Aden Creed's haunting, in the damned falcon. And the bear? A shiver ran down Wind River's spine. No, not the bear. Better to weather the newness than watch Elkhorn being torn to pieces bit by bit.

Daisy's looked about the same from the outside except for a sign that said DAISY'S FRENCH SALON. Wind River tethered the Appaloosa to the picket fence and took a deep breath. There was one thing that had changed for the better. If Daisy could advertise, the world had to be a little better off. Wind River folded his arms and gazed with fond recollection at the whitewashed frame house with the deep-blue stained-glass windows that had always reminded him of two eyes framing a nose that was the double door.

She'd have new girls, no doubt. French, maybe. Wind River's loins began to itch in anticipation, and he closed his eyes to prolong the sensation. When he opened them, a stout but appealing woman dressed in black and wearing a stylish pillbox hat with a feather held in a jeweled clasp was coming down the steps. When she reached the gate, Wind River swung it open for her, doffed his hat, and flashed her his most lascivious grin. "Don't run off, honey," he said, wondering why Daisy had taken on a woman so old. "The best is yet to come."

The woman's eyebrows rose. Her shoulders squared and her breasts jutted imperiously. "I beg your pardon!" she hissed, and hurried away, nose in the air.

Wind River closed the gate after him, hoped that what the

woman lacked in friendliness and youth she made up for in experience. Hoping, too, there'd be some younger ones, he hurried up the walk and entered Daisy's without knocking.

"Hide your women, guard your kin! I've . . ."

Three stern ladies with frightened eyes stared at him with alarm. They were all middle-aged and unattractive. They all wore hair curlers, and a layer of mud covered their faces

"Lord!" Wind River exclaimed, backing away from the gorgon masks. "Lord, Lord!"

Daisy emerged from a rear room that had once been an extension of the parlor. She was a big-boned, soft-featured country girl whose fifty years rode easily on her broad back and thick arms and shoulders. She had been born on a farm, had run off to Denver as a girl to lead a wild life, and had then brought some of it to Mountain City until the changing mores of a dying frontier forced her to alter her style drastically.

"Oh, no," she groaned.

"Daisy!" Wind River said, relieved to see not only a familiar face but a human one as well.

Daisy flashed a knowing smile at her concerned customers, all new arrivals to Mountain City. Before Wind River could speak again, she snatched him by the arm and propelled him into the back room. There Wind River caught a glimpse of a fourth woman customer sitting beneath a large metal contraption that was connected to her head by a tangle of looping wires. Her eyes were saucer-wide, whether because she was experiencing some indescribably painful procedure or simply because Wind River had frightened her as much as she had him, Wind River had no way of knowing, for he was immediately womanhandled out the back door.

"Hey," he protested, struggling.

"Shush!" Daisy pushed him down the back steps and, hands on hips, glared at him. "That'll be just about enough out of you, Wind River," she said angrily.

"What the hell, Daisy!" Wind River's feelings were hurt. Why was he being treated so shabbily? "I brought enough for a good time. Name the price. Hell, it's been so long I don't even know if I can remember how it feels."

Daisy looked perplexed, then incredulous as Wind River

went on. "I mean it, Daisy. Name your price." He dug into his poke, pulled out two good-sized nuggets. "These here ought to weigh out pretty good."

"You mean you ain't heard?" Daisy said, softening.

"Ain't heard nothin', ain't smelled nothin', ain't touched or felt nothin', by way of a woman since the spring of '24." He held out the nuggets. They shone dully in the afternoon sun. "Hell, Daisy, I'm here for a good time," he whined. "I don't want no sass and gimme-gaw."

"Oh, Jesus, Wind River." Daisy laughed. "Ain't you the berries! I ain't in the trade no more."

"Gimme a young gal with flashing teeth," Wind River rhapsodized. "Gimme one with firm legs and a smile like sundown. Gimme . . . What?"

Daisy walked down the steps, curved Wind River's fingers around his gold, and patted his closed hand. "I ain't in the trade no more. Them days is over with."

"I don't understand." Wind River's voice had a desperate quiver to it.

"I took me a mail-order course. Hairdressin' and all the rest. Ordered and bought the equipment, and went into a respectable business for myself."

Wind River looked as if he'd been kicked in the head by a horse and hadn't yet fully revived. "But I brought gold," he mumbled.

"Mountain City is growin', Wind River. The lead mine's goin' full blast and people are movin' in as quick as they can build homes. People who don't know or couldn't care less about the past. There's a fortune to be made if a girl sets herself up right. Ladies like to look nice wherever they live. Don't you see, Wind River?" she finished plaintively.

"Two of the best I ever found," Wind River said, holding out the nuggets again. "Saved 'em just for you."

Daisy sighed. "You ain't even listenin' to me, Wind River." She wagged her head, brushed her bangs away from her eyebrows. "Look, why don't you go on. Buy yourself a bottle or two," she said in a kindly voice. "Dream, old-timer. Have a good time. That's what I do. I gotta go." She spun on her heel and hurried back inside without a backward glance.

Wind River stared at the back door. He would have marched after her and demanded his rights had Daisy not outweighed him by fifty pounds and packed a harder punch. He kicked at the dirt, but when that proved as useless as staring at the door, stuffed the nuggets into his poke and walked around the house to collect the Appaloosa.

Slowly he trudged back toward the center of town. Wind River felt lost, forsaken by time and circumstances. The streets were growing crowded, people were staring at him, the swaybacked old Appaloosa, and the rickety, pieced-together wagon Wind River's ears burned with shame. He was a relic, a curiosity. A spook, the boys and girls said.

But what did they know? he asked himself. The Piggly Wiggly loomed on his right. Bright lights burned. A young man dressed in a suit and carrying a sack full of groceries emerged. Had that boy ever been forced to live by his wits? Had he faced a pat hand and bet his last dollar on three lowly treys? Had he stared down the maws of smoking guns, braved the winter mountain snows? Hell, no, he hadn't. Could he build a fire or live off the land? Make his own medicine, find his own meat, blaze his own trail if need be? Hell, no, he couldn't. Wind River was twice the man at seventy-one as the whole lot of town-raised, panty-waisted, smirking younkers. And if they thought they had him down, they were as mistaken as a pup dog trying to hump a bull moose.

I'm the Wind River Kid, the old man thought, his teeth grinding. Let 'em have their French salons and their god-damned Piggly Wigglys filled with a bunch of useless trash and lard in puny little one-pound bricks. He'd learn it all and beat them at their game, the way he had in the old days. Nobody kept the Wind River Kid down. Not for long.

"Help you?" a younger version of Lewis Weldon, only with hair and without a chaw, said from behind the counter as Wind River walked into the store.

"Your pa."

"In the back," the boy said, jabbing a finger toward the rear door.

Weldon was digging a long, narrow hole inside the front

door of the barn. When he saw Wind River, he climbed out, wiped the sweat from his face with a rag. "Well," he said. "What do you think?"

"You plannin' to plant someone right there in the open?" Wind River asked, thinking perhaps Lewis had joined the rest of the town and gone plumb, stark raving mad.

"What?" Weldon looked at the hole, back to Wind River. "That there's a grease pit."

Wind River shook his head. "Seems like an almighty strange place to keep grease in."

"Keep grease in?" The storekeeper's belly shook with laughter. "Jesus, Wind River, but you take the cake. Where you been, anyway? You drive your car over this hole," he explained, "then I climb down inside and work on the underneath."

"You don't drive my car over no hole," Wind River said, still dubious. "Don't have one and don't plan to get one. Not so long as there's horses. That one ride you give me last year was enough. 'Course I could lead my Appaloosa over that hole. You'd see a sight more than grease then," he added with a chuckle.

Weldon snorted. The mountains were full of old-timers who'd never make their peace with the new age, who didn't recognize progress even when it hit them in the face. "Look, Wind River, I don't have time for this. Is there something I can do for you?"

Wind River jangled his poke. "If a fellow was interested in finding himself a couple of bottles, would you know where he might look?" he asked.

"Well, now." Lewis grinned. "That's different. I wouldn't want to break the law, of course, but I just happen to have a few real pretty bottles. Mind you, I don't know what's inside them, but they're right nice. Maybe even collector's items. C'mon back here. Watch your step. Don't kick dirt in my hole."

The rear of the barn was already beginning to look like a garage. A pair of shiny new gas pumps in one corner waited to be installed. New workbenches had been built. A ladder reached into the rafters, where someone had been stringing electric wire. Wind River followed Weldon, stood to one side as the storekeeper pressed a panel on what turned out to be a false-fronted cabinet. The doors swung outward on hinges. Weldon reached inside and pulled out two corked and wax-sealed quart bottles. "That'll be one dollar."

Wind River opened his poke, peeled a single off what remained of his roll. "This better be good, for a dollar," he said, tucking the money in Weldon's shirt pocket and taking the bottles.

"Good?" Weldon said, his feelings hurt. "It'll frizzle your hair and curl your toes." He turned to close the concealed door. "Preston St. Vrain made it. You ever hear of anybody making better hooch? Hell, the devil himself couldn't improve on that stuff. You recall that last batch? . . ." He looked around, found that he was alone. By the time Lewis picked his way past the boxes and assorted junk, the Wind River Kid was disappearing around the corner of the store. Weldon jumped into the grease pit and resumed digging. A few seconds later he caught a glimpse of the Appaloosa, Wind River, and his dilapidated wagon heading up Silverado. Weldon leaned on his shovel, clucked sympathetically. "Crazy old coot," he said, remembering the Wind River Kid of old and suddenly wondering whether all the progress was worth it or not. But there wasn't really time to think about that. After all, he had a grease pit to dig.

7

Lode Benedict was mad, and in his wrinkled, bedraggled, unwashed state, no one had ever cared to approach him and ask why. It was just as well: he wouldn't have answered. Madness locked out the past, dulled the present, and denied the prospects of any future at all. No more impenetrable wall could have been designed or built.

Lode drooled, too. He had since shortly after his lower lip had been badly mauled by a fox terrier owned by the Mountain City marshal in an unfortunate incident. Lode had been sleeping off his latest drunk in a cell that the marshal had failed to close when the dog snuck in and vented its nasty temper on poor Lode. Half drunk himself, Doc Bufker had stitched the wound, and ever since, Lode had drooled through the hole where the stitches hadn't taken.

Wind River handed Lode the bottle. Lode nodded and took a swig, scratched a pine needle out of his hair, and handed back the bottle. The whiskey was better than he usually got, although he was only faintly aware of the difference. A placid smile on his face, he blinked his eyes and stared at the moon. The moon winked at him, and he winked back.

There had been a time when Wind River wondered why Lode was the way he was. Wind River stared at the bottle, stared at Lode, and pondered. For ten years he'd been checking up on Lode every time he came to town. Not that

Wind River could do much, of course, but every little bit helped. What would happen, he wondered bleakly, when he left and never came back? Who would keep an eye on Lode Benedict? Unable to think of an answer, he stared at the moon as it balanced on the branches of the pine tree he was sitting against. When the moon blurred, he looked downslope to Lode's cabin, and beyond it to the twinkling lights of Mountain City. His throat burned from the contents of Lewis Weldon's collectible antique bottle. "I'm dying," he groaned.

Lode stared at the moon and winked.

"I just realized it. Awful for a man to go this long and not realize it. Seems a fellow ought to see it coming in snatches and pieces, not all at once. It isn't fair." He belched, and the fire caught him for the second time. "Ahhh, shit. What is?"

Lode frowned, winked more emphatically.

"Piggly Wiggly," Wind River said scornfully. "Piggly Wiggly." He tilted the bottle and swallowed holy hell. "Daisy used to have such long, sweet-smelling hair. Cut it off. She looks more like a man than any two men I know."

The moon finally winked back.

"I don't want no part of it. Her or her sign."

Lode smiled. It was nice to have a friend. The moon was a nice friend. His heart full, he winked again at his friend.

"Progress," Wind River mumbled, slipping off the tree trunk and falling onto his side. "Piggly Wiggly." He cradled the bottle in the crook of his left arm and curled into a fetal position. "I'm scared, Lode. Scared."

Lode looked away from his friend the moon, down at his other friend, the old man who always came to see him and treated him nice. Softly, he covered him with the blanket he had brought to sit on, returned to his cabin, and went to bed.

The moon winked.

8

Wind River woke up on the back of his horse, surrounded by trees. More or less woke up. Dynamite was exploding inside his head. His mouth tasted like a buzzard's nest. His stomach was host to a witches' brew churned by the fire in his gut. The Appaloosa was plodding through a small stand of golden aspen that was too bright to look at. Wind River felt something hard knock against his thigh, realized it was a bottle. In the dim recesses of his mind, he remembered a second bottle he'd stashed in the wagon. He tried to recall just how he had managed to hitch up the wagon, saddle the horse, mount, and ride off. Maybe Lode had helped him.

The Appaloosa stumbled. Wind River fought to keep his balance, held on for dear life. His hip was killing him, and he remembered he'd slept on the ground. That must have been it, he thought, rubbing his forehead and fighting down the rising nausea. Sleeping on the ground brought on bad hangovers. A little hair of the dog that bit him was what he needed. A gas pocket expanded in his gut. Maybe the whole dadgum dog, he reconsidered.

There wasn't much left. Wind River cocked one eye at the bottle, popped the cork with his teeth, and spit it out. Tilting his head back, he swallowed. It felt as if he'd stuck a knife into his stomach.

"Where we goin'?" he rasped, not really caring.

The Appaloosa ignored him, picked his way through a dry stream bed, and emerged into a clearing.

"See if I give a damn," Wind River said, shading his eyes. It was around ten o'clock in the morning, according to the sun. That was kind of strange, though, because mountains rose ahead of him and if they were heading south and east the mountains should have been petering out. Wind River stiffened in the saddle. Morning, hell. It was afternoon! "Whoa!" he yelled, hauling in the reins with a mighty tug. "You're goin' north, you damned-fool horse! Whoa!"

The Appaloosa pawed at the air, dug his hind legs into the soft, grass-covered turf, and kept to his own course.

Wind River held on, sawed on the reins. North! Goddamn! The fool horse was taking him back to Elkhorn. "No, we ain't gonna go that way. No, sir! Hold it!"

Once in the spring, once in the fall, they made the round trip to Mountain City and back again. The pattern had been the same for the last sixteen years and was deeply ingrained in the Appaloosa. It didn't make any difference what Wind River wanted. The Appaloosa knew where he was supposed to go and was diligent in his obstinacy. Deviation from routine was not part of his world. The fight went on in grim silence, slowly seesawed back and forth between man and horse. Wind River drove the blunt clubs of his bootheels into the Appaloosa's flanks, jerked mightily on the reins. The aging stallion gave way and veered around to the west, then got the bit into his teeth and headed north again. The wagon bounded over an exposed root, hit a rock, and slewed to the side. Miraculously, the wheels stayed intact. Wind River considered dismounting and leading the animal, but the Appaloosa speeded up enough to give him second thoughts. They passed out of the clearing and hit the trail north through the pine forest.

The Appaloosa was winning. Wind River's hangover was forgotten and he began to panic. He shrieked for the horse to stop, cursed the shady aspects of its origins, cursed the day he had bought it and the three ounces of gold dust it had cost. Unconcerned, unconvinced, uncooperative, the Appaloosa plodded forward. Ducking a tree limb, Wind River caught a mouthful of mane for his trouble. He reached forward and bit the stallion's ear. The Appaloosa let out a shrill scream and bolted forward. Behind him, the wagon swayed and careened dangerously until, winded by his short but ever northward run, the Appaloosa slowed again.

Wind River gave up and rested. Elkhorn was still miles to the north, he was still on the cutoff trail he'd blazed years earlier that saved a good dozen miles from the wider road used by the ore wagons and stagecoaches in the old days. Three miles ahead, he'd run into the crossover to the stagecoach route and would be forced to make a decision. If he kept to the side trail, there'd be nothing he could do to keep the Appaloosa from heading straight back to Elkhorn with its bear, with Aden Creed, with its memories. If he could talk the horse onto the crossover, his choices were more varied. He could go onto the stagecoach road, let the horse have its head, and end up in Elkhorn. He could follow the same plan, but keep right on through town and try for Lincoln Pass before the first storm hit. He could stop at Lazy Girl Spring for the night and then try to get the damned animal disoriented enough in the morning to cross the stagecoach road and strike the trail through Angel Valley and over Temptation Pass. If he was lucky enough, they'd be far enough south to hit the road to Idaho Springs and Denver before the Appaloosa figured it out, and then it would be too late.

The closer they came to Lazy Girl Spring, the better the last plan sounded. By the time they camped for the night, Wind River's outlook was positively rosy. "Stupid damned beast," he said, tethering the Appaloosa in the center of a patch of good grass. "We'll see who gets the last laugh." Later, wrapped in a blanket and lying in front of his fire, Wind River watched the stars and dreamed of the days to come. The roundabout route would slow him down, but he didn't really care, even looked forward to it. The last time he'd been through Angel Valley had been back in the eighties, and he remembered a beautiful waterfall where he'd spent the night with a dance-hall girl who had be-friended him. "Ah," he sighed, sleepy and already dozing off. "Those were the days. Those *were* the days." At last he slept, with the clear sky over him and the whispering pines comforting him.

The morning sky was gray and ominous. There had been a good inch of snow during the night. A vicious wind barreled through Angel Valley and across Wind River's campsite. The Appaloosa stood with its tail to the west and Wind River hunched over the fire he'd built in the lee of a deadfall. He held a cup of black coffee in his gloved hands and ruminated on his ill-fated luck. The first storm of the year had hit sooner than expected. Visions of Denver dissipated as rapidly as the steam from his coffee cup.

A snowflake drifted past his shoulder and settled on the oily surface of the coffee. Wind River stood and shaded his face. The storm had blown in from the west. Angel Valley was a meandering, dull shadow that led right into the teeth of the wind and snow. He had food enough, of course, but there was no telling how long he'd have to camp out, and he wasn't sure his bones could take the punishment. The snow-capped peaks in the north looked tantalizingly close, yet were in reality too far to reach before Lincoln Pass closed in. In that distant sky, clouds that had built up while he slept swirled and boiled. If he tried there, he'd freeze to death. To the east, flying low, a huge V of geese heading south gave their beauty to the morning, gave it freely in contrast to Wind River's sour mood. Their song, a chorus of joy and sorrow unending, had set Wind River's heart racing once, when as a young man he had been immune to the real meaning of change. He watched the geese. The Appaloosa stamped his hooves and impatiently pawed the ground.

"You knew all along," Wind River grumbled bitterly. He finished his coffee, tossed out the dregs. With the change in weather, his choices had shrunk to two. He could wait out the storm in Elkhorn or return to Mountain City, be a spook, and get drunk with Lode. It was some choice. "Okay, horse," he said, resigned. "Elkhorn it is. But only until the storm breaks. The first snow won't last long. It's only tempo-rary."

He washed out cup and pot, stowed them in the wagon. He saddled the Appaloosa, lashed the lodgepole pines tightly to the horse's flanks, and made sure the wagon was running freely. He mounted up and moved out. By the time he'd backtracked to the cutoff trail, his hands felt like cold clay in his gloves, his heart like a block of ice in his chest. His teeth clenched, he sang against the cold.

> "Her soul was a ribbon that no man could tie,
> Her demeanor was gentle, her manner was shy,
> And I was a young man, so brave and so bold,
> And I was a roamer who yearned for the gold.

> > So farewell, Lorena,
> > It's free I must be.
> > Farewell, Angelina,
> > and sweet Rosemarie.

> The ladies of Frisco were cultured and gay.
> They cried how they loved me and begged me to stay.
> But I was a young man with hard calloused hands,
> And I had a taste for the far distant lands.

> > So, farewell, Lorena,
> > It's free I must be.
> > Farewell, Angelina,
> > and sweet Rosemarie."

The song, an old one he'd sung when riding alone as a young man, went on and on. In the end, of course, the young man left and never again saw Lorena, Angelina, or sweet Rosemarie. In the old days, Wind River had thought the song was ineffably sad. Now he just sang because it was cold and because he needed something to do to while away the time on his way back to Elkhorn, where he didn't really want to be.

> > "So farewell, Lorena.
> > It's free I must be.
> > Farewell, Angelina,
> > and sweet Rosemarie."

"If it wasn't for the snow," he muttered when the song ended. "If it wasn't for the goldurn snow."

9

The cutoff trail met the stagecoach route three miles south of Elkhorn. The old road was an undisturbed white avenue slippery with snow and hidden mud, and the going was slow. The sun had set an hour earlier when the Appaloosa paused on top of Damnation Hill. Below, Elkhorn looked like little more than strangely rectangular shadows, only briefly revealed as buildings in what little moonlight made its way through the heavy clouds.

Snow flecked the stallion's mane with diamonds, brushed the back of Wind River's neck. "Come on, horse," he said, too tired and cold to curse. "The last mile's the easiest." He poked at the animal's ribs, leaned forward. "Mind you watch that loose shale. Be ice on it, probably."

The Appaloosa didn't have to be told. Tired himself and looking forward to getting out of the wind, he picked his way down the hill and actually speeded up along Main Street. For a second, Wind River thought he smelled smoke, but dismissed that as the product of an overactive imagination. Besides, reality was more disquieting. Two more buildings, the newspaper office and Widow Guthrie's dress shop, had been torn apart. Knowing full well it was the work of the bear, Wind River shuddered and blamed the cold. "Well, we're back," he said, dismounting in front of the livery. "All thanks to you." The doors creaked open on rusty hinges.

"Wait just a goldurn minute," he added when the Appaloosa nudged him between the shoulders. "You want to walk in on a sleepin' bear? Bein' stubborn I can understand, but don't turn damned fool to boot."

Wind River stepped inside, groped for the lantern kept by the door, and lit it. A little drift of snow had collected under a broken board in the north wall, but other than that, nothing looked different. The Appaloosa hadn't waited, was already at the mound of hay piled against the back wall. "You're lucky we didn't take everything with us," Wind River said, digging some oats out of the tin and dumping them in the trough. The stallion nickered and pushed his master's hand out of the way. "Hay's mighty slim eating after a ride like that."

A light skim of ice had formed on the water trough in the corral. Wind River broke through it, brought a bucket of water inside, and set it in the holder next to the oats. He loosened the lodgepole pines, backed the wagon away from the horse. "Least we'll sleep warm tonight," he said, returning to remove the saddle, bit, and bridle. "Guess I can thank you for that, too, can't I." The horse munched on oats, paid no attention. "Just the same, don't get feelin' too uppity. We're leavin' come the end of this storm. You just wait and see." Wind River threw an old blanket over the horse, then sorted through the load on the wagon, filled a burlap sack with what provisions he'd need for a few days, and found his bedroll. "Keep an eye on the rest of it," he said over his shoulder. "Any coyotes come in and start nosin' around my grub, you kick 'em out pronto."

Wind River closed the livery door and started for Muenster's Funeral Parlor before remembering the broken door that let the wind through. He'd need a warmer place tonight. He veered toward the hotel. The snow, still spotty, was the beginning of a first-rate storm. Flakes kissed his cheek, melted, and ran through the thick stubble of his beard. Others followed, finding his lowered head. The wind tugged at his hat. Burdened by the load he carried, bent forward by the cold and the stiffness of the ride and the pounding the stallion had given him when they had fought for the right to decide where they were going, Wind River hurried down Main Street. From somewhere high in the mountains, a wolf howled. Wind River clutched the burlap sack and his bedroll, peered apprehensively to his right at the remains of the barbershop. Animal shapes lurked in the deep shadows, sparked his imagination, and filled him with fear. Scar. Avenging bear. Wind River held his breath. The damn grizzly might be anywhere, watching, waiting....

Creed hadn't showed up to watch him ride in, Wind River suddenly remembered, grasping at any straw that would take his mind off the bear. Probably looking at me, though, and laughing to boot, he thought. It wasn't the first time the Wind River Kid had left for good, only to show up again a few days later. Well, he'd see who had the last laugh when the storm let up. Tonight was another story. Wind River was too damned cold to argue, too tired to put up with the farts and snide comments that Creed would bring to any conversation.

Two doors led into the Great Northern Hotel: the main one to the lobby, a side one directly into the dining room. Wind River quietly scraped his boots and, keeping an eye out for Creed, tiptoed down the porch to the side entrance. To his right, a sudden gust of wind ripped loose a board in the already mangled barbershop. Wind River jumped and, chased by a sudden premonition of danger, as if Scar himself were looming out of the dark to attack, darted inside and slammed the door behind him just as a shrill scream of terror split the silent depths of the dining room. Wind River's heart leaped to his throat. Before he could move, an orange light followed by a deafening explosion lanced out of the darkness.

"*Jeeee-suuuuusssss!*" Wind River yelled, lunging to one side. He slammed into a chair and fell over a table as the gun fired again. And again. And again. The arm of a chair behind him exploded in a shower of wooden slivers. Something whined past his head, smacked into a table. A porcelain vase that had weathered a landslide unscathed was obliterated, smashed into a thousand pieces. Wind River screamed and a high-pitched voice screamed in answer, and the gun fired and fired and then was silent.

His ears rang, his mouth tasted like gunmetal. Trying

desperately to escape, Wind River crawled around captain's chairs and under pedestaled tables. Suddenly the room brightened as the door to the lobby flew open and a man carrying a lantern ran in from the lobby. "Lainie, what the hell?" the man said. He held a revolver. The amber light from the lantern spilled across the frightened, huddled form of a girl in front of the fireplace. She pointed in the direction of Wind River, who was peeking around an overturned table.

"Hold it right there, you bastard," the man snarled. "Goddamnit, Lieght, you don't quit, do you?"

The voice sounded distant through the ringing in his ears. Wind River wondered at the name and took a chance. Hands aloft, the veins on his temples standing out, he willed his rubbery knees to straighten and showed himself. "Don't shoot," he said, his voice trembling. "I ain't no Lieght."

"It just went off," the girl said meekly. She was crying and her slim hand was weighed down by a .45-caliber Browning automatic pistol. "I didn't mean … It just went off."

Roman looked surprised to see an old man with skinny wrists and shaking hands poking out from his sleeves. "What the hell?… An old man. Just an old man." Quickly, not trusting his eyes, he set the lantern on a table and stepped outside its glow. "Who the hell are you, pops, and what're you doing here?"

Wind River remembered the smoke he'd smelled, wished he'd taken heed. He studied the young man, saw a fair-haired, tall, and broad-shouldered youth who was acting tough to cover up how scared he actually was. The girl, Wind River could see now, was pale-skinned and had hair like filaments of jet cut in long bangs over deep brown, frightened eyes. She was dressed in a light-green filmy gown cut above her knees. Her legs were slim, albescent lines of flesh.

Roman waved his revolver in Wind River's direction. "I ain't gonna ask again, pops. Who are you? Who sent you?"

"They call me the Wind River Kid," Wind River said, his eyes swiveling to the gun. His fingers splayed wide and he poked them higher into the air. "Don't shoot, mister."

"Kid? Kid?" Roman's voice cracked with tension. A forgotten Lucky Strike between his lips bobbed up and down as he talked. Crouching, he ran to Lainie's side, traded guns with her, and immediately began to reload the automatic. "Well, Kid, you're trespassing, you know. Get killed that way." The magazine snapping into place and the snick of the slide being pulled back were chilling sounds. "Lieght sent you, didn't he? Sent you in first. He's with you—out there waiting."

"Trespassin'?" Wind River said, incensed in spite of his fear. "Trespassin', by God!"

"Where is he? On the front porch? At the side? Keep out of the light, Lainie. Keep an eye on him." Roman zigzagged through chairs and tables to the lobby, appeared a moment later, and made his way along the wall to the open side door.

Wind River looked over his shoulder, saw Roman down on one knee, the automatic extended in front of him as he peeked around the door onto the porch and into the street. "You're wastin' your time," he said, trying to be helpful. "There ain't nobody there. And I don't know no Lieght, whoever he is."

Roman acted as if he didn't hear him. Abruptly he sprang through the door and disappeared. A moment later Wind River and Lainie could hear his footsteps on the front porch, then returning to the side door. "Only one set of tracks I can see," Roman said, coming in and closing the door securely after him. He appeared a little calmer as he kicked the snow off his shoes and brushed it off his jacket. "Maybe he's telling the truth, after all."

"Hell, yes, I'm tellin' the truth," Wind River snorted. "This here is my town and I'm the only one who lives in it. My town! You're the ones who are trespassin'."

"Ahh, nerts to you, too, old man." Roman stabbed out the Lucky in an ashtray designed for fifty-cent cigars and threaded his way through the tables. "You got a gun?" he asked, quickly patting Wind River's sides and pockets. "Go on, put your arms down before they fall down. Hell, Lieght would have to be pretty desperate to use the likes of you." He walked across the room to the fireplace, held out his hands to warm them. "Damn! I wish I'd given you the .38 in the first place. We can't afford to waste bullets."

Lainie sat heavily in one of the armchairs in front of the

fire. She looked terribly tiny and fragile with her legs curled under her and her hands tightly clutching her shoulders. "It wasn't my fault, Roman," she said in a pleading voice. "It just kept going off." She shuddered, held out the .38 to Roman. "Here. Take this one, too. I don't want a gun. I'm afraid. Look what I almost did."

Roman ignored her, walked to the window facing the street. "One set of tracks. Unless there's some other old coot holed up here." He glanced over his shoulder at Wind River. "How do I know there ain't, huh? How do I know that five minutes from now Bronco Billy won't come through that door with guns drawn and blazing like in the movies?"

"'Cause I told you so," Wind River said sullenly. "Nobody but me here, and hasn't been for years. 'Course, you could go out and see. Go out and don't come back."

"Don't get too smart, pops," Roman said. He turned to watch as Wind River crossed the room, grabbed his bedroll and bag of provisions, and started for the lobby door. "Going somewhere?" he asked in a conversational tone that was tinged with menace.

"Puttin' up my things."

Roman intercepted him halfway across the room. "What things?"

"Just my bedroll and such," Wind River said, keeping himself between the bag and the young man.

"Leave it on the table."

"Why? It's mine."

"We'll see," Roman said. He reached around Wind River, grabbed the burlap sack, and spilled the contents on a table. "Well, I'll be damned," he said with an added whistle. "And such, he said. Such isn't bad at all. See there, Lainie? Look at all that food. The Kid"—he chuckled even as he said it—"the Kid here is a real find. A diamond in the rough."

"Roman?..." Lainie said, chiding softly.

"Forget it, baby. We didn't buy near as much as we needed in that stupid hick town. What do you think we'll eat if we have to hide here longer than a few weeks? Pine cones?"

"We can pay you, Mr. ... uh ... Kid," the girl said, harsh and embarrassed at the same time. "We have money."

"Lainie!" Roman exclaimed, stricken. His gangster image crumbled and he looked thoroughly worried. Lainie cringed in her chair. Roman stuffed the food back in the burlap sack. "All right. You're alone. I'll buy that. Still, no one asked you to come here, but you did," he said, reverting to the clipped tones of the tough gangster he imagined himself to be. He hefted the bag, grinned approvingly. "So be it. Just stay out of our way and we'll stay out of yours."

"What am I supposed to eat?" Wind River asked lamely.

Roman didn't answer. "There's enough for all of us, isn't there, Mr. Kid?" Lainie said, filling in the awkward silence. "And when the storm lifts, you can always buy yourself some more. We'll see to it, won't we, Roman?"

Roman looked away. Wind River studied the girl. Deprivation wearing face paint and fake pearls. He knew the type.

Lainie stood. "There? You see? Now." She set the .38 on a table and clapped her hands, as if thoroughly satisfied that everything had been solved. "Now. I'll make us some coffee. Papa always said I made good coffee. Things won't seem so dreary then." She started toward the kitchen, stopped, and turned in the doorway. "I'm sorry for shooting at you, Mr. Kid." She looked pained and terribly unsure, and her attempted smile was a total failure. "Really, I am."

Wind River stared at her as she left. Only when the kitchen door swung closed did he steal a glance toward the Hawken rifle hung above the hearth. It was still loaded. If he could get at it . . .

"What are your looking at?" Roman asked harshly.

Wind River pointed at the fireplace. "You let that fire out and you'll freeze your tail off tonight."

Roman stared at him, then walked to the fire and added a few logs. A column of sparks whooshed up the chimney.

The initial, sharp edge of his fear dulled, Wind River watched him. The boy was in trouble, he was certain. Nobody swaggered around with such exaggerated toughness unless he was afraid of someone or something. It was an attitude Wind River knew well. "You runnin' from the law?" he asked.

Roman twisted violently to one side, glared at Wind River a moment, and then looked straight ahead into the darkness.

The glow of the fire revealed the profile of a grim smile on his face. At last, he stood and turned his backside to the building flames. The dull glow of the lantern twenty feet away across the room barely lit his face as he stared at Wind River in open hostility, as if by blaming the old man for his troubles he might escape self-recrimination.

"Here it is!" Lainie said as she posed in the doorway. Coffeepot in one hand, three cups in the other, her forced cheerfulness forced a wedge into the tension between the two men. "Nothing like hot coffee," she said, starting toward the fireplace, "to take the chill off . . . Damn!" she exclaimed as one of her heels caught in a crack in the floor and she stumbled. Wind River and Roman both hurried to help her, Wind River grabbing and juggling the hot coffeepot and Roman saving the cups and Lainie herself from a bad spill.

Her attempt had been well-meaning but abortive. A heavy silence, almost palpable in its weight, filled the dining room. Lainie recovered enough to pour the coffee, handed a cup to Roman first and then one to Wind River before helping herself and, shivering in her light dress, moving close to the fire. "I wonder if it's snowing in Denver?" she said wistfully, her brown eyes dreamy and soft.

"It better be," Roman growled, as if wishing made it so. None of this had gone as he had planned, and it was all his fault because he hadn't had the stomach to do what had to be done. All his fault. He tasted his coffee, tensed as Wind River grabbed his cup and started toward the side door. "Where do you think you're going now?" he asked, reaching out and grabbing Wind River by the sleeve of his coat.

Wind River glanced down at Roman's hand, back into the young man's face. "I got a bed in the funeral parlor up at the end of town."

Roman's eyebrows raised. "Funeral parlor? Jesus, you really are crazy. You hear that, Lainie? He sleeps in a casket, all ready to go."

"I do not," Wind River retorted angrily. "Sleep in a bed like everybody else."

"Not tonight," Roman said in an authoritative tone. "You sleep right here where I can keep an eye on you."

Wind River pulled his sleeve from Roman's grasp. "You

know, for a young man you got enough sass for the entire state of Colorado."

"Look, Mr. Kid," Roman snapped, "Lainie and me don't need nothing from you. Especially —"

"Except my food. You need my food, remember?"

"Especially back talk. Now, if you're so tired, crawl into a corner somewhere and go to sleep. Just stay out of the way and don't try anything you'll be sorry for."

"Like mindin' my own business?" Wind River asked.

Roman rolled his eyes, considered gagging Wind River. "For a start, yeah. Look. Is there a garage around here?"

"Garage?" Wind River actually laughed, then stopped abruptly. "Is that how you got here? In a car?"

"How do you think we got here in this weather? Walked?"

"I'll be damned," Wind River said, realizing for the first time that they must have arrived only hours before him, and that if he'd only taken the stagecoach road he would have known and been able to avoid them. "Ain't never been a car in Elkhorn before."

"Well, there is now," Roman said between clenched teeth. "And it's outside getting snowed on, so if you don't mind" — his face was turning red — "I'd appreciate it if you'd tell me where I can put it inside."

Wind River scratched his head and considered. "There's the livery," he said finally, just as Roman was about to explode with frustration. "I reckon it'll fit. 'Course, that's where my Appaloosa stays. If he don't take too unkindly to the smell, I guess you can put it in there."

Roman walked into the darkness by the lobby door, returned with a heavy coat. "Where is it?"

"Up the road. Last on the right," Wind River said, pointing.

"Won't do us any good buried under the snow," Roman explained to Lainie, shrugging into the coat. He handed her the .38 Colt revolver and rechecked the Browning automatic before thrusting it into his pocket. "You keep an eye on him, baby. One shot ought to take care of him if he gets any ideas."

"I haven't had an idea in years, boy," Wind River said, his yellow teeth worn and crooked in his smile.

Roman stabbed a finger in his direction. "Good. You just watch it. Remember," he said from the door that led to the kitchen and the back of the hotel, "she shot once. She'll shoot again."

Lainie held the gun in both hands. Wind River didn't so much as move. A few seconds later they heard the back door slam, followed by the sound of a motor grinding, then starting, and a car driving down the alley. "The boy has an edge to him," Wind River said as the sound faded. "I suppose time will wear it smooth."

Lainie smiled nervously and nodded her head in agreement. "You just don't understand him," she said. "It's pretty scary out here, not knowing if or when Mr. Lieght . . ." She paused, unsure of how much to reveal.

Wind River relaxed, sidled toward her. "Not knowing if or when Mr. Lieght what?"

"I don't think I should tell you. He might not like it."

"Suit yourself," Wind River said, angling toward the fireplace and the Hawken. Lainie backed away a step, but kept the gun on him. Wind River was close enough if he moved quickly. The girl didn't look like the type to shoot him down in cold blood. She had just been frightened before. All he had to do was lift the leaden weights of his arms. All he had to do was shed the sodden, chilling knowledge that he was a coward, a defeated man afraid even of a little girl. "You mind pointin' that thing somewhere else?" he asked, sagging into one of the chairs in front of the fireplace.

The gun wavered, moved no more than an inch to one side. "You don't have to worry," Lainie said. "I'm very good with my hands." Her face brightened. "I worked in a seamstress shop in Denver and can make just about anything a needle and thread can make," she went on proudly. "Roman and I met at a dance contest. He was watching from a table, looking so cute and tough. He isn't really, but he would hate for me to tell anyone. He was a driver for Mr. Lieght."

"Lieght?" Wind River asked. It was the fourth time he'd heard the name.

Lainie shuddered. "I don't like Mr. Lieght. He can be very frightening. But Roman always said that Lieght was only a beginning, and that he would eventually move up in the world . . . Mr. Lieght's world, that is." She shook her head dolefully. "It all sounded terribly exciting at first, but after a while, when Roman and I were seeing each other regularly, we . . . we began to worry about what we were getting into. Roman tried so hard not to mind, but sometimes a conscience can be a terrible thing."

She sat across from him. Wind River tried and failed to remember the last time he had sat in the company of a pretty young woman in the dining room of the Great Northern Hotel. Lainie's polished fingernails drummed on the table. She bit her lower lip. "Gosh, this place is spooky. I can't stand it when it's this quiet, you know what I mean? I guess that's maybe why I talk so much, huh?"

"You never know," Wind River said, thinking of Creed for the first time since walking through the door and being shot at. He looked around surreptitiously.

"Anyway," Lainie went on nervously, "Roman began to think about leaving. I wanted him to, so I guess it was as much my fault. He said we'd need money. I had some saved, but it wasn't enough, so Roman figured out a way for us to get some more from Mr. Lieght." She looked down at the flimsy flapper outfit she was wearing and sighed. "I hadn't ever done anything like that before. Honest, it was . . ."

The side door swung open and a cold gust of air followed Roman into the room. Snow glistened and melted on his head. He stamped his feet and shook the snow off his arms. "Not a soul. Town's deader'n a doornail, thank God." He strode across the room to the fire, pulled off his coat, and threw it over an empty chair before relieving Lainie of the .38. "Guess we can rest easy, after all."

The fear had gone out of Roman's eyes, but Wind River wasn't fooled for a second. The boy's cheeks were still sunken from lack of sleep and too much tension. Wind River had seen that look before. He had seen it in a mirror. "My Appaloosa take to your car all right?" he asked.

"You got me," Roman said, reaching for his still full coffee cup. "I guess so. I thought you were going to find a place to sleep."

The room was warm. Wind River was tired and convinced that neither Roman nor Lainie meant to harm him if he kept out of their way. With his bones comfortably warm, the last thing he wanted to do was venture out into the snow. Relieved, he leaned back in the chair. "Right here by the fire will be fine with me," he said.

"Not too close," Roman said, pointing to a pile of blankets he and Lainie had brought with them. "We're putting our bed down here."

Wind River groaned, stood, and stretched. He started for his bedroll, then stopped. "I had a hard ride and been cold all day," he said. "You mind if I eat some of my food first?" he asked, sarcastically emphasizing the "my."

"There's some of our pork and beans left over in the kitchen," Lainie said.

Roman groaned and glared at her. Lainie returned his stare with a defiant look. Wind River grinned despite himself and followed Lainie into the kitchen. "Don't think I'm taking sides against Roman, Mr. Kid," she said, stirring the beans and shoving the pot and a bowl toward him. "I just feel bad for almost killing you."

"Shoot me first and then give me my last meal." Eating right from the pot, Wind River ladled a mammoth spoonful of beans into his mouth. "You got the order all wrong there, girl," he went on, chewing at the same time. "Where I grew up, it was the other way around." He swallowed, took another bite. "Good beans. Just a touch of molasses."

The compliment pleased her, and Lainie repaid it with a shy smile. "I can cook. I guess that and sewing is about all I'm good for. Well . . . " She looked flustered, at a loss for words. "I do like to watch a man eat, but I guess . . . That is, Roman will be wondering what took me so long."

Wind River watched her leave, lit into the beans with a vengeance. Once the edge was off his hunger, he checked the door to the dining room and, cursing the boards that creaked underfoot, tiptoed over to the pantry. He jimmied the door loose from the jamb and swung it upon its rawhide hinges. The bottle he kept there for emergencies was hidden underneath the lowest shelf. He popped the cork and took a long swig. "Whee-unhh!" he said under his breath.

The whiskey parboiled his Adam's apple but cleared his head and loosened the logjam of beans weighing his stomach to the floor. If Lainie didn't sew any better than she cooked, he mused, she was a lost soul. He fought back a belch. The rotgut liquor had started his metabolism working, had kicked the internal engine into a renewed if sluggish life. Wind River tilted the bottle to his lips and took another snootful, then doubled over in a fit of coughing. He'd no sooner recovered enough to return the bottle to its hiding place and close the door than Roman appeared in the kitchen. "C'mon, old coot. Time to drive the pigs to market," he said.

Wind River wiped his hands on a nearby washcloth and dabbed at his mouth, betraying an etiquette once practiced in the finest dance halls and gambling parlors in the West. "Good beans," he said, for lack of anything better.

"Jesus!" Roman said, exasperated. "I'm glad you liked them. Now, are you ready to flop or not?"

Wind River didn't know what driving the pigs to market meant, much less flop, but there was no question that Roman meant for him to return to the dining room. Not knowing quite what to expect, he waited while the younger man blew out the lantern, then preceded him through the door. Lainie was already wrapped in a cocoon of blankets in front of the fire. A second pallet lay at her side. Wind River saw that his bedroll had been placed under a banquet table halfway across the room.

"There you go, old-timer," Roman said, jerking a finger toward Wind River's bedroll. "Nighty-night, Mr. Kid. Don't let the bedbugs bite."

There didn't seem to be much choice in the matter. Wind River bedded down, watched as Roman rolled into his blankets and blew out the last lantern. The only light left in the room came from the fireplace. Wind River squirmed around, tried to get comfortable on his side, finally lay flat on his back. From across the room, he could see the glow of a cigarette and hear Lainie and Roman talking softly for a moment, followed by silence. "Mr. Kid," Wind River muttered dourly, already drifting off. "Old enough to be his grandfather and not a lick of respect."

The last thing Wind River remembered before he fell asleep was wondering about driving those pigs. There weren't any pigs in all of Elkhorn. None at all.

10

The Wind River Kid sat up, instantly awake, and almost hit his head on the underside of the table. Groaning, he looked around and remembered where he was and why. He wasn't alone anymore. Not by a long shot. The population of Elkhorn had tripled.

Someone had waked in the night and put more wood on the fire, for it glowed cheerfully. Wind River squirmed out from under the table and, sitting uncomfortably on the floor, pulled on his new ostrich leather boots. He stood painfully and rubbed a cramp out of his hip. It was a hell of a thing to make an old man sleep on the floor, he brooded, pulling on his coat and hat. A hell of a thing.

Roman and Lainie were bundled in individual blanket cocoons and sleeping beside one another in front of the fire. Wind River approached, peered down at them with the air of one watching a secret he isn't supposed to see. Lainie seemed less innocent than she had the night before, as if awake she worked at appearing naïve, sweet, and inexperienced. Asleep, her mouth took on a sensuous fullness and her bosom rose and fell with each even breath. She was a woman in repose, a child awake. Roman snored faintly. In sleep, he looked boyish, as if his churlishness was every bit as much a façade as Lainie's innocence. His curiosity suddenly piqued, Wind River took a second to study him. In the soft light of the fire, Roman bore a remarkable resemblance to someone in Wind River's past. He tried to put a finger on it, grasped for a face and a name, and, in so doing, lost both.

Wind River shrugged. Buttoning his coat and pulling down the earflaps on his hat, he moved soundlessly into the lobby, and, hoping the sudden draft of cold air didn't wake the sleeping couple, onto the porch. The morning light was gray and dripping under a heavy overcast. The temperature had risen and was hovering around the freezing mark. The prior night's snow had turned to a mixture of rain and sleet, and a glaze of ice covered everything. Icicles hung from the overhanging roof and left him with the impression that he was standing in the maw of some gigantic beast. Across the street, more glassy fangs hung from the roof and naked beams of what was left of Widow Guthrie's dress shop. There was little wind.

Wind River sucked in a lungful of damp air, pulled his coat closer around him, and walked to the back of the hotel to relieve himself. When he returned, he smelled the medicine smoke and looked over to see Aden Creed sitting in long-legged discomfort on a straight-backed chair that was tilted against the front wall of the hotel. Creed was bundled in a Hudson Bay blanket that had been cut and then sewed with deerhide thongs to serve as a loose-fitting capote. A hood covered his bald pate and obscured his face in deep shadow. His nose hooked out from the fabric, and below that the bowl of his pipe and part of the stem could be seen. "Winter's cuttin' her teeth," he said.

Wind River studied the icicles and nodded. "You might have warned me," he finally said, by way of response.

Creed looked at him questioningly. Wind River stabbed a thumb toward the interior of the hotel. "Oh," the mountain man said. His pipe bobbed up and down. "Ain't my business to warn or not to warn."

"Just what the hell is your business, then?"

"No more, no less than I'm doin'."

"Why do I ask?" Wind River sighed, staring at two small pools of water that had dripped from Creed's capote onto the board porch.

"Yes," Creed sadly agreed. "A rheumatiz sort of day.

Have to be careful. A fellow could catch his . . ." He puffed on his pipe, not wanting to pursue that train of thought. "What are you going to do about them?"

"Don't know," Wind River admitted, shaking his head dolefully. "I only come back to get out of the storm." He craned his head out from under the porch and looked at the sky. "Looks like she might clear up pretty quick," he predicted hopefully.

"Not in the passes. Snow up in the lonesome. I been there. Three-foot drifts. Deeper, some places."

"Well, I ain't goin' through no passes," Wind River said, idly turning over ideas of how to trick the Appaloosa into going south from Mountain City. "Head south instead. Only the first storm of the year. Damn. They took my food."

"Can't put up with that," Creed said matter-of-factly. "Any ideas?"

"Not a one, yet."

Creed sucked laconically on his pipe. "Man your age needs food real steady in weather like this. You'll have to do something, you don't want to freeze to death."

"I'll do something, damn it. Now leave me be."

"Life's harder than five-card stud, ain't it? A man has to know the rules before he sits down. And when he does sit, he has to play the hand dealt him, play it to the bust." Once again, the pipe bobbed up and down maddeningly. "Ain't right for a man to let another play the final hand and take the loss."

"*Aaaaarrggghhhh!*" Wind River grabbed a chair from the other side of the door and hurled it at Creed. The chair hit Creed's, splintered with a crash that was muffled by the gray, water-logged air. Wind River doubled over at a sudden explosion of pain in the small of his back. When he finally managed to straighten up, Creed was standing in the street. Rain seemed to have no effect on his pipe.

"Testy," the mountain man said. "No need to get a burr in your blanket."

"You aren't any damn help at all," Wind River said, wincing and rubbing his back.

"That's not my job."

"Well, what is? Just what the hell is?" Wind River

shouted. He raised his hands and eyes to the charcoal-gray heavens in supplication. When he dropped them, the street was empty and Creed was gone. "That's right, disappear on me," Wind River complained. The aroma of burning cherry bark clung to his nostrils, and he blew his nose to get rid of it. "Ah, hell. I'm gonna see to my horse."

Behind him, a shadow in the dining-room window moved and a tattered curtain fell back into place. Not quite sure what to make of what she had seen, Lainie hurried across the room to the warmth of the covers. "Roman?" she whispered. "Roman?"

"Wha? . . ." The dream didn't want to go away. Roman was in Mountain City, almost twenty years ago. He was in a warm house, sitting on his grandfather's lap. There was no trace of the religious fanatic in the old man in those days. Instead, he was given to laughter and the telling of tales meant to excite the imagination of a five-year-old. More importantly, he smelled good. The heady aroma of yeast and flour and honey clung to his clothes and hands, and hinted of hidden cookies and small, boy-sized cakes or pies cooked especially for a grandson. "Wha?   ." Roman repeated as a squat, bullet-headed figure in a gray overcoat intruded into that fairy-tale, never forgotten past. "What?"

"It's the old man. Mr. Kid," Lainie said breathlessly.

Roman sat up, noted Wind River's empty blanket. "What about him?"

"He's outside talking to himself. Arguing. I've been listening." Lainie's eyes were round with wonder. She cuddled closer to him for protection. "He even yelled and threw a chair. I looked for someone else, but he was alone. He was just standing there in the rain, talking."

"So what do you want me to do? Call Mr. Hearst and have him run it on page one?" Roman lay back down, put an arm around Lainie, and pulled her to him. "For Chrissake, Lainie, the old fart's nuts. Probably been up here for years living like one of the bears, eating honey and ants and hibernating in the winter."

"Oh, Roman, stop it."

"Forget it. He's harmless enough, so let him be." Roman slid his hand inside Lainie's blouse and found her breast.

Lainie shoved away, but he caught her, brought her back to him, and nuzzled her ear. "Mmm. You taste good."

Lainie tried halfheartedly to get away. "Roman, no. We haven't finished talking." She giggled in spite of her anxiety. "Will you stop it!"

Roman reached deep inside the covers, slid his hand between Lainie's knees. "I should have let him go to his damned casket last night. I got so hard thinking about you that when I rolled over I almost broke it off."

"You should have done something then, while he was asleep," Lainie whispered. Her skirt was riding up to her waist and she tugged at the blankets to make sure they were covering her. "What if he comes back in now?"

"The sight'll give him a heart attack," Roman said, chuckling. He rolled on top of her, worked at the buttons on her blouse. "No. I take that back. He's so old he won't know what we're doing."

Lainie tried, but couldn't respond. "Do you think Mr. Lieght will find us?" she finally asked, her voice a whisper against his neck.

Roman's ardor collapsed. He rolled off her and lay staring at the ceiling. "Why'd you have to say that?" he asked in return.

"Because I'm scared. I think about him." She shuddered, pulled the blankets tight around her against a coldness that no blankets could help. "I keep hearing him say that no one ever took anything from Harry Lieght before, and that we'd never get away with it."

He'd said that and more. That he'd hunt them down, that he'd find them and make examples of them that no one else would forget. "I should have killed him," Roman said. "I had the chance. I should have. The only way to be sure was to squeeze the damn trigger." His voice turned harsh and grating. His hands were clenched into fists and his eyes were squeezed closed. "If he does find us, if I see him first, I will. I'll shoot first and ask questions later. I swear, I'll kill him the next time."

Lainie had seen a dead man once, and had been sick for a week. Even the thought of Roman shooting anyone made her queasy. She had, as usual, said too much, and regretted it. Too late, she propped herself on one elbow and looked down at him. "But he won't find us, Roman," she said, exuding brightness and false confidence. "I mean, you said no one knows about this place, at least not in Denver. So he can't find us." Trying to bring him back, she leaned over and kissed him on the lips. "I'm sorry, Roman. I talk too much. How you ever put up with me, I don't know."

His eyes remained closed, and he seemed to have shrunk into himself.

"Roman, let's do it now. Please?" She reached down between his legs and touched him. "Please? I'm not afraid. I want to. We're safe. I just know it, Roman."

Roman pushed her away, rolled onto his stomach, and stared at the fire that burned not nearly as intensely as his fear. Safe? What was safe? Elkhorn wasn't on the map, but Harry Lieght had his ways. Beside him, Lainie had curled into a ball with her back against his side. He felt her shake. She was crying silently. As he listened, he could hear the rain turn into sleet and beat against the walls of the Great Northern Hotel.

It was a hell of a way to start a day. Lainie was crying, and so were the clouds. Somehow, Roman wished he could, too.

11

Harry Lieght was a driven man. From the moment Roman
Phillips and his sheba had left him bound, gagged, and
trussed like a guinea hen waiting for the butcher's knife, he'd
lived, breathed, eaten, slept, and fantasized retribution.

The owner of the boardinghouse on Colfax Street had
found Lieght about an hour after Roman and Lainie's departure. An hour had been more than enough time to lay out, in
meticulous detail, a plan. The plan took into account the fact
that others, whose money his treacherous apprentice had
stolen, would be looking for him. Lieght did not discount the
power of those other men, but neither did he spend a great
deal of time worrying about them. They would get their
money back: of that he was certain. With, he grimly promised himself, interest.

Harry had taught the boy, and knew how he would think.
He wouldn't go too far for the first few days, would lie low in
a safe place and let the opposition burn itself out searching
before he moved. By nightfall, over a dozen men who could
be trusted not to tell his superiors what had happened
had fanned out over Denver with orders to find his Lincoln
and Roman and the girl, not necessarily in that order.
While he waited for news, a torpedo who owed him a
favor was out buying a new Model T and getting a New
Mexico license plate for it. A Ford was a terrible come-

down after the Lincolns and Cadillacs a man of Lieght's station was used to driving, but there was nothing to be done. In the first place, his cash reserves were low and money was going to be tight until he got back the bag Roman had stolen. In the second place, a Ford, because it was common and less apt to be remembered or described, gave him a certain secure sense of anonymity.

The first concrete results of the search came the next morning in the form of a message from Pink-Eye Paul, a derelict Lieght had once bailed out of the city jail. Lieght's Lincoln had been spotted at a used-car lot on the western end of town where, the owner said, a young man answering Roman's description had traded it for a thousand cash and a 1920 Model T runabout. Half an hour later, Lieght put the next stage of his plan into effect when he visited his tailor and was fitted for a suit he was assured would be ready by noon. At ten, he entered a clerical supply shop on Bernie Street. By two in the afternoon, outfitted in every visible way as a minister, he visited Roman's mother.

Mother and son had been at odds with each other since Roman had left the Holy Light Divinity School in Colorado Springs to pursue a career amid the unholy gaiety and excitement of Denver. Lieght, in manner unctuous, hesitated to state the exact nature of young Roman's difficulties, but hinted that Roman was in trouble with the law and in danger of losing his immortal soul. The Divinity School, while irritated with her son, was in no way desirous of completely abandoning him to Satan and his minions, though. It would appreciate any information about her son that Mrs. Phillips might be willing to confide, the better to shepherd the wayward sheep.

The ruse worked to perfection. Amanda Phillips, earlier an agnostic insofar as she had ever thought about religion, had married Zechariah Phillips, whose father, Malachi, had once been a Pentecostal preacher. Fanned by an apostate father, the fire of zealotry that burned in Zechariah soon spread to his new wife, and Amanda, born anew in the Blood of the Lamb, embraced the charismatic movement with a fervor unforeseen by her husband and became, within months, Sister Amanda of the Holy Divine Single True

Word of God Bible Church of Colorado Springs. There had been those among Amanda's friends who predicted the new-found relationship with hell and brimstone and strange tongues would never last as much as a year. They were wrong. Amanda's conversion took and stuck through thick and thin, through the birth of a son and the death of a husband. And when the polite and wholesome emissary of the Lord called upon her and asked questions about her son, Amanda, moved by the good reverend's concern, spilled her soul and her family's past.

One item in particular intrigued Reverend Jones, for so Lieght called himself. Roman's grandfather, the minister, now deceased, had lived in a town called Mountain City. Reverend Jones's gentle but insistent questions elicited even more of interest. The grandfather had originally come from a place called Elkhorn, a small mining community in the craggy timberland above and aloof from the beaten path. In the grandfather's youth, Elkhorn had been a wild and woolly place, but it had since been abandoned and had become a ghost town. Mrs. Phillips had never visited there, but remembered many stories of it, because Roman and his grandfather were close and it was the old man's habit to sit in front of a fire and regale his grandson with tales of tragedy and high drama from the town's heyday.

Only when he had already said goodbye and was about to leave did the Reverend Jones bring up the subject of Elkhorn again when he suggested, as an afterthought, that perhaps Roman had gone there. Mrs. Phillips thought the idea amusing, but dismissed it out of hand. Elkhorn was such a lonely, out-of-the-way place that she couldn't imagine anyone ever going there, especially her son. The reverend concurred. Then he and Sister Amanda prayed together.

By late afternoon, Harry Lieght, his holy duds discarded, drove out of Denver. Beside him on the seat was a sack lunch, a bottle of French brandy, and a map of Colorado with a circle drawn around the town of Mountain City.

12

Mud like rich, dark chocolate sauce oozed over the sides and down into Harry's shoes. His feet, wet inside black knit socks, made soft, sucking sounds with each step. Mountain City seemed devoid of life in the gray and rain-drenched early-morning light. Lieght shook his left foot and continued down Silverado Street until he found a place that was open. Grunting with relief, he stepped under the porch of Vertina's Café, brushed the slick wool surface of his coat that glistened wet from his walk in the rain, and entered.

Inside, Nick Vertina eased his elbows off a counter that ran the length of the diner. Of the twenty stools, none were occupied. A pair of grizzled local hang-arounds hunched over a week-old copy of the Denver *Post* glanced up from their places at the single table at the rear of the café and stared with mutual curiosity at the newcomer. Nick swept a hand across his thick, black, oily hair and sauntered toward Lieght. "Help ya', bub?"

"Drove my car into a ditch," Lieght said. He pointed with his thumb down the road leading out of town. "Is there a garage around here?"

"Lewis Weldon is trying to be," Nick said with a chuckle.

Lieght stepped back to look through the window in the direction of Nick's nod. "The blue-and-white sign?" he asked.

"You got it," Nick said. "Weldon Auto Supply and Parts." He paused, looked at Lieght's shoes, and grinned. "Walk far?"

"Yes."

"Have a cup of coffee and rest your dogs."

The smell of hot coffee permeated the air. Lieght slogged over to the counter and sat. "Thanks. I could use it."

Nick slid a heavy white cup and a spoon across the counter. " 'Fraid I'm fresh out of cream. Sugar?"

"Yeah." Lieght stirred in a heaping teaspoonful, wrapped his hands around the warm cup. "Live around here long?" he asked idly.

"Long enough to be as old as I am."

One of the local yokels, a burly, black-bearded man who looked as if he might have been a lumberjack, guffawed.

Lieght ignored him, took a swallow of his coffee, and burned the roof of his mouth. "That ought to be long enough to know if a young couple came through last week sometime. Sort of blond, tall kid in his twenties and a pretty, black-haired girl a little younger. They'd of been driving a '20 Lizzie runabout."

Nick didn't answer right away, took a long second to wipe a smudge off the counter. "Someone you know?" he finally asked, guardedly.

"My daughter," Lieght said. "Run off with a lounge lizard. I'm trying to find them and have reason to think they might have come through this way. Maybe I can talk some sense into her. At least make sure the cake-eater marries her proper."

"Kids," Nick said, shaking his head and taking Lieght's cup to top it off. "Too bad. Too bad," he sympathized. " 'Fraid you came a long way for nothing, though."

"How's that?"

"He means," the big man with the beard chimed in, "that no one ever comes through here. They either come to Mountain City or they don't. There just ain't no through, 'cause there's nowheres to go through to. The road stops."

"That's funny." Lieght looked a little confused, the way a city slicker ought. "Fella down in Idaho Springs told me about a town up on the divide. Place called Elkhorn."

"Jee-sus. You got to be kidding, mister." Local number two had a whiny voice, and looked like a smaller version of his companion. "Nobody but nobody goes to Elkhorn."

"Tate's right, buddy," big beard said. "Him and me hunted some elk up that way, and the place is dead. There's an old stagecoach road that starts up at the north side of town here in back of the school. Two days there on a fair horse, and then nothin' but fallin'-down shacks and houses and such for your trouble."

"That and coyotes and wolves and a bear or two," Tate added helpfully. "Them and the Kid, that is."

"The Kid?" Lieght asked, interested.

"A crazy old coot." Tate laughed scornfully. "Hermit, sort of. Lives on his lonesome. Works the tailings of the mines around those peaks for what silver or gold he can find, and traps and sells skins for cash to the Sears, Roebuck. Comes down a couple times a year to buy supplies. Speaking of which." He wet his lips and scratched under his cap. "Where'd you say your car was?"

"About a mile back," Lieght said.

"Me and Newkirk here got us a wagon and team. No work today. We could hitch a line to her and haul her into town for you. Ford, you said?"

Lieght looked at Tate, figured Newkirk, the big man, would end up doing all the work. "A new '27 with New Mexico plates," he said, deciding what the hell. It didn't matter who did what as long as he got the damned thing fixed. "How much?"

"Five bucks?"

"Agreed. You can bring it to Weldon's."

Newkirk glowered at Tate for bargaining him right out into the rain and mud. He almost tried to up the price to five apiece, but at the last second noticed Tate wink at him. He wondered what the smaller man was thinking, then looked at the city slicker and decided what the hell. The damned fool was willing to pay a day's wages for a few hours' work. "And you can make sure that five-spot is waiting for us at Weldon's," he said, rising and starting out. "Get your ass in gear, Tate. This was your idea."

"Pleasant," Lieght said when the door closed behind

them. He pulled a half dollar out of his pocket and flipped it onto the counter. "This Weldon fella be there now?"

"Ain't never anywhere else," Nick said. He shagged the half, dropped it into the till. "Those two will do your work, but don't turn your back on them without putting your wallet up front. Blue-plate special at lunchtime. Keep me in mind."

"Right." Lieght pulled his hat down low over his eyes, buttoned his coat, and started for the door. "Thanks for the coffee."

The rain had turned into a steady drizzle. Neither hurrying nor taking his time, Lieght strode up the road toward Weldon's, knocked what mud he could off his feet, and walked in. The store was evidently in the process of renovation, for boxes and large parts and shelves in various stages of construction cluttered the floor.

"Won't open until next week," a voice said from the back.

Lieght closed the door and waited a moment until his eyes adjusted to the gloom, then walked quietly to the rear of the store, where he found a middle-aged, balding man working on a set of ledger books. "You Lewis Weldon?" he asked.

"Yeah . . ." Weldon looked up, startled. "Thought I heard you go out," he said, groping for his peach tin. "Not going to be open until next week."

Lieght unbuttoned his overcoat, pulled a wallet out of his breast pocket. While Weldon watched, he extracted a twenty-dollar bill, placed it in the ledger like a bookmark, then closed the ledger.

Weldon stared at the crisp features of Andrew Jackson, looked back up to Lieght. He saw a city-bred man well under six feet tall but broadly built in the shoulders. His hair was clipped short to his scalp. Square, chiseled features framed ice-blue eyes. His head fit to his trunk by a short, bull neck. As best as could be seen under the coat, the rest of him was as chunky and solid as a rock: a barrel chest, thick waist, and powerful thighs all left the impression of density and mass. A trail of muddy footsteps led from the doorway to the rear of the store and the visitor. Weldon didn't complain: twenty dollars would clean a lot of floor. "What can I do for you?" he asked.

"Name's Lieght. Got a '27 Lizzie being towed into town.
Guy in the café down the way said you had a garage."

"He said that, did he?"

"That's right."

"Who? Nick Vertina?"

Lieght took a deep breath. He had better things to do than
trade small talk with a hick storekeeper. "I guess. Sign said
VERTINA'S CAFÉ. Can you —"

"Well, he was wrong. Gas pumps'll be in tomorrow and
the garage part won't be finished for another week." He
waved a hand to indicate the mess that surrounded Lieght.
"Parts I got, if I can find anything. What'd you say the
trouble was?"

"I'm a businessman, not a mechanic," Lieght said, con-
trolling his temper. When Weldon only looked at him, he
sighed in resignation and went on: "I don't know. The
damned thing slid off the road and hit a rock or something. It
won't run."

"Wish I could help you, Mr. Lieght," Weldon said with
maddening slowness. "I just —"

"There isn't a mechanic in town?"

Weldon shook his head. "My boy tinkers, but he's only
good for small stuff. You need anything major done, Idaho
Springs is the closest place. Fella by the name of Slim
Underwood has a shop there."

"Phone him and tell him to come up."

The storekeeper considered that, scratched his scalp with
his pencil. "That'll take some cash. It will cost him time to
get up here. Slim's good, but he isn't cheap."

Lieght's patience snapped. "I have money, Mr. Weldon,"
he said in a cold voice. He leaned over the counter, fixed
Weldon with an equally icy stare. "What I don't have is time
to waste watching you not earn the twenty-dollar bill I just
gave you."

"Now, there's the trouble," Weldon said, coloring but
holding his temper. "You city fellas all think alike. You think
you can come up here and snap your fingers and order us
about." He shook his head. "I can't rightfully complain about
the road and the cars that run on it 'cause they're gonna be

how I make a living, but it does sometimes seem that the people who drive them are a hotheaded lot. Come in here waving money around like it has gone out of style, wanting everything done yesterday, talking to your elders like they was — "

"Who?" Lieght demanded, cutting him off.

"What?" Weldon said, taken aback.

"Who are you talking about? Besides me, that is."

Weldon was puzzled, a little frightened, by Lieght's intensity. "I don't know what you're talking about," he said cautiously.

Lieght took out his wallet, extracted another twenty, and put it with the first one. "My daughter has eloped with a man of whom I don't approve. I intend to find her and bring her home to Albuquerque," he said, planting the lie so the coppers wouldn't be looking for him in Denver. He described Roman and Lainie, told him that Roman's grandfather had lived in Elkhorn, and added his suspicion that the pair had gone there to escape an outraged father's wrath.

"I'll be damned," Weldon said, delighted to be privy to an exciting piece of scandal. "Old Malachi Phillips's grandson. Never did think that family would come to any good. The girl stayed in the car while the boy came in here and bought three extra tires for that little runabout he was driving. Saw them stop at a few other shops. Hell, I figured they'd head back to the city. They weren't dressed for around here, that's for sure." He took the twenties out of the ledger and tucked them into his vest pocket. "Be crazy, of course, but they just might have gone up there."

"I need a car," Lieght said.

Weldon looked dubious. "I don't know about that. Only a few in town. Might have to wait until you get yours fixed."

"No. What about a wagon?" Lieght had found them and he was anxious to get on with it. "A horse, even," he added.

"A horse?" Weldon cast a skeptical glance at Lieght's clothes. "No offense, mister, but do you know how to ride?"

"I'll learn. Do you have one?"

"My son does. Out back. You could use it, I guess, but not in those clothes. Weather's just nasty down here, but up there it'll be colder'n a witch's tit. Snow, too. I let you go, they'd be after me for murder. If they ever found your body."

"Damn it!" Lieght said, slamming his fist onto the countertop with enough force to crack the wood.

Weldon jumped back in surprise and terror, almost swallowed his tobacco. "Of course, if you're set on it, I guess I could fix you up." The man was mad. Mad but well off. Forty dollars was a nice feeling, tucked away in his pocket. Weldon's eyes narrowed with the thought of how much he could add to them. "It'll cost you, though. Fifty dollars more, for everything, plus another hundred deposit on the horse."

Lieght added it up, arrived at the preposterous figure of ninety dollars. Weldon was getting away with highway robbery, but there wasn't anything to be done about it. Not if he wanted his ten thousand, plus whatever cash was left over from his Lincoln. Not to speak of the pleasure of slowly killing Roman Phillips. He took out his wallet for the third time. "For this kind of money," he said, counting a hundred and fifty dollars, "you forget you've ever seen me if he comes back here. And remember to let me know."

"Done," Weldon said. "Follow me."

Ninety dollars was a great expediter. An hour later, Lieght was dressed in a pair of ill-fitting boots, long johns and rough work clothes, a coat, and a slicker. The horse stood saddled and waiting in the barn. Weldon had added a bedroll, a ground cloth, and a sack of provisions. "Now, a mile out of town the trail forks. The right hand takes you on a trail old Wind River found, but it's hard to follow sometimes. The left hand is the old stagecoach and ore wagon road. Loggers still use the first ten miles or so of it, so it's in pretty good shape. Keep to it and you won't get lost. As for the horse, pull to the left when you want him to go left, to the right when you want him to go right," he instructed. "Kick him in the sides when you want him to hurry, and haul back on the reins when you want him to stop. Make sure he gets plenty of water, and give him a double handful of those oats twice a day, morning and night."

Lewis Junior glared at the city slicker who had usurped his

place on old Tony's back. Lieght ignored him and stared malevolently at the horse.

"You'll get there tomorrow night at the soonest," Weldon went on. "You aren't back in a week, we'll send someone to look for you."

"I'll be back," Lieght said, swinging awkwardly aboard and taking the reins. "You can bet on that." Weldon opened the barn door. As instructed, Lieght kicked the horse in the sides, and rode off into the curtain of mist, north, toward the school and the logging road to Elkhorn.

The first and last time Harry had ridden a horse had been twenty-two years earlier at a public park in Chicago. He had not enjoyed the experience then and was not enjoying it now. He tried to adjust his weight, but to no avail. Every step the horse took jolted his spine, and his testicles ground together painfully no matter how he sat. The logging road, two deep ruts worn in the wilderness, looked passable by auto if it was drier. And if his damned cheap car hadn't broken down, wedged in a muddy grave.

The weather grew colder as the road rose along the mountainside. Some time long after the trail forked and Mountain City was well out of sight, Lieght stopped to give the horse a breather. His pocket watch said three in the afternoon. He had been enduring the elements for the better part of a day. "Half-cocked is half-assed," he muttered, a lesson he thought he had learned long ago. Bleakly, he assessed his situation while chewing on a biscuit. His toes were getting cold and his fingers beginning to lose their sensitivity inside the heavy leather gloves. Lessons learned in the trenches in France had helped him keep dry, but they didn't make up for a lack of adequate clothing. At that, the clothes Weldon had supplied would have been warm enough if it weren't for the inactivity of sitting on a horse. If it got too much worse, he'd have to get down and walk for a while. At least on the level spots, if there were any.

Drab greens and ominous blacks of trees ran together in the slate-tinted air. Gray sky, gray sleet. Gray clouds like ashen eyebrows furrowed in anger. Stupid stupid stupid stupid went the refrain in Lieght's mind. Roman was up there, somewhere ahead. He wasn't going anywhere. He was hiding. It was stupid not to wait for the car, for dry weather, for the right moment. It always came down to the right moment. Isn't that what he had always said? Wait for the right moment. Stupid to have trusted Roman, even if it had seemed like a good idea at the time. Hire a driver, a young kid willing to learn, willing to wait his time. A man didn't just snap his fingers and find himself with Harry Lieght's reputation. It had to be earned and, once earned, protected. That was where he had failed, where the stupidity entered the picture. He should have spotted all the signs: the kid's big talk, the look in his eyes, the hesitation to carry through when the work got rough.

"You should have killed me, boy," Harry said aloud, repeating the warning he'd given Roman just before he was gagged and left to endure the humiliation of being found tied and helpless to a chest of drawers. Furious, he jerked the horse's reins, pulled the animal's head around as he mounted. "You should have killed me."

The road left the gentle slopes and cut through rougher country, angling back and forth on itself through a series of mild switchbacks. The temperature had stayed below the freezing mark at that elevation, and a heavy glaze of ice covered the trees. Sagging branches and weathered trunks took on the appearance of crystal in the wan light. The surface of the road had frozen. Underneath, the mud was still wet and slippery. An occasional branch torn down by the weight of the ice lay across their path. The horse was sure-footed, the going slow.

There were, perhaps, another three hours of daylight left. Lieght beat his hands together to warm them, let the horse have its head as they went around yet another switchback. He had just about decided to start looking for a place to spend the night when a sharp cracking sound startled him. The horse stopped abruptly. Lieght looked around. Just ahead of them, its thick trunk scarred by a lightning strike and its barren branches bowed beneath the weight of the ice, a huge oak tree hung over the trail. The horse's ears were perked up, his right leg raised in midstep. Suddenly, with what sounded like an explosion, the tree split in half.

Wide-eyed, Lieght watched helplessly as a thirty-foot length of bristling branches and shimmering ice fell toward him. The horse backed violently, reared in terror as the tree barely missed it and smashed into the road. Pieces of ice showered horse and rider. Lieght leaned forward and clutched at the rearing animal's neck in an attempt to stay on as the horse, still on its hind legs and backing, slipped off the edge of the trail. Frantic, it spun against the heavy weight of the man on its back, only partially regained its balance, and leaped over the trail below. Lieght closed his eyes as he and the horse hurtled downhill between two white pines and snapped a six-foot piñon in half. For one moment more, he was on horseback. For another, a more dreadful span of time, he was airborne, with the ground rushing sickeningly past underneath him. When he finally hit and rolled, the .45-caliber Browning automatic he carried in a shoulder holster tried to bury itself in his ribcage.

Lieght forced himself to relax, tried not to fight against the fall, especially as, with mind-wrenching clarity, he saw a monstrous ponderosa pine racing up the slope toward him. A second later, pain exploded through his midsection and head, and he came to an abrupt and jarring stop. Dazed, his mind only half working, he saw the horse, miraculously unharmed, racing homeward along the trail. At least that was what Lieght thought he saw. He had his doubts, though, because the horse was upside down. As were the trees, the earth, the sky, and Harry Lieght.

13

The freezing rain had at last subsided, but left behind jagged remains that clung to the town of Elkhorn and reflected the gray light. Above the cover of lowering clouds, the sun was in the far west. Whether one looked to the north or south east or west, the trees sagged under a coat of ice. An ever-constant gloom hung in the air. Wind River's breath, as if stricken with some dolorous malady, sank to the earth. Ignoring Roman's call to stay close to the hotel, he walked up the north slope toward the graveyard. Wind River had managed most of his life well enough without taking orders, and had no intention of obeying the shouted demands of his upstart, unwanted guest. He did not believe Roman would shoot him. After all, the youth and his girlfriend were hiding, which meant they were afraid. Wind River knew full well what fear could do to a man, what a fearful man would and would not do.

Fear. He'd been so angry at the invasion of his town that he had forgotten. Fear came to him as he stared at what time had left of Lucie Jean Marckham's skull, though. Fear as cold as the ice that had collected where the little girl's eyes had been. The sockets had filled and frozen into round, saucer-shaped pools. Tiny droplets had collected and run off to form pointed icicle teeth that fringed the bony lips. The whole skull shone with a glassy brilliance.

The bear had not been satisfied with Lucie Jean alone. More bones lay scattered about. "He was busy last night," a voice said, followed by the the snick of a knife cutting into wood.

"Curse that bear," Wind River said, not even looking at Creed. "What does he want? What does he want with the dead?"

The body first, creased with tiny nicks for ribs. Creed concentrated on the flanks before moving on to the more delicate work of carving legs. "Bear's business," he said, matter-of-factly.

"Hasn't dug up yours yet," Wind River noted, tapping Creed's stone with his foot. "You got a smart-ass answer why that is?"

The sound of whittling stopped. Creed didn't like anyone kicking his gravestone, especially Wind River, who had bought it. "No," he said with more effort than was evident, and abruptly started cutting the notch that would separate the deer's antlers.

Wind River stared at the bones. He turned around and looked down on the ruined buildings that the bear, Scar, had torn apart. Roman was walking toward the graveyard. As gradual as the slope was, the young man breathed heavily. City life did that, Wind River thought, trying to ignore him. There were more important events to ponder. Elkhorn was being destroyed board by board. Wood and bones, all destroyed.

"He's after me," he said with horrifying clarity, with realization as bitter as vomit lodged in the throat. "He's after me. The graves, the town, and then me. When there's nothing else left, me." He spun around. "That's right, isn't it, Cre—"

The mountain man was gone. A chill breeze sent the shavings he'd left behind tumbling toward the evergreens. The same breeze stirred branches and needles. Each, with its thin layer of ice, responded with a tiny, tiny creak or groan that multiplied by millions, sounded like an infinitude of specters whispering back and forth. Specters of bears, born and unborn and long ago dead, of Lucie Jean Marckham and all those who accompanied her, of those who had fallen to Wind River's gun . . .

"Old man!" Roman yelled as he approached the cemetery "When I tell you . . ." He stopped short, stared at the graves, at Wind River. "What the hell is the matter with you?"

Wind River turned his back on Roman and started down the slope.

"You dig up those graves?" Roman asked, falling into step beside Wind River.

"Scar did," Wind River corrected. "Aden Creed—nobody you know, left here before you was even born—used to scare me with tales of the grizzlies, how the miners hunted them for food when the elk and deer was scarce or gone. Scar was the last and meanest of the old silvertips. He was maimed by Creed's hand. Hated men and still does. It's kept him alive after all these years." Wind River paused, cocked his head in thought. "Or maybe he's dead like Creed," he mused. "Dead and come back."

"Jesus!" Roman said, edging away from the old man.

"He should be after Creed. Creed's the one that pulled the trigger. I never did no harm to that hellish thing. But he's back and after this town and everything in it. Me." Wind River turned to Roman. His red-rimmed eyes were alive with a mad gleam. "And now you, boy. Scar will be after you, too. Hee hee, you picked the wrong place to hide. You hear that? You traded purgatory for perdition!"

"Aww, horsefeathers. You're a crazy old fart."

Wind River laughed madly. Roman glanced over his shoulder to the frozen bones they had left behind them. Edgy, he hurried to catch up to Wind River: a madman was better company than no one when bones were lying about. They didn't stop until they reached the top end of Main Street, when Wind River suddenly pulled up and, his head back, searched the sky. Roman followed his gaze for a moment, then gave up and looked around. To his right, a wooden foundation marked what remained of a building. It seemed familiar to him, for some reason. Curious, he angled toward it. Few boards remained standing. There was no evidence of a roof. At the far end, a cracked and tilted pulpit leaned on weakened supports. In its own way, it reflected the rather helter-skelter spirituality of the whole town. His grandfather's stories rushed back, and suddenly Roman remembered.

Behind him, Wind River did, too. "Reverend Phillips!" he said, awed. "Now I place the face." His brow furrowed. Was this another specter come to haunt him? Weren't Creed and the bear enough? Frightened and confused, he backed away. "But you're too young! It ain't fair. Ain't fair at —"

"His grandson," Roman said. "And no reverend when I knew him. Just a baker down in Mountain City. He used to tell such stories." He took in the town with a sweeping glance, shook his head in dismay. "Christ, he made it sound like . . . like . . . Ah, hell. I don't know. And here it is just a bunch of fallen-down buildings along a poor substitute for a main drag, and with a screwy Methuselah for the big cheese."

Wind River blinked. He wasn't sure what Roman had said, but it sounded like an insult. "Are they all like you?" he asked.

"Who?" Roman asked in return.

"Out there." Wind River pointed to the horizon beyond the mountains. "Are they all as bitter and full of bluster and bullshit and talk so's a person can't understand what in tarnation they're saying? Are they all like you?"

The question lacked meaning. Roman stared with comtempt at Wind River, stared at his boots, muddy and puckered with strange, wart-like protuberances, ranged up the coarse denim work pants to the heavy, soiled, fleece-lined leather coat, to the half-inch-long, gray and grizzled beard, to the rheumy eyes and the heavy lumberman's cap.

"Well?" Wind River insisted when Roman didn't answer. "Are they?"

"Nerts to you," Roman said, his hands on his hips.

Wind River thought about nerts. It was the second time he'd heard the term, and he still couldn't decipher its meaning. "That's what I was afraid of," he finally said and, sick to his stomach, turned away to stare with glazed eyes over Rampage Valley. Suddenly all the future was tinted with an ominous shade of doubt, and his ability to escape was uncertain. Cold seeped into his spine, and unable to remain in Roman's presence, he started walking stiffly toward Muenster's Funeral Parlor and the bottle he had hidden there that morning. He needed something to fight the chill and bolster his courage. He needed a friend. One was waiting to be uncorked.

Roman watched Wind River walk away from him, wondered why everything had to go wrong. Elkhorn was deserted? In a pig's eye. All he'd wanted was to find a quiet place to hide for a while, and look what happened: he was stuck with a half-crazed old coot who talked to himself, who communed with bones, who talked of ghosts. Hell, they ought to have gone straight to San Francisco, driven the Model T into the ground, and taken a train the rest of the way. They hadn't, though, which was what came from being too clever. The only thing to be done was to keep busy and make the best of an awkward situation.

"Keep busy," he repeated to himself, striding purposefully toward the stable. "Do something," he muttered, inside and untying the rope that held the cardboard valises to the left running board luggage rack.

The Ulysses S. Grant Suite had a fireplace, a bed that hadn't fallen in, and most of the windows intact. By dark, Roman had carried in enough wood to keep them comfortable for a few days. He had cannibalized the windows in two other rooms in order to replace the two broken panes in the suite. He had cleaned out the wardrobe and put his and Lainie's clothes in it, even swept the floor with a drape taken out of the next suite. The legless washstand was propped up on bricks; an unbroken pitcher, washbasin, and a pair of chamber pots had been found, washed out, and installed. He'd even located a couple of foot warmers, which he placed by the fire, ready for the night. Pleased, he carried the portable Victrola downstairs and put it in the dining room so they could have music with their meals, and then decided to finish checking out the rest of the upstairs rooms.

Night was falling rapidly and the temperature was dropping. Every step produced a symphony of creaks and groans, especially on the fourth and top floors, where the old building had been most subjected to the ravages of time and weather. The candlelight was fitful as multiple drafts from broken windows and shutters pushed and sucked at the flame. Twice, in spite of his cupped hand, the candle was blown out, and the darkness from inside and out mingled. Each time, his ears sensitive to the slightest sound, Roman hurried to relight it.

The truth was, he was unnerved. An ancient, irrational fear of the old man's imagined ghosts followed him through the corridors, past the dust-covered drapes of purple velvet, through the rooms where the most successful of men had entertained their ladies and plotted the acquisition of fortunes. Thin-legged tables of once polished maple, fragile in the delicate craftsmanship that only in the last few years was being replaced by mass-produced monotony, shuddered as he passed. Spiderwebs parted at his touch. He froze as he entered the final room, the one marked 418, in the northwest corner. There, barely visible in the faint light from the candle, a pair of eyes glared at him from the corner. Roman's breath caught in his throat, stopped there by his leaping heart. "Lieght!" he gasped, unable to move.

Lieght was trussed and then tied to the bureau, just as he had been in the boardinghouse in Denver. The same words the mobster had spoken then now echoed through Roman's memory. They promised retribution and death unless Roman squeezed the trigger of his revolver and sent the soul of Harry Lieght merrily on its way to hell. In that moment, again, Roman relived the knowledge that reality was far more difficult than fantasy. In that moment, he recognized the difference between tough talk and the macabre, frightful domain of those who act. Was it a moral choice? Was he unable to overstep the streak of decency ingrained in his character by the years in Sunday school and church, by all those hell-and-brimstone preachings, by the repeated admonitions of mother and father, by the innate awareness, even, of right and wrong? Or was he simply afraid? Harry Lieght, bound, gagged, and glaring, daring the hand that held the gun. Roman's finger curled around the trigger had been paralyzed. He had seen Lieght kill a man, heard him talk of killing others. Surely there could have been no great evil in ridding the world of such a monster. And yet ... And yet ...

Lieght's eyes blinked, suddenly rose, and came toward him. Roman's arms raised to fend them off, and he bent backward. His face was twisted in near-apoplectic terror. "Waugh-o! Waugh-o!" The harsh cry was sudden and strident in the enclosed room.

Roman's throat worked spasmodically, but no sound emerged. He backed into the edge of the door, and only then, as his head rapped sharply against the wood, saw the winged form of the great horned owl as it veered to one side, banked steeply, and disappeared out the open window.

Not Lieght at all. A trick of the imagination, the transformation of owl to man. Roman made himself laugh, made himself walk across the room. The owl had been perching on a wooden valet's helper. A mere trick of the imagination had transformed him into Lieght. Roman looked down at the pile of bones and hair balls littering the floor underneath the valet and realized with a shudder that Lieght and the owl had one thing in common: each was a predator, each hunted and stalked his prey. Neither would hesitate to kill. Not for one second.

Sobered, Roman backed out of the room, walked to the stairway, and paused to drum his fingertips on the balustrade before starting down. The lesson to be learned from the owl was important, but the analogy between man and owl went only so far, and it would be a mistake to imbue it with too much meaning. A man was not a hare or a grouse. Roman was not a complete and utter fool. The owl hunted indiscriminately, taking whatever prey appeared. Lieght was faced with a much more difficult problem, for he sought one individual among millions. Yet Lieght was more intelligent than the owl. Owls didn't ask questions. Lieght did, though, and would collect information, analyze, and then act with a degree of certainty that no brute animal . . .

"Enough. Jesus, enough!" Roman said, shakily lighting a Lucky. "You gotta quit that." He stopped on the landing above the lobby, sat on the top stair, and forced himself to think logically. Lieght was a hundred miles away, would have no clue as to which direction they had taken. He and Lainie had time and money. Ten thousand, almost eleven, really, would give them a start. They could buy a house somewhere and start a family. Maybe even in Mountain City. Roman liked the mountains, and Lieght would never think of looking so close. He'd think they'd gone to the West Coast, or New York, maybe.

Then again, maybe pigs had wings, too. Or ducks had hooves, or whatever it was they said. "Oh, Christ, I'm tired of being tough," he muttered.

"A penny for your thoughts." Lainie's voice drifted up from the darkness below.

Roman could see her silhouetted against the light spilling onto the lobby floor from the dining room. He moved the candle to one side. "I don't have thoughts," he said, trying to match her lightness of tone.

"Everybody does. Maybe I didn't offer enough."

"Maybe life doesn't offer enough."

"Oh, la de da. Aren't we the deep one, though."

"I won't be made fun of!" Roman snapped.

Lainie laughed shrilly. When she spoke, her voice was brittle. "Then don't *be* funny."

Roman wished he could see her face. Something was troubling her. "What the heck has gotten into you?" he asked.

"I thought you'd never ask." Pent up for too long, the words tumbled out. "It's cold and miserable and I haven't stepped outside all day and I've burned a pot of beans and charred a pie I was going to surprise you with and I'm making a perfectly botched mess of things. And I went outside once to use the outhouse which was terribly cold and when I was squatting over the seat something bit me and I don't even know what it was but I have a nice lump on my leg and if it was a spider I hope it wasn't too poisonous and I also managed to get a splinter in an especially private place. And when I came inside I unwrapped my records and broke 'If You Knew Susie,' which was my favorite one. And the fire went out just now because I forgot to put wood on, and to top it all off and make this just a perfect day, you, Roman Phillips, have been grumbling and growling and prowling around and acting nasty and ill-tempered and downright wretched all because you couldn't commit an act of murder, because you couldn't bring yourself to Mr. Lieght's level. Well, I'm as frightened of Harry Lieght as . . . as anyone, but let me tell you something, if you had murdered him in cold blood I surely wouldn't be here and I surely wouldn't care about you because you wouldn't be the same Roman Phillips I loved. That Roman Phillips would be dead, at least inside, and good riddance. But you didn't and you aren't and I'm scared, but I'll be damned if I'd have it any other way, even if you haven't said three words to me all afternoon long."

She stopped, paused to take a breath. Suddenly she felt stupid. It had all poured out so rapidly. What had she said? She tried to remember, but was too confused to think any longer.

Tension clung like mist to the distance between them. Roman had neither moved nor spoken. Lainie thought that perhaps she ought to say something else, but was uncertain of where to start. At last, the candle moved. In its light, the sad amber face at the top of the stairs didn't look angry at all.

"I love you, Lainie," Roman said.

"Oh." Lainie blinked, felt the weight of the day slipping off her shoulders. "Oh!"

His hand was beckoning. Her steps weightless, Lainie climbed the stairs. When he put his arm around her, they did not speak again, only moved quickly to the Ulysses S. Grant Suite. Neither of them cared that the bedclothes were musty.

Exhausted, Wind River had gone to bed with the birds Safely bedded down in Muenster's Funeral Parlor, he slept soundly for three hours before his dreams took a turn for the worse. He was dressed all in black, sitting at a table and watching Paunch Pepperdine study the cards fanning out from his fist. The year was 1892, it was the first of March. The town was Dry Out, Nevada. Wind River had turned thirty-six earlier that year, and was growing weary of the life he had chosen and the violence that dogged the path of a man with a shootist's reputation.

The game didn't feel right. Paunch was a wolver and stunk of the wild and could not play cards worth a damn. Worse, he was a poor loser, exactly the kind of player Wind River made it a policy to steer clear of.

"Open for a five-dollar gold piece," Paunch growled, staring across the table.

Wind River looked at his hand and the two aces and two deuces he held and knew to his soul it was a winning hand. He knew equally, however, that he had to get rid of it and let Paunch have the pot. Knowing when to lose was as much a part of the game as knowing how to win. Wind River added up the table, calculated just how much it would take to leave Paunch a few dollars up, and decided that then was the time. "Call," he said, sliding his bet across the green felt. "Two cards," he added, and traded his aces face down for a nine of hearts and a seven of clubs. His face fell just ever so slightly.

Paunch took two cards, immediately bet another ten dollars, which Wind River hesitantly raised twenty. Paunch's chin jutted out and he stared at Wind River, then at his own cards, and finally called. When Wind River showed his deuces, old Paunch guffawed and flung down his pair of queens. "I knew ye was bluffin'!" he yelled "By damn knew it!"

"You caught me there, Mr. Pepperdine. I thought I had you," Wind River said with a silent sigh of relief. He dropped the stub of his cigar into a spittoon and pushed back a little from the table. "Well, we're even stephen and I haven't eaten supper, so I guess I'll call it a night."

Paunch's face turned ugly. "The hell, bucko," he said, his voice rumbling ominously. "I done sat here and watched you have your way with me for three hours. Now my luck's changin', I ain't about to watch ye skedaddle."

Wind River saw the trouble coming, saw it barreling down like a steam locomotive on the fast side of a pass, and no way to jump out of the path. "I'm beat, Mr. Pepperdine. We're even up. You maybe even won a couple of dollars. That's where I call it quits."

Pepperdine made a guttural sound like a wolf caught in a trap. His growl started as Wind River stood, grew louder as he walked away from the table. Men stepped back, cleared a path as Paunch's growl turned into a roar. His thick neck bulged with fury and his lips curled back to reveal black stumps of broken and decayed teeth. Drawing a huge bowie knife from the sheath at his waist, he kicked over the table and charged across it. His huge frame catapulted forward with astonishing speed for his size and the amount of whiskey he had consumed. Wind River, in one fluid motion, turned, drew his revolver, crouched, and fired, shot Paunch Pepperdine twice in the stomach and three times through the lungs. The last bullet struck square in the wolver's heart, and still the man had enough momentum to knock Wind River flat on his back and enough strength to bury his knife up to the hilt through the pine flooring next to Wind River's left ear.

Wind River woke in a sweat, the same sweat he had felt at that moment, thirty-five years earlier, when he shoved Paunch Pepperdine's inert, lifeless body off his. The same cold chill, the same gut-churning fear clutched him as it had two nights later when he learned that Paunch's kin were after him. It was then that the Wind River Kid knew he had used up his luck and had lost his courage. There hadn't been anything left to do but run and hide. And he was hiding still.

Trembling, he uncorked the bottle and nursed at it. Only when it was half empty did he fall asleep again, this time too stuporous to dream.

Sometime beyond midnight, Roman woke up. The Ulysses S. Grant Suite was quiet save for the occasional pop of the fire and the soft, even sound of Lainie breathing. When he realized that she, too, was awake, he propped himself on his elbow and ran the palm of his hand over her breasts, then kissed each one twice. Lainie pressed his face against her flesh, and they lay together in the full and solicitous gentleness of lovemaking.

"Joanne Elaine Brewster. What kind of a name is that for a girl?" Roman asked.

"A perfectly good name, silly."

"I like Joanne Elaine Phillips better. Has a ring to it, don't you think?"

Lainie laughed and held him close. "Yes, I do. A perfect ring."

"You do?" Roman rolled his eyes back, tried to see her face. "Maybe the old man could marry us, then. Sort of like the captain of a ship."

"Poor old man. Don't make fun of him."

Roman sighed in mock seriousness. "Probably wouldn't take, anyway. Hey!" He extricated himself from her arms, looked down on her again. "What the heck. My grandfather was a pulpit pounder. I ought to be able to do the job myself. I mean, if the son of a preacher's son can't marry somebody, who can?"

Lainie made a face. "Now you're making fun."

"You think so?" He took her hand. "Do you, Joanne Elaine Brewster, take me, Roman Phillips, who isn't much, to be your lawful wedded husband, to have and to hold, to tell him when he's being a fool and back him when he's right, to give him courage and strength to be something more than what he is, for richer or poorer—probably poorer—until death do you part?"

"I do," Lainie said, her voice husky. "I do, Roman. I really do."

"And I do, too." Roman grinned widely. "By the authority vested in me, inherited from my grandfather, the right Reverend Malachi Phillips, I pronounce us husband and wife!"

Lainie pulled him down to her and kissed him. "Congratulations, Mr. Phillips. You're a very lucky man."

"Thank you, Mrs. Phillips." He kissed her on each eye, on her forehead and nose, again on her lips. "I know."

Later, in the quiet of the warmth, Roman, to himself, intoned the final lines of the marriage ceremony as he remembered it. "What God has joined," he whispered under his breath, "let no man rend asunder."

14

In the autumn of the aspen, winter had whispered hints of its approach and then left. The morning was clear, the sky a sapphire blue and dotted with milky opal clouds. It was cold, but enough above freezing to send the icicles of the day before dripping noisily from every eave and folded roof and weather-worn overhang. Now and then one would fall with a sharp, tinkling explosion that, to the west, was blunted against the mountain and, to the east, faded in the thin air over Rampage Valley. The shattering of ice spears was a happy noise, Lainie thought, as she broke some eggs, beat them to a froth, and dumped them into a hot skillet. "Well," she said, glancing up as Wind River walked through the back door, "Roman is out looking for you."

Lainie he could take. Roman was a different matter, and little more than an uneasy truce existed between them. "I don't doubt it. Probably wants to kick me lame," Wind River said, rubbing the redness from his eyes. His stomach growled. He crossed to the coffeepot, grabbed the handle, and yelped. "It's hot," Lainie cautioned.

Wind River grimaced at her, wrapped his shirttail around the handle, and poured a cup of coffee. He noticed with satisfaction she had traded her flapper dress for a pair of Roman's trousers, a sensible if baggy change. He took a sip and made a wry face. "Oh, God! You threw out the grounds."

"They were three inches deep in the bottom of the pot."

"Of course they were," Wind River exclaimed. "It took me a da . . . darn long while to build up to it, too. Blast it, woman, I had it just right."

"You needn't yell," Lainie retorted heatedly. "It took me a pretty while to scrape it all out. Such scum!" She shivered. "Brrr! I almost threw up."

"Oh, you did?" Wind River stared bleakly at the weak excuse for a brew. "Well, you oughta know that's the way to make coffee. A little salt every once in a while, an egg shell now and then, and keep adding grounds so the old mellows the new. Hell, if a body's gonna make coffee, they oughta make coffee and not ladies' fancy sippin' tea."

"You may call it coffee, Mr. Kid," Lainie said, her eyes narrowing dangerously, "but civilized people would call it warfare."

Wind River walked to the sink, ceremoniously poured half his coffee down the drain. "Miss," he said, drawing himself up, "I have got four things to say to you."

Lainie folded her arms across her chest. The wooden spatula she held in one clenched fist waved like a scepter. "Oh?"

"Yes." He posed importantly. "One, you are not in civilization. Elkhorn is not civilization, never really was, never wanted to be, and the world is better for it. So don't talk of civilized. Two, you leave them grounds in the pot. It's my grounds and my pot. I fix the well and pump the water, and I chop the wood for the stove. Three, don't call me Mr. Kid. It makes me want to slap leather. Wind River will do just fine."

Not waiting for any reply, he marched to the pantry, found the emergency bottle, topped off the tepid brew with hellfire. While a wide-eyed Lainie watched, he took a sip, nodded his approval, and started from the kitchen.

"That was three," Lainie said, stone-faced against what she considered an unwarranted attack.

"Huh?" Wind River said, pausing at the door.

"You said you had four things to tell me. That was only three. What's number four?" Her smile was a model of sarcastic sweetness. "I'm sure it must be as important as the others."

"Yeah." Wind River scratched at his whiskers, paused dramatically, then nodded toward the range and the smoke rising from the skillet. "Your eggs is burnt."

Lainie spun around and, with a muffled cry of consternation, ran to the stove and stared down at what looked to be a bubbling yellow and black pancake. "Oh, damn!" she said, and closed her eyes and sighed. When she turned back to place the blame on Wind River, it was too late. He was already out the door.

Which was how he had planned it, and which was a damned good idea, he thought, congratulating himself when he heard the cast-iron skillet smash against something, accompanied by a cry of anger from Lainie. It served her right, though, for ruining his coffee. A morning without a decent cup of coffee was like a claim without color, pretty damn near useless.

Still, as he stood on the hotel porch and lit his morning cigar, Wind River felt as if a great weight had been lifted from his shoulders. As far as he could tell, old Scar had not come to town during the night. Nothing new had been destroyed and there weren't any fresh tracks in the sodden earth. The whiskey had perked him up. The mountain air felt fresh and balmy, and his lungs invited it in with full, deep breaths. If the temperature held, the trail south would be clear again in a couple of days and dried out enough for the wagon.

Wind River scowled, mulled over his escape plans. A lot of doubt had crept in during the last couple of days. If Lainie and Roman were representative of what he'd find in the outside world, he wasn't sure he even wanted to go through with it. But that was only an excuse, he admonished himself. They were only kids. Denver, for starters, was full of people. Folks couldn't all be alike. Some of them had to be sensible. In any case, the alternative to leaving was staying, and he surely didn't want to do that. All told, life really was like a game of cards. A man had to play the percentages, and the percentages mitigated against staying. Not counting himself, and Roman and Lainie, who would be gone soon, Creed and Scar were one hundred percent of the population of Elkhorn. Even if only ten percent of the outside world consisted of sensible folks, the odds for finding a kindred soul were far better out there. Resolved, Wind River checked the sky for the falcon, stepped off the porch, and started up the street to the livery. He hadn't looked in on the Appaloosa since his return to Elkhorn, and if the animal was going to be at the peak of health for the trip, he'd need feeding.

The best-laid plans don't always work out. Wind River was almost to the livery when he noticed Aden Creed standing in front of a motte of quaking aspen on the western slope.

The mountain man had his hand raised and waved Indian-style, with his palm outward and held aloft to show he held no weapons. When Wind River automatically waved back, Creed turned, took a step or two up the mountain, and beckoned for him to follow. "In a pig's eye," Wind River said, realizing Creed was on the trail to Silvertip Falls.

"Where the hell have you been?" Roman said, coming out of Muenster's. He carried the Hawken and looked irritated.

"If it's any of your business," Wind River said, "I went down to the hotel for my morning coffee." He spat to one side. "A lot of good it did me."

Roman stepped into the street and glanced at the slope behind him. "Who were you signaling?"

"Son-of-a-bitch wanted me to follow. I know where, too, but I ain't goin'."

"Who?" His throat tight with anxiety, Roman studied the slope. He saw nothing but yellow grass, evergreens, and a stand of aspens, golden in the morning light. "There's no one there."

"He was," Wind River assured him.

"Who?"

"Creed, damn it, boy. Aden Creed."

Roman looked suspicious. "Who the devil is Aden Creed?"

Wind River drove his right fist into his left palm. "That's it! You hit it, by God!"

"Hit what?"

"The devil, of course." Wind River nodded knowingly. "Now, why didn't I think of that myself? Creed and Old Beelzebub! One and the same."

Any doubts concerning Wind River's sanity were erased. "Beelzebub, eh?" Roman asked with a sly wink. "Guess you're the only one he shows himself to, eh?"

"Wouldn't know about that," Wind River said. "Don't matter, really. I just wish he'd stop. Dry up and blow away. That's what folks're supposed to do, aren't they?" For the first time, he noticed Roman was carrying the Hawken. "You like that rifle?" he asked caustically.

"Ah . . ." Roman looked down guiltily.

"Almightly loose when it comes to other folks' belongings, ain't you?"

"This old relic?" Roman asked.

"That old relic'll blow a porcupine right out of its quills at five hundred yards," Wind River pointed out.

"Then it's a good thing I took it, isn't it?" Roman said with a grin. "Wouldn't want you to get any ideas."

"Squeeze that trigger and you'll get an idea or two." Wind River reached out and carefully pushed the muzzle to one side. "It's loaded."

Roman pulled his finger off the trigger. His face blanched. "I didn't know . . ."

"Well, you woulda, if you weren't so damn wet behind the ears. That there's a Hawken .50-caliber rifle. Cap and ball. Used to belong to Creed. In case you get an urge to fire it off, it shoots just a little bit to the left. Has a kick like a Missouri mule, too."

"I can handle it." Roman sniffed, raising the rifle to his shoulder and aiming at the weathervane on the livery roof.

Wind River looked in the direction Roman was aiming and caught a glimpse of a brown speck drifting lazily over the treetops. "Damn!" he exclaimed, and took off running for the livery.

"Hey!" Roman yelled, startled. He lowered the rifle and followed Wind River, reached the doors ahead of him.

Wind River darted inside, bent double, coughed, spat, and coughed again. "High mountain air"—he paused, gasped, breathed heavily two or three times—"makes for hard shuckin'."

"What the hell was that all about?" Roman asked, almost as breathless as Wind River.

"A fella . . . can't be . . . too careful . . ." Wind River leaned back against something cold and metallic. "What the hell?. . ." he yelped.

An answering whinny sounded from a stall at the back of the stable.

"Thunderation!" Wind River said, staring at the battered and dented runabout. Giving the car a wide berth, he circled to the horse. The Appaloosa rolled his eyes and snorted his complaint at having to share his home with the mechanical monstrosity. "Easy, boy. Easy," Wind River said, stroking the horse's neck. "That thing"—he pointed to the car—"made it here without bein' drug?"

"Sure did," Roman said proudly. "Easy as falling off a log."

Wind River warily approached the car, wished again he'd taken the main road. "Looks like it fell off more than one," he said, tentatively kicking one of the tires. A great hunk of dried mud fell off the fender. "Yours, huh?"

"Bought and paid for."

"With the money you took from that Lieght fella?"

"How'd you? . . ." Roman's look of pride turned to embarrassment, then anger. "Lainie?" he asked.

Ill at ease, Wind River nodded yes.

"I might've known," Roman snorted. "How much did she tell you?"

"No need to get your nose out of joint, young'un. I've been down the same road myself, and far and long enough to be able to read sign when it's plain as day. If she hadn't felt like talkin', I would've known sooner or later. Maybe not exactly, but close enough." He kicked the running board. More mud fell off. "All that metal, all them dollars, and that thing still can't take you where my horse can go. Pretty soon they'll be makin' metal men to ride their metal automobiles, and regular flesh-and-blood folks won't be needed at all." Wind River shook his head in sorrow and walked to the rear of the stable, where the Appaloosa was pawing at the door to the corral. "Nag's got more sense than most," he said, unbolting the door. High-stepping and obviously relieved, the stallion trotted out into the corral. "He don't even want to be in the same room with such nonsense."

"That nonsense will take me a lot farther than that old hay burner you call a horse," Roman said, miffed.

"So I heard tell," Wind River agreed. "But there's not a man alive can convince me it'll take a two-foot-wide trail along a mountainside."

"Well . . . maybe not that," Roman admitted. "But anywhere else. And faster, too."

"Maybe so, maybe not," Wind River said. "'I'll tell you one thing, though. There ain't no such thing as fast in these mountains. Only far and hard."

Roman wiped the water gauge with his sleeve. He looked supremely confident. "Elkhorn's far enough," he said with a grin. "As for hard, I made it here, I can make it back."

"When?" Wind River pressed. "You ain't got enough food for winter. Not even with mine thrown in. Don't let the sun fool you, boy. Winter's coming. Real winter. Not just them little flurries we had. If you got half as much sense as sass, you'll get out while the weather holds."

"Don't you worry about me," Roman snapped. Deep down, Wind River's warning worried him, but he wasn't about to admit it. "I can look after myself."

"And the girl?"

Roman stiffened, then abruptly started for the door. "When I want your advice, old man," he said in a huff, "I'll ask for it."

Wind River took a couple of steps after him, laid a hand on his arm. "I wouldn't go outside right now."

Not even slowing, Roman shook off Wind River's arm, stepped into the street, and headed back to the hotel. He got no farther than the second mudhole when, with a rush of air and a wild screech, a blur of feathers and talons slammed against his head.

"Jeee—sus!" Roman shrieked, going straight up in the air. His hands flew out, his feet made running motions in the air. When he landed, off balance, he pitched face forward in the mud. "Gaw-dhaaam!" he cursed, lunging to his feet. Above him, Roman's hat firmly gripped in its talons, the falcon screeched and swooped upward in a triumphal arc. Roman shouldered the Hawken, sighted on the speeding bird, and squeezed the trigger.

Boooommm!
The sound of the explosion raced to the mountainside, returned about the time Roman hit the mud seat first, skidded, and, his legs kicking high, rolled onto his back. Before the echoes had faded over Rampage Valley, the falcon had angled gracefully into a cloud and disappeared. Wind River disintegrated. His eyes streaming tears, his hand holding his side, he watched Roman struggle to his feet. The boy was dripping brown, coming and going. Mud streaked his face and matted his hair. Mud oozed from his shirt and trousers. A great glob of it had been forced under his belt when he had skidded backward. "I know . . . I know . . . When you want my advice . . ." Wind River gasped, "you'll . . . you'll . . ." Too weak to go on or even stand, Wind River staggered back and sat on the running board of the runabout.

The quiet in the street was preternatural. All Roman could hear was a great ringing in his ears. His head hurt where the falcon had hit it, his right shoulder where the Hawken had slammed into it. He was soaked. A slow stream of mud slid down between his buttocks. He shifted uncomfortably, discovered he was standing ankle-deep in more mud. Holding his toes stiff so he wouldn't lose his shoe, he eased one and then the other foot out. The Hawken lay to his right where he had thrown it. Stunned and humiliated, he grabbed the rifle and slogged toward the hotel.

Lainie appeared on the boardwalk. Roman stopped at the bottom of the stairs and looked blankly at her. Her mouth moved, but e heard nothing. jskloaly, he climbed the steps, slipped on the smoot boardwalk, and managed to stop in front of her. "If you ask—" He paused, blinked. Even his own voice sounded strangely distant. He opened his mouth wide, worked his jaw. His ears popped, but the ringing didn't stop. "If you ask if everything is all right," he finally said, "I'll strangle you."

The laughter from the stable was infectious. "Yes, dear," Lainie said, barely managing to keep a straight face. His legs stiff, his shoulders back in an approximation of dignity, Roman marched past her and into the hotel. Desperate, almost choking, Lainie put her hands over her ears to block out Wind River's laughter and breathed deeply until she gained control of herself. At last, her own amusement transformed into a downcast look of common concern, she followed Roman's tracks inside.

15

Harry Lieght stumbled and his knees stabbed into an upthrust chunk of granite shaped like a foot. He grunted, stood, and continued walking. The pain slowly penetrated his numbed senses and registered on his brain. "Ouch," he said, after half a minute. He reached down to hold his knees, walked bent over that way for another minute. "Shit!"

His toes were a memory. His legs felt like stilts, frail appendages that made walking a precarious business. Lieght wiped a forearm across his forehead, realized he was sweating. His breath clouded the air. His head ached and his cheeks were flushed with the war paint of fever. He had trouble keeping his eyes in focus, and fought back delirium. How long he'd been walking he didn't know, but it seemed forever. How long he could continue he didn't know, either. In a sense, it didn't matter: he was functioning on instinct alone, and had been since he had struck his head against the tree. He sneezed, lost his footing, and tumbled into a wash. The pain was slow to come, but excruciating when it arrived. He thought someone had torn his elbow out of his arm.

"Shit-eating mountain," he gasped. The earth tried to hold him down. His lungs burned. He willed himself to his feet, stood tottering in front of a wall of root-laced dirt.

"This is Harry Lieght!" he roared, pulling the automatic from its shoulder holster and firing into the dirt. A root exploded, a clump of dirt fell. Lieght swung around and blasted a circle of pockmarks until the .45 clicked on empty. The mountain was still there. Defeated, he slumped to his knees and balanced on his hands. "This is Harry Lieght," he repeated dully, over and over again, panting, his mind almost blank. Somewhere he found the strength and pushed himself erect again. He stood, fell down, stood. He roared profanity after profanity. He fell, and sneezed.

How long he lay there he didn't know, but it was getting dark when he finally roused himself. A wall of dirt to either side hemmed him in. Puzzled, he stood, and stumbled forward down the gully until he found a place where he could climb out. At the top, he found himself in a grove of pine trees. He bent double in a sneeze that ended in a deep, lung-searing cough, then straightened and started walking again. He plodded through the stand of timber and emerged from it along a deer trail, unrecognizable to him, but a lucky choice all the same. Five minutes later, from the top of a rise, he glimpsed the lights of a cabin.

Lieght's head spun. He sneezed and fell down. "Stop it!" he shouted, gripping the earth. When the spinning slowed, he managed to stand once more.

It was a slow and awkward dance, played out in the dim light of dusk amid the towering pines and monstrous boulders on the side of the mountain. For every step Lieght took forward, another wandered to the left or right. His path was angular, then a looping, drunken arc that took him back to where he started. At last, when he brought his wayward progress under a semblance of control, the cabin appeared to recede, to slide away from him. Half falling, he ran. He wanted to catch the cabin, anchor it. Sneezing, bent double, he fought for balance, and only at the last second straightened in time to crash shoulder first into the door.

He had it! The cabin was real! A hard and tangible object. A wild elation surged through the murkiness. Lieght stepped back a pace, grabbed the latch, and felt the door give way beneath his weight and warm air rush forward to kiss his cheek. He placed one foot in front of the other. He walked an imaginary tightrope through the door and inside.

Never had warmth meant so much. He had survived. The

showed their faces? Wind River peeked around the corner of the ruined barbershop. The Great Northern Hotel looked quiet enough, but a fellow never knew, and a lifetime of living on the thin edge had taught him to consider the odds. The idea hit him like a flash. Even if they did hear him, they couldn't follow him in an automobile that didn't work! All he had to do was remove a few parts and they'd be stuck. What parts or how he'd get them off he wasn't sure, but it didn't really matter. One or two were sure to be important enough. Besides, he thought with a sly grin, he might even be able to build up his stake a little, after all. The three extra tires Roman had tied onto the back of the car would be the perfect starting place. All he had to do was switch them to his wagon and then sell them to Weldon when he got to Mountain City.

The brilliant blue bowl of sky overhead was empty of hunting falcons, but Wind River still hesitated. The little girl, Lainie, posed a real problem. He'd known a thousand like her when he was younger and had never given a one of them much thought, but times had changed. Unlike Lainie, who was a frail little thing, those girls had been toughened by the frontier. They had all wanted something. Always. Lainie, on the other hand, just to be nice, had walked up to the funeral parlor the night before and brought him an extra blanket, then invited him to breakfast the next morning. She'd even taken the trouble to tell him she hadn't emptied the grounds from the coffeepot. He'd smiled at that, after she was gone. Roman Phillips, though, was a different matter. It was true that the first rule was to look out for yourself and the devil take the hindmost, but the boy had overstepped the bounds of decency with that bag of grub. Wind River freely admitted he'd been guilty of a few indiscretions in his day, but he'd never stooped so low as to take an old man's food. The hell with Phillips and the girl. They had money and leg power. Let them hike into town, buy a horse and supplies. That wasn't any more than Wind River was going to have to do.

Rechecking the sky and the hotel, Wind River walked quietly across the street to the livery and slipped through the partially open doors. Morning light streamed in the back door and silhouetted the runabout. Wind River began to undo the knots on the rope holding the tires, then stopped, hearing Creed announce himself in the usual way.

"Wolves," Creed's voice explained from the shadow of a stall.

Wind River ignored him, finished the first tie, and started on the second.

Another fart echoed resonantly through the barn. "More wolves."

"Okay. Okay," Wind River said, stepping around to the side of the runabout.

The mountain man was sitting on Wind River's saddle. The peaked cowl of his Hudson Bay blanket capote gave him an especially spooky quality. "Ow-oooooo," he said, raising his arms at the same time. "I am the Ghost of Christmas Future."

Wind River snorted. "You don't look like him to me."

Creed shrugged, pulled the cowl off his bald head. "Maybe. Maybe not." He pulled out his pipe and lit it. "Busy, huh?"

"You might say," Wind River said guardedly.

"A man's always busy when he starts a new career."

"What the hell's that supposed to mean?"

"Never knew you for a thief before, Kid."

"Now, see here—"

Creed held up a hand, blew a perfect smoke ring in the still air of the livery. "Won't change a thing. Thievin's thievin'."

"And so's fair's fair, damn it," Wind River said defensively. "They took my food, which, as you'd know if you'd been there, I didn't ask them to do. My food, their tires. It's the cut of the cards."

"Cards?" Creed snorted. "The cards are yellowed and curled, Kid. The game is over. Can't you understand that?"

"Not for me," Wind River insisted doggedly. "I can always buy a new deck, and that's just what I plan to do. I been cooped up in this town so long that I forgot there's the whole rest of the world out there. Bigger, grander places than Mountain City. With people, too. Real live people."

"Oh, Lord, Kid. Lord, Lord, listen to you." Creed shook his head sadly. "You spent seventy-one years playin' a lone hand, and now you're talkin' about people." Slowly, he walked around Wind River, looked him up and down. "I don't know," he finally said. "Maybe you're right. You never did get past a card game when it come to people. Played 'em for what they was worth, used 'em as you saw fit, walked away from 'em when they run out of anything you needed or wanted."

"That's not true," Wind River said quietly.

"It ain't?" Creed asked. Deliberately, he opened his coat, unbuttoned his shirt, and bared his chest. Three puckered bullet holes, ugly and swollen in the dim light, marred his flesh. "Ain't it?" he asked again in the hushed silence. "Butch and Dupree Pepperdine. You recall them?"

Wind River turned his back, leaned against the runabout for support. "Close your shirt, Aden. Get dressed."

"And let you do the same thing to them kids? Leave 'em stranded up here, not knowin' a thing about mountains or mountain weather, with winter comin' on?" Creed shook his head stubbornly. "Not goin' to let you do it, Kid. Not gonna let you walk away from this table."

"Oh, you aren't?" Wind River said, whirling about to face Creed again. "Well, let me tell you somethin'. You ain't no durn sky pilot, and I don't need your advice or your lettin' or not lettin'. I'm the Wind River Kid, damn it. That's some-thing. What the hell have you ever done to be so durn high and mighty?"

"I went to Silvertip Falls, for starters. Which"—Creed emphasized with a stabbing forefinger—"I wouldn't of never had to do if you'd taken my advice in the first place."

"So that's it!" Wind River crowed. "You're galled 'cause I took Angelina's way."

Creed's head wagged back and forth. "Not galled, Kid. Just disappointed. All them years I'd wanted a son to be proud of, and what I ended up gettin' was a gambler and a shootist with half a dozen men's lives in his pocket. No gettin' around it, Kid, you turned out bad. You plain took the wrong way."

"Oh, I did, did I?" Wind River's voice dropped. His face was pale, the veins on his temple stood out. "You want to know what else I took, Creed?"

"No," Creed said quickly, backing away a step.

"Angelina, that's who." Wind River's voice shook with black and ugly triumph. "I put it in her up to the hilt and let go. She had as much of my seed as yours in her. And she said I was better, too. Younger and stronger. She felt sorry for you and let you diddle her, but it was me who kept her fire goin' and kept her happy. She said I was a natural with the cards and the ladies, and what I didn't know, she taught me."

Creed was trying to fill his pipe, but his hands were shaking so badly that he spilled the tobacco. "Don't want to hear about it," he mumbled. "You're hittin' low. Don't want to hear it."

"Then get. Get out and leave me alone."

The two men stared at each other for a long moment. Dust motes danced in the sunshine from the open rear door. At last, Creed turned slowly and started out the barn, but then stopped. "I'll git," he said dully, turning toward Wind River. His face was dark against the bright light. "I always wanted me a son, Kid. You came along and gave me the chance. Thickheaded, selfish whelp you were, I promised myself I wouldn't fail, and I ain't about to."

Wind River was suddenly tired, didn't even care anymore. The whole argument was ludicrous, a waste of time. "I ain't your kid, Creed," he said quietly. "We ain't kin. Just leave me be. I can take care of myself. A man has to rise up pretty early to put anything over on the Wind River Kid."

"Not more than an hour early, I'd say."

"What the hell . . ." Wind River quit, snorted in disgust. "Never mind. You quit makin' sense long ago."

"They took the horse."

For one startled moment, Wind River thought he hadn't heard right. Suddenly he was moving, running past Creed. "Son-of-a-bitch!" he swore, looking wildy around the empty corral. The Appaloosa was indeed gone. They'd fooled him! He'd been tricked by a couple of . . .

He raced to the gate. Clearly visible in the dewy grass, the horse's tracks led across the meadow below the graveyard and the trail north toward Lincoln Pass. "Why the tarnation didn't you tell me?" Wind River asked, stalking back to the barn. "Least you could of . . ." He stopped. Creed had disappeared. "That's right!" Wind River yelled. "Run off when I need you, you long-tooth, sop-eared son-of-a . . ." He sputtered, unable to remember the rest of the epithet.

Wind River's heart sank. Creed had mentioned an hour. The Appaloosa wasn't fast, but he did eat up ground in his own plodding way. They'd be four miles away, and every step of it uphill. Wind River was stuck, bamboozled, and betrayed. Righteous indignation welled in his chest. Roman and Lainie had snuck away with his horse and left him stranded! Conveniently forgetting he had intended an identical fate for them, Wind River yanked determinedly on the brim of his cap and looked around for a means of vengeance.

Vengeance? Hell, he had to catch them first, and there wasn't anything in town to be rode other than the runabout, which was impossible. In the first place, he didn't know how to drive, and in the second, they'd hear him coming and pull off the trail long before he got to them. Third and last, as it dawned on him, made him shiver: they had guns, and he didn't.

So that was that. His choices had narrowed down to two. He could stay in Elkhorn and starve, or hike it alone to Mountain City. Without the Appaloosa. Stupid horse, anyway. "Durned near useless," he said aloud. "Wouldn't run if his tail was on fire. His fault I'm in Elkhorn. Better off without him."

But damned if that wasn't another chunk of time gone. Sixteen years they'd been together. Animal hadn't been two years old when he'd bought him. Left an empty spot, all right. Different if he'd died, maybe. Understandable. But to have him stole? That was almost more than a man should have to take. Defeated, his years weighing on him, Wind River allowed himself the luxury of self-pity.

"Durned car!" he yelled suddenly, kicking one of the wheels, striking out at the one object Roman and Lainie had left behind. "Dad-burned, evil-smellin', ugly heap of gopher shit."

He stopped as suddenly as he'd begun, looked around to see if Creed was watching. Slowly, the idea taking shape in his mind, he circled the machine, tentatively touched one fender, and pulled his finger back as if burned. Desperation breeds desperate measures, he thought. Angelina had said that once. Or maybe Creed. Wind River drew himself up, took a deep breath. He stopped in front of the automobile and stared at it. The headlights stared back passively. "You don't scare me," Wind River said, bridling. "I've saddled and forked a bronc or two when the going got rough, and the town too hot to quibble over rightful ownership, so by the devil's back flap, I reckon I can ride you."

A Ford would go anywhere a horse would. That's what they said. The one in front of him had negotiated the trail to Elkhorn and would drive it back to Mountain City. All Wind River had to do was figure out how. Head cocked to one side, he studied the machine. Lewis Weldon had taken him for a ride through and around Mountain City in a similar model. Driving hadn't looked too complicated. Kind of like riding a horse in some ways. Instead of pulling on the reins to go left, you turned the wheel left. Same for right. Feeling cocky, Wind River slapped the hood. "You and me, machine," he said, the old confidence intact again, "is going to Mountain City!"

It would be easy. He'd spend a while learning how to drive, then pack his gear, rest up, get a good night's sleep, and start bright and early in the morning. Once he got to Mountain City, he'd tell Lewis he'd traded the runabout for the Appaloosa and all his gear, plus a good map of how to get through Lincoln Pass. And then, by God, either trade for another horse or just drive right on through to Denver. "Wouldn't that be something!" he said aloud. "Drivin' into town with my good duds on, sittin' up there pretty as a picture!"

The years that had weighed so heavily only minutes before fell away as fast as winter's worries on a spring morning. Feeling better than he had in months, Wind River walked around to the driver's side and started to get in, then remembered there was no door there. "Can't fool me," he chuckled, hurrying around to the other side and climbing in. "Can't put anything over on the Wind River Kid. Let's see, now . . ."

It had been a year, but any mind capable of recalling the

fall and configuration of a deck of cards could certainly reconstruct the simplicity of a mere machine. Wind River sat behind the wheel, shut his eyes, and concentrated. The automobile Weldon had driven had been his first and he had been eager to demonstrate his knowledge of it. Sentence by sentence, Wind River ran through the storekeeper's monologue. "You got to have the brake on, first of all," Weldon had said. Wind River experimented with the brake, figured out how to squeeze the handle and release it, then set it again. "The spark, this thing here"—Wind River's hand touched the little metal rod to the left of the wheel— "is important. Damned crank will kick and break your arm if you don't shove it up before you try to start it."

There was a great deal more, some of it contradictory. The three pedals on the floor were a bit of a mystery, but one Wind River was sure he could figure out easily enough once he got moving. At last, deciding it was then or never, he set the spark and throttle, turned on the ignition key, and climbed out. A strap held the crank in place. He unhooked it and pulled out on the little ring Weldon had called the check or choke or something. The first few times he tried to turn the crank it kicked back at him, but at last the engine popped, then popped again, and finally caught with a groan and a rumble. Still halfway crouched over, Wind River suspiciously eyed the machine, at last straightened as it bellowed into full-blown life.

"Glory be!" Wind River shouted, flush with excitement. "Alive and smokin'!" He ran around to the driver's side and fiddled with the spark and throttle, then back to the front to hook the crank in its strap and push in the little ring. "Nothing to it!" he yelled above the roar.

Intoxicated, he climbed back into the car, slid over behind the steering wheel, and let loose the brake. Immediately the car jerked and started rolling forward. Coolly, Wind River shoved the left foot pedal halfway in. The transmission was in neutral, the auto rolled to a stop. So far so good, he thought, relieved. Ready for the next step, he took a deep breath and shoved the pedal clear to the floorboard. In low gear, the auto lurched forward through the open rear doors of the barn and into the corral.

"Yippyyy-yiiiii!" Wind River hollered. He twisted the wheel to the right, the runabout turned right. He twisted the wheel to the left, the damned thing turned left. That figured out, he pushed up on the throttle and slowed, pulled down on it and went faster. Exuberant, he pulled his foot off the left pedal. In high gear again, the car sprayed mud and headed straight toward the livery. Wind River's face paled as the barn loomed. Twisting frantically, he aimed for the open doors, managed to squeeze between them. "Whoa!" he shouted, pulling back on the wheel. "Whoa, whoa, damn it!"

It was one thing to remember how to drive when he was sitting still, quite another at twenty miles an hour inside a barn. The runabout clipped a stanchion, tore off the right rear bumper, smashed through the partially closed front doors, and shot into the street. Throttle half open, he was almost to the steps of the assay office before he recovered enough to twist the wheel to the left. The auto tipped menacingly but stayed upright. Wind River held on through one full circle, then another; at last had the presence of mind to try to straighten it out. Twisting on the wheel, he inscribed a perfect double S up Main Street before circling in front of the church and heading south again.

If God had wanted man to go that fast, he would have given him four legs and hooves, and had him eat oats seven days a week. Used to a more sedate pace, Wind River's vision blurred. Buildings sped by. His back was pressed against the seat, his arms were stiff, his hands clutched the wheel. Without quite knowing how, he found himself rolling down the boardwalk in front of the sheriff's office. He ducked as the runabout mowed down a post, cringed as the awning collapsed behind him with a resounding wheeze of anguished wood. "Whoa!" he shouted again in vain, bouncing over the debris left from the Widow Guthrie's dress shop. "Whoa!"

Nothing helped. The runabout ascended the bank steps, bounced off a pillar onto Main Street, and headed for the Jo-Letty Restaurant. His lips drawn back in a silent scream, Wind River twisted viciously on the wheel, almost overturned again, and charged on a diagonal course for the Great Northern Hotel.

"Oh, hell!" Wind River moaned, pulling on the wheel in time to level off and skim the front porch. Suddenly the Appaloosa appeared at the mouth of the alley. It bore two riders whose faces were framed in horror as the Model T bore down on them. The Appaloosa reared and pawed the air as the runabout shot past under his raised hooves, then fell over backward, dumping Roman and Lainie into the alley. Whinnying in terror, the animal rolled to its feet and ran for the woods.

Wind River ducked. By the time he dared look up, he was on a collision course with the funeral parlor. He grabbed the wheel to brace himself and then turned around without letting go to look for Roman and Lainie. The car responded abruptly, turning in a tight circle around his sitting log and throwing Wind River against the right-hand door before straightening itself and heading down Main Street again. Appalled, Wind River planted his feet on the floorboard and clamped his hands on the top of the windshield. Sweat-caked dust clung to his face. His eyes were wide with disbelief and incomprehension. The car was driving itself, jouncing from one mud hole to the next.

Suddenly Roman appeared in the mouth of the alley. "Help!" Wind River croaked, gripping the windshield more tightly. "Heeeeeellllllp!"

Roman limped into the street, prudently retreated to the porch of the Great Northern Hotel. "Get behind the wheel!" he screamed. "Get behind the wheel!"

Somehow, Wind River obeyed. "What do I do?" he pleaded. "Tell it to stop!"

"Put your left foot on the left pedal!" Roman shouted, running toward the car. "Shove it halfway in!" The runabout swerved toward him. He turned and raced back to safety.

"Whoa!" Wind River yelled, at the same time trying to follow instructions. He stepped on the left pedal, felt the runabout start to slow as it dropped out of high gear into neutral.

"Put your right foot on the right pedal and shove it down as far as it'll go!" Roman directed at the top of his voice.

Wind River obeyed, felt the car slow even further.

"Now shut down the throttle!" Roman yelled. "It'll stop. Keep your left foot …"

The engine roared, the whole vehicle shuddered as Wind River pulled the throttle lever all the way down, as he thought Roman had instructed. "What?" he yelled, unable to hear the boy any longer and turning to try to see him.

The car swerved. "Foot! ... Foot, damn it!" Roman screamed frantically, running away again.

Confused, Wind River pushed as hard as he could on both feet, applying the brake and dropping the transmission into low gear at the same time. The competition was unjust. The rear wheels on the runabout had never been designed to hold the car against the power ratio of low gear. Engine racing, metal brakes squealing and smoking, Wind River frozen to the wheel, Roman desperately trying to catch up, the car lurched inexorably forward.

"Oh, no," Wind River whispered. The front wheels hit the porch steps, bounced once, and came down on the second step. "Oh, no! Whoa!" The rear wheels dug in, pushed the car up the next two steps and onto the boardwalk. "Please!" Wind River moaned as the front bumper broke through the boarded-up swinging doors of the Twin .45 Saloon.

The runabout pressed on. At the majestic speed of five miles an hour, it obliterated tables and chairs. Two tires blown, steam spouting from the broken temperature gauge, it battered through the bar. Engine at full rpm's, it undercut the back shelves. Unsupported, the mirror teetered, fell forward, and smashed, showering Wind River with thousands of shards of glass.

That crash was nothing compared to the one that followed. Even before the sound of breaking glass had faded, the whole building, already weakened by age and the slide that had partially undermined it in the past, began to tilt. One rotten support splintered, then another and another. Slowly, to the unabated roar of the motor and the rending of boards and timbers, the Twin .45's supports gave way and the building, Model T, and Wind River went crashing down the slide to join the houses that had been swept to destruction years earlier. Doors and windows agape, the swinging sign swaying gently in the clouds of dust that arose from below, only the false front of the building remained.

The silence, after all that incredible noise, was awesome. Roman and Lainie gingerly stepped to one side and peered over the edge. "He's dead," Lainie whispered faintly.

A board moved, then another. "No such luck," Roman growled, sickened by the destruction of his car. "Hey! Where are you going?"

Lainie paused, already over the edge of the slide. "To help him, of course. Come on. We can't just leave him there."

"He helped himself to my car. Let him help himself out of it."

"Roman!" Lainie's lips pursed. Below, a muffled groan came from the jumbled remains of the Twin .45. Immediately Lainie's brow furrowed in concern, and not waiting for Roman, she scrambled down the slide.

Roman raised his hands in a helpless plea. "Okay," he sighed, and let himself over the slide to follow Lainie.

The whole wreck shifted precariously. Like the work of a mad genius, timbers jutted at crazy angles to wedge each other in an interlacing network of wood and twisted metal. Sharp splinters threatened the most careful probing hands. It took twenty minutes to strip away the top layer of debris and discover that the car had borne most of the punishment, for the four-by-four timber that had stove in the hood and torn off the radiator had also protected Wind River. Carefully, Roman and Lainie cleared out the right side of the seat, helped Wind River slide over, and then lifted him out.

"Are you all right?" Lainie asked solicitously.

Wind River was white with dust. His coat was torn and his hat missing. Dazed, he looked around, blinked, and then peered at Roman. "Shouldn't take a man's horse," he finally said.

"We just went for a ride," Lainie explained.

"We didn't *take* it," Roman added, glaring at Wind River.

"Shouldn't take a man's horse," Wind River repeated. Stiffly, he leaned on Lainie for support, then let go and began to climb up the slide. "Shouldn't take a man's horse," he said again, thinking that was the first time he'd said it.

Worried, Lainie followed him, helped him again when his knees temporarily gave out halfway up the slide.

Behind them, Roman sat heavily on a timber and watched

the steam rise from the broken radiator. "You crazy geezer!" he suddenly shouted, rising and shaking his fists at the dust-covered figure disappearing over the edge of the ravine. "You're crazy, you hear? Crazy! Ahhhhh . . ."

It was a waste of time. Disconsolate, he sat again and stared at the broken boards and shattered timbers and demolished runabout. Now they were stuck. Really stuck. His shadow shrank into his body as the sun climbed higher overhead. There was no way out. The Wind River Kid, the town of Elkhorn, heaven itself, had conspired against him.

"Awwww, nerts!" he finally said, and wearily began the long climb out.

17

Lather hung on Wind River's beard in clumps, ran in streaks down the half of his chin that was naked. Wind River angled the straight razor and dug into the scruffy, steel-colored bristles on the left side of his jaw. "Gawd Almighty," he groaned as the four-week-old fringe resisted. He jerked involuntarily. "You're supposed to cut 'em off, not pull 'em out," he muttered, inspecting the razor for the sixth time. "She could at least have given me a sharp one. I've seen keener edges on a shovel. Keep out!" he yelled, raising his voice in response to a knock on the door.

The door creaked open. A small foot appeared, then a pair of hands holding a huge, steaming kettle. "I told you to keep out," Wind River repeated, panicking. "I'm in the tub, damn it. You can't . . . Oh, shit! . . ." Dropping the razor on the floor, he ducked low into the water and pulled a cloth over his privates.

"It's all right," Lainie said cheerfully, ignoring him. She raised her left elbow. A pile of clothes dropped to the floor. "I had three brothers, all younger. I used to bathe them, too."

"There ain't gonna be any of that 'too' business in here. I'm bathin' myself."

"Watch your feet," Lainie said. She tipped the kettle and sent a stream of water into the tub.

Wind River squawked, pulled his knees up to his chest. "You're boilin' me, girl."

"No sense in trying to wash in cold water. Hot makes the dirt come loose."

"Dirt, hell," Wind River complained. "You re cookin the skin right off my feet."

Lainie set down the kettle. "I took the liberty ot going through your stuff and finding some clean clothes for you," she said, picking up the bundle she'd carried into the room. "Hope you don't mind."

"I do. You got no right meddlin' in my belongings."

"I was just trying to help." She laid out clean long johns, coveralls, and shirt on the bed, gingerly started picking up those he had taken off. "These are full of dirt and splinters. I'll wash them out for you tomorrow."

"I'll do it myself," Wind River said hurriedly, starting to reach for them and then remembering he was naked. He sank quickly under the water. "Don't need no maid. Been doin' for myself long enough."

"Honestly, Wind River, your gratitude knows no bounds."

"If that gimmegaw chatter means I ain't almighty gracious about havin' you and that bad-tempered son-of-a-buck here in my town, you're right."

Lainie rolled his dirty clothes into a ball and threw them into the hall, then came back for the kettle. "I thought Roman handled himself quite well today, considering you wrecked his automobile."

"Weren't any of my doing," Wind River protested. "Damn contraption wrecked itself. I just went along for the ride, is all."

Lainie fought back a grin. "I'm certain that will make Roman feel better."

"Didn't have nothin' to feel so uppity about in the first place. It was him who stole my horse."

"We went for a ride," Lainie explained patiently, for at least the fourth time since she had helped him to the hotel and demanded he take a bath.

"Yeah?" Wind River slowly extended his left leg. The hot

water felt good on his cramped and aching muscles. "Around here we call that by another name."

"There is no 'around here' anymore. You're talking about fifty years ago. Things have changed since then. We live in a civil world."

"Civil world, huh?" Wind River nodded. "If it's so almighty civil, how come you two are hidin' out up here in the mountains?"

Lainie pursed her lips. "That's different," she finally conceded.

"Different? Different?" Wind River hooted. "It ain't different at all, and when you get to be my age and have some wisdom, you'll see it never will be. No matter how many goddamn Piggly Wigglys they build."

"You, Mr. Wind River Kid, are the most aggravating man I know," Lainie said, marching to the door. Half out, she turned and grabbed the knob. "But that's all right. I like you, anyway," she added with a tinkling little laugh, and closed the door behind her.

Wind River blinked the water from his eyes. He shrugged, scratched at his head, and winced as he touched the bruise on his skull where a board had clobbered him as the Twin .45 collapsed around his ears. "I wish she hadn't said that," he grumbled, reaching for the razor. Half of one side to go and he'd be set for another month.

The water was still warm when he woke up. One eye opened slowly, then the other. Briefly confused, Wind River looked around, remembered the wreck and the bath. He sat up. There was a crick in the back of his neck where it had rested against the rear edge of the tub. The fire was bright, the room warm. The kettle sat on the stool next to the tub. Lainie must have warmed the water while he slept.

That was strange. He never slept in the . . . What was it? Morning? Afternoon? More like noon, he decided, from the way the sun lay on the windowsill. Dripping, he stepped from the tub, stood in front of the fire, and toweled himself dry. Strangely enough, he felt good. The ache in his left leg where he'd hit the brake handle and the soreness in his chest where he'd bounced off the steering wheel seemed to have disappeared. The knot on his head was still there, but that was a minor inconvenience compared to what could have happened to him. Something else was different, though. Something he couldn't quite put his finger on. He felt buoyant, younger. There was a new spring to his step. The air looked brighter, smelled a little fresher. Mystified, he walked to the mirror and stared at himself.

A little paunchy here and there, skin white and on the wrinkled side. He breathed deeply, held in his stomach, and turned sideways. "Not bad," he chuckled, slapping his belly. "Over seventy, with the body of a fifty-year-old. And a mind half that! 'Farewell to Lorena, It's free I must be . . .'" Singing, Wind River strutted to the bed, quickly pulled on the clean long johns Lainie had brought him, and then stopped with them half buttoned.

"That's it!" he said. "The dadgummed bath! Well, I'll be . . ." A bath that late in the year? How long had it been? He bathed every spring usually, maybe once or twice more during the summer if the notion hit him. In the old days, when he was riding high, he bathed at least once a week, sometimes more often, depending. And in perfumed water, too. Lilies of the valley. He'd forgotten how good it felt to get rid of the dust and sweat, how much better to pull on clean duds. Whistling, he looked for his socks and found them draped over his boots. "Would you look at that!" he said glumly, inspecting the boots. Not a week old and they looked the worse for wear already. He was about to wipe them on the bedspread when he realized it, too, had been changed. Quickly he looked around for something else, then stopped short when he spied the wrapped mound of cloth in the wardrobe.

"Old and wise, hell," he muttered, realizing for the first time which room he was in and wondering how he could have failed to notice before. "Blind's more like it." It was Lainie, of course, taking advantage of him when he was still stunned from the accident. She had all but dragged him upstairs and threatened to strip him herself unless he undressed and climbed into the tub. He had hoped never to see the damned gun again. Mesmerized, he bent down and unwrapped the cloth, picked up belt and gun, and let his fingers run over the worn ivory grip.

Strange, how just touching it affected him. Wind River automatically glanced around, looking for Creed. Every time he held the gun, the mountain man showed up. It was almost as if ghost and man were bonded through that gun, as if the cold metal formed a bridge between the ghostly world Creed inhabited and the real world where Wind River lived. "Shouldn't have told him about Angelina," Wind River muttered, slightly ill at ease. "Hurt his feelings sure enough."

But that didn't make sense. Not even to Wind River. Ghosts didn't have feelings like regular people. Still, the mountain man was nowhere to be found. Wind River grinned, began to feel a little easier. Just to see what would happen, he held the belt around his waist and then checked the room again. "Well?" he asked "You there?"

Nothing. He listened for a fart, didn't hear anything. He sniffed the air. Nothing again. There had to be a reason. Things didn't just go along the same way for a quarter century and then change abruptly for no reason. But what? Why? Nothing was different. At least he didn't think so.

The damn quiet was getting to him. Making him feel edgy again. Creed wasn't there, and yet his presence . . . something that felt like him . . . The gun? Was that it? He'd forgotten how heavy it was on his hip, how the weight shifted as he walked. He'd been used to that, once, as accustomed to it as he was to a hat or a pair of boots. Still holding the belt closed with his hands, Wind River walked to the mirror and stared at and through himself to another Wind River Kid.

The bump on the head, he thought, aware of what was happening and yet unable to tear himself away. The year was 1892 and he was middle-aged, tired, and on the run, punishing his horse in a wild and headlong flight, breaking the animal's heart, riding it to death in Rampage Valley. He hadn't felt safe until he'd reached Elkhorn. There, his dignity and untarnished reputation outwardly intact, he had strolled nonchalantly up Main Street and asked for the best room in the Great Northern Hotel.

He hadn't gotten the best. Only the second best, but

Wind River hadn't complained. The bed was soft, the furniture heavy, the air fragrant with the perfume of beautiful women. Creed had come the first night, in that long ago. Snuck in the back way so the clerk wouldn't notice him, and crept up the servants' stairs lest one of the guests discover him and sound the alarm. Stable bums weren't tolerated in the Great Northern Hotel, even though its day was drawing to a close. Wind River had heard the knock, and cautiously opened the door.

"I seen you," the mountain man said without preamble. "Knew you'd come back one day."

"Aden Creed," Wind River said. "I figured you would have been dust and bones long ago." Holstering his gun, he backed into the room and gestured for Creed to enter.

Transfixed in the mirror in 1927, Wind River watched and remembered, saw Creed framed in the doorway as if it had been only the day before. He was a weather-beaten, ashen-faced man of seventy who coughed frequently and whose skin covered his bones like a threadbare suit.

"Not yet, boy. Not yet," Creed said, choking on his laughter.

"What do you want? I've had a long hard ride."

Creed wiped the pinkish spittle from the corners of his mouth. "You mean run, don't you?"

Wind River's eyes narrowed. "Watch it, old man. You're forgetting who I am."

"You're forgetting I know *who* you are," Creed retorted. "Maybe more than you do. A father knows his son."

"We aren't kin, Creed," Wind River said in a tight voice. "We never were."

"I took you in. I fed you. I helped you grow and showed you the trail. That makes me kin," Creed said, his voice shaking.

Wind River sat on the edge of the bed, poured a double shot of whiskey, and emptied it down his throat. Creed licked his lips, but had not yet sunk low enough to ask for the drink that Wind River wasn't going to offer on his own. "I just come to see you," he managed to say in spite of the cough that racked his body.

"Now you have. Close the door on the way out.'

"I come to see if all the stories I heard about the Wind River Kid was true."

"Depends," Wind River said, pouring himself another drink, "on what stories you heard."

"That he's a cold-as-ice shootist, a gambler, and a whoremonger."

Wind River sipped at his whiskey. "You've had your share of sin, Creed."

"But never for the pure love of sin. I never did no man harm without thinkin' that what I was doin' needed bein' done, and was right at the time."

"Don't judge me, old man."

Creed's eyes didn't waver as he looked into Wind River's. "Somebody has to. I reckon there's none more fit than me."

"Go to hell."

"No." The mountain man took a step forward. "I done my best with what I had. Hell is for them who've done their worst."

"Git!" Wind River snapped, grabbing the shot glass and throwing it at Creed.

Creed ducked. The shot glass hit the wall behind him, bounced off, and rolled halfway across the room before it stopped. "You're Satan-bound, boy," he said, pointing an accusing finger at Wind River. "And you'll carry perdition around with you a long time before you die."

"Get out, damn it! Go back to your stable or wherever the hell they let you sleep!"

Creed nodded. He wagged his head and his eyes turned moist. "They'll find you, you know."

Wind River came off the bed as if he'd been stabbed. "What are you babblin'?"

"They'll—" Creed coughed. A glob of pink phlegm flew from his mouth onto the Persian throw rug. "They'll find you," he repeated. "They always do."

"Damn you!" Wind River shouted, in the same instant drawing. The navy Colt sprang to his hand, pointed at Creed's belly. "Damn you, Creed."

Creed never so much as looked at the gun. Instead, he stared into Wind River's eyes with the same intensity as if he were looking into his soul. "I'll be around when they do," he said when he heard the whisper of metal on leather as Wind River slipped the revolver back into its holster. He turned and left the room.

"I don't need you or anybody else!" Wind River shouted, grabbing for the bottle and knocking it off the table.

Thirty-five years later, his gunbelt dropping to the floor, he spun to catch the bottle as he had before. There was nothing there but the sound. Wind River rubbed his temples, but the sound wouldn't go away. It wouldn't go away. Trembling, he kneeled on the floor and wrapped the gunbelt in its cloth. And in that simple action came simple revelation. He saw exactly what had to be done. Morning would be soon enough. His heartbeat slowing as he calmed, he set the bundle on the table and started pulling on the rest of his clothes.

"What?" Roman asked, more interested in the money on the table in front of him than in what Lainie had said.

"He was right, heaven help me," Lainie called from the kitchen.

Roman arranged the ten piles in a neat row. Each held a thousand dollars. Once again, he counted them, tapping each with his forefinger, then glancing toward the foyer. Having the ten thousand out in the open made him nervous as a virgin in a whorehouse. It didn't do to tempt temptation, and he'd feel a lot better when it was hidden. All he could do was hope the bank vault was so obvious that no one would think of looking there. "Who?" he asked, making conversation.

"Wind River." Lainie entered with the coffeepot and a handful of clean cups. "I'm beginning to like the coffee."

"Yeah. Pretty soon we won't need to drink it," Roman said, stirring sugar into the black brew. "Just call it. The damned stuff will crawl out of the cup and into our mouths on command." He smiled to show her it was a joke.

"Silly." She stared at the money. It was the first time Roman had taken it out since their arrival in Elkhorn and the sight triggered mixed emotions. Ten thousand dollars was either a miraculous opportunity for a new life or a deadly bait that would draw Harry Lieght to them. "I still wish you'd stay," she said, trying to sound gay and failing miserably. "Or that we could go together."

"You'll be safer here," Roman said, and lowered his voice to add, "Especially if the old man thinks you don't know where I've hidden the money. Just don't let him know and everything will be fine."

"It's so quiet, though." Lainie shuddered. A city girl, she was as unnerved by the silence of a ghost town high in the mountains as she was by the thought of Harry Lieght. "I mean, what if a bear or a mountain lion or something—"

"He's lived here over thirty years," Roman pointed out. "Crazy, maybe, but he's healthy as a coot and tough as nails. That wreck would have killed most men."

"Well, maybe . . ." Lainie's fears, however, were legion, and not easily dismissed. "What happens if Lieght's in Mountain City?"

"I'll just have to take my chances," Roman said flatly.

"I'm scared, Roman."

Roman got up and walked around the table to massage Lainie's shoulders. "It's going to be all right, baby. I'll be gone five days, six at the most, and get back here before the next storm hits. We'll sit that one out and then leave before everything closes in totally for the rest of the winter. Depending on how Mountain City feels to me and how much snow there is, we'll either go south, skirt the town, and catch a bus in Idaho Springs, or head north and across the pass, then east to Boulder, where we catch a bus or train to Cheyenne and then Laramie, where we spend the rest of the winter. Boulder's kind of dangerous because it's so close to Denver, but I think we can pull it off. I'll let my beard grow and you can—"

"You're gonna need help either way you go."

Roman whirled in surprise as Wind River entered from the foyer. The old man was dressed in clean clothes. His shoulder-length white hair made him look like a real frontiersman, a dime-novel Wild Bill Hickok, maybe; or a Buffalo Bill Cody. Roman shook his head in disbelief, grudgingly hoped he'd be in as good shape when he was Wind River's age, whatever that was. "I thought you were asleep," he said sourly.

"Was. Not anymore. Don't want to sleep my life away." Wind River set a bundle on the sideboard and crossed to the table. "My oh my," he said, casting an appreciative eye over the stacked bills. "Robbery's a funny habit for a preacher's boy."

"I'm not a preacher's boy," Roman said, miffed. He sat back down across from Lainie. "The preacher in the family was my grandfather."

"Close enough." Wind River nodded. He reached out and gingerly removed a crisp new fifty from one of the piles and held it to the light. "Pretty color, green, I've always said."

Roman plucked the bill from Wind River's fingers, replaced it on the pile. Wind River shrugged, pulled out a chair, and sat. "Thanks for keeping the fire going," he told Lainie. "Room gets right cold for a man sitting in a tub."

"Are you feeling all right?" Lainie asked, concerned.

"Right as a trout in mayfly season."

"Better than my runabout, I guess that means, huh?" Roman said sarcastically.

"Can I have some of that?" Wind River asked, pointing at the coffee. "Water under the bridge, my boy. Water under the bridge. Just one of them piles ought to buy you a new one." He'd counted them when he'd walked in, but made a show of counting them again. "You got ten."

"Just remember that, too, old man," Roman said, moving the money away from Wind River's side of the table. "I got them. Not you. Me and Lainie."

Wind River accepted a cup of coffee from Lainie. The sight of their fortune had worked a transformation on him. He hadn't seen that much money in three decades. His eyes twinkled with the prospects and possibilities. One pile, one thousand dollars, roughly ten percent, would fix him up in good shape. He smacked his lips. "Excellent coffee, my dear," he said, shedding years and reverting to the Wind River Kid of old, the smooth-as-silk operator who could talk a trey into becoming an ace. "A truly superlative brew. Nectar of the gods." Roman was looking at him strangely.

Wind River winked. "Of the gods, don't you agree, partner?"

Oh, Jesus, Roman thought with a sinking feeling. The lump Wind River had taken on the head had turned him batty. "You taken leave of your senses, old man?" he asked gruffly, at the same time scooping the stolen money into the leather valise Lieght had used for his collections.

"On the contrary, my boy. I have only just found them." Wind River clapped his hands, rubbed them together vigorously. "Nickels, dimes, quarters, and halves. Get it?" He watched the money disappear, knew it would reappear in good time. "Well, down to business!"

Lainie was staring open-mouthed at Wind River. "Everything's all right, baby," Roman told her. "Don't worry." He turned deliberately toward the old man. "I'm not your partner and we don't have any business," he said, enunciating the words clearly. He stuffed the last bills into the valise. "And if I catch you sniffing around this money, there'll be hell to pay."

"There's always hell to pay," Wind River said, stating a simple fact he'd learned longer ago than Roman's and Lainie's combined ages. "Nothing in life is free. Which brings me to my services. Services easily—"

"I think you'd better eat something," Lainie broke in. "I'll fry some bacon." She rose, looked at Roman, and shrugged her shoulders. "I read somewhere that old men are supposed to eat."

Wind River caught her before she could leave the table. "Not so fast, girlie," he said firmly. "I'm gonna need your help here."

"I think that wreck must have scrambled your noodles," Roman said with a snort of disgust.

"Hear me out and then decide." Wind River guided Lainie back into her chair, went on with barely a pause. "You was talkin' about headin' north. Now, that's a good plan, except for one problem. The only way north, especially at this time of year, is through Lincoln Pass."

"Right," Roman said with a self-satisfied smile.

"Aha!" Wind River crowed, one finger raised. "But north what? Northeast? Northwest? Due north? And when you get there, the trail branches four ways. Three of 'em go through a hundred miles of wilderness. Only one to Boulder. Choose wrong and you'll end up froze until spring thaw, and then buzzard meat. Next year this time the wind'll be blowin' through your hollow skull." His eyebrows beetled as he looked directly at Lainie, who seemed more affected by his words than did Roman. "Sort of whistles," he added, leaning toward her. "As it goes through the eye sockets. Which have been pecked clean— after you're dead of course."

The description was altogether too graphic. Lainie shivered, as Wind River had known she would. "He makes a lot of sense, Roman," she said, brushing her bangs away from her eyes.

Roman shrugged. "So we go south. Go around Mountain City and then—"

"Where's around?" Wind River interrupted, his voice low.

"You know." Roman waved his hand vaguely. "Just cut off the trail, then back onto it," he explained lamely.

"Over what creeks or rivers? What about the Plates? You ever hear of them? What about Rib Roast Valley? You know how to get out of it? This ain't a Sunday promenade you're talkin' about, you know."

Roman's brows knotted. He had no doubt Wind River was exaggerating, but was beginning to think he'd better not take a chance. Especially given the look on Lainie's face. "And you, of course, know the way," he said.

"Like the back of my hand," Wind River assured him.

"*Both* ways?"

"North or south, east or west," Wind River said, folding his hands on the table. He thought he heard the *flick flick flick* of cards being slapped on a table, but when he looked around, the room was empty and the sound faded. He stared at Roman.

Roman glanced at Lainie, who was obviously alarmed at the prospect of the wind whistling through her empty eye sockets, pecked clean after she was dead, she hoped, and not while she lay helpless, bruised, battered, and bleeding. Buzzard meat. "How much for this valuable service?" Roman finally asked, ceding the battle if not the war.

"A thousand dollars," Wind River said quickly. "One of them little piles."

"Nerts to you."

Wind River blinked. "Does that mean yes or no?"

"It means you're full of goat droppings." Roman moved the valise a little farther away from Wind River to emphasize the point. "You owe me a 1920 Ford anyway, remember?"

His coffee was getting cold. Wind River stared into it, drummed his fingers on the tabletop. He looked out the window. The wind had come up. Dust swirled in the street, making the buildings across the road hazy. "Tenderfoot have a hard go up there. Have to pick the right time to leave. Need someone to show you how to live through the snow and the cold. Seven hundred and fifty dollars. Half in advance."

"That's it, then," Roman said, standing. "Sorry, old man. I'll be back in a few days with the mules, honey. A few weeks after that, we'll just go right back through Mountain City. The way we came in. The hell with Lieght." He jerked a thumb toward Wind River. "And this one, too."

"It isn't safe," Lainie said in a tiny voice.

Roman glared, wanted to signal her to shut up, but Wind River was watching him.

"Well, it isn't." One hand fluttered to her face, touched her cheek, traced around her left eye. She couldn't forget. "Please, Roman?" she pleaded.

She had lived in Denver all her life, had looked at mountains in the distance but never set a foot on one. The *Post* carried stories, though. SEVEN LOST IN MOUNTAIN STORM. AVALANCHE KILLS NINE. EIGHTEEN-FOOT DRIFTS FOIL TRAVELERS. In all truth, Roman couldn't blame her for being afraid. He was himself. A little, at least. And if anything happened to her . . . The thought was too unpleasant to follow to its conclusion. Slowly, he walked around the table, laid his hands on her shoulders, and bent to kiss her forehead. "Okay, honey," he said, and then, straightening and looking Wind River in the eye, "five hundred dollars payable when we say goodbye. That plus the runabout you wrecked makes your asking price. Fair enough?"

A broad smile added creases to Wind River's face. His hand shot out. "You just made the best dingle-berry deal you ever made, younker."

Roman shook his hand.

"Now that we're partners," Wind River said, unable to take his eyes off the valise, "how's about a —"

"We aren't partners," Roman corrected. "You have your life and we have ours. Once we're out and you're paid, that's it." He helped Lainie up, pulled the .38 out of his belt, and handed it to her. "I'm going to go out and hide this now. You keep an eye on our guide here and see that he doesn't follow."

Lainie started to protest, but Roman shushed her with a finger on her lips. Hesitant, she took the gun and let him guide her to the fireplace.

"You can keep your head turned toward her until I'm out of sight," Roman said to Wind River. "I'll be outside. Somewhere."

Wind River turned as directed. Behind him, he could hear Roman's footsteps, the sound of the door and the wind, and then silence again. For a fleeting second he considered turning to see which way Roman went, but then decided there was no need to muddy the waters. He'd be able to track him in any case. If the damned wind let up, that was. "You mind if I sit?" he asked.

Lainie kept both hands on the gun. "No."

"You can relax and point that somewheres else," Wind River said. "I ain't gonna try anything. Makes me nervous."

"Me too," Lainie admitted. "But Roman said—"

"Roman said," Wind River repeated with a sad wag of his head. "That boy's a hothead, girl. Gonna get the both of you in trouble. Now, if it was me— Why, what's the matter, girl?"

A tear rolled down Lainie's face. She wiped it away with the back of her hand. "Nothing," she said in a tiny voice.

Wind River leaned back, folded his arms. "Pretty girl like you don't cry for nothing."

"I . . . I don't want him to go," Lainie said between sniffles.

"Oh." Wind River looked at his boots. " 'Fraid?" he asked gently.

Lainie looked embarrassed, bobbed her head up and down.

"Of me?"

Her head shook no.

"Can you multiply in your head?"

"What?" Lainie asked, taken aback.

"What's three hundred and sixty-five times thirty-five?" he asked.

Her tears forgotten, Lainie stared at him. "How would I know?"

"Bein' a gambler, I have to do ciphers in my head. Three hundred and sixty-five times thirty-five is . . ." He paused, closed his eyes momentarily, ". . . exactly twelve thousand seven hundred and seventy-five. You know what that is?"

"No."

"That's how many days I been here. Most of the time alone. Now, if your Roman is gone six days, that's only one, let's see . . ." He paused again, this time squinted at the ceiling. "Six into twelve thousand . . . into twelve is twice exactly, into seven is once, carry one, into seventeen . . ." His face lit up. "Six days is only one two thousand one hundred and thirtieth of the time I already been here. You can do that." His voice was soft, even tender. "I ain't gonna let nothin' happen to you, Lainie. You'll be just fine."

The gun lowered. Lainie sniffed once more, wiped away the last tear. Her lips quivered, but she forced them into a tight little smile. "I guess you think I'm pretty silly, huh?"

"Naw. Just misinformed, is all." Wind River thought it best not to mention Scar. "Most dangerous thing we got around here is that falcon. As for him, all you got to do is—"

The front door opened and the wind whistled through the foyer. A few seconds later, it slammed again and Roman entered the dining room. "You can turn around if you want," he said. "Everything all right, Lainie?"

"Sure, Roman."

"Good. I'll keep an eye on him now." He took the .38 from Lainie, tucked it in his belt. "Say, you been crying?"

Lainie laughed, her special little laugh that meant that everything was all right "Of course not. I just got something in my eye, is all. Guess I rubbed too hard."

"Shouldn't do that. Let the tears clean them out." He put one arm around her and gave her a quick hug. "I'm hungry. Anything for lunch?"

"Sure, Roman."

Roman watched her go, slipped the gun in his belt. "Wind's blowing pretty strong. Kicking up a lot of dust. I guess if you stick around inside for a couple of hours or so, it'll be pretty hard to see where I went."

Wind River shifted in his chair. "Dang the money," he said, angry. "I'd never up and take it and leave that little girl all alone."

"Easy to say," Roman said with a shrug. "The rain has to fall, the sun has to shine. Fire is different. It's best to throw water on it before it starts."

"Good words," Wind River said dryly. "Clever. That what Mr. Lieght taught you?"

A slow smile spread over Roman's face. "That and more," he said cryptically. "Admit it, Wind River. If it was your ten thousand, you'd worry. You can't blame me for being careful. Coffee?"

There was no getting around that, Wind River had to admit. "Drunk my fill," he said, deciding not to push his luck. The ten thousand would show up again sooner or later. "Too much at a time is bad for my innards. Comes to all of us."

"I imagine so," Roman agreed, sipping and making a wry face. He looked over at the bundle on the sideboard. "What's that?" he asked, curious.

Wind River's eyes darted to the cloth, back to Roman. "Nothing."

"Really?" Roman had let himself relax. A little too much, he thought. Slowly, cautiously, he stood and walked toward the sideboard. "Let's see what nothing looks like."

"Leave it be!" Wind River said, his voice low and threatening, so different that Roman glanced around to be certain it was the old man who had spoken. "It doesn't concern you."

Roman's eyes narrowed and his shoulders hunched. "I don't much like secrets, old man," he said, reaching for the fabric.

"Keep your hands off, boy!" Wind River snapped, his hands on the back of a chair, ready to pick it up and use it as a club.

Roman paused, looked around again.

"Like you said, you got your life and I got mine." Wind River's voice was flat, distant, almost hollow, as if he spoke from the bottom of a well. "That's part of it, and you ain't gonna touch it."

"Lunch in a minute," Lainie called from the kitchen. "Pick a table. I'll be right in."

Roman glanced over his shoulder, decided there was no reason to cause a scene, especially in front of Lainie. His gaze met Wind River's as he stepped away from the sideboard. "Exactly," he said, his voice oddly gentle. The kitchen door swung open again and Lainie entered with a tray. "That nag of yours know the way to Mountain City and back?" Roman asked, as if nothing had happened between them.

"Better than you do," Wind River said. "Shorter way than you got here, too, you give him his head." He pushed the chair closer to the table, swiped at the dust that covered it, and took the tray from Lainie. "And he rents for ten dollars a day."

Roman scowled, sat, and took the plate with the fattest sandwich.

Pleased with himself, Wind River hurried around the table and, with an exaggerated display of gallantry, helped Lainie with her chair.

"Thank you," Lainie said, smiling up at him.

"Pleasure is mine, girl," Wind River said with a grin. He had a way out and five hundred dollars at the end of the trail. And once he was finished with the damn gun, there was only one thing left to do: try to recall the route over Lincoln Pass.

18

Harry Lieght was certain he was awake. The pain in his head and throat and chest told him so. Pain didn't lie. Not about being awake. You didn't hurt in your sleep. He'd learned that on a number of different occasions. The last time had been some years ago, but he remembered. Vividly. So vividly that he thought it was ten years earlier and that he had just been beaten to a near-pulp by Andy Northouse. His head had hurt then, too, as had his hand where he'd broken it against Andy's head and his leg, where Andy had broken it with his steel-toed boot.

His eyes liked the darkness, but he opened them anyway, blinked against the heat, and stared at his hand. It looked all right. That was confusing. He flexed his leg. It worked, too. But his head still hurt. That didn't make much sense. If he could just sit up ...

He tried to pry himself from the bed. The slats beneath the mattress creaked. The pain behind his eyes stabbed toward the side of his head and left him sweating. Harry Lieght wasn't one to give up without a fight, however. Pain was an old enemy he'd faced too many times before. The only way a man beat pain was to face it head-on, refuse to acknowledge it. Groaning, he pushed himself upright and willed his legs over the side of the bed and onto the floor.

Christ! They were tearing his head off! The walls tilted

crazily. The floor bucked under his feet. The roof caved in. Harry collapsed back on the bed to avoid being crushed. The roof flew back into place. Harry coughed. Air squirmed through his throat and trickled into his lungs. He was burning, on fire. Except for his feet, which someone had immersed in a bucket of ice. "Ahhhhhh," he said. Someone had etched his throat with a sharp instrument and then rubbed salt in the wound. Damning the pain, he coughed and spat. "Ahhhhhh." It was easier that time, so he struggled through his name, repeating it several times without making a sound. When he had the name down, he tried for a sentence.

A cold rag distracted him. A grimy hand with heavy, spatulate fingers wiped the coolness across his face. Beyond the coolness, a face hovered in the air above him. The face was disconnected and looked like a balloon that had been stitched together with pulsing colors. After a while, the coolness on his forehead stopped moving and was gone. It was replaced by more coolness that sat there like a weight and drained the fever from him. A trickle of cold water ran down the side of his temple, worked its way past the top of his ear. The pain reached out for it, and Harry closed his eyes again.

When he opened them, he was alone, and remembered his name easily. "Harry. Harry. Harry." A name easy to repeat. He turned his head and stared at the wall to his left. The wall was made of logs instead of boards. The logs were sweating, the moisture bringing out the colors in the damp wood. He had never known there could be so many shades of brown.

"Where?" he wondered, his mouth barely moving. "Where?" The word was almost as easy to say as Harry. Both went trippingly on the tongue.

The devils inside his head picked up their hammers and went back to work. Losing consciousness, Lieght tried for a sentence.

"Harry, my boy, what have you got yourself into?"

19

Roman had said goodbye when the sun was still below the horizon. The Appaloosa saddled and waiting, he and Lainie had stood at the end of the street and watched the snow-covered mountain peaks rise into the light. Snowdrifts glowed below the brightness with a light of their own before fading into rich purple lusters and then the black green of the forest. Their heavy coats separating them from each other, Roman had held Lainie close for one last minute. And then he was gone. Hands dug deep into her pockets, her breath forming clouds to briefly match those few bumping along overhead, Lainie watched until he was out of sight across Damnation Hill. Lonesomeness settled on her like a cloak to be unwillingly worn until his return. She could taste his kiss as she trudged back up the street to the Great Northern.

The morning wore on at an interminable pace. Lainie drank coffee. She looked out the window. She scrubbed the skillet and breakfast plates, just for something to do. She thought about the money and what it would buy, cranked up the Victrola, and placed a record on the spindle. In scratched but exuberant tones, Johnny Marvin began singing "Ain't She Sweet."

Six days to go. Lainie thought about doing her nails, but decided to save them for later, when she got really desperate. She considered her clothes, too. The trousers Roman had given her to wear were baggy and too long. Ugly. If the day warmed up, she'd put on her favorite flapper outfit. Maybe that would perk her up. Not maybe. Positively, she thought, hurrying to the window to check the sky.

It certainly looked as if it would get warm. The sky was bright and clear, a clean, gentle blue. Sighing, Lainie sank to the floor and rested her chin on her forearms, her arms on the windowsill. She wondered if any of the girls at work missed her. They had all thought the idea of her eloping with Roman was just the most exciting thing. It had been at the beginning, before it turned scary. Now it was only boring. Boring, boring, boring . . .

Johnny Marvin's voice reverberated in hollow appeal off the walls of the dining room. There was no one to talk to. The multitude of empty chairs and tables made her feel even more lonely. No cars or people passed outside her window. The only sign of life was Wind River standing on his front porch and checking the sky for the falcon. Lainie craned her neck for a better view. The old man had a bundle under his arm, the same one he had had the night before. While she watched, he stepped off the porch and disappeared down the alley between the funeral parlor and the wrecked barbershop.

That was funny. "Ain't She Sweet" ended in a series of repetitious clicks that brought Lainie running before the needle wore down any further. Hurriedly she grabbed her sweater and, pulling it on, ran through the kitchen to the back steps and up to the landing. Wind River was standing between a pair of old and sagging wagons, looking around in the manner of one who wants to make sure he isn't being followed. Stranger and stranger, Lainie thought, her boredom forgotten. Ducking below the window, she ran back downstairs and peeked out the servants' entrance door.

Wind River had disappeared. Lainie chewed her lip, pondered whether she should follow or not. Deciding that listening to "Ain't She Sweet" one more time would certainly drive her out of her mind, she stepped out the door Invading Wind River's privacy might not be very nice, but at least it wouldn't be boring.

A breeze stirred the aspen grove where the street turned into a trail. A bouquet of golden leaves that flickered like sunlight on a lake showered down. Almost invisible in a tan buckskin coat, Wind River walked through them and disappeared again, this time up the trail.

Lainie ran quietly past the decrepit wagons, into the luminous, translucent shade cast by bright-yellow leaves trembling from ivory-colored branches. She walked on a carpet of crinkly leaves covering the moist humus laid down in earlier years. She did not know that the humus was a death warrant of sorts, that one day sprouting from the thick, rich layer, tiny pine saplings would, in unfeeling recompense, steal the sun and crowd out the aspen.

Wind River was there, and then he wasn't. Lainie played hide-and-seek at a discreet distance, tried to make as little noise as possible. The trail led upward and to the right. Sometimes it faded, for it had not been much used in recent years, but always she picked it up again. Once, she thought she had indeed lost it for good and slumped exhausted to the ground. She was tired and breathing heavily. The only sound came from within her: a faint ringing in her ears and the soft whoosh of her breath. Nothing moved between the thick, heavy boles of the pines that towered over her. The trees behind her formed a solid wall that blocked her view of the town.

For one of the few times in her life, she knew true panic. She had been afraid of Lieght, but Roman had been with her. This fear was different. It hollowed out a deep pit in her stomach and constricted her chest at the same time. It populated the forest with creatures that peered around trees at her and licked their chops and unsheathed their claws. An image came to her of wind whistling through empty eye sockets. Her breathing became ragged. Her arms pressed against her abdomen as if she were ill; she rocked forward on her knees and squeezed her eyes closed.

Nothing roared. Nothing coughed or sprang or pounced. When Lainie at last opened her eyes, she discovered, no farther than a foot from her nose, a deep imprint in a patch of moss. Surprised, hope welling in her as rapidly as had panic, she traced the outline of a boot heel. The moss was bright

green and soft as a powder puff. As she watched, the com-
pressed tendrils in the heel mark uncoiled as slowly as a
watch spring. Almost crying with relief, she realized that she
hadn't lost the trail but was on it. Wind River was still ahead
of her somewhere. Eyes bright, Lainie scrambled to her feet
and searched the way ahead. A narrow spot between three
rocks marked the trail. Not worrying about finding her way
back—any direction downslope would eventually lead to
Elkhorn—she struck out for the rocks.

Once past the rocks, the slope gradually leveled. The
trees thinned, too, and Lainie's spirits brightened in direct
proportion to the added light that found the forest floor. The
silence was less oppressive. Birds sang, a jay, she thought,
and she could hear the steadily increasing roar of falling
water. The sound increased with each step forward. Moving
quickly to catch up, Lainie rounded a bend, stopped short,
and ducked behind a huge ponderosa pine.

She was on the edge of a small glade in the middle of the
forest. The roar she had heard came from a thin ribbon of
water that spilled off a mossy granite shelf twenty feet above
an ice-sheened pool that, like the central diamond in a
cluster, dominated a grassy clearing bounded with pine on
her side and autumn-gold aspen on the other. The pool was
at least fifty feet across and twice as long. Narrow at the base
of the falls, it widened out at the other end, where an old
beaver dam caught and held the water before letting it spill
into a tinkling, yard-wide stream that disappeared into the
trees. The waterfall formed a veil across the rocky wall of
granite. The spray from the mist cradled a rainbow drawn
from the pool and imbued with a life of its own. Not more
than ten feet from the base of the falls, Wind River stood
with his back to her.

Lainie held her breath, darted to her right, farther away
from the path, and hid behind another tree. Why, she wasn't
sure. She was guilty of no crime, and yet seemed instinc-
tively to know that Wind River wouldn't appreciate her
presence. He wasn't exactly acting strangely, but he wasn't
acting what Lainie would have called normally, either. His
buckskin coat looked darker, as if he had been in the water,
but his overalls and boots looked dry. The bundle was

nowhere to be seen. Her attention reverted to Wind River, who was backing away from the edge of the pool and talking.

"That's it, Creed! You got it now. That's what you wanted, ain't it?" His hands fell to his sides and his head turned from side to side, cocked, as if he was listening for an answer. When none came after a long moment, he pointed to the falls and spoke again. "It's in there, like I said I'd do. I don't want to see it again. Good riddance. Done is done. All I want to do is forget." With that, he turned and walked away, leaving the clearing by a second path.

Lainie waited until she was sure he was gone, at last emerged from behind the tree and stepped into the clearing. What upon first view had appeared as a cathedral now took on some of the aspects of a haunted house. The waterfall hissed. The wind-stirred aspens clacked one against another like dried bones The rainbow faded and brightened in a slow, Cheshire-cat wink. Wind River had brought the bundle there and left it. And spoken to whomever he had given it.

Or had he? Lainie couldn't have explained why, but she was certain Wind River had been as alone in the glade as she was. Slowly she approached the falls. His footprints were distinct in the soft dirt and tiny bar of sand. There were no others. Tiptoeing, she followed them almost to the base of the falls. They disappeared at the edge of a rocky ledge that led into a hollowed-out grotto behind the water.

"Darn," Lainie said, torn between entering and fleeing. "Darn." She stuck out one hand. The water was like liquid ice. The spray hit her cheek. Her skin tingled from the cold. She should have known, though, There wasn't much choice, hadn't been since she'd seen Wind River disappear down the alley between the barbershop and the funeral parlor. Covering her head with her hands, she jumped onto the ledge, took two quick steps through the spray, and ducked into the grotto.

The noise was remarkably subdued inside. Lainie caught her breath. Seen through the water, the pond, with its thin skim of ice, and the trees, green and gold, looked like a vision seen in a dream. Every surface inside was damp, subjected to a continuous spray. And on a small rock ledge at the very rear, almost lost in the darkness, lay the bundle Wind River had carried there. Money? Gold? Something from his past, she was sure. Something he was ashamed of, from the way he had talked. Almost afraid to touch it, but knowing she would, Lainie reached out a tentative finger. The ancient velvet, worn smooth by age, was damp and clammy, felt almost like skin. Her hand jerked back involuntarily, reached forward again.

"Silly," Lainie said aloud, her voice sounding strangely hollow and muted. "Just pick it up. It's not going to hurt you." Resolute, she leaned forward and pulled back one corner of the velvet, then another.

"A gun! Why ever?..." The bone handle gleamed faintly in the dim light. Gingerly, Lainie picked up the holster. The leather was old and cracked but still supple. A dozen cartridges filled the loops centered in the leather. Turning so the light was better, she pulled out the gun. It was heavy, the barrel faintly blue. Six bullets filled the chambers. The handle was carved with coiled snakes and worn smooth as piano keys. A gun. What had he said? "I don't want to see it again. All I want to do is forget."

Because he had, sometime in the past, killed a man? Was that who she had seen him talking to? Was that why he had lived alone in Elkhorn all those years? Because he was afraid the authorities would catch him, maybe even hang him?

But Wind River, for all his eccentricities, seemed so harmless. Eyes wide, Lainie stared at the instrument of death. It was a little like the first time she had seen the gun Roman had taken from Lieght. She had been frightened then, too, when she heard it was the same gun that had killed a man. And to think that she had actually shot at Wind River with it! Oh, God, she thought, her stomach churning. If she had killed the old man . . . She imagined the same guilts and fears that plagued Wind River plaguing her. She envisioned herself haunted by the ghost of Wind River as he was haunted . . . She shuddered uncontrollably and almost dropped the gun. Her fingers felt stiff and awkward. But for fate, she and Roman might have been driven mad by worry and shame, and passed their days hiding, always hiding. Poor Wind River. Sad old man. How silly to have been afraid of him, when all he wanted was to forget.

She almost left it there, almost wrapped the gun and left it on the misted stone altar. But Roman had to see it. He had to know, to see the symbol of the consequences they had almost brought down upon their own heads. The money they had stolen was blood money. What sort of life could be built on that? A life like Wind River's? A life of hiding and fear and lonely madness?

Lainie held the gun tightly to her stomach, tried to figure out what to do. It was too late to take the money back. It wasn't Lieght's. It wasn't theirs. She didn't know the answer but had sensed the question and knew what she must do. Roman would see the gun, but not at the risk of offending Wind River. She would hide it in the only safe place she could think of, with the money, and, when Roman returned, confront him with it and her thoughts. Uncertain if that was indeed the right course, yet somehow relieved, she held the velvet cloth over her head and ducked out of the grotto.

The trip downhill was easier than the trip up. Afraid she might run into Wind River or get lost if she followed the path he took, she retraced her steps through the heavy pines, past the rocks and moss, and entered the grove of trembling aspen. Twenty minutes later, she stopped to rest at the edge of the aspen grove, where the trail ended and the unnamed street that intersected Main Street began. Elkhorn lay basking in the sun. Lainie sat cross-legged in the golden leaves. The weather-beaten buildings looked almost pretty from a distance. She couldn't see the splinters, the broken boards, the gaps and holes and dust. When she closed her eyes, the scene came to life with miners and storekeepers and businessmen and children all bustling about, talking and laughing and working against the backdrop of Rampage Valley and mountains so beautiful they took away her breath, even if they were lonely and sometimes terrifying. If only Roman were with her, she thought, and then opened her eyes as the fantasy was broken by a door slamming shut.

The sound of boots drumming on the boardwalk carried through the crisp mountain air. A second later, Wind River appeared in front of the barbershop. He was dressed as before, but had added a dull-gray cap. Strangely enough, he stopped in the middle of the street and just stood there, as if waiting for something.

"Farewell to Lorena,
It's free I must be ..."

Singing. He was singing! Lilting, raucous, carefree, the words floated up the hillside to Lainie. Always before he'd been sour and grumpy, but now he sounded happy, as if a great weight had been taken from him. That was the gun, Lainie knew, wishing she could ask him what had happened and how and when, wishing she could share her own fears and new resolve.

Suddenly she caught her breath. Streaking from high across the blue expanse of sky, a growing dot that became the falcon was diving toward Wind River. Lainie tried to call out, but there wasn't time. Wings flared back, hardly more than a blur so great was its speed, the bird sped toward its prey and struck.

Clang!

Stunned, the falcon veered off awkwardly and fell to the ground. Wind River stumbled but kept his feet. The pot he had on his head flew off and hit the ground, spinning. Dazed and wobbling, the falcon reeled about in the street.

"Got you that time, you feathered devil," Wind River crowed, scrambling for the pot. "I seen you from the window and I got you! That makes it complete!"

The bird sort of cawed or coughed, Lainie couldn't decide, and clawed itself into the air just ahead of the flung pot. Wind River hopped up and down, called in glee. "And don't come back!" he shouted. "You hear me, bird? Don't come back!"

The falcon fled in a zigzag course toward the safety of the tall pines. By the time he was out of sight and Lainie looked back to Main Street, Wind River had disappeared among the trees north of town. Only his voice lingered, singing that incessant song about sweet Rosemarie and the gold fields and being free.

20

Roman had never known that stars could be so bright. Now they were pressing close enough to touch, now so infinitely far away that imagination didn't suffice to name their distances. Either way, loneliness made them brighter. He was camped in a scooped-out U made of granite somewhere along Wind River's cutoff route to Mountain City. In front of him, his fire was burning down, but his legs and butt hurt too much to get up and put on more wood. Besides, he'd need what was left in the morning if he wanted hot coffee. As Wind River had suggested, he had cut pine bows and spread them in a rectangle, over which his ground cloth lay. He was out of the wind, unless it shifted, and wrapped in three blankets. The temperature was below freezing, he imagined, but the dry air felt merely brisk. At first he had worried about the cold, but as the pine boughs insulated him from the ground and the blankets trapped and held his body heat, the worry had faded. He felt almost serene.

The trip from Elkhorn had been a strange one, in a way. He had spent the first few hours worrying about leaving Lainie behind, but gave that up when he stopped to eat a bite for lunch and became preoccupied with starting a fire, feeding the horse, and looking for water. By three in the afternoon, under a warm blue sky and a sun that forced him to remove his coat, he had grown quite blasé. Wind River had been right. The horse would do all the work and all he had to do was go along for the ride.

The strangest part was being away from Lainie. They hadn't been together that long—only a little over a month, but time enough to make him accustomed to having her near, to feeling her occasional touch, to hearing her voice. He couldn't remember being happier, even with all the doubt and fear and tension. Certainly not at the Holy Light Divinity School. When he thought about that, which wasn't too often, he wondered why he'd ever gone. His father's death had been the main reason, he supposed, for it was shortly thereafter that his mother had started pushing him to go into the Lord's work. Lord's work, indeed. Hour after hour of dull classes. Latin, Greek, Bible studies, all of them boring beyond description, all of them spent wishing he were somewhere else and at the same time feeling guilty because he wasn't listening, wasn't paying attention, and so was thwarting his mother and by extension blackening his father's name. Elocution, declamation, oratory. Learn to say "Gaaawwwdddaa" for God. Rise on toes, extend finger, draw out vowel. Give 'em the picture of hell, boy, and arrest them in their sinful ways. And the drone of the reader working his way through the Bible at dinner and the interminable prayers and the communing with his Maker. The beetle-eyed doctor of theology Warren Stanley Barthanson, Jr., a virulent Elijah, questioning, incessantly probing the state of Roman's soul. The constant reminders to watch the collection plate. Oh, how he hated the hypocrisy—both his and theirs to an equal degree.

It hadn't been hard to leave, once his mind was made up. Funny, how things happen. For Roman, it had come during a church-history class. Brother Harmon Beech was lecturing on Martin Luther, thumping the lectern with his fist as he recounted the nailing of the theses to the church door. *Thump.* "The first stroke of the first nail in the coffin of the Roman Catholic stranglehold on the world." *Thump.* "No more worshipping of idols." *Thump.* "Reform which, once started, could not be stopped because"—*thump!*—"God himself would not let it be stopped!"

The thumps went on, but Roman had stopped listening.

Each thump was, for him, another nail in the door that held him prisoner. Before he knew what was happening, he had closed his books and stood up and walked out the door, just like that. Walked out the door and to his room, packed his bags, and went away, just like that. And never looked back except to wish he had left sooner.

Roman watched the last tiny finger of flame wink out, tossed his cigarette butt into the coals. A thin shaft of smoke rose in a straight line until it reached the top of the rocks, then crinkled into gradually increasing corrugations until it dissipated completely. Flat on his back, he watched the stars again. A year sooner, a year later; at least he had left.

He ended up in Denver, because that was where the first ride he caught took him. Any other city would have done as well. Three days after he arrived he had a job as a carpenter's helper. Six days later, broke and hungry because the job had come to a halt when the contractor ran away with the money, he had fallen into a life of crime by the simple expedient of driving a load of shingles from the job site and selling them to another contractor. From there, one thing led to another, and he might as well never have seen the inside of a church. The smiling, clean-cut, well-mannered, devout paragon of virtue had become a cynical, tough-talking, cigarette-smoking, unprincipled small-time hood on his way up in the harsh world of bootlegging and numbers and fast bucks by whatever means. Within six months he was working for Harry Lieght, and six months after that, having witnessed the brutal death of a man, actively comparing the stupidity and emptiness of a life of crime to the futility and boredom of a life of religion. Worst of all, he couldn't see a way out. Other than having some knack—but little experience—at carpentry, he could find no place in that great in-between world where he might fit.

Lainie, of course, had been his salvation. He had known the instant he had first seen her in the dance hall that there was indeed a place for Roman Phillips, because he intended to make one, come hell or high water. That "hell or high water" turned out to be stealing ten thousand dollars from Harry Lieght didn't occur to him until later. By then, he was so crazy in love with Lainie he would have robbed Al Capone himself if he had to. Harry Lieght was bad enough, though. No turning back, Roman thought, chilled now, and not from the night air. Keep to the plan, he told himself. Stay out of sight and hope for the best. Ten thousand dollars would last a minimum of two years even if he went to school to learn a trade. By that time, they'd have new names, be safely established in some town Lieght had never heard of, and maybe even have a family.

A kid! Now, wouldn't that be something. Maybe even name him after his grandfather, Roman thought, his mind wandering. Christ, he was tired. He shifted slowly, favoring the raw spots the saddle had worn on his behind and the inside of his thighs. Damned car, anyway. Stuck under a broken house. He yawned, tried to stretch his legs, and gave up. Be sore in the morning.

What was that? Roman jerked from sleep, rose on one elbow, and listened. The sound kept on, a slow, steady munching. The horse. That was it. Oh, but he had the heebies! Heck with 'em. Too tired to think much more. Stupid, anyway. The Lord took care of th … Now, where did that come from? There was no answer. He was asleep before his head touched the mat of pine boughs.

"You did right to bring me here," Dr. Taft said as he touched the blankets around the bundled-up figure of Harry Lieght. "That was real good of you."

His face sallow in the lantern light, Lode Benedict appeared wholly disinterested, the more or less permanent set of his expression. He scratched beneath his floppy gray hat and flicked whatever he found there from between his fingertips. The reins of the team dangled limply in his grasp as he held the horses for the doctor.

Lieght coughed. Taft shook his head, leaned over the side of the buckboard. "Don't you worry, now, Mr . Lieght. Like I said, you've had a bit of a concussion and a nasty cold. Just lie still. We're going to take you over to Mildred Smith's. She takes lodgers and I use her place as a sort of hospital when there's someone who needs attention they can't get somewhere else. You'll be fine there. Rest and food is what you need and we'll see that you get plenty of both. Another week and you'll be good as new." Taft limped around to the front of the buckboard, paused to cluck in despair at Lode's ramshackle cabin. "You saved his life, Lode," he said, speaking as he would to a child. Taft decided he'd bill his new patient enough extra to cover some new clothes and a week's worth of groceries for Lode. Seemed fair enough. "Now, the next time you come to town, you be sure to come see me. I'll have a little surprise for you, okay?"

Lode nodded. Taft climbed into the buckboard, took the reins from Lode, and clucked to the horses. Behind him, Harry Lieght coughed weakly and stared up at the same stars that Roman was sleeping under.

> "Yippi ti and away, a drover's life for me.
> As I drive my cattle on the lone prairieeee."

In the quiet of the cold hills, in the whisper region below the spiked peaks, Roman Phillip's lone voice bounced off granite shelves and echoed across the sweep of lesser hills to the east and south. Two hours earlier, his only song had been a moan of despair as his aching muscles and saddle-sore rump reacted with excruciating pain to the jolting gait of the Appaloosa. An hour's riding though, if not curing his ills, had alleviated them to the point where the pain was bearable. The mountain air was responsible for the rest.

"Whoa!"

The Appaloosa stopped and craned its neck around to study Roman, who swung down from the saddle. The Appaloosa and Wind River had never stopped there before, and the altered routine was confusing. Eyes wide, teeth searching for the bit, he tried to keep on but was snubbed up short when Roman looped his reins around a small pine.

"Yippi ti yiii!" Roman hollered, cupping his hands to his mouth.

"... ti yiiiii ... ti yiiii ..." his echo responded.

"How about that, horse?" Roman asked, proud of himself. "Pretty darn good for a tenderfoot, right?"

The Appaloosa looked at him with as dour an expression as a horse could muster.

Lost in a childhood fantasy generated by the dime novels

of Western adventure he had consumed voraciously and secretly as a youth, Roman stretched, stood spraddle-legged with his left thumb hooked in his belt, tipped his hat forward, lazily snagged his canteen from the saddle horn, and took a long pull from it. He hunkered down on his heels, lit a ready-made, and left it dangling from his lips. The smoke drifted past his eyes as he squinted across the bright hills lit by a butter-yellow sun.

"Well, Old Paint," he finally drawled, stubbing out and shredding his cigarette butt, "I reckon we better hit the trail."

Roman untied the reins and mounted. The Appaloosa needed no urging, actually broke into a trot. Still living in the Old West, Roman rode tall in the saddle, trying for a sober, melancholy, William S. Hart look.

They were closer than he'd thought. Reining in the Appaloosa on the next crest, he looked down on Mountain City. "Well, I'll be damned," he whispered, patting the horse's neck. "We made it."

And then it hit him. He couldn't fool himself any longer. Brave words to Lainie and playing cowboy were all well and good, but when it came right down to it, Mountain City was dangerous. Roman hadn't so much as mentioned the name of the town, even to Lainie, but Lieght was no fool. If a way could be found to trace them there, he would have found it. And if he had found it, Roman realized grimly, Lieght might well be waiting.

"Well, here we go, horse," he mumbled to himself, memorizing the lay of the land in case he had to made a rapid escape. He debated leaving the Appaloosa tethered among trees to keep from drawing attention to his arrival, but reconsidered immediately. He would invite as many questions if he arrived on foot. The only course, when all was said and done, was to ride in and take his chances. "Back to the real world."

The schoolyard was empty, but he could see children's faces turning to stare at him through the open classroom windows. The horse plodded down Silverado Street. A trio of old-timers playing checkers in the early-afternoon sun in front of the barbershop watched him pass without interest. A wagon driven by a ragged local slithered through the drying mud. A scant half dozen men and women, none of them city people from the way they dressed, hurried along on workday errands. Roman's nerves were keyed to a pitch, but hard as he tried, he could find nothing threatening or out of what he imagined was the ordinary.

Weldon's had changed. The front porch had been removed. In its place sat two shiny gasoline pumps. Roman tethered the Appaloosa to the nearest pump and sauntered inside. "With you in a minute," a voice from one side called in answer to the clanging cowbell that hung over the door. "Hold it right there while I nail it, now." A hammer struck a nail, then wood. "Hold it, damn it! I can't hit a moving target."

Roman winced. The storekeeper was missing as often as he was hitting. His eyes slowly adjusting to the dim light, he stepped over a crate, swerved to avoid a pile of quart oil jars. The transformation of Weldon's General Store into a garage and parts store, already in progress when he'd first come through town, was virtually complete.

"Now, that's the way it's supposed to go. Won't hold a dadgummed thing, crooked."

"It wasn't all that crooked," Lewis Junior complained. "A half inch isn't gonna—"

"I'm not even going to argue with you about it," Weldon said. He sounded tired and out of sorts. "There isn't enough time in the day. You get those forms off that concrete in the pit?"

"I would've if you hadn't called me in here to—"

"Never mind. Git. I got a customer. You can straighten up the rest of these in the morning." Lewis appeared at the end of an aisle, squeezed behind the counter. "What can I—" he looked surprised when he saw Roman. "Well, I'll be," he said, unable to believe his luck. Mr. Lieght would pay for this. Good money, too. "It's you."

"Yes, sir," Roman said noncommittally.

"Malachi Phillips's grandson, right? Dawned on me after you'd left." Weldon untied the nail apron he was wearing and dropped it on the counter. "You chew?" he asked, pulling out a plug.

"No, thanks," Roman said politely. "I need some mules."
Weldon took his time while his mind raced. Word that
Lieght was safely back in town had spread like wildfire.
Weldon had inquired and learned the man would not be able
to move about for at least another three days, if not more. At
least that was Mildred Smith's diagnosis. Still, Weldon
wished he could get to him. "Mules, eh?" he said, biting his
tongue to keep from asking why.

"Yes, sir. You know anyone who might have some to sell?"

"Maybe, maybe not." One eyebrow raised. "That's it!
Your grandfather used to have that place up in Elkhorn.
Doubt there's much left of it now. You find it?"

"Maybe, maybe not," Roman said, not quite so politely.
"Who wants to know?"

Weldon laughed. "Just being sociable, son. Just being
sociable." He spit into the peach tin and changed the subject. "Mules, eh?"

"Mules," Roman repeated, trying to keep the tightness
out of his voice. "At least a pair. Three would be better."

Weldon spit again, squinted in thought. "Well, let's see,"
he said with maddening slowness. "Joe Nusken down at the
livery might know of some around. Cost you, of course."

"Nusken at the livery," Roman repeated. "Thanks." He
turned to leave, noticed a dusty counter filled with an as-
sortment of folded jeans. "You got any girl's sizes in there?"
he asked, pointing.

The storekeeper's eyes narrowed. "Might." He pulled at
his chin. "I already sold them all to Lulie Harskell down at
the ladies' shop, but that doesn't mean I couldn't let you
have a couple."

Roman was already rummaging through the pile. He
selected a couple of pairs that looked as if they'd fit Lainie
and peeled a five-dollar bill off his roll. "This cover it?"

"You got some change coming," Weldon said, trying to
think of how he could glean some more information for
Lieght. He fiddled with the cash register, turned over the
problem, and came up short. "Here you are. Fifty cents."

"Thanks." Roman stuffed the money into his pocket,
tucked the jeans under his arm. "Oh, yes," he added casually.
"I almost forgot to ask. I talked to a fellow about maybe

meeting him up here." Roman's eyes never left Weldon's. "Not too tall, husky build, short hair. Name of Lieght."

"Well?" the storekeeper said, spitting into the tin again.

Roman watched closely but saw nothing to alarm him in the storekeeper's eyes. "Well, did someone like that come through looking for me?" he asked, beginning to hope his fears had been unfounded.

"Naw," Weldon drawled, easy now that he'd had time to concoct a story. "City guy came through, but he was a drummer selling parts for Nashes. I told him there weren't any in town and he left. Didn't look like this fellow you're talking about, anyway. I can keep an eye out for him, though, if he shows up," he added helpfully. "Anything you want me to tell him?"

"I guess not," Roman said, surprised at how calm he sounded when all he wanted to do was shout with relief. "I'll be gone myself in a few days. I'll see him back in Denver in a couple, three weeks. You mind pointing out the livery?"

"Straight down the road, first street to your right, at the end of the second block. You can't miss it," Weldon said, following Roman to the door and then stopping to stare at the Appaloosa. "Hey, where'd you get that horse?"

Roman held the door open for Weldon. He could feel himself grinning, but didn't believe it, he was so tense. Anyone watching would have thought they were old buddies. "Rented it from an old geezer up in the hills. Charged me a tenner a day for it. You want the truth, I think I was suckered."

Weldon apparently had lost interest. "Beats walking," he said, watching Roman mount. "Hope you find your mules."

"Many thanks," Roman said, waving over his shoulder. If he hadn't been so blissfully pleased with his good fortune, he might have looked back a moment later to see Lewis Weldon lock the front door of his store and walk briskly down the street. And if he'd kept watching, see the storekeeper enter a white, two-story house with a sign out front that said: MILDRED SMITH. ROOM AND BOARD.

Finding the livery was an easy matter. Buying mules not so. One was available immediately, but two more had to be brought in from a farm outside town. Roman used the

time to rent one of Nusken's wagons and go to the Piggly
Wiggly. By the time he returned with the supplies he
needed, Nusken was waiting with bad news. The pair of
mules he'd expected to bring back wouldn't be available
until late the next afternoon. Roman was forced to content
himself with lessons on how to load and unload a mule by
himself.

"Almost seven o'clock," Nusken said as he watched
Roman set down the last pack. "Looks like you got the hang
of it. Good thing, too. A man shouldn't go into that country
unprepared. If you ask me, he had it comin' to him."

"What's that?" Roman asked idly, leading the mule into a
stall. "Who?"

"C'mon, I'll buy you some coffee."

Roman slammed the stall door, hurried out to the front of
the livery to join Nusken. A slow tension was building inside
him. His fingers felt stiff, his knees watery. "Don't mind if I
do," he said in a carefully controlled voice. "Who was that
you were talking about? The one who had it coming to him."

"Some guy from New Mexico. Albuquerque, they say.
Looking for his daughter and the young feller she'd run off
with." Nusken led the way toward Silverado. "Come into
town one day last week. Lewis Weldon rented him a horse
and some gear and turned him loose headin' north. Damned
fool should have known better. Fools, rather. Both of 'em"

Roman felt weak all over. That Albuquerque business
might have fooled Weldon and the others, but not him. God!
If it was Lieght ... He shook his head. "Jeez. I hope it wasn't
somebody I know. I was supposed to meet a friend here. You
get a name?"

"Nope. Lewis is bein' close-mouthed about it. I reckon
the name'll get out in a day or two, though. Seems the city
slick made it back to Lode Benedict's place. They carried
him over to Mildred Smith's last night." He chuckled.
"Damned if I'd like to be sick at Mildred's. Whole town'd
know everything about you, sooner or later, that mouth of
hers. I recall the time when ..."

His voice droned on, but Roman paid only enough attention to answer with an occasional grunt, or a yes or no. His
stomach was all butterflies one minute, felt like someone

had dumped a load of gravel in it the next. They ate, but what he couldn't remember, went to a bar and had a beer, but all it did was bloat him. Not until nine did Nusken run down. "Well," he said with a yawn, "I got to be up and about early. Mind you, now." One stubby forefinger poked at Roman's shirt pocket. "Sleepin's all right. I've bedded down in many a pile of hay. But no smokin' inside. That livery'd burn to the ground in ten minutes."

"I won't," Roman promised. "See you in the morning?"

Nusken laughed. "If you're awake that early. Hell, boy. I'm there before the sun, these days. Way it has to be if a man runs a stable." He frowned at Weldon's, three blocks up the street. The new gas pumps sat like prim sentinels in the glow of the new sign over them. "Which I might not be doin' for much longer, way things are goin'," he added. Nusken sighed, belched, and started down the street. "See you."

"Right." Roman's smile crumbled and he sagged against the post holding up the roof over Little Georgie's Bar. The strain of appearing calm for the last two hours had caught up with him. His supper rose to his throat. Gagging, he leaned over and vomited against the wall, leaving a puddle of beer and stew steaming on the ground.

"Easy now," he told himself, wiping his mouth and repeating the phrase over and over again until the suggestion took. His breathing slowed. "You still don't know. Not for sure. It might not be him."

Might was about as slim a chance as a snowman dancing through hell. He had to know, and there was only one way to find out without arousing suspicion. The street was empty. Nusken had pointed out Mildred Smith's boardinghouse. Breathing slowly at last, Roman sauntered toward it and stopped a half block away.

Mountain City went to bed early, as a rule. Only one light in the boardinghouse was on upstairs, three down. A dog barked off to his right. Roman shushed it, walked up the street at a natural pace, then ducked low behind a hedge that ran along the front of the house. When he was sure no one had seen him, he poked his head up high enough to see. The first two windows opened on the dining room. "Oh, God, don't let whoever it is be on the second floor," he whispered, creeping along the hedge. Inside the third window, a drummer sat working on his books in what looked like a sitting room. Roman crossed the lawn in a crouching run, hid behind a tree at the side of the house. A light was on at the rear. Poised for flight in case someone should call out, he tiptoed past another tree, stopped behind a third.

A lace curtain obscured the window. Against it, he could see the shadowed silhouette of a man. When the man leaned over, something dangled from his neck. Roman caught his breath, edged up to the side of the house, and slowly peeked around the corner of the window. From that distance, he could see through the curtains. The man he had seen a moment earlier was bending over a bed, obscuring Roman's view. Roman held his breath, pleaded silently for him to move. At last he straightened. "Your fever is down and your chest sounds better than it did last night," Roman heard the figure say in a voice muffled by the window. "A concussion that severe plus what damned near amounted to pneumonia would have killed a man with a less hardy constitution. You're lucky. Another week of rest and Mildred's food, and I think we can have you on your way. As long as there are no complications, of course," he added, walking away from the bed.

There was more, but what he said next, Roman had no idea. His eyes were glued to the bed itself and the man lying in it. Harry Lieght.

21

Wind River watched the sky turn the color of a bluebird's egg, pale blue speckled with gray. A deeper violet tinged the treeline. Across Rampage Valley, Diamond Peak glittered in the late sun that still shone there. A pair of coyotes down by the jail were rousing themselves for their nocturnal wanderings. Plaintive howls and shrill yippings filled the coming night air. Wind River was standing among the graves where he'd been hard at work since the middle of the afternoon. Four of the sites Scar had rooted up had been filled back in. Three more, dark blotches in the earth, remained unfilled. "There are moments in a man's life that it doesn't do to recall," Wind River said to Cow House O'Reilly's skull as he gingerly dropped the bleached cranium into the hole and began scooping in dirt.

"You reminded me of *Hamlet* just then," Lainie said.

Wind River turned and suffered her a glance, then resumed filling in the grave. "Don't know him," he said between shovelfuls.

"The play," Lanie explained. "You never saw Shakespeare?"

"Nope. Him neither. He a friend of this Hamlet feller?"

"He's the author!"

Wind River snickered to himself. Dadgummed girl

thought she was so all-fired smart. Hell, yes, he knew who Shakespeare was. Troupes used to go all around the West in the old days. He'd taken in a play called *Othello* once, but didn't understand it, didn't like it, and never went to see another because it was a waste of time when he could be making money. "Arthur who?" he asked innocently. "Dang, girl, but sometimes you and that boyfriend of yours make about as much sense as diggin' a stock tank in alkali."

"Shakespeare wrote the play *Hamlet*," Lainie explained slowly and clearly. "And in it, Hamlet, who was a prince, talked to a skull named Yorick, just like you were doing."

The hole was filled, but Wind River kept on, mounding the dirt higher. "Don't know about Yorick, but I wasn't talkin' to no skull. I was readin' this here marker." He whacked the loose dirt with the bottom of the shovel a couple of times for good measure and then picked up a slab of weathered wood on which was carved:

COW HOUSE O'REILLY
BORN ? DIED 1879
THERE ARE MOMENTS IN A MAN'S LIFE
THAT IT DOESN'T DO TO RECALL

Lainie read the tombstone as Wind River hammered it into place with the flat of the shovel. "Like what happened the other morning?" she said.

"Which other morning?"

"When you . . ." Lainie almost mentioned the pond and the falls, but then thought better of it. She thought quickly, found a substitute. "When you drove the car into—"

"Mighty cold up here," Wind River said, interrupting to change the subject. "The wind cuts right across these graves. A hell of a note, to shiver for all eternity. 'Course, it beats fryin', I reckon." He glared at Lainie. "You sure you ain't gettin' chilled?"

"Meaning you don't want to talk about it?"

"There's hope for you yet, girl."

"Okay. I won't." She hugged her knees, stared at the ground in front of her. "It's just that I've got to talk about something. I'm lonely, Wind River. It feels as if Roman's been gone a year." She pushed her bangs out of her eyes, swung her arm out in a wide gesture. Rampage Valley was already a deep shadow. The bare wooden buildings in Elkhorn were rapidly fading from gold to a deep umber. "I don't know how people stood it, living up here, making a town in this emptiness."

"We had our times," Wind River said, his eyes twinkling. He scraped a layer of mud off the shovel with the heel of his boot. "Anyway, that's why it's called the High Lonesome."

The hush that dusk brings was falling over the hillside. Somewhere, far off, an owl waked and tested its voice. Lainie shivered a little, smiled to show she wasn't afraid. "That was nice of you."

"Huh?"

"There's hope for me yet. That's about the nicest thing you've said as long as I've been here."

Wind River stuck the shovel in the ground, pressed his palms against the small of his back, and pushed. "Ah!" he grunted, grimacing when his spine popped. "Better." He appraised his handiwork, the four mounds of earth that covered the sad, toylike bones he'd returned to their places of rest. "Good thing it's gettin' dark. I'd probably be damned fool enough to keep on."

"Who dug them up?" Lainie asked.

"Not who. What. Scar. A devil of a one-eyed silvertip grizzly. He's gone now, though, so you don't have to start worryin' all over again. Chased off by the winter, I reckon. Probably holed up in a cave somewheres. I'd find him and finish him if I knew how to track bear worth a damn. Creed would know how, but he isn't around either, bein' dead and all."

"Oh," Lainie said. That Creed was dead, she understood. That Wind River believed this man Creed spoke to him, she also understood. But the two earlier times she'd tried to learn more, Wind River had changed the subject immediately. She shrugged, decided he'd tell her more in his own good time. "Like they say, 'There are more things in heaven and earth, Horatio.'"

Wind River raised his eyebrows. "Horatio? He another one of them . . . what's-his-name fellers?"

"Shakespeare! For heaven's sake, Wind River. You aren't so smart, either. At least I've been exposed to some culture."

"Yeah," came the sarcastic answer as Wind River started for the trees. "Well, I'm smart enough to know that we better get down off this hill before it gets any darker." He reached into the top branches of a wind-stunted cedar and pulled out a pair of skinned and dressed squirrels. "And I'm smart enough to trap us some fresh meat for supper tonight, too," he added, walking back to Lainie. "And if that ain't enough, I'm all-fired smart enough to show a certain city-bred gal who has the special talent of changin' perfectly good bacon into kindling how to make Damnation Stew."

Lainie grimaced as he held out his hand to help her up, reached delicately around the shiny, stiff carcasses to catch his wrist instead. "Well, I . . ."

"Come along, girl." Wind River pulled her to her feet, turned to pull the shovel out of the ground and swing it over his shoulder before starting down the slope. "I've done my duty to the dead. It's the stomachs of the living I'm after saving now."

Lainie matched him stride for stride. "By the way," she asked, halfway down the hill, "how can you be sure you put all the right . . . remains . . . together in the correct graves?"

Wind River stopped abruptly. Obviously he wasn't sure. His mouth open, he looked back up the hill, then at Lainie. "That's a hell of a thing to say," he snapped, and strode off again.

They proceeded in silence, Lainie pleased with herself because she'd finally been able to throw him, the Wind River Kid mentally reviewing the afternoon. Not until they reached the beginning of Main Street did the irony of it all hit him. Lainie looked at him out of the corner of her eye when he began to laugh. "Now, wouldn't that be something," he said, his head bobbing up and down in glee. "I wonder what the Widow Guthrie would say if she thought that some of Cow House wound up in her bed."

Meat, wild onions sautéed into softened transparency, and red chili pepper along with a dash of salt was the traditional, basic recipe for Damnation Stew. Anything else depended on availability. Springtime, he usually added wild asparagus, chopped and quartered. Gave the gravy a bit of a green cast, but the taste was worth it. Kind of a nutty flavor, Wind River always thought. Potatoes and carrots were always good, too, although finding fresh had been a problem for the last thirty years. One good thing about Roman and Lainie: they'd been fool enough to pack them in. Wind River was grateful. Mint, basil, thyme, even cumin, which pushed the whole concoction to the chili side, were acceptable. Hell. A good Damnation Stew would take anything a man could throw into it and still turn out just fine.

Wind River bent low, moved his nose inches above the steaming kettle. He stirred the mixture with a long-stemmed wooden spoon. "Close," he muttered, admiring the way the chunks of dark squirrel meat bobbed among the carrots and potatoes. "Real close."

Lainie's stomach growled in anticipation: the aroma had long since overcome her initial reluctance to eating squirrel in any shape or form. She finished setting the table and walked to Wind River's side. "Close enough to be finished?" she asked hopefully.

"Not quite." Wind River shook his head, took a cautious sip of the steaming gravy, and held out the spoon for Lainie. "Nothing like lots of fresh air and exercise for an appetite," he added, eyes a-twinkle. "Hunger's better than salt."

Lainie sipped, closed her eyes in appreciation. "Mmmm. You were right about the whiskey. I take back what I said."

"Gives it body," Wind River said, finishing off what was in the spoon. "Still lacks a crucial ingredient to bring it up to snuff, but I reckon I got no choice but to serve it up half dressed if we want to eat tonight."

"I've watched you toss a little of everything in the kitchen into that pot. What in heaven's name could it lack?"

"Pant'er. I ought to have trapped me a mountain cat—shot," he added pointedly, "but you'll remember I ain't been left no gun—and put part of him in the pot to sort of offset the squirrel taste."

Lainie made a face. "I'm certain it will taste fine without adding pant'er," she said quickly, hurriedly bringing both bowls to the stove. "It'll be just fine the way it is. Before you get any more ideas."

The kitchen was warm and close, the top of the stove a cheery red, the lantern light soft. Lainie nibbled on a soda cracker and stirred her stew to let it cool a little. Wind River attacked his in a more frontal manner, blowing briskly on each spoonful and then moving it around in his mouth so it wouldn't scald his tongue. It was peaceful. The snap of crisp crackers, spoon and bowl noises, the occasional wind sound seeping through to remind them how lucky they were to be inside and protected. Suddenly Lainie sat upright and listened intently. "What is it?" Wind River asked, instantly alert.

"I thought I heard Roman."

Wind River crushed a handful of crackers into his stew. "Hell, girl, he's only got to town yesterday. Take a day or two to round up mules, and another two to get back here."

"I know," Lainie said, her stew forgotten. "It seemed to take forever in the car. We weren't sure of the way and the weather was getting colder." She shivered a little, remembering. "Camping out was horrid. I was cold, and every noise in the dark sounded as if it could be that awful Harry Lieght."

The crackers made the stew a little mushy for Wind River's taste. He got up to refill his bowl. "This Lieght fellow sounds like the original curly wolf," he said, juggling the hot ladle.

"Roman was young and out to conquer the world," Lainie said dreamily. "I guess with Mama dying and all, supporting Pa until he drank himself to death, I kind of needed somebody who thought he could do that, I was so down. Anyway, Mr. Lieght drove fast cars, wore spiffy clothes, and ate at all the right places. He seemed to have the world by the tail. I guess with his background and all, it was just natural Roman

wanted to be like him. He said that when Mr. Lieght offered
him a job driving, it was the best thing that ever happened to
him. He was so proud he didn't even care how Mr. Lieght
made his money." She shrugged. "I can't complain about
that, though. I didn't, either. I was as bad as Roman. When I
met him, all I could see was the outside: how neat he looked,
how he threw money around."

"And how did Lieght make his money?" Wind River asked
between mouthfuls.

"Well . . ." Lainie leaned forward conspiratorially. "Since
we're sort of partners and everything's jake between us . . . I
don't think Roman would want you to know, so you have to
promise not to tell him I told you."

Wind River's nod was perfunctory.

"Anyway, one night about a week after we'd met, Roman
told me all about him. He works for the mob. Sort of a
collector or carrier. He makes the rounds of the businesses
in Denver and collects the monthly dues they pay for protection."

"Protection against what?"

"Against what happens if they don't pay." Lainie tried a
spoonful of stew, continued stirring. "If a storekeeper de-
cides he doesn't need what the mob calls 'insurance,' Mr.
Lieght visits him after hours and has a talk with him. Driving
Mr. Lieght around was a big break for Roman. Sitting in that
big Lincoln while Lieght collected the money and then
delivered it to the Big Cheese seemed harmless enough,
too, and even exciting. But one night, he was brought along
on one of Mr. Lieght's special visits. When it was over,
Roman came to Miss Clayze's boardinghouse and snuck up
to my room. He was white as a sheet, and scared. I was
scared too, 'cause I'd never seen anyone shake so hard. First
he got sick, and then he talked. I held him, and he talked and
talked and talked and talked." A sad little smile warmed her
face as Lainie remembered. "That's when I knew I loved
him, I guess. Knew for sure, anyway, and that he loved me."

"And?" Wind River prompted.

"Well, he wanted to quit, but was afraid to. That's when
we got the idea of stealing the money so we could get far
enough away that Mr. Lieght could never find us. Mr.

Lieght had begun to trust Roman sort of like a son, although that's a horrible thing to say, so it was pretty easy to do. One day, when they'd gone to this hotel kind of place where Lieght had a meeting with some businessmen, Roman waited until everyone but Lieght had left and then pulled a gun on him and tied him up and took the money Lieght was supposed to deliver to his boss. We never knew who that was, but figured it was somebody terrible, because Roman had once asked Mr. Lieght why he didn't just keep the money he collected and Lieght said there was no place he could spend it and live."

"But he was durned fool enough to do it, anyways," Wind River said, awed. "I don't know. That boy's either a total idiot or has more sand than the Sahara."

"We were sort of hoping that Mr. Lieght would be too busy avoiding his associates to bother with us," Lainie explained lamely.

Wind River knew better. He'd seen Lieght's kind before. Like Paunch Pepperdine, they didn't give up, just kept on coming. His mouth felt dry, as if it were stuffed with cotton. "Nothing changes much, I reckon," he said, trying not to let the fear show. "Every two-bit town I been in all my life had somebody like that. Sometimes they was the law, too." He shook his head, gazed sadly into the remains of his second bowl of stew. "Talkin' about 'em, this Lieght fella, sort of sours a man's appetite."

"I agree," Lainie said, suddenly animated in an attempt to overcome the pall she had cast over the meal. "I'm tired of thinking about him and sick of worrying. He can't find us here, and soon we'll be even farther away. Let's not mention him again. I'd rather eat."

Her brows knotted in thought, then smoothed rapidly as she took her first bite. A second bite followed, then a third and fourth as she dug in with obvious relish. Wind River watched her as unobtrusively as possible, and chuckled underneath his breath. Damnation Stew got 'em every time.

The fire in the dining-room fireplace crackled merrily. Supper sitting heavily in their stomachs, old man and young woman stretched out in chairs pulled opposite one another, much as Wind River had sat on many another night with Creed. Firelight danced an aura of throbbing light halfway across the room. Night wind pressed against the shutters and made the warm interior seem all the more cozy. "They call it Damnation Stew . . ." Wind River's voice drifted off as he stared at Lainie and thought how nice it was to sit across from a pretty girl. She was one hell of an improvement over Aden Creed. He hoped Roman took his time finding the mules.

"Because?" Lainie said.

"Hmm? Oh, yeah." Wind River settled a little deeper into the chair, regarded his cigar. "Well, I got the recipe from Lymon Bascomb, also known as the Waco Kid."

"There certainly were a lot of kids out West. Didn't anybody ever grow up?"

"Do you want to hear this or not? It's a term of respect Like you'd call a padre padre, or a minister reverend, or a doctor doctor. There was Billy the Kid, the Mobeetie Kid, the Waco Kid, the Arizona Kid—now, there was one for the books. Arizona took the whole state for a handle. The Tucson Kid and the Yuma Kid, a rough pair if I've ever seen one, didn't take so kindly toward Arizona bein' so uppity, so they gunned him down one night in a backwater town up in the Christmas Mountains."

"And there was the Wind River Kid," Lainie added, as Wind River lapsed into the silence of memory.

"Yeah. Him too." Wind River roused himself, went on with the story. "Like I said, the man who sort of taught me Damnation Stew was the Waco Kid. The Waco Kid was a gunman pretty famous for his work during the Hill County War down in Texas. I was tryin' my luck in San Antone at the time, givin' a good account of myself at the tables and ridin' high when I met Waco, or, you might say, our paths crossed. I didn't think much of it at the time, winnin' bein' natural to me and all, but I guess old Waco kind of took exception.

"Now, you ought to know that the Waco Kid, before callin' a man out, would make up a whole mess of Damnation Stew and invite the man he was fixin' to gun down to sit with him and eat sort of a last meal. The night after I took his roll, I was in Felicia's Cantina, which was where the high rollers come to pay their respects to my way with the cards, when Waco come in and began cookin'. Felicia had her a big ol' fireplace to take the sting out of the blue northers that come rippin' through that part of the country, and Waco set up shop right there over that fire. He didn't have no pant'er either, and made his apologies for havin' to substitute *cabrito*."

"*Cabrito?*"

"Baby goat. Now, you gonna listen or not?" Wind River asked, glaring at her.

"Sorry."

"Anyway, ol' Waco had it figured out down to the last shake of a saltcellar. It had worked before, Lord knows. After he'd gone through all that rigmarole and set a bowl of stew on the table in front of whoever he was after, the poor soul would be shiverin' in his boots so bad that when it came time to start the music, he'd be too strung out to dance."

"And you were the one he was inviting to dinner," Lainie said, caught up in the story.

"None other." Wind River smiled lazily, enjoying the effect the story was having on her. "I was the one and only on the guest list."

"What happened?"

"We ate," came the simple answer. Wind River pulled himself up to a sitting position, stuck out his elbows as if he were sitting at a table. "The two of us stared at each other across the table"— his right hand mimed the action —"and shoveled away the stew. Folks down San Antone way still talk about that meal. The two of us eatin' our fill." He got up, moseyed toward the fire real casual like. "I even went back for seconds. I think that's what got to him. Waco had never met a man who could eat Damnation Stew with him and have the gumption to go back for seconds." Bent over in front of the fire, he froze. "I heard him shove away from the table all of a sudden like when I was facin' the kettle and knew—" His look back at Lainie was almost parenthetical, but he mainly wanted to make sure she was paying attention. She was. He turned back, held out his right hand. "He was goin' to make his play early. I had the ladle in my right hand, whirled, and"— Wind River pivoted with the grace of a ballet dancer. His right hand shot out, then dropped to his waist, drew an imaginary gun, and extended toward Lainie— "hit him with a faceful of his goddamnation stew!"

He was crouched in the pose of a gunfighter. Lainie sat, her arms around her knees, perched on the edge of the chair. "And?. . ." she asked breathlessly.

"He wasted his first shot," Wind River said, straightening up. "I didn't, of course." He holstered the imaginary pistol, shrugged. "Directly they hauled him out, I got my seconds."

"And that's what we ate?" Her knees still drawn up, Lainie scooted back in her chair. "Brrr. Sort of a bloodthirsty dish."

"Good vittles is good vittles, whatever the source, even if you have no use for the cook."

Lainie looked a little dubious. "I don't know, Wind River. I just can't picture you as the cold-blooded gunfighter. I wonder if you aren't pulling a city girl's leg just a little bit?"

Wind River studied her a moment without speaking, then ambled back to his chair. "Yeah. Maybe it was just a dream I had a long time ago. Seems real enough now, though. But dreams have a way of doin' that, when you want them to bad enough." He stared into the fire.

The episode had been real, he knew, because if he closed his eyes he could still see Waco flying backward and smashing through the table. He could see the cards and money flying, and what was left of Waco's stew spilling onto the floor. He could still hear, too, the roar of the pistols and the ungodly collision of mushrooming lead against flesh. The smell of the gunpowder, the whine of the bullet, high and to his left, the ugly *hunhh* sound Waco made as the impact forced the air out of his lungs, the surprised look in his eyes, the . . . Every infinitesimal detail, etched forever on his memory. Roman would know, would have an idea, at least, if he had seen a man die. But not Lainie. And all the words in the good Lord's world were insufficient to convey to her what death looked, smelled, sounded, tasted, felt like. "Where'd you cache the money?" he asked her, dragging himself out of that particular morass by his own bootstraps.

The look on Lainie's face changed. "Why do you ask?" she said, unaware of Wind River's true feelings.

"Thought I might take a look at it. Haven't seen the likes in a while."

"And I thought you were a high-rolling gambler."

Wind River sank back into the easy chair. "Been a while, girl. But those were the days," he reminisced. "Cards are like women, you know. You have to know when to press your luck."

"And what a game you're playing!" Lainie added sternly.

Wind River snorted. Damn, she was learning. Girl might make it yet, he thought.

"Game? Game?" Wind River asked. "I've seen pots, and won 'em, too, with the right cards or the right bluff. I played for stakes that make your roll look like a Chinaman's wages. Plenty of times. Why, I've won thousands, and next minute, lost every cent I had. I've had me more days' and nights' worth of pure God-almighty hellacious good times than you got years to your name. Tasted more sweet slidin' whiskey, went to see the elephant, kissed the girls, danced me more fandangos, been hot, cold, drunk, sober, and loved every dadblasted minute of it. I've . . . Where you goin'?"

His answer came in the form of clicking gears as Lainie wound up the Victrola. "You'll see," she said, thumbing through the few discs stacked to the side. Of the five records, four were vocals. The last was an instrumental, a Charleston. She slipped it out of its jacket and put it on to play. A drumroll, a crash of cymbals, and a salute of horns blared from the speaker.

"Now, wait a minute . . ."

"I'm calling your bluff, old man," Lainie said, advancing on Wind River. A predatory smile transformed her face. "Let's dance."

Wind River's mouth dropped open. "You're plumb loco, girl!" he squawked as Lainie grabbed his wrists and yanked him to his feet.

"Ba ba ba bahm bahm!" Lainie sang, dragging him to the center of the room.

"What the! . . ."

"Ba ba ba ba bahhh!" She kicked high, crouched low, shimmied her shoulders in time to the music. "C'mon, Wind River! Let's see your stuff!"

Wind River planted his feet, refused to move. "Hell's bells, girl, I don't got the foggiest notion of what you're doin'."

Lainie grabbed his hand and spun him in a circle. "The Charleston!"

"What the hell's the Charleston?" Wind River shouted over the music.

Lainie kicked her heels backward, crouched with her hands on her knees, and wiggled toward him. "This."

Jesus! Her knees were going one way, her feet another, her hands yet another. Wind River tried to figure it out but gave up. "Looks like the conniptions to me . . . Oops!" he said, once more spinning, almost falling, then caught and spun in the opposite direction.

Her grip was unrelenting. The band played hot and heavy, brass on brass, the beat irresistible. Wind River, more as a matter of self-defense than anything else, tried a few steps and found he could no more follow Lainie's sudden, explosive, and completely unpredictable movements than he could track goose down in a blizzard. But what the hell, he suddenly decided, catching her fever. Hadn't he danced the fandango with enough *señoritas* in his lifetime? And was he going to let a slip of a girl show him up?

Hell, no! Wind River let out a wild, blood-curdling war whoop and jumped into the air. He kicked out with his feet and bayed like a wolf in heat. Lainie gave a start and jumped away. Wind River shot her a wicked wink and kicked over a table. He jumped the pedestal and landed in a sweeping bow directly in front of her.

"Dancing, is it?" he hooted. Rising, he grabbed her hand and held it high. "If it is, if that's what you want, little gal, then follow the devil! Yeee-ha!"

Wind River slapped his thigh and spun Lainie around. He lifted her off the ground with a resounding slap on her bottom. He clapped his hands and dallied in a circle, then broadened the range of his steps to take in the whole dining room. He hooted like an owl and yelled like a Rebel at Shiloh. He kicked his heels and dodged tables and leaped clear over chairs. He landed light as a butterfly on his toes, stomped hard enough to raise dust, and danced toward the girl, who was laughing so hard she could hardly stand, and then gasping as he swung her from the sideline into the middle of the action. He twirled her around and pulled her back and forth and caught her in an embrace and spun her back the other way. Lainie slowed long enough to start the record again and then, caught in the spirit of the dance, began to mimic his movements.

Wind River howled, and Lainie answered with a wild yell.

And they danced.

And they laughed.

And they danced.

"It makes it sound so late at night when the logs go pop like that."

Wind River studied Lainie. Legs tucked under her, she was curled up in the easy chair across from him. Both had sat in quiet reverie for more than an hour, enjoying the unvoiced pleasure of each other's company. Orange firelight transformed their faces into fluid, friendly clown masks. The lines and creases in Wind River's face were emphasized by a warm smile. "That's because it *is* late."

Lainie smiled back sleepily. She knew it was after midnight. "Well, I certainly worked off that bowl of stew."

"There's plenty more. Be some left when your man shows up too, probably."

Silence. Breathing. Peace.

"I guess I'd better go to bed," Lainie finally said, stifling a yawn.

Too lazy to answer right away. The clock ticked, tocked. A minute passed. "Think I'll sit awhile," Wind River said, slow and relaxed.

Lainie nodded sleepily, stood, and took a step toward the stairs. "Wind River?. . . Ah . . ." She paused, groped helplessly for a more substantive parting.

"Yeah?"

He looked so friendly, so safe. Like an old Santa Claus, resting at last after a thousand trips around the world. There was a lump in Lainie's throat, and for a moment, inexplicably, she thought she might cry. "Nothing," she said quickly, adding a bright little smile so he wouldn't see how she felt. "Just good night, I guess."

Wind River's hands rested lightly on the arms of the chair. His knuckles looked big and bony, even to him. "Night," he replied softly.

Lainie walked across the room, stopped and turned around, and came back. She knelt by his chair, leaned forward, and kissed him on the cheek.

Wind River couldn't begin to remember when anyone had kissed him like that. He stared at her, let his right hand touch her hair, push her bangs out of her eyes. "If I could have crossed your trail about forty years ago," he said, his voice all gravelly, "we could have had us a time, girl."

"A swell time."

"Fourth of July, every day."

"Uh-unh. No," Lainie said, shaking her head. "Not on Mondays, Wednesdays, and Fridays."

"Oh?" Wind River's brows raised quizzically.

Lainie rose and left, turned at the doorway. "We would have saved them for Christmas."

She was gone, her footsteps light on the stairs. Wind River continued to stare into the fire while the clock ticked and tocked. While he watched, the logs shifted and popped, sending a ruby ember sailing through the air to land at the edge of the hearth near his foot. He lifted a bootheel to stamp it out, but then, his foot hovering over the ember, changed his mind. Eventually, the coal faded, and died.

22

Harry Lieght sat up, swung his legs over the side of the bed, and stood. The room started to spin, but he focused on the window-shade pull until the walls and window slowed and stopped. His left leg touching the mattress for support, he walked slowly to the foot of the bed and caught hold of the brass knob on the bedstead. "So far, so good, Harry," he mumbled. Sweat ran down his sides and his knees trembled. "Don't stop now."

The brass was cold to his touch. He picked up one foot, set it down carefully, then repeated the sequence. Damned if he'd shuffle, he reached the other end of the foot of the bed and pulled himself around the corner. Only three feet to go and he could rest. Five steps. He counted them, concentrating on each, and finally twisted to his right and sat heavily. For a moment, he thought he was going to throw up, but the nausea quickly subsided, which he took as a good sign. His strength was returning, thanks to Mildred Smith's home cooking.

A drop of sweat ran down the side of his cheek. Harry wiped it away, adjusted the gauze the doctor had wrapped around his head. The damned bandage had kept him awake half the night before with the tape tugging at his ears and hair. Stitches or no stitches, he wasn't going to try sleeping another night with it on. The hell with it. A man was as sick as he let himself feel. He pushed himself back on the bed, saw his pajama cuffs had rolled down over his feet, and stretched forward to pull them back up to his calves. Mildred's deceased husband had been a tall man. Not as broad at the shoulders, though, Harry thought, unbuttoning the tops and fanning himself with them.

A knock sounded at the door. Lieght tensed. Well enough to remember that there would be those looking for him in the same way and for the same reason that he was looking for Roman Phillips, he scooted up in the bed so he could reach the porcelain pitcher on the nightstand. It wasn't much, as weapons went, but better than nothing. "Come in," he said.

The Widow Smith entered, took one look at him, and made a beeline for the bed. "Mr. Lieght!" she exclaimed. "The doctor told you in the strictest terms not to exert yourself."

"It's Harry, remember?" he said, letting go of the pitcher.

Mildred Smith set down the tray, punched up the pillows, and pushed him back against them. "You are taking liberties, Mr. Lieght."

"And you love it, don't you?"

Lieght's pajama tops flopped open, revealing a hairless chest ridged with muscles. Mildred tried not to look as she pulled the sheet over him. "You have the nerve," she said, flustered. "Here only two days and already acting like the king of the roost."

She was buxom, a little thick-waisted, and had a pretty face that would have looked good on a cameo. Lieght's eyes started at her thighs, rose upward to her hips, waist, breasts, and finally eyes. "I fell on my head," he said, feeling the life stir in him and knowing he was going to get better a hell of a lot faster than any of them thought, "not my pecker."

"Harry!" she exclaimed, shocked. "I mean, Mr. Lieght. Really!"

"Oh, come off it, Mildred." He stared into her eyes without blinking, held her to the side of the bed by mere suggestion. "You've been married, you know what the story is." His head jerked in a gesture that took in the rest of the house. "They've all gone to work. I heard them clumping down the hall." He reached up and cupped one of her heavy, round breasts through the black dress. "We're alone."

Mildred jumped away from him as if burned. Trembling, her breathing labored, she covered her breast with one hand. "Mr. Lieght . . ." she finally said.

His eyes narrowed.

"Harry, then," she quickly amended. "You simply must behave yourself. You and your city ways are . . . entirely out of place . . . in this house."

"And have been for too long?" Lieght asked, knowing she was enjoying the interplay. He stretched, and his pectorals, silken smooth, leaped and bulged.

Mildred's face turned beet red. "You do not own this place, Harry Lieght," she said with difficulty.

"No. You do," Lieght agreed, managing to sound contrite, but never letting his eyes stray from hers. "And what you say goes. Nothing happens here" — his voice, low and taut with animal sexuality, rumbled in his chest— "in this room and in this bed—unless you want it to. And whatever does happen is nobody's business, nobody's decision but your own."

"Well, that's good, because nothing's *going* to happen," she declared emphatically, at the same time bursting into a flurry of activity. She straightened his covers again, though they didn't need straightening, poured him a fresh glass of water. "And if you keep up that kind of talk, I'll send you back to Lode Benedict."

Lieght winced comically at the idea, drawing a laugh from her.

"Here. Drink this," she said, handing him the glass. "I'm supposed to see that you get plenty of liquids."

Lieght took the glass, made sure his hand touched hers. "You're the boss," he said, noticing she held on longer than necessary. He leered at her over the rim of the glass as he drank.

Head cocked to one side, Mildred regarded him seriously. She didn't believe for an instant that he had given up, but that was because she did not want to believe. She had been alone for five years, left to lie in a lonely bed by a none too bright husband who was careless enough to eat his lunch in the path of a falling tree. In those passing, passionless years, work had taken up most of her time and energy, but now strange feelings were waking inside her. The stirrings had begun two nights earlier when Dr. Taft had brought Lieght to her and she had bathed him. Sick as he was, his body was magnificent, and later on, clutching her blanket in a taut fist, she had waked damp and quaking from an erotic dream. Frightened, she had tried to pretend nothing had happened, and swore to be as coldly professional with Lieght as she was with the meanest lumberjack or drummer.

Resolve was not foreign to Mildred Smith. She had always been a forceful woman, one not given to being dominated, one used to having her own way. But this time, resolve was short-lived. Supine, recovering from overexposure, a nasty bout with a severe cold, and still feeling the effects of the concussion, Lieght still exuded a blatant, uninhibited sexuality that threatened to overpower her quickly unraveling self-control. From the moment she walked into his room the next morning, and each time she saw him thereafter—to take his temperature, to bring him food or liquids, to straighten his bed—the palms of her hands broke out in a sweat and her heart raced insanely. And from the first time he looked into her eyes, it was impossible not to know what he wanted from her. Though she was proud of the reputation she had guarded jealously for the past five years, it was becoming more and more difficult for her not to respond.

Lieght had had his way with enough women to know exactly what she was thinking. "Anything else you want me to do?" he asked, pointedly staring at her breasts.

Mildred refilled the glass, left it on the bedside table. "I'll let you know," she said, surprised at her own coyness, and blushing again. She drew herself up, became all business. "Oh, yes. Mr. Weldon is here to see you again. I had him wait downstairs in case you were feeling poorly, but I see the error of my ways. A man as quick with a tongue as you are can certainly have visitors."

Their little game was over, Lieght knew. For the moment, at least. His manner changed abruptly and he dismissed her with a wave of his hand. "Send him up," he ordered. "And see we're left alone." Mildred obeyed without question. Pleased, Lieght helped himself to a cup of coffee, noted that his hand barely shook. A strong man with a strong constitution recovered quickly.

Lewis Weldon entered the room after knocking. Fidgeting nervously, his fingers toying with the brim of his western hat, he stood by the door. His ears were wind-burned from the cold. "My Lord, you are looking well," he said. "Dr. Taft's business will pick up once folks see what he did for you."

"Taft, hell," Lieght growled, setting down the coffee cup. "I'm doing it myself."

"Maybe. Just the same, you can thank your lucky stars Lode didn't bring you to Doc Bufker." He snickered. "Though I guess he wouldn't've, seeing as it was Bufker who sewed his mouth all crooked that time the marshal's dog chewed on him. Oh, yes," he added, approaching the bed to hand Lieght a small roll of bills, "here's your deposit on the horse. Thought you'd like it back."

Lieght's voice was flat and emotionless. "I'm not interested in a medical history of Lode Benedict," he said, tossing the money on the nightstand without counting it. "What about the boy? Anything new? Still in town?"

Weldon shook his head. "I don't know what all he's been up to, because he didn't come by my place again. He did get the mules, though. Nusken brought them in late yesterday. The boy must have got up early this morning, because he had them loaded and headed up Silverado and out of town when I was shaving. Been gone at least two hours by this time."

"Back to Elkhorn?"

"Don't see where else he could go, heading that way and riding Wind River's horse. Like I said yesterday, if you're still worrying about your daughter, there's no need. Wind River might be a little touched, but he knows more about living in those mountains than most people around here have forgotten. With his savvy and all that food young Phillips packed out, that girl of yours is safe as she could be."

"It's not safe I'm thinking of!" Lieght roared, pounding the bed with both fists, putting on a show for the storekeeper. A slow smile of diabolical intent backed Weldon away from the bed. "You have any daughters, Weldon?"

"No!" Weldon blurted, the word popping out of him like a cork out of a bottle. He gulped. "A son. Two sons, that is."

"You'd better tell them to be careful with whose daughters they play around with," Lieght said, his voice a menacing rumble again as he stoked the storekeeper's fear. The reaction was predictable. A quick shake of the head, the Adam's apple bobbing. Lieght could almost hear Weldon's gut rumble. Fear did that to most men. For others, like himself, it was a food of sorts, sustenance. Under the circumstances, a curative. He almost laughed, decided instead on the barest hint of a smile. The same smile a snake used before it struck. Oh, they knew. The victim always knew. "And what about my car?" he asked suddenly, changing the subject. That was part of the technique, too. It kept them off stride. "Is it fixed?"

Weldon wet his lips, stared at his boots, then his hands. He adjusted the crimp in the crown of his hat, looked over Lieght's head and out the window. "No," he said.

Lieght sighed. "Why not?"

"Nance and Newkirk never brought it in. I guess when they heard you were lost, they just figured that Ford was theirs by forfeit."

"You guess."

"Yes, sir." Weldon's hands were sweating. He wiped them off one by one on his trousers. "I was going to go out there, but ... Well, I'm just surprised Nick Vertina even let you hire them. Newkirk's a wild one, and big enough to have things his own way. Nance is mean as sin when he's been drinking. Pure 'D' mean. Nobody'll hire either one of them except during prime logging season, and then everybody who's strong enough to miss his foot when he pees works."

The soft popping sound was Lieght's knuckles. "Well, now ..." he said, flexing one finger at a time.

Weldon's eyes bugged and he hid his hands inside his hat. He couldn't stand the sound. "What I could do," he said, a little too loudly, "is ask Bill Langly to go out there. He's the town constable and that cabin they live in is inside his jurisdiction, I think. If it isn't, I'll see that he notifies the sheriff down in Idaho Springs, so you needn't worry."

"I won't." Lieght interwined his fingers, turned his palms out, and finished with one collective pop. "You tell him about any of this yet?"

"No. But I figured on—"

"Don't. I'll handle it myself."

"But—"

"I have other arrangements in mind," Lieght snapped, his patience wearing thin. "Forget about the car." He leaned forward, and his flat, humorless smile hinted of awful promises that reawakened the fear in Weldon. "Forget about everything," he said, oh, so slowly and clearly. "That's the least you can do for the money I paid you. You *capisce*, my friend?"

Weldon didn't understand what *capisce* meant, but the message was clear His throat was so dry he couldn't swallow without it hurting. There was more to the city stranger than met the eye, but none of it was Weldon's business. And frankly, he admitted privately, he didn't want it to be because Lieght frightened him too much. Nodding, his head bobbing up and down, he backed away from the bed and, glad to wash his hands of the whole affair, hurried out the door.

Harry Lieght watched him go, grinned wolfishly, and settled back to another cup of coffee. Outside, the shadows clocked the morning as they shrank under the trees. With each passing blade of grass, Lieght felt better. He was regaining his strength and he had a plan. He couldn't remember what had happened to his gun, but that was no problem. Weapons were always available. What was more important was the plan, simple to the point of elegance. Sinking into himself, he visualized its every facet, watched it as he would a movie on the silver screen. He was so engrossed, he did not hear the Widow Smith enter his room, nor see the tray laden with sandwiches and a glass of milk. He paid no attention when she arranged the bedside table, didn't even look as she unbuttoned her dress, slipped out of it, and climbed into his bed.

He noticed her then.

23

"Wind River? Wind Riverrr!"

Lainie waved her arms, moved farther into the street, and called again. She could see him halfway up the tree-dotted slope that led to the graveyard, standing silently, facing Rampage Valley. It was the second afternoon after the night they had danced and laughed together, and ever since then he had avoided her. What was eating at him, why he had retreated into brooding silence, she couldn't imagine. Wind River was a puzzle to her, plain and simple. She wasn't about to pester him, though. If he wanted to be alone, so be it. She had no intention of making a nuisance of herself. No intention at all, even if she was half out of her mind with loneliness.

"I'm going crazy!" she shouted. "Do you hear? I'm going crazyyy!"

". . . going crazyyy . . . azyyy . . . azyyy . . . azyyy . . ." the hills replied.

Whether Wind River didn't hear or only pretended not to hear, Lainie couldn't tell. Either way, he didn't answer, only walked away, uphill. Feeling more foolish than before, Lainie started walking down Main Street, kicking clumps of dried mud, raising little puffs of dust. She had to do something to take her mind off the interminable waiting and the crushing boredom.

Impulsively, she turned toward the Gold Nugget Saloon. The steps creaked, the boardwalk answered. The swinging doors groaned on their hinges and screeched in agony as she eased them back into place. The interior was dimly lit by a hole in the roof. Lainie stared silently at the cobwebs. To her left was a waist-high bar running the length of the north wall. The rest of the space was littered with the debris of decades: tables and chairs both broken and sound, shards of amber and brown and green bottle glass, shiny slivers that crunched underfoot. Peeled and faded posters decorated the walls. Some advertised melodramatic productions of years gone by: *The Villain of Dry Gulch. Bess of Bandera. The Hero's Dilemma. The Kidnapped Bride.* Other more brightly colored lithographs touted the benefits of sundry elixirs, her favorite, after a quick inspection, Dr. Bent's Formula Tonic. The amazing nostrum was guaranteed to cure grippe, bowel disorders, tooth disease, various debilitating male and female dysfunctions and ailments, and had actually grown another leg for a Civil War amputee. As proof of this miraculous claim, a series of drawings showed a Yankee officer being wounded in battle; recovering, minus a leg, in a wheelchair; and finally dancing with his loving wife at a dress ball in Washington, D.C.

"Can't dispute proof like that." Lainie chuckled.

Her voice sounded strangely out of place in the oppressive stillness. Almost as if the room didn't want voices, as if it had grown so unused to the sound of humans that its walls shrank back from the contact. Pensive, Lainie walked to the bar and leaned on it. Behind the bar, a cracked and dusty image of herself looked back at her.

"Why?" she whispered, hurt. Two days — well, two full days at midnight — and he hadn't talked to her. Not because she was ugly. Her clothes were nothing to brag about, certainly, but her face was pretty. Something she had said? But she hadn't said anything. They'd parted friends that night, and the next morning he had greeted her with silence. If she could divine the reason Wind River was avoiding her, she might be able to approach him with some sort of rebuttal, but he hadn't given her a clue. Only silence.

Pride darted like fire through her veins. "Well, what do I

care?" she said aloud. "Crazy old man. Who needs him?"

She sighed, tapped her fingers on the bar. She did, that's who, and felt guilty for demeaning him. Liked him, too, moreover, and what of it? So maybe he was crazy. Maybe she was, too. All her old friends would think so, to see her now. She was improperly married, had been an accomplice to a theft, was hiding out like a common criminal, wearing men's clothing, traipsing up and down mountains, living alone in a ghost-ridden, ancient, falling-down hotel. But was that really her? Had Joanne Elaine Brewster, the girl in the flaking, dusty mirror surrounded by the gilded gold of long ago, changed that much? Were her friends right? Had she become, as they would certainly say, a lady of mystery, a woman of the world?

"No," she whispered to herself. "Still just a seamstress from Denver, no matter what has happened." A woman not of mystery, but of cross stitches and hems and button loops. They were fools, she and Roman, to try to be more than that. But maybe God had an extra sprinkling of sacred providence for fools. More than a sprinkling, she amended. A bushel basket might be in order.

Sighing, she turned away from the bar and, looking down, discovered her arms were dusty from wrist to elbow. It figured, she thought, taking in the room. Dust, broken tables, broken chairs, broken bottles. Broken. That was a good word for Elkhorn. Her life, too, she thought, conjuring up her father's dark, kind face. He smiled at her and she felt her heart swell with longing. She had been short-tempered with him in his last days, heaped guilt on him in proportion to the pain she'd endured as he slowly degenerated in an alcoholic blur. Her father nodded forgiveness. Or was that merely wishful thinking?

I stitch other people's ragged edges, she thought. I mend their tattered clothes. I have about as much value as ...

God, she loathed self-pity. But there was nothing else to do in Elkhorn.

It was the girl. That was the trouble. The girl. And the kiss he could still feel moist on his cheek. And knowing she was young and had her whole life ahead of her, while his was far behind. Face as craggy and weathered as the peaks, eyes of flint, lips of frozen metal, Wind River watched the dull, anvil-colored advent of the coming storm leech the last of the blue tint from the spectacle of the sky. When a man lived in the mountains long enough, he could feel change coming a long way off.

"Man lives here long enough, he learns to feel the changes coming a long way off," Creed said, stealing Wind River's thoughts and farting in the process. "Wolves," he added. Razor-sharp, his knife peeled away minute curls of wood.

"Be fine with me if you took them damned wolves somewhere else," Wind River grumbled, out of sorts. He shook the shavings off the tops of his feet. "And keep your trash off my boots, too, old man."

"Old!" Creed exclaimed. "I ain't old."

"You're older'n me."

"Bullshit!" The mountain man marched over to his grave, pointed down at the cross. "Seventy years, it reads, and you're seventy-one. You can see for yourself. Add it up. Seventy years old when Butch Pepperdine put the punc'tiation at the end of my sentence."

"That was thirty-five years ago," Wind River scoffed. "Seems you would've forgot all that crap by now."

"Forgot, hell!" Creed roared. "Jumpin' hallelujah, boy. That was an all-fired important day in my life, seein' as it was the last. Days like that sort of tend to stick to mind. Which," he added archly, "you'll find out for yourself one of these days."

Wind River wouldn't be baited. "Thirty-five plus seventy is a hundred and five," he said, the numbers on his side. "You gonna tell me it ain't?"

"What if it is? Them last thirty-five don't count. You can't make 'em."

The first rule was, when you have an edge, don't let it go. "Can and do," Wind River said with a smug smile. He drew the number in the air with his forefinger. "One . . . hundred . . . and . . . five, by God."

Creed's head ducked, the way it did when he was thinking hard. "You're wrong, Wind River," he said, his voice strangely soft. "Plumb wrong. You're countin' all the years, but all the years don't count. It's only the ones when you can feel the sun warm on your cheek that count. It's them when a man's breath turns his beard into a bib of ice during the winter months. It's them with women hot and clawin' your back, and then all of a sudden smooth like a glacier pond and callin' your name loud enough for only you to hear. It's them when you're so dadgum tired you can't even feel the blisters your boots has worn on your feet, or so almighty filled with the fire of far horizons you're ready to take on all comers and have enough grit left to face the varmint in his den. It's them when you're full enough to sleep and empty enough to be kept awake, them with tears and laughter and lovin' and hatin', and bein' *alive*, Wind River. Alive!"

He looked down at the stag he was carving, and in his passion had deantlered. "Rest don't count, boy. Don't count 'cause all they are is emptiness and loneliness, and the wind blowin' through you like it does the trees." The bitterness seeped through his voice as pitch seeps through pine bark. "Sounds prettier in the trees, Wind River. Lots prettier."

"Well," Wind River said, melancholy now and not wanting to be. He kicked a pine cone, watched it bounce off a rock and roll all wobbly downhill toward town, where, barely seen in an upstairs window of the Victorian Palace, a tattered yellow curtain wafted outward on the breeze like an invitational flag waved by one of the girls who used to live and work there.

"Better follow it, old son," Creed said in a hollow voice. "Pine cone knows the way you ought to go. Better get inside. It'll be dark soon."

"I ain't afraid of the dark."

"No. But you will be."

Wind River snorted, walked away.

"They still don't count, Kid. Them thiry-five years never wore a single line in my face," Creed shouted after him. "It's the livin' years that age a man! You hear me, Kid?"

Wind River didn't respond. Creed dug his fists into the deep pockets of his capote. Above him, the clouds crawled slowly by, like slugs on a gray wall. The world was donning its mourning rags. Autumn was a corpse, winter the coming king. And Creed, alone now in the graveyard where his bones lay six feet deep, watched them with angry eyes and cried out.

"Weeeelllll!?"

In the hotel kitchen, Wind River heard. And walking across the street, her shoulders hunched against the cold, Lainie paused and listened to the rising north wind scream through the hotel eaves. It almost sounded like a voice, or a scream. Hurrying then, she shivered and continued on her way.

Lainie ate stew. Wind River ate stew. Lainie's spoon scraped the bowl. Wind River's coffee mug clattered on the table. That was supper.

Dark had come to stay the night. In the dining room, Wind River sorted out and piled the load of wood he had brought in. Lainie fiddled with the Victrola. The crank turned, wound tight, but the table refused to rotate when she released the catch. Something jarred loose on the bumpy ride from Mountain City must have finally broken. Peeved, she gave the machine a sharp slap and pursed her lips. Nothing happened. She wiggled the release three or four times. Still nothing . "Damn!" she said, brushing back her bangs and beginning to pace the room. "I wish I smoked."

Wind River watched her out of the corner of his eye. "Nothing to be done about it, girl," he finally said, throwing a log into the fire and adjusting it with the toe of his boot.

Lainie glared at him, continued pacing.

"I know the feeling. Been there myself. It's like runnin' a bluff with the last coins to your name and sensin' the fellow across from you is fixin' to sweeten the pot and bump you right out of the game. Right out. And there you sit, not knowin' what to do, knowin' there's nothing you can do."

"Roman could fix it if he was here."

"Maybe so," Wind River admitted. "But he ain't. Weather kickin' up like this ..." He shrugged, left the sentence unfinished.

"Damn. I wish I drank."

"Wouldn't do no more for you than smokin'. Tell you what, though." He squeezed past her, headed for the kitchen. "Wait right there."

"I thought I might take a little walk to the other end of the room," Lainie said sarcastically. She could hear him rummaging around in the cabinets and drawers. "Whatever you're up to, it better be good," she hollered.

"Good as the other end of the room," Wind River said, coming back with a deck of cards in one hand and a box of matches in the other. He pulled a table in front of the fire, lit a cigar, and motioned for Lainie to sit across from him. "Matches are sort of tame, of course, but bein' as we don't—" He stopped, struck by a miraculous idea. "Damn! I plumb forgot! Don't suppose you'd want to bring out that money you hid, would you?"

Lainie rested her chin on her fists and slowly shook her head. "It won't work, Wind River."

"Won't, eh?" He dumped the matches on the table, divided them two to one in her favor. "Didn't think it would." He patted the deck of cards. "A California prayer book," he explained, spreading them out, gathering them in.

"Four suits for the four gospels, and all that?" Lainie asked.

"You got it, girl." Wind River beamed. "Now, honey, I am about to win every match you have to your name." He riffled the deck. "I trust providence has acquainted you with the illustrious game of five-card draw?"

Lainie sat up and squared her shoulders. "My father used to play. He taught me the rules."

"A wise and exemplary man," Wind River entoned. His palm reverently covered the deck. He fanned the cards face down across the surface of the table, closed the deck, flipped it, spread it face up, and briefly glanced at it. "All there," he announced, sliding the cards into a pile with his right thumbnail.

Two or three or ten times a winter, when the snow was

high and Wind River was on the verge of cabin fever, he brought out the cards and played with them. On those empty, white-filled days and nights, he dealt high, dealt low, cut out aces and treys, as his fancy chose. But a man had to practice every day to be good enough to play with the best, for the muscles, tendons, sinews, and bones to recall the minute movements with absolute precision. Those days were gone for good, though. The Wind River Kid was no more than a rusty deft, barely good enough to impress Lainie. He scooped up the deck, cut with his left hand alone. He held his hands apart. The cards literally exploded from one palm to the other. "That's the way we used to do it," he explained with a satisfied grin, and shuffled quickly, twice.

"Let's clear the air. Before we begin in earnest, *muchacha*, one brief hand of Mexican Sweat, a game taught to me by the *vaqueros* of old Mexico, where they have the courage to gamble and did so every day. A land of hot-tempered women and hotter-tempered men." The cards flew as he talked. "Five . . . six . . . seven cards dealt face down. You go first; turn over a card and bet if you want. Then it's my turn, and I keep turnin' up cards until I got you beat on the board, and then I bet, and it's your turn again."

Lainie's first card was the ten of spades. She bet one match.

"Now that's a sensible bet," Wind River said, calling and turning over an eight, a three, and another eight. "A pair," he said, betting four matches.

"Call," Lainie said, feeling reckless. She turned over an ace, a jack, and another ace.

"There you go," Wind River laughed. "Got my little pair beat. Bet 'em, girl!"

Lainie didn't fear losing. At least not matches. "Ten," she said, shoving them in.

"Normally I'd fold right now," Wind River said, "but seein' as it's just a *friendly* game . . ." He flipped a jack, a deuce, a five, and, his final card, another eight. "Three of a kind. Well, well . . . Let's see. You got three cards left an' a pair of aces . . . I'll bet"—he glowered at her, made up his mind rapidly—"five matches."

"And ten more," Lainie said, catching the spirit.

"Call. Turn 'em over."

"Seven of spades," Lainie entoned. "Darn! Three of diamonds." She looked at her hand, to Wind River. "An ace, right?"

Wind River gloated. "That's what it'll take. Wanta bet an extra ten?"

"Ah . . . No!" Lainie said, turning over the last card. "Oh, damn!"

"What?"

"I mean darn!" Lainie said, staring down at her losing pair of aces.

Wind River raked in his winnings. He laughed, shuffled the cards, cut the ace of spades, shuffled, cut the ace of spades again. "Old ace of spades keeps comin' up," he said, shuffling again and cutting the ace of hearts. He frowned at his mistake, then brightened at discovering the cause: Lainie had taken the spade ace somehow, as he proved by reaching out and plucking it from behind her ear. And what was that? The ace of diamonds behind the other ear?

"Mercy, girl! Shouldn't oughta hide cards that way. Win a hand but lose a gizzard. No percentage, girl. No percentage."

"Deal," Lainie said, laughing.

He did, the cards spinning out with dizzying speed. Lainie lost sixteen matches, then four, then nineteen on a hand she knew would win. She won two on a hand that should have won more, then lost those two plus eighteen when she thought she had caught him bluffing and he laid down three tens to beat her aces and fours. "Elk River is what they call them three tens," Wind River said, picking a piece of tobacco off his tongue. "Mighty good to me over the years. Won the precise amount you and the boy took off that Lieght fella with it once. Little town of Spur, in west Texas. Rode out of there the next morning with more money in my bedroll than the bank had in its vault. Fiesty young cowboy met me on the trail a few miles out of town and tried to talk me out of it." He grinned wickedly, remembering. "Didn't, of course."

"You killed him?" Lainie asked, horrified.

"Naw," Wind River drawled, dealing again. "I give him my saddlebags. The cheap ones full of cut-up newspaper."

He nodded toward Lainie's hand. "Hold 'em a little closer to your belly," he instructed. "Be surprised how much a fella can see without too much trouble a'tall."

The advice seemed to help. Lainie won two small hands, folded the next before Wind River could bet, then won again. Cagey, Wind River fed her three queens, then a fourth on the draw. When she raised him, he bumped back and watched the excitement light up her eyes. Another two raises and she raked in as many matches as she'd lost since they'd started playing.

Wind River figured she was as off guard as she'd ever be. "Where's the money?" he asked, hoping she'd answer without thinking.

Lainie opened her mouth to answer, then stopped. A slow smile played at the corners of her eyes. "What?" she asked innocently, not looking at him.

"Where's the money, dadburn it?"

Lainie concentrated on separating her newly won matches into piles of ten. "I don't know," she said.

"Oh, come on, girl!" It was beginning to look as if he'd let her win almost fifty matches for nothing. Wind River put a rein on his temper. "Now, I know, and you know, that you know where it is."

"Of course," Lainie said. "It's hidden."

"I *know* that." He took a deep breath. "I ain't goin' to take it. Hell, I wouldn't do that for the world. I'm just curious, is all. You can tell me."

". . . fifty-one . . . fifty-two . . . fifty-three," Lainie said, pushing the last three into the center of the table for her ante. "No, I can't. Roman hid it."

"Hrumph!" Fifty-three matches! To a girl! "Blackfoot!"

"Blackfoot?"

"An Injun. A Blackfoot Injun. You'd 've made a good one."

"I don't know anything about black-footed Indians," Lainie said, shuffling. "Are you going to ante?"

Wind River pushed in three matches, sat with his fists on the edge of the table. She knew. Knew damned well where it was. "Yeah," he said, furious at being beaten at his own game. "Are you goin' to deal?"

Her victory was short-lived. Lainie's pile of matches

dwindled slowly but surely. Talk was limited to bets and the spare vocabulary of poker. Lainie was down to her last pile of ten matches when Wind River stopped in the middle of a deal and cocked his head to one side. "What?" Lainie asked.

"Shhh!"

Lainie strained to listen. At first she thought she was hearing the wind, but then the sound repeated itself, louder this time, unmistakably the coarse bellow of a mule. "Roman!" she whispered, rising from the table and racing toward the front door. "Roman! Roman!"

Roman was tethering the Appaloosa to the hitching rail in front of the hotel. Behind him, on a lead line, stood three mules. Lainie gave a cry and ran into the street. Roman caught her as she wrapped her arms around his neck. "You all right?" he asked, his throat hoarse from the cold ride.

"Now," Lainie said. "I thought you'd never get here."

"Neither did I." He pulled the glove off one hand and cupped her cheek. "God, you're a sight for sore eyes."

"Your hand is freezing."

"My everything is freezing." He shielded her from the cold with his body and kissed her again. "Oh, Lainie, Lainie. You don't know . . ." He stopped himself just in time. How frightened he had been, he had almost said, but it wouldn't have done to frighten her in turn. There was time. A week, the doctor had said. He'd heard him. Three more days, at least, before Lieght could start out after them, and by then they'd be long gone. "Hey!" he said with a laugh. One arm wrapped around her, he started up the steps. "We better get you inside before you turn into a chunk of ice. How's the old man?"

"The same," Lainie said, starting to shiver. "He's been teaching me things."

"Oh? What?"

"How to make Damnation Stew. How to play Mexican Sweat."

"Glad I asked," Roman said, fighting the wind for the door.

Wind River was standing in front of the fire. Roman shed his coat as he walked across the room. The two men appraised each other for a moment, then shook hands. "Hello,

Wind River," Roman said, genuinely relieved to see him again. "Thanks for taking care of her. You both look fine."

"Glad you made it all right," Wind River said, secretly proud of Roman, even if he couldn't figure out exactly why. "Rough trip for a greenhorn. When'd you leave?"

Roman stretched, held his hands above the flames, and rubbed them briskly. "Three days ago. Damned mules."

"They can be a trial, 'less you know how to treat 'em," Wind River admitted.

"I learned," Roman said grimly. "Finally took a pine bough to them this morning. Never thought I'd see the day when I'd say that horse of yours is fast, but he sure is in comparison to them." Roman paused, looked a little embarrassed. "Ah, Wind River?"

"Yeah."

"You, ah … Well, would you mind taking them to the barn?" He grinned self-consciously. "So Lainie and I could be alone for a few minutes?"

"Sure," Wind River said, his good nature souring. Lainie's man was back. He went to the kitchen, came back with his coat on. "All right with you two, I'll go ahead and sleep up to Muenster's tonight."

"Bought a bottle for you," Roman called to him. "It's in the top pack on the lead mule."

There was some hope for the boy yet, Wind River thought, pausing in the lobby to pull on his gloves. He looked back through the dining-room door, saw they were already on their way up the stairs. "Lord, Lord," he said, pushing through the front door onto the boardwalk. "What I'd give for a — " He stopped dead in his tracks, stared in disbelief at the mules. "A white one!" he whispered under his breath. He took the steps slowly, walked gingerly around the mules. Two were mud-colored, but one was the color of dirty snow. "A goddamn white mule," he repeated, glaring at the Appaloosa. "How come you let him do that?" he asked.

The stallion chomped on his bit and rolled his eyes in indignation at being tethered to a hitching post as if he were a mindless colt. "Serves you right," Wind River said, loosing the reins and throwing them over the horse's neck. "And just for that, you can take 'em to the barn, too," he added, slapping the Appaloosa on the rump.

Anixous to get out of the wind, the Appaloosa started, and stopped immediately. "What the? . . ." Wind River looked back. Forelegs planted firmly, neck stretched against the strain of the line, the lead mule had decided he wasn't going anywhere. "Git on! Hie up!" Wind River shouted, jerking on the line. Nothing happened. Slowly, cussing every step of the way, Wind River walked hand over hand down the line and looked the recalcitrant animal square in the eyes. "Knothead," he said, raising one foot. The animal's eyes twisted sideways as he caught the motion. "You see that foot? I ain't no city boy. Now you get along or I'll capital 'P' personally kick your ass up around your ears so that every time you break wind you'll hear cannon fire. You savvy?"

The mule rolled his eyes in baleful fashion, but took a step forward. "That's better," Wind River said, clucking to the Appaloosa to move him along. "Me and you'll get along just fine, long as you remember I don't take no puckies from no mule."

The barn was warm compared to Main Street. Happy to have something useful to do to take his mind off Lainie, Wind River lit a lantern and set to work. He pulled off the Appaloosa's saddle, rubbed him down, gave him a pail of oats and a bucket of water. He tied the mules in the open center of the livery, unloaded them, cringing when he had to touch the white, then led each into a separate stall for feed and water and a quick rubdown with an old tow sack. The supplies stashed in the tack room, the bottle Roman had bought tucked safely under his arm, he surveyed the scene, blew out the lantern, and left the way he had come.

The wind had changed, was kicking in from the south and bringing warmer, moist air. A light snow had started to fall. Wind River closed the livery doors, leaned against them, and opened the bottle. He always liked it when it started to snow. It was as if the snow brought a hush over the world, as if everything stopped for those few minutes to make sure the first flakes hit the ground without hurting themselves. The whiskey tasted smooth and burned with a slow fire. Not like the rotgut he usually bought, Wind River realized, taking a second, slow sip and by way of thanks tilting the bottle in the direction of the hotel.

The upstairs windows were dark black rectangles against the lighter wood. "Know what they're about," Wind River muttered wistfully. "Got me a case of Cupid's cramp myself." Feeling sorry for himself, he wondered exactly when his life had taken such an empty turn, when the future had passed him by and left him alone and standing on an empty street in an empty town—1892, when he first returned to Elkhorn? 1900, when the century changed? Something about a century changing. Horns, whistles, shouting, hugging and kissing. Only no one had invited him. 1910? Been a war around then. No, that was later on. Came with the cars and even aeroplanes he'd heard of but had never seen, except in pictures. And worse, too. Like Luke Welch, down in Mountain City. He'd gone off to that war and come back with his lungs half rotted away. 1920? Tarnation, but they spun by fast, and him not even realizing how fast until a pair of younkers came through to show him how different he'd become. Them and the Piggly Wiggly and Daisy turnin' a perfectly good whorehouse into a beauty parlor and the damned government takin' away all the good whiskey . . .

"Least there's some hope on that score," Wind River said, taking another snort and then perking up his ears.

"What's that?" he said, stepping into the street.

The south wind hummed, carried the faint sound of a piano. Wind River cupped his ear, heard it again. A piano, sure enough, playing a rinky-tink melody. The music sounded as if it came from the Victorian Palace, but the ornate gambling hall, saloon, and brothel had been empty for three decades. Impossible, Wind River thought, his brain all muddled by the whiskey and the night and the loneliness. Utterly, totally impossible, except that he heard it.

Heard the music. The music! The bottle forgotten, he dropped it and took off at a stiff-legged run. The piano player kept on playing. Not really a tune Wind River could make out, but who cared? All that counted was hurrying before it stopped. Was he dreaming? he wondered. "Don't care!" he panted, stumbling on a frozen rut. "Don't care. Just don't want to wake up if I am."

Not until he had held Angelina in his arms one more time. Oh Christ! Spanish Angelina, her full sweet body ripe as cherries in the fall, fragrant as wild mint. Angelina of the pert, high breasts, of the sloe eyes, black and smoldering with lust. Angelina with fingers as deft as any gambler's, with strong thighs and firm buttocks, with flicking tongue that left a man with memories that lingered like a fever all his days.

Wind River's boots clattered on the boardwalk. He hit the door, kicked it open, and rushed inside, where the fetid, musty scent of waiting women assailed him. He stopped dead still, sniffed the air for Angelina's perfume, and thought he found it. "Angelina!" he called.

He could barely distinguish the battered shapes of the once gaudy furniture, barely discern the fancy adornments beneath the accumulation of dust. Did she answer? Was that her laugh from beyond the parlor curtains?

"Angelina!" he whispered, rushing across the room.

"Angelina!" he cried, thrusting aside the curtains.

"AAARRRROOOAAAOOO!!" Ten feet of devil-eyed, bristle-backed grizzly, remnants of the piano still caught in his razor-sharp claws, blocked the doorway.

"Jeeeesssussss!" Wind River shrieked, and ducked as the talons swept over his skull and tangled in the curtains. The drapes fell on top of the fire-eyed behemoth.

"Goddamn!" Wind River bawled, hitting the front door at a run that would have shamed a younger man.

The grizzly tore the curtain from his head and bellowed a deafening challenge. Front legs swinging in great arcs, he splintered the parlor door and lumbered through the front room, leaving demolished chairs and tables in his wake.

"Yeee-owwww!" Wind River shouted, racing toward the hotel. Behind him, the front wall of the Victorian Palace exploded outward and Scar rambled in pursuit. Wind River's lead shrank as the bear gathered steam.

"Ain't gonna make it," Wind River's mind screamed. He could smell the animal's stench, hear his clawed pads hitting the ground and his heavy breathing. He envisioned himself being torn to shreds, tossed and mauled. The hotel might as well have been a mile away. Pain knifed through Wind River's side and he felt himself slowing. Not this way, he thought. Not this ...

He stumbled, pitched forward at the same time an explosion rang out from the balcony of the hotel. Wind River rolled to one side, caught a glimpse of beautiful blossoms of orange flame, and recognized the sound of a heavy gun firing. Above him, Scar reared and bellowed, caught at the slugs scoring his hide, and, howling in pain, veered and loped into the safety of the alley. Seconds later, the hills echoed to his thrashing among the trees as the brute lumbered off to lick his wounds.

Spent, Wind River lay in the street, watched as Lainie and Roman ran from the hotel to his side. "Damn critter's back," he gasped as they helped him to his feet. "Nothin's changed. Creed was foolin' me. Tryin' to trick me into stayin'." His side hurt, his legs felt like rubber. "Won't let go," he muttered. He sagged, was aware he was losing consciousness, but didn't care. "Won't let go ..."

He could hear them talking, knew they were caring for him. Cold changed to warmth as he was laid on something soft. Lainie's face filtered through the haze. Her voice sounded hollow, as if she were far away. "Do you think he'll be all right?" she asked, tucking a blanket around him.

"In a while," Roman said. Wind River could barely hear him. "Heat up some coffee. He'll need something warm to drink. I'll watch him."

The pain in his side was going away. Lainie disappeared, too. Roman was sitting at a table next to him. He was doing something with his hands. Wind River decided he was in a chair in front of the fire. He stared into the flames, tried to wet the inside of his mouth with his tongue. "It's back," he finally croaked.

"What?" Roman asked, getting up and going to Wind River's side.

Wind River looked at him, struggled to focus. Roman had a gun in one hand, a rag in the other. That explained it. Cleaning the gun. Hope for the boy yet. "It's back. The devil bear." He struggled to stand. "It's back."

"Wait a minute, Wind River," Roman said, gently pushing the old man back into the chair. "He's awake, Lainie. We could use that coffee now," he called.

"Come back for me," Wind River insisted. "Scar's ghost."

"It sure as hell looked like a real bear to me," Roman said. "It ran like a real bear, sounded like a real bear. If it was a ghost, you crazy old fart, how come my bullets drove it off?" Roman shook his head, not without sympathy. After all, he had his own nemesis, who was altogether real.

"Ask her," Wind River said, nodding toward Lainie, who had just come from the kitchen. "She seen the graveyard. What he done."

"It was just a bear, Wind River," Lainie said, handing him a cup of coffee.

"No such thing as 'just' a bear. Least not that one." Wind River stared accusingly at Roman. "First you buy a white mule, then Scar shows up, all in one night."

"What's the matter with a white mule, for Chrissake?" Roman asked.

"A white mule is what they call a gambler's ghost."

Roman looked puzzled. "Who?"

"They, damn it!"

"Well, it's all 'they' had to sell. I took what I could get."

"It's all comin' together," Wind River said, ignoring his coffee. "That silvertip grizzly wants this town and then he wants me. He's walkin' death brought by the white mule and Creed both. The longer I stay here, the shorter my time."

"Silvertip Falls," Lainie whispered, nudging Roman. "That's where it got its name. From the bear."

Wind River's stare had become dreamy, as if he focused not on the young couple before him but on a drama in the past. "I figured to be safe here in a dyin' town, but the Pepperdine brothers followed me and found me. I tried to bluff my way out, told 'em I'd face 'em at Silvertip Falls." He nodded, visualizing the scene. "I was afraid, so damn scared I couldn't even manage a good sweat. The dry scares are the worst. Your flesh feels like a dead man's. Cold and dry as last year's fallen pine boughs.

"I went to Silvertip Falls, all right. Waited for the Pepperdines in a cut in the rock behind the water. Butch and

Dupree Pepperdine showed, right on schedule. What I figured was they'd wait awhile and then leave, assuming I'd left town, but I hadn't counted on Aden Creed." Wind River's voice sank to a mere whisper, so Lainie and Roman had to lean close. "He come to stand with me, only he found himself alone. I couldn't move. My nerve was gone, used up, so I just stood there and listened while Creed called their hand."

Wind River stopped. His eyes were misty, and when he leaned back and closed them, a tear was squeezed from one and ran down his cheek. "Christ, but he was magnificent," he went on. "He fired his Hawken and killed Dupree right off, then charged across the creek, right into Butch's gun. I could see the bullets hittin' him, slowin' him but never stoppin' him, saw him take three rounds in the chest and one more in the gut. Somehow, though, he made it to the other side and caved in Butch's head with the barrel of that Hawken before he fell." The old man rubbed a hand across his eyes, blinked them open. "He died slow. Layin' there turned toward the falls like he could see me hidin' in that cut, he died slow. And the shame of it has kept me here since." He sighed. "The Wind River Kid." He snorted in disgust. "Blue lightning with a gun." He stared into the flames. "The Wind River Kid."

24

Three in the morning and miles from Elkhorn and an old man's nightmares, Harry Lieght stood flanked by two small pines and watched in silence until he had memorized the landscape. The cabin, set just where Mildred had described, was a comfortable-looking rustic structure built of logs and hidden from the road to town by a screen of young pine and old aspen rising into the night air like so many arrows half buried in the snow. Behind the cabin and to the north side, a low shed and a single-story barn blended into the side of a hill. A silvery banner of smoke rose in a thin line from the stone chimney at the rear of the cabin before catching an updraft and being whisked out of sight. No movement against the cabin windows, no sign of a dog. The whole scene was peaceful and serene, as it should have been.

Lieght's footsteps crunched in the snow as he rounded the cabin and walked into the shed. As predicted, the Model T rose out of the shadows before him. Satisfied, he went on to reconnoiter the barn, whose occupants, two horses and two mules, nickered softly but otherwise ignored the intruder. Keeping low and to the deepest shadow, Lieght crept back to the Model T and reached into the back seat to lift the cushion. "Good," he grunted in satisfaction, pulling out a tommy gun and a round ammunition drum. Crouching, his back to the car, he seated the already loaded drum and chambered a round. The bolt made a dull click that was muffled by his coat. He made sure the sound had gone unnoticed and only then, armed, reached back under the seat to remove and pocket the three extra boxes of shells he'd secreted there. Two hundred rounds, double the number he'd need under the direst circumstances, might have seemed excessive to some, but Harry liked the margin. He had learned a long time ago not to take any chances.

"Damn!" he muttered under his breath, and smothered a sneeze with his coat. Quickly he popped a honey lozenge inside his cheek and sucked on it. Both the doctor and Mildred had been indignant to a fault when he had told them he was leaving three days before he was declared fit, but that hadn't stopped him. Four days in bed were enough, and he was well enough to function. The lingering cold wasn't severe or debilitating enough to decrease his efficiency as long as he took care not to be heard coughing or sneezing at an inopportune moment.

Any further delay served no purpose. Lieght kept to the shadow of the shed as long as possible, cut across the narrow open space to the cabin, and crept to the nearest window, which he immediately dismissed because it was covered with frost. Bolder, he circled the cabin to the opposite side. The panes in that window were frosted, too, but not as heavily. A small half-moon shape in the top of each allowed him to see in. Both men—the larger, Sim Newkirk; the smaller, Tate Nance— were asleep. The cabin was a single large room lit by a kerosene lantern turned low for the night. A table with plates and bottles and scraps of food sat in front of the fireplace. Clothes and harness and tools hung from pegs hammered in the walls in a haphazard arrangement. A Winchester pump rifle hung on a rack, handy above the door. No other weapons were visible.

Humming "Cemetery Blues," Lieght fished in his pocket and brought out a stick of dynamite he had bought from Lewis Weldon that afternoon. Tommy gun tucked under his arm, he took out a match and striking stone, lit the fuse, and then smashed out one of the panes with a circular stroke of the gun and tossed the dynamite into the cabin. The fuse was rated for one minute, but looked short enough to blow the dynamite much sooner. Lieght caught a glimpse of Newkirk sitting bolt upright at the sound of the breaking glass before he ducked out of sight.

"Sheeeiiiittt!" two voices cried in unison.

Feet hit the floor and the latch rattled. Lieght waited out of sight around the corner of the cabin. Newkirk, by virtue of size and the ability to manhandle Nance, was the first out, but Nance was right on his heels. Neither wore shoes, and both were wearing frayed long johns. Tate Nance slipped and ate snow, scrambled to his feet, and followed Newkirk to the safety of the trees, where they both turned and crouched, waiting for the explosion.

"Good morning, gentlemen," Lieght said, stepping around the corner and silhouetting himself against the open cabin door. "Remember me?"

"Oh, nooo!" Nance moaned. Lieght's face was hidden in shadow, but his build and voice were unmistakable. "It's that Lieght fella. The one with the car."

"What the hell?. . ." Newkirk sputtered.

"So it is. We meet again, right, gents?" Lieght stepped to one side, held the tommy gun so they could see it, and advanced again.

Newkirk looked at the cabin that had yet to blow, at Lieght, and, realizing he had been tricked, back to the cabin. "You son-of-a-bitch!" he growled, taking a step forward.

Lieght raised the gun. "It'll be the last thing you hear, my friend," he said. "Where you were will be just fine."

Nance turned white and scurried away from Newkirk. "Sim! Jeez, watch it!" he yelled.

Newkirk's hands shot into the air. "I ain't doin' nothing. Don't shoot, mister!" he pleaded, backing away.

"That's better. Just remember. Try something like that again and I'll turn you into ground meat." Lieght jerked the muzzle toward Nance. "You. I will count to three. If you're not standing next to our large friend here, I'll be forced to—"

"Don't tell me!" Nance shouted, hurrying to Newkirk's side.

Lieght smiled, didn't say anything. Newkirk and Nance

waited, began to hop from one bare foot to the other. Cold crept up their legs. They put their hands in their armpits, took them out, and rubbed their upper arms. Lieght watched impassively.

"Hell!" Newkirk finally bawled. "I'd rather be shot than freeze to death."

"We was goin' to give you your car," Nance blurted, "but we thought you was dead. That's the whole of it, mister. Honest. We was just keepin' it safe. Why, there wasn't anyone around glad as us to learn you was safe and sound. Hell, I even told Sim here that—"

"Shut up, Tate," Newkirk muttered. "I seen his kind in the war. He cares about that car about the same as he cares about squashin' a bug. Don't mean a thing."

"You're smarter than you look, Newkirk," Lieght said. "Just like going to school, those trenches. The difference between us is, I liked it and studied hard." He slung the gun over his shoulder, turned, and nonchalantly started walking toward the cabin. "Long enough," he called back to them. "If you want to keep your toes, that is."

Newkirk and Tate followed at a distance, slowed when Lieght entered the cabin. "Let's run for it," Nance whispered.

"Where?" Newkirk asked. "Barefoot and half naked, we ain't got a chance." He gave Nance a push. "C'mon. I'm cold enough."

They hurried to the warmth of the cabin. A few minutes later, they were warming their backsides and groaning as their feet thawed. Lieght sat in a chair in the center of the room, toyed with the stick of dynamite while they dressed. "They'll stop hurting faster if you'll rub them," Lieght said, tossing the red cylinder over the table and into the flames.

"Gahhh!" Nance yelled, hitting the floor.

The hollowed-out stick of dynamite just sat for a moment, then burst into a fierce, brief flame as the oily paper and the residue of the dynamite burned.

"Stupid," Newkirk said, shaking his head. He stood on his left foot, massaged his right, and tried to figure out how he might reach the Winchester.

"Works every time," Lieght said.

"I imagine so." Newkirk switched feet, kept his eye on the machine gun. "But why?"

"A talk."

"Talk you could've had for a lot less trouble," Newkirk said. His eyes flicked upward to the gun on the wall, back to Lieght. "I don't take kindly to frostbite, Mr. Cityslick."

"The name is Lieght. Mr. Lieght to you. And I don't take kindly to thieves." He slouched back and let the muzzle of the tommy gun drop toward the floor. "Now, do you want to consider us even and go on from there, or would you rather try for the rifle over the door and lose all that money?"

Newkirk's eyebrows rose like two furry caterpillars arching themselves over a twig. "What money?" he said, the rifle forgotten.

"The money I'll pay you and your friend to enter my employ."

"He means go to work," Nance said.

"Shut up!" Newkirk snapped. "How much money?"

"Five thousand dollars apiece." Lieght shrugged, as if the sum meant little to him. "It's a one-time deal, of course, but if you work out and are interested, I can steer you to some people who might want to use you on a project or two of their own."

"Five thousand," Nance whispered, awed. "Jesus H. . . ."

"You're jokin' us," Newkirk said.

"I never joke about money. Well?"

Newkirk scratched his beard, glanced at Nance. The smaller man licked his lips nervously, at last nodded. A slow grin spread over Newkirk's face. "All right," he finally said with a facetious chuckle. "It's a deal. Who do we have to kill?"

Lieght smiled.

25

Lieght was riding Newkirk's horse, which left Newkirk the dappled jack mule, because the jenny didn't like to be ridden. The jack's gait was about as smooth as a pile driver, but the logger didn't mind that much. And anyways, Tate's horse was too damn small to confiscate. Newkirk was thinking about the fortune, the mother-loving fortune he was coming into, and mentally calculating all the things those beautiful five thousand dollars would buy. As far as the job itself, Lieght's explanation of why he wanted Roman Phillips and his girlfriend dead was of no concern to him. They'd made their own bed and would have to lie in it. People died every day. He himself had killed enough times in the war: twice more wouldn't make much difference as long as he was careful and no one found out. He slowed, held up his hand to stop Lieght and Tate, then rode out onto the logging road.

Mountain City was two miles behind them and the snow was unmarred. By nightfall, or earlier, the signs of their passage would likewise be obliterated. Just off the road, Lieght sat hunched in his saddle. Farther back in the trees, Nance and the pack-laden jenny brought up the rear. Satisfied that all was well, Newkirk pulled his hat low around his ears and settled in for the ride. "Well, let's go," he said, and pointed the jack's head north.

The cold and snow made the going difficult. Lieght was

thankful that Newkirk's horse was bigger and stronger, more sure of itself and calmer than Weldon's nag. The section of switchbacks where he'd had trouble before was ahead of them. This time, though, he wouldn't be the first in line, and would have help if there was an accident. Lieght checked the blanket wrapped around the tommy gun that lay on his lap, made sure that none of the heavy flakes that drifted down through the trees was getting onto the metal.

Bastard winter, he thought, sneezing and cursing the mountains under his breath. Christ, the things a man did in the name of his reputation. It was worth it though, in the long run, for however uncomfortable, the elements were working for him. Newkirk had assured him before starting that even if the snow kept up for a week, the way down would still be negotiable even if, at the higher elevations, the passes were closed. That meant that Roman Phillips was trapped. As were Newkirk and Nance, as far as that was concerned, for although they were a temporary necessity, they were also totally expendable. They didn't know it yet, but they were going to have to spend their money in Elkhorn, because those two were never going to make it back to Mountain City.

The three men stopped in the middle of the morning for coffee and a rest, again at noon for lunch. Newkirk led the way to a spot off the trail where a mountain freshet fell into a sheltered nook in the rocks and, while Nance checked their mounts' hooves and gave them a bite to eat, got a fire going. Being out of the wind was the best part, but a hot tin of beans followed by nearly boiling coffee came in a close second. Their stomachs full, their ears thawing, they sat on logs around the fire and warmed their gloves before starting out again. Lieght stared into the distance. Newkirk dozed sitting up, opened his eyes when Nance started laughing softly. "What's so damned funny?" he asked.

"Just thinking," Nance said, suppressing another laugh and almost choking. "Five thousand dollars! Five thousand, Sim!" He grinned, licked his lips in anticipation. "Man, oh, man! You know what I'm gonna do? I'm gonna find me the seven best-looking whores in Denver and have one a day for a week straight. The one I like the best I'll keep, move on to another town, maybe Albuquerque, and start over. Keep adding and subtracting until I got me the seven best blue-chip chippies west of the Mississippi and then, savin' one a day for myself, put the rest to work."

"Shit," Newkirk said with a snort. "You won't be able to get it up after the first two days."

"Oh, you just wait and *see*! Practice is gonna make me more perfect than you ever thought possible. What are you gonna do with your share, Sim?"

Newkirk poured himself the last of the coffee. "Leave these damn mountains and put as much distance between me and you as I can get, peckerhead."

"Awww," Nance groaned, pretending to be hurt. "And here I thought we was partners, Sim."

"A man with five thousand dollars don't need no partner, right, Mr. Lieght?"

Lieght didn't answer, only looked at him, then away to the north again.

Newkirk suppressed a shudder. He had seen hollowed-out, expressionless eyes and faces gray as the grave before. Invariably, they belonged to those who saw other men as nothing more than numbers or things or obstacles. Suddenly five thousand dollars was an insignificant amount in comparison to his life. Still, it wouldn't do to let the others see that he was worried. Pretending an enthusiasm he didn't feel, he threw out the dregs of his coffee, rose, and began to kick snow on the fire. "Time, Mr. Lieght," he said, pulling on his gloves. "We better move it out."

"Shit," Nance said.

"Shut up," Lieght ordered, rising stiffly and holding out his coffee cup.

Newkirk took it, but was careful not to look at the man from the city then, or during the rest of the afternoon.

The sun never did come out. The day remained drab, with visibility limited by the snow and the thick trees. The going was slow and sometimes treacherous, hard on men and animals alike. Newkirk's mind became as numbed as his fingers and toes. The others would be having the same problems, he knew, only more so, for the jarring gait of the jack kept him awake after a nearly sleepless night. By dusk, they were all ready for hot food and sleep.

Getting ready for the night stirred them out of their lethargy. Newkirk took care of the horses and rigged a lean-to out of lodgepole pine boughs. Nance gathered wood, fixed a fire, and cooked the beans and fried the bacon and brewed the coffee. A taciturn Lieght pitched in to help gather more boughs for the floor of the lean-to before laying out their ground cloth and bedrolls. By the time the food was ready, he had built a small rack over the fire and was warming dry socks for himself. The war had taught Sergeant Harry Lieght more than how to kill: it had also taught him how to live in relative comfort in hostile surroundings.

They ate in silence, gulping down the food while it was still hot. Afterward, their feet and hands as warm as their full bellies, they sat and stared into the fire and smoked and drank coffee laced with the whiskey Lieght had brought. There was little wind, the night was silent, all sound smothered by the snow except for an occasional metallic click as Lieght cleaned and oiled his tommy gun. "How many rounds does that thing hold?" Newkirk asked, jerking a thumb toward the round magazine.

"Fifty," Lieght answered briefly.

A boy and a girl and a hermit, an old fart everyone knew was crazy and harmless as Lode Benedict back in town. "Think that's enough?" Newkirk asked sarcastically.

"It'll do the job," Lieght answered, rapidly sliding the bolt back and forth.

"Then how come you need us?"

"To get there," Lieght said placidly, reading Newkirk's mind.

"And back?" Newkirk asked.

The logging road was easy enough to follow, but Lieght had spent his day memorizing landmarks just in case. Returning alone to Mountain City would be a piece of cake. "And back," he added reassuringly, lying easily. "Besides, it always pays to have an edge, no matter how good you think you are. Don't underestimate those people. They're armed, remember."

"The boy and the woman, maybe," Nance broke in, speaking for the first time since he'd announced that the meal was ready. "Not the old man. Newkirk and me see him up there when we go hunting. He don't even carry a gun. Scared of 'em."

Lieght made sure the stock was firmly seated, snapped the ammunition drum into place. "So what?" he said, giving the gun a final wipe.

"So he's loony." Nance spat into the fire. He didn't mind a scrape as long as the odds were right, which usually meant that Sim Newkirk was around, but he'd never touched an old honker like Wind River and didn't like the idea of starting. "I don't mind earning my five thousand, mind you. It's just that ol' Wind River don't count for coonshit."

"I'll tell you what," Lieght said, his voice as low and dangerously flat as when he'd invited Newkirk to try for the Winchester. "Let's pretend he does." His eyes held Nance's across the fire until the smaller man blinked and looked away, then glanced at Newkirk. The bearded logger concentrated on his coffee. "Good," Lieght said, standing. "Think I'll get some sleep. We reach Elkhorn tomorrow night, right?"

Newkirk shrugged, looked up at the sky. "With this weather slowing us, I doubt it. Maybe the morning of the next day."

Lieght mentally tabulated the days he had been gone. By now, his employers in Denver would have issued contracts for his life. To stop the process, he had to return to Denver with the money and the body of the one who stole it. Time was running out, though, for as certainly as he had found Roman Phillips, the others would find him. "You said—"

"I know what I said," Newkirk admitted, ill at ease. "But I didn't count on so much snow." He glanced up: Lieght was staring at him with unblinking, expressionless eyes. Uncomfortable, Newkirk looked away. "I . . . I don't know," he finally conceded. "Maybe if we push it."

"That sounds better," Lieght said, already walking toward the lean-to. "We'll push it."

26

"Creed!"

Roman heard Wind River's call and walked to the front
door of the hotel It had been snowing intermittently since
the night before when Roman had saved the old man from
the bear, then all the tedious gray day, and now at dusk was
far from abating. Without a breeze, the flakes fell silently in
one vast, all-encompassing curtain that obscured vision and
muffled sound.

Lainie, on the stairs, saw Roman at the door. "He isn't in
his room," she said, worried. "He didn't move all day long,
and all of a sudden he isn't there."

"I know," Roman said, jerking a thumb toward the street.
"He's out in the street calling his pet ghost. Jesus, Lainie.
Much more of this and I'll get the willies for sure."

"Creed!" Wind River bellowed again. His voice, muted
by the heavy snow, took on the elemental quality of pine
boughs rustling or distant coyotes mourning the passing of
the night.

"Hadn't you better try to bring him in?" Lainie asked.

"He took the Hawken. It wasn't loaded, but who knows
what the old coot has hidden in this town?"

"He might catch his death."

"Creed!"

Roman scratched the back of his neck, weighed the situation. "Could be, I suppose. Maybe that's what he's trying to do. Ah, hell," he said grudgingly, admitting to himself, if not to Lainie, that he was concerned about the venerable gunfighter. He shrugged into his coat and buttoned it. "I'll go. I'll never hear the end of it if I don't."

Wind River didn't know and didn't care who was looking for him. Brandishing the Hawken rifle like a club, he strode down the street through snow so thick he couldn't see the buildings to either side of him. "Creed," he challenged. "You lying, tricky bastard, show yourself."

"I'm right here, son."

"I ain't your son, damn it. Never was."

"We're blood kin, younker. The closest kind."

Wind River squinted, tried to follow the voice, put his feet to the path. Was that a movement? He swung, struck empty air, swirled flakes in the gun's wake. "You lied."

"Not true."

"The bear . . ."

"I never said the bear was gone. He won't leave until he's done what he has to do. Him and those that come after him."

"Then it isn't Scar. Either way, you lied." Wind River stalked through the curtain of white. Flakes melted on his cheeks. The water ran down his neck and onto his chest.

"Bears have a long memory, Kid. One dies, one is born. From cub to fang and claw to cub again. The favorite haunts, the special hates, all handed down. So it is Scar in a fashion. It's nature, too, and you can't kill nature without killing yourself. Drive off one bear, kill him, another will take his place. Another Scar. Whether you kill them or yourself, either way ol' Grizz wins, because either way you lose. Of course, there is one thing a man can do."

"Which is?"

"Enjoy losing," Creed's voice replied, drifting to him.

Wind River swung at a shadow and nearly fell. Breathing heavily, he stumbled forward and only barely regained his balance. "Where in blazes are you?" he howled in anguish.

"Right ahead of you, Kid." Creed's laugh sounded like dry bones rustling in a grave. "Right straight ahead of you."

"That a lie, too?" Wind River asked. Groping with the Hawken, he shuffled forward until the barrel touched something solid. Another step or two and Angelina's Victorian Palace, the foremost promontory of an unreal city, loomed large in the whiteness. "You got the bear with you?"

"I don't need no bear, younker."

Wind River stalked forward until he could make out the ruined front wall. A great gaping black wound left by the grizzly's hasty exit marred the false façade. Wizard like, tall and gaunt under the peaked cowl of his capote, Aden Creed appeared in the mouth of that wooden cave. Wind River walked up the steps and raised the rifle.

"Clubbed with my own gun. Now, isn't that a hell of a fate," Creed sneered.

"All these years with everything goin' just fine, and then all hell breaks loose. Why, Creed? What do you want of me?"

"The tally sheet doesn't balance, Kid. I'm callin' what's due me."

"Ain't nothing due you, damn it to hell."

"Oh? What about the days I had left, days to feel the sun on my face, to wander the old places, to live ..." Creed shook his head. "Sorry, Kid. A debt is a debt."

Wind River was sweating in spite of the cold. "The hell it is. I didn't ask for your help in the first place. Didn't need it then and don't now. I don't need anybody."

"You seem mighty stuck on that little girl."

"You leave her out of it," Wind River squawked, shaking the rifle.

"And that boy as well. He's got the sass, but you've taken a shine to him, too."

"The devil I have! He don't mean a thing to me."

"Now, that's the Wind River Kid I know," Creed said with heavy sarcasm. "Dangerous bein' your friend. Especially when there's lead flyin'."

Talk of flying lead made Wind River nervous. His lips tightened. "You still ain't told me what you want," he said, getting back to the original subject.

"Don't you know yet? See it shapin' up? I stood in your place, Kid. Can't you guess the next step?"

Wind River's face paled. "The only step I take is to get out of here as far and fast as I can. After I send you back to perdition or wherever you cut loose from, that is," he said, brandishing the rifle and advancing on Creed. "Go on, damn it! Get back or I'll . . ."

Aden Creed grinned. He pulled open his coat, dug his fingers into his buckskin shirt, and ripped it open. Wind River froze, his eyes fixed in a stare at the purplish puckered wounds disfiguring the mountain man's bony torso. As in a trance, his mind reeling with horror, he watched as the bullet holes began to seep a hideous yellow ichor.

"Wind River," a voice said from his rear, and a hand grasped his shoulder. Wind River shrieked and swung the rifle. Behind him, Roman ducked, dug his shoulder into Wind River's belly, and at the same time looped one arm around him. With his free hand, he grabbed the gun before Wind River could swing again. "It's me. Roman. You crazy old coot! Take it easy! It's me!"

"Leggo! Help! Help me, Creed!"

The words weren't out of his mouth before Wind River realized what he'd said. The knowledge was like a dash of cold water, more frigid by far than the melted snow that ran down his back. He'd asked for help! Again! And from Creed. The fight drained out of him. "Who?" he said, barely able to hold the rifle.

"Me. Roman." Roman stood, gently took the Hawken from Wind River. "You all right?" he asked, peering into the old man's face.

Wind River stared at him dully, then slowly turned away and looked at the Victorian Palace. There was nothing there. Nothing but the ruined front of a decrepit, musty building. "Yeah," he finally said, his voice a hoarse growl in his throat. "Yeah. I'm all right. Can we go back now?"

"Sure," Roman said, slipping his free arm around Wind River's waist.

Slowly, almost painfully, his mind a confused blur of racing images of bears and mountain men and graves and Pepperdines, Wind River sagged against the younger man, and let himself be led up the street to the Great Northern Hotel.

27

Roman rubbed oil along the barrel of the automatic. The feel of the blued metal made his skin crawl, as if he were touching the hand of Harry Lieght himself. It was Lieght's gun, after all, and Lieght was very much on his mind. Roman wondered what he had seen in Harry Lieght, then chided himself for those same thoughts. He had seen what any fool sees: wealth and everything wealth could buy — luxury and power and a life lived far from the holier-than-thou dead end of a fundamentalist theological seminary. Not that he could lay the blame at anyone else's door, of course. His matriculation in the Holy Light Divinity School had been his father, Zechariah's, last wish, his final effort to atone for a baker in Mountain City, a sour old man elbow deep in flour and powdered sugar instead of fire and brimstone.

Roman frowned, rolled his head to loosen his neck muscles. Tension always accompanied thoughts of his sternly disciplinarian father, who, unable to outgrow the trying childhood he had endured, inadvertently saw to it that his son experienced the same difficult youth.

The checkered pattern on the metal, no-nonsense grip was worn smooth in places from years of use. Absentmindedly, Roman used his thumbnail to clean out the deeper grooves. As he did so, his mind climbed the stairs in the old house on Binkley Street to where his father lay dying, his lips flecked with spittle and his flesh the color of a gray dawn. He heard his mother sobbing and repeatedly assuring her husband that his last wish would be granted and that her son's life would be dedicated to the service of the Lord. Roman saw the doctor lean forward as the dying man made a sound like sawing wood. It was too much to bear. Sobbing, fleeing from the horrid rasping sound, Roman bolted from the room and ran down the hall, pleading, as he passed the painting of Christ on the stairs, for Jesus to save his father.

"I will live a good life," he promised, knowing his father was dying because Roman himself was a sinner. "I will try to be good, Jesus," he vowed over and over again. "I will become one of your ministers."

He hadn't wanted to three days earlier, and he didn't want to again before the month was out. "Well, the best intentions," he said, his voice heavy with sarcasm as he slapped home the magazine and gave the butt a final polish. "At least I tried," he added, recalling the mind-numbing hours spent in the knowledge that he hadn't the stuff of heaven. Nor of hell either, he thought, realizing how alien his association with Lieght seemed now.

"Mother, father, and Harry Lieght," he snorted, disgusted. "Always trying to be who I'm not, and always for somebody else." At least that part of his life was over. He might be a fugitive from the courts of heaven, hell, and hard times, but he was on his own, none other than plain and simple Roman Phillips. A frightened Roman Phillips, to be sure — if his plan didn't work and Lieght found him, he wouldn't be anything for very long — but Roman Phillips nonetheless.

"Roman?" Lainie called, entering from the kitchen. "You in there?"

"Jesus, Lainie," Roman exploded, juggling the automatic and getting new fingerprints all over it.

"I'm sorry," Lainie apologized, hurrying to him and kissing him on the forehead. "I didn't mean to startle you."

"I wasn't startled," Roman snapped. "You just took me by surprise, is all." He rose, jammed the automatic in his belt, and handed the .38 to Lainie. "Here You'd better keep this. I'll be back in a few minutes."

"What's going on?" Lainie asked suspiciously.

"Nothing's going on. I'm just going to give the mules a little extra food." His eyes avoided hers. He had never lied to her before. Leaving out Lieght wasn't exactly a lie, but he didn't have the heart to scare her with the whole truth. "They'll need it. We're leaving in the morning."

"So soon?" Lainie asked, surprised. "But I thought —"

"Well, don't!" He was taking out his own fear on her, and he didn't want to do that. Roman grinned self-consciously, forced the irritation out of his voice. "Look, baby, we've been here over two weeks," he explained calmly. "It's time. Just like we planned in the beginning, okay?"

He wasn't telling the truth. Not all of it. She could tell. Lainie stood her ground. "But we made other plans, too, and I don't think Wind River is well enough to travel," she pointed out. "Besides, he says the passes are all snowed in."

"Wind River says!" Roman snorted. He caught Lainie's shoulders and pulled her to him. "He's been here a long time. A little longer won't hurt him. Don't worry about him. We don't need him, he doesn't need us." He talked quickly. "It'll be a piece of cake. We'll go south, around Mountain City — it isn't all that hard to do; I checked it out — and into Idaho Springs, where we sell the mules and catch the first train west. Another week and we'll be in San Francisco. Maybe go up the coast to Oregon or Washington, right?"

Lainie pushed far enough away from him to look into his face. Fear of the unknown, the untold, that which was so evidently being left out in spite of his almost frantic sincerity, clouded her eyes. "There's more, isn't there, Roman?" she said quietly.

"More?" Roman looked hurt, then serious. "I'm not going to let anything happen to you, Lainie. You know that. I love you too much. Hey! What is this? The third degree?" He turned her around, gave her a playful swat on the fanny, and headed for the door. "To work, woman. Supper. We'll pack after we eat."

Lainie didn't move. "Mr. Lieght is coming, isn't he?" she said with great effort.

Roman stopped. Unable to bring himself to face her, he leaned against the doorjamb and stared into the empty lobby. "He's in Mountain City," he finally said. His shoulders sagged and he bit his lower lip. "He got there over a week ago."

"And?" Lainie prompted.

"The guy at the store where we bought the tires sold him some clothes, rented him a horse, and pointed him this way. The horse threw him, I guess, but he made it back to town. He was hurt and sick, but you know Harry. Tough as a board. Tuesday night, I listened outside his window and heard the doctor tell him he'd be up and about in a week."

"But that was five days ago!" Lainie said, aghast. "We'll be heading right for him!"

The Bible said that the truth had the power to make men free. Roman wasn't sure about that, but it did make one feel better. Eager to reassure Lainie, he hurried to her and took her hands. "No," he said, shaking his head. "I've got it all figured out, Lainie. Remember, there are two ways down from here to Mountain City. The way we came the first time, and the path Wind River discovered. Lieght will go the first way because it's the only way he can go and not get lost. Meanwhile, we'll have taken Wind River's way. The two come together a few miles north of Mountain City, and I've got a spot all picked out. We'll get there, camp out, and watch the road. It'll be perfect. All we have to do is wait. When Lieght goes up the road coming here, we'll wait awhile and then go right on down the road in his footsteps. By the time he gets here and back, we'll be long gone!"

"And Wind River?" Lainie asked dully.

Roman shrugged. "He stays here, of course."

"To face Lieght all alone?" Anger flared in Lainie's eyes. "You didn't think about that, did you?"

"Of course I did. Jesus, Lainie, what do you take me for?" It was all going wrong. All he'd tried to do was keep her from getting upset, and she was twisting everything around. "Lieght isn't going to do anything to Wind River. Why should he? All Wind River will do is tell him the truth, that we left three or four days earlier. Lieght will be pissed, but not at Wind River."

Lainie picked at a cuticle, studied it assiduously.

"Look, baby, I *like* Wind River," Roman went on, groping

for more arguments. "The old buzzard keeps things from getting too dull, what with his imaginary friends and assorted bears, horses, and birds, but you gotta consider. He's an old man locked in his ways, still living in the nineteenth century. Christ! If we take him with us we'll have to *keep* him with us, because if he ever does take a look at the world out there he'll be so lost he won't know what to do. Believe me, leaving him is by far the lesser of two evils." He cupped her chin, looked her in the eye, and spoke very convincingly because it was the truth. "Because if he's with us and Lieght does find us?..."

The sentence dangled unfinished in the air. Lainie lowered her eyes. The lesser of two evils. The episode at Silvertip Falls flashed across her mind. She had thought then that their crime would come back to haunt them as Wind River's had his. Now it had, and Wind River was going to be the first to stand in harm's way. Roman's explanation and assurances notwithstanding, the old man's life lay in Harry Lieght's hands, placed there by her and Roman. Involuntarily she shuddered. "I wish I knew what was going to happen to him," she said, in little more than a whisper. "It's like him paying for what we did. I hate it, Roman, and I'm scared for him." Her eyes tearing, she pleaded with him. "We can't do it this way. We just *can't.*"

"We have to, Lainie," Roman said, adamant in the face of her tears. "Look. I'll tell you what. Lieght may be mean, but never without reason. We'll tell Wind River what's going to happen before we go. That way he'll be prepared and can tell Lieght everything he knows about us, except where we're going, which he won't know. Believe me, Lieght won't hurt him. Probably even give him something for his trouble. I *know* the man, Lainie. I'd lay bets that I'm right. And to make up for whatever grief we've caused him, we'll give Wind River the five hundred, just like we said we would. Hell, I'll even throw in one of the mules and the stuff we won't need, now that we're leaving. After Lieght is gone, Wind River will be sitting on easy street. Well?" he asked hopefully. "What do you think? Is it a deal?"

The first lie is always the most devastating. If he'd just told her the truth to begin with . . . "You're sure?" Lainie asked, reluctant to believe him.

"As positive as I can be," Roman said emphatically, sensing that anything more would be a mistake.

Lainie studied her torn cuticle a moment longer, at last sighed deeply. "Okay, Roman," she finally said. "If you say so, I guess it'll be okay."

"I know it will," Roman promised, relieved. "Hey!" He touched the corners of her mouth. "A little smile, huh?"

A little smile was all she could muster. "Sure, Roman."

"And supper when I get back?"

"It'll be an hour at least."

"That's my girl. And you'll see. It'll be all right."

The door swung shut behind him. "It'll be all right," Lainie repeated, heading for the kitchen. And Wind River? She'd never know what happened to Wind River. And hated to think of what was going to happen to them. Roman had no idea how fertile was the seed of distrust he had sown. She had hoped they wouldn't lie to each other. There was just no escaping the past. Lieght was bad enough, but what had come between her and Roman was worse. Mechanically, she pumped a pot full of water, added a couple of sticks to the fire, and set the water on to boil. Listlessly, she shoved the coffeepot a little closer to the heat, rinsed out a cup, and dumped in a spoonful of sugar.

She'd have to tell Wind River, of course. She dreaded that. The poor old man. He was like no one she had ever known, and for the first time, standing alone in the kitchen, Lainie realized how much he had come to mean to her, how deeply she cherished him. His funny, old-fashioned way of talking. His directness. How sweet he could be, how irascible. She had to chuckle in spite of herself, recalling how upset he'd been the day she'd cleaned out the coffeepot, and again, two days later, when she'd scoured his favorite cast-iron frying pan. His sense of honor, his independence, even his almost childlike qualities.

Roman was right about one thing, though, she had to admit. He'd get along. Oh, she didn't doubt he'd be disappointed when he learned they were leaving without him. It was so painfully obvious that he wanted to accompany them. Roman had been right about that, too, she was forced to concede. Wind River would never be happy in a big city. The contrast of Elkhorn to Denver had been a shock to her system, and she was young. Transporting Wind River from the nineteenth to the twentieth century would be even more of a shock, given his age and set ways.

But she couldn't tell him that. Saying as much would be a terrible insult. They'd done enough harm intruding on his life without compounding matters, and she loved him too much to upset him with that kind of truth. Her mind made up, Lainie got a coffee cup for him while she rehearsed what she'd say. The part about Lieght would be enough. Convincing him shouldn't be too difficult. She'd just ...

"Oh, my God!" she said aloud, almost dropping his cup as the realization hit her that she was going to lie to Wind River exactly the way Roman had lied to her. And for, she further realized, exactly the same reason: his own peace of mind. The irony was almost too much. God, but she'd been a silly fool. Of course Roman had lied. What else was he to do if he didn't want to scare her half to death? It was all so simple when she looked at it that way. So damnably simple.

Relieved, she poured Wind River's coffee, hurried up the stairs to his room, and knocked on the door. "It's me, Wind River," she called, opening the door when she heard a croak that sounded like "Come in."

His overalls and shirt baggy on his spare frame, Wind River was sitting in a chair by the window.

"You shouldn't be up," Lainie chided gently.

Wind River snorted. "I shouldn't be down, is more like it. This room smells like last year's hoorah. Stretched out in bed there, I began to feel like one of them durn flowers that folks press between the pages of a book. Them old and brittle flowers. The dead ones."

"I guess you know what's best," Lainie said, handing him the cup. "Here. I brought you some coffee. It's fresh."

He motioned her to be quiet. "Hear that?"

"No." Lainie looked around apprehensively. "What?"

"Scar." Wind River nodded knowingly. "That grizz is out

there calling. I think Creed put him up to it. Wants to have it out once and for all, to see if I'm gonna stand up or turn tail."

"I hear the wind," Lainie said.

"That's 'cause your ears are still in Denver, gal." He looked out the window, then glanced back. "Now there, by God, is the name for you. Denver Gal. Should've thought of it before. A mighty fitting handle, if I do say so myself."

There was no sense in putting it off. "Wind River?" Lainie said, clearing her throat. "I thought I'd better tell you. We're leaving tomorrow."

"Can't," Wind River said matter-of-factly. "The passes are closed."

Once started, all she could do was rush through it as quickly as possible. "We're not going through the passes. Roman's thought it all out, and he and I are going back to Denver. He thinks that that way will be better, all things considered."

Wind River held on to the cup with both hands. "We ain't goin' together?" he asked, disbelief written on his face. "But we got to."

Lainie walked to the other window in time to see Roman emerge from the barn. "I'm sorry, Wind River, but we can't take you," she said, hoping the lie had been as difficult for Roman as it was for her. "There's a good reason. Harry Lieght is looking for us. If he finds us, it will be bad enough. But if you're with us ..." Her voice broke. "I just couldn't stand to see anything bad happen to you, Wind River. I just couldn't. Don't you understand?"

She'd learned to make coffee, at least. Keep that with her the rest of her life. Wind River took a sip, set the cup down before he spilled it. "I understand," he said dully, keeping one ear cocked for the bear. It was still out there somewhere, waiting. "You don't want some crazy old fart slowin' you down." He tapped his right temple with his forefinger. "All I got to say is, now you're thinkin', Denver Gal. You and Roman both. Now you're thinkin'." The north wind moaned, rattled the glass, set it chattering. "You better get on downstairs and fix your man some grub. You two got a long haul tomorrow."

"Wind River? . . . I'm . . . I'm sorry," Lainie blurted, fleeing from the room before the moisture in her eyes became full-fledged tears.

"What for?" Wind River said softly. Alone. He leaned back against the side of the window, let his head rest on the bunched-up, faded curtain. "Harry Lieght for you, a devil bear for me. Life is a cut of cards, so don't be sorry. I'd do the same thing and not even look back. Not once." He wiped a forearm across his eyes. "Not even for you, I'm afraid, Denver Gal."

28

The last brief flurry had stopped shortly after dark, and now a waning moon peered fitfully between the scudding clouds. With the clearing sky came intense cold. By morning, there would be a thick, heavy crust on the damp snow carpeting the ground. Two-thirds of Elkhorn's population had gone to bed earlier, though a light showed underneath their door. Over half the night had passed since then, and still Wind River remained by the window. The glass emanated a chill that crept into the room and largely overcame what feeble heat the dying fire generated. Wind River's breath clouded on the panes as he peered uphill to the graveyard, where, now and again, the moon illuminated the markers. Wind River knew them by heart, for even as he had dug too many of the holes and lowered too many of the boxes, so had he carved too many of the names and messages their markers bore. They had been at peace until the bear showed up. Cursed bear, prowling through the night, scratching, digging, rending. And Creed, too, for that matter. "*Goddamn* Elkhorn," Wind River cursed, knowing he never should have stayed to watch the town dry up and turn to rot.

Creed farted.

Wind River turned and wrinkled his nose. Smelled more like rotten eggs every day.

Chip chip chip. Tiny hooves forming on tiny legs. *Chip chip chip.*

Why had the bear come? Why revenge after all this time?

Creed rocked in the chair by the bed. The chair creaked. The rungs cut deep furrows in the flimsy carpet. *Chip. Chip.* The antlers took shape. *Chip chip chip.*

Wind River's bones creaked like the chair, but he got up without speaking to Creed and walked out of the room. The hall was quiet, the better to hear the bear. Denver Gal thought it was the wind, but Wind River knew better. Outside, a warped board popped. Bending, it exerted force on a rusty nail. The nail squeaked, squeaked again a moment later. And again. Wind River imagined a stone tossed in a well, how a man waits to hear the comforting finale when it at last strikes bottom. Stealthily, step by single step, he crept downstairs and into the lobby. He'd waited long enough, he thought, opening the door a crack and squeezing through it. Scar or whatever, let the bear come. Let it be ended one way or the other. The board groaned, the nail squeaked.

"Bear?" Wind River whispered.

There was a brief quiet scuffle somewhere in the black depths of the town. Wind River pinpointed the movement. It came from the alley between the sheriff's office and the general store. "Bear?" he called softly. "Ain't got the stomach for it, after all? Come on out. I come to call your hand, be it bluff or aces full. I can't take it no more, so do your worst."

Nothing. The board did not groan, the nail did not squeak.

"Bear!" Wind River called, more forcefully.

Cold steel pressed against the nape of his neck. Before he could move, two shapes materialized in front of him. Wind River gasped, froze in surprise. What in God's name had he conjured?

"Clam it," one of the shapes said.

Wind River squinted, made out a man in a gray fedora and a hound's-tooth overcoat. The man held a gun like one Wind River had seen in a picture in Lewis Weldon's store. Motioning his shorter companion to stay put, he drew close, stuck his face right up to Wind River's. "Where are they?" he asked.

"Jesus, mister, I — " The world exploded. Above him, the cloud lurched and stumbled. Wind River felt himself falling. The snow cushioned his fall, but when he tried to get up, he felt a boot pressed against his left wrist.

A face hovered over his. "I'm going to break this one first," the man said. "Then I will break your right one, and then your knees. Then I will leave you. I am not without generosity. You will have your life for as long as you can drag yourself around. For the last time, where are they?"

They. Roman and Lainie. Wind River's mind whirled crazily, stopped at the name Harry Lieght. Oh, Jesus, he thought, not wanting to tell but frightened beyond belief. He couldn't. Not that. Not betray them.

The pressure on his wrist increased.

"Hey! There's a lantern glow in one of the windows," Newkirk said, pointing upward.

"It ain't them," Wind River blurted out much too quickly, too emphatically.

Lieght grinned. "Thanks," he said, lifting his foot off Wind River's wrist. "Newkirk, come with me. Nance, help the old man up and bring him inside. Where's your courtesy?"

"I left it in Mountain City." Nance grinned. He grabbed Wind River by the shoulder and hauled him to his feet. "Come on, old-timer. It will be morning soon. Wouldn't want folks to think you spent the night in the gutter."

"There ain't no folks," Wind River groaned, grateful for the darkness that hid his tears of shame. Why couldn't he ever do anything right? He'd failed them as he'd failed Creed.

"Just ghosts, huh," Nance said with a chuckle. "You don't know how right you're gonna be, old-timer. Let's go."

Lieght and Newkirk were upstairs before Nance and Wind River got moving. Lieght's tactics, as they had been two nights earlier at the cabin, were designed to terrify and give an insurmountable advantage. He pointed the Thompson machine gun at the door. Automatic gunfire turned the lock to shrapnel and shattered the quiet. Before the reverberations died, Lieght kicked open the door and walked into the room. "The girl will die first," he announced, leveling the tommy gun at the startled couple in the bed.

The fire and the lantern gave off enough light to see by. Adrenalin pumped through Roman's system. His heart racing, he bolted upright and grabbed for the gun on the bedstand, then froze. Lainie screamed, sat up, and pulled the cover over her breasts. Her face bloodless, she stared at Lieght.

"That's right," Lieght said in a monotone. "The gun, now. Very slowly. Fingers out and hand away, like a good boy."

Roman's fingers splayed wide open as ordered, and his hand moved reluctantly away from the automatic. Lieght smiled, walked around the bed to the table, and retrieved the gun. "Well, well," he said, falsely jovial. "Imagine that. Now, what's *my* gun doing *here*?"

Roman felt a hollow spasm of pain center in his gut.

"Get dressed," Leight snapped. "You first," he added, gesturing menacingly with the tommy gun at Lainie. "And hurry, or I'll have Mr. Newkirk here help you."

Lainie swung her legs out from under the cover and, thankful for the dim light, walked naked across the room to her clothes. "Good girl," Lieght said as she stepped into her shoes. "Now over there in the corner while Romeo takes his turn."

There was no arguing. Not with a tommy gun on him and Newkirk's rifle trained on Lainie. Glad they were still alive, Roman tried to marshal his thoughts while he dressed. Whoever Lieght's helper was, his intent was obvious from the way he watched Lainie. It was too late to worry about himself any longer. Lieght had him and that was that. There had to be a way to free Lainie, though. There had to be some way.

Finished dressing, he stood ramrod straight as Lieght approached him. "It's nice to see you again, Roman. I missed you," he said, patting his ex-helper on the cheek, an affectionate gesture were it not for his eyes, as loving as molten lead. "Now. Why don't we all go downstairs and have a little chat."

Roman and Lainie led the way. In the dining room, unable to meet their gaze, Wind River sat huddled by the fire. Another man, holding a gun of his own and Roman's .38, found in the kitchen, watched over Wind River. Roman cursed himself for not keeping the pistol at his side, then realized it would have done him no more good than the automatic had.

"Lanterns," Lieght said, interrupting Roman's train of thought. "Well, come on," he added harshly, when no one answered.

"The two on the mantel have kerosene in them," Roman said. "There are three more in the kitchen."

"Light them," Lieght said, tossing a box of matches to Nance. "You." The gun pointed at Lainie. "We've had a hard ride. Get some coffee going."

"I'm hungry," Nance said.

"Something to eat, then, as well," Lieght added. "Just make sure it's hot."

"I'll watch her," Newkirk volunteered, grabbing Lainie's arm. Lainie pulled free and started for the kitchen under her own volition.

The first lantern caught. "Nice," Nance said, watching her with an approving stare.

Newkirk leered at him over his shoulder. "Not half as nice as she was a couple of minutes ago. You missed the real show, Tate," he taunted just before disappearing through the kitchen door.

Tate Nance hurriedly lit the second lantern, tossed the match into the fireplace. "You think Sim is gonna need help watching the doll?" he asked hopefully.

Lieght hadn't taken his eyes off Roman. "Shut up and stand by the door," he ordered. "Keep your eyes on the old man."

"Ah, hell, Mr. Lieght. He's a harmless old geezer."

"Watch him, I said."

"Sure, sure. You're the boss."

Stove and cooking sounds filtered in from the kitchen. The fire hissed briefly. Lieght surveyed the room, noted empty tables and faded lithographs and torn tapestries. And no money, which didn't really bother him because he had no doubt Roman would tell him soon enough.

"How did you find me?" Roman asked suddenly, breaking the silence before he screamed.

Lieght's glance was heavy with contempt. "You're stupid, you know that, Phillips?" His left hand slammed down on a table. "Jesus Christ, but you're stupid! You know how long it took me to find you?"

"No," Roman said, not even wanting to hear.

"The next day. Not even twenty-four hours and I knew where you were. Sister Amanda spilled the beans, kid. Jesus! A broad like that for a mother? No wonder you're so stupid."

"I was smart enough—"

"To what?" Lieght shouted, his face an inch from Roman's. "Take a bag of money from me? That's smart? Shit. You'd fuck up a wet dream. In the first place, you should of kept the Lincoln and shagged some new plates for it. Hell, nine o'clock the next morning I knew what you were driving, the plates, and what direction you were headed. Next, you should of gone where there's lots of people, not some half-ass ghost town with nothing more than that"—he gestured contemptuously to Wind River—"for protection." Lieght shook his head. "It's too bad, Phillips. I thought I taught you better than that. Like I said, you should of killed me when you had the chance."

Roman gritted his teeth. "Yeah. I guess I should have," he said, glancing at Wind River. "What did you do to the old man?"

"Do? To him?" Lieght's laugh was flat and without humor. "Not a thing. He was most cooperative. Even directed me to your room, didn't you?"

Wind River squirmed uncomfortably in the chair, kept his attention riveted on the floor.

"Didn't you!" Lieght repeated, stepping toward him.

"I'm sorry, young'un," Wind River mumbled. "There was three of 'em, and I—"

"Let him go," Roman said, sounding infinitely more brave than he felt. "He doesn't mean anything to you."

"He don't mean anything to nobody," Nance said from the door. "They call him the Spook back in Mountain City."

"Shut up, Nance," Lieght said, without so much as a glance at him. "Where is the money?"

"Hidden," Roman said, realizing he had some leverage after all.

Lieght slashed upward with the Thompson before the word was fully out, driving the barrel into Roman's groin. His face contorting, Roman collapsed, curled into a ball, and tried to suppress the agony. Lieght placed the gun on the table and took the automatic from his pocket. "An automatic is like a child," he said, working the slide and ejecting a cartridge. "It must be cared for." A slow smile played over his face as he removed the clip and replaced the single shell. "Very nice. At least you kept it clean and loaded. Too bad it didn't do you any good."

Roman managed to rise to his hands and knees. His breath whistled in his throat and his testicles felt swollen and on fire, but he wasn't going to grovel. Not in front of Harry Lieght. Cold sweat beading on his forehead, he pushed himself to his feet and, supported by a table, managed to remain erect.

Lieght's stare was clinical, dispassionate. At last he shrugged, tucked the automatic back into his coat pocket. "All right, Phillips. Morning soon. You'll tell me then."

"Go to hell, you bastard," Roman croaked, speaking itself an agony. "You'll never find the money. I can take anything you can dish out."

Lieght yawned. The last two weeks had been murderous. He glanced at his fingernails. They were actually dirty. He needed a bath and a manicure. A woman would be nice, too. Most of all, he needed the money. "Maybe," he said, yawning again. "But can she?" he asked, nodding toward the kitchen. "Can *she?*"

Ignorant of how his weight threatened to crush the fragile legs, Sim Newkirk perched on a stool and watched Lainie. She had a nice ass. Wiggled even when she sliced bacon and laid the marbled strips in the skillet. The temptation was too much. The next time she bent forward to add wood to the stove, he did too, and ran an approving hand across the contour of her hip.

"Don't you ever do that again!" Lainie snapped, whirling, holding a split piece of firewood like a club.

Newkirk laughed, grabbed her wrist. "Honey, I don't know how you come by that boy out there, but I'd say a hellcat like you needs a real man." He squeezed until she dropped the kindling, which fell to the floor with a heavy thud. "Lucky for you it ain't too late. A word from me will set everything jake. Hell, a gal built like you has got enough to knock a fella clean off his feet."

"Let me go!" Lainie said fiercely.

"Let you go? Awww, honey . . ." Newkirk jerked her toward him, and as he did, Lainie kicked the weakest leg of the stool. Already strained to the breaking point, the leg splintered. Newkirk's weight did the rest. With a cry of surprise, he let go of Lainie, threw up his arms, and pitched over sideways.

Lainie grabbed for his rifle. Newkirk kicked at her ankles and knocked her down. Lainie scrambled away on all fours and collided with the stove, knocking the chimney loose. By the time she could get to her feet, Newkirk was lunging for her. The jolt when he hit the stove knocked the stovepipe free, dumping a cloud of ashes and soot into the room. Backpedaling, then turning to run, Lainie bumped into Lieght, who had entered to see what all the ruckus was about. "Let me go!" she shouted as Lieght hauled her, squirming and kicking, into the dining room. "Let me go!"

Covered with soot, Newkirk charged out of the kitchen. "The bitch!" he howled. "Let me at her! The goddamn —"

"Hey, pickaninny. Where's your mammy?" Nance shouted, doubling over with laughter.

Newkirk blinked back the tears and tried to rub his eyes clean. "You shut your damn mouth," he roared, and then dove behind a table as Lieght fired a burst from the tommy gun.

The noise was deafening. Everyone froze in place as plaster and wood showered down from the ceiling. "That's better," Lieght said in the sudden, utter quiet that followed. He shoved Lainie toward the chair across from Wind River. "Now you. Sit down and shut up. You've caused enough trouble. You, Newkirk. Get back out there and fix the stove. Take the old man and have him do the cooking. Maybe you'll be able to keep your mind on business."

Looking for all the world like an end man in a minstrel show, Newkirk poked his head up from behind the table, then quickly rose. "Come on, you old fart," he said, hauling Wind River out of his chair. "You heard the man."

By the time the stovepipe was fixed and the kitchen cleaned up enough to use, the eastern sky was gray with dawn light. Tired, Wind River watched the water come to a boil, dumped in a double handful of coffee grounds, and started on the bacon. An hour later, as the first rays of the sun touched the rooftops, everyone had eaten. Newkirk dozed in a corner, Nance had gone out to check the horses. Lieght sat across from Lainie, Roman, and Wind River, and slowly sipped on his third cup of coffee. He appeared relaxed and off guard, but Roman knew better than to underestimate him. Harry Lieght might relax from time to time, but he was never off guard.

The front door opened to let in a chill draft. "Jesus, it's cold out there," Nance announced, stomping his feet and heading for the fire. "Snow's frozen hard as ice."

"It is ice, you prick," Newkirk mumbled, half awake.

"The horses?" Lieght asked.

"We'll have to wrap their legs if we don't want them to get all cut up going through the crust. They're fine and dandy, though. Fed 'em and watered 'em. They're ready to go when you are."

"Excellent," Lieght said.

The atmosphere in the room changed subtly as Lieght rose from the chair and walked around the table to stand behind Roman. Lainie clenched her hands together, sought Roman's knee with hers. Wind River tried to look over his shoulder without turning his head. Roman jerked involuntarily as the muzzle of the tommy gun touched the back of his neck.

"Well well well," Leight said. "It's that time of day,

Phillips. I don't like to ask more than twice, you *capisce?* Where's the money?"

It had come. All the eternity of waiting suddenly seemed like a mere blink of the eye. Roman closed his eyes, didn't answer.

"Stubborn, isn't he." The gun pressed harder, forced Roman to bend forward. "Newkirk."

"Yeah?" The logger grinned, uncoiled from his chair.

"Take her upstairs."

Newkirk's grin widened. "You mean that?" he asked, hardly believing his luck. "What I think you mean?"

"If you have to ask, maybe Nance ought to go first." Enjoying himself, Lieght played the game of fear and terror to the hilt. "What do you think, Phillips? Who gets her first? Newkirk or Nance?"

"Now, wait a minute . . ." Newkirk said, moving toward Lainie.

Nance intercepted him before he got there. "Hell, first is fine with me," the smaller man snickered in gleeful anticipation.

"Son-of-a-bitch!" Roman snapped.

Leight paid no attention. "No opinion, then. Okay, what about you, girlie? Which one do you want first? The big one or the little one?"

It was all Lainie could do to keep from screaming. "Please," she whispered. "Please please please please . . ."

"I'll tell you what then. Both of them. They can flip a coin. Loser gets to hold her down while I keep an eye on the brave and bold Mr. Phillips." He didn't have to see Roman's face to know the effect his words were having. "Unless he wants to go along to watch, of course, in which case we can make a regular party out of—"

His stomach was churning and the taste of vomit was vile in his throat. The words, the ugly, filthy words, went on and on. "Wait!" Roman said. "Okay. Okay. Wait."

"Ah. The voice of reason." Fear always worked. As long as the threat was real, they all crumbled sooner or later. Lieght sniffed, took his handkerchief, and blew his nose. "The third and last time, boy. Where is the money?"

"Lainie and Wind River," Roman said. "They go free."

"Take the girl upstairs."

"She doesn't mean anything to you. Neither does he. The money is what you want. That and me. You let one of those apes touch her, if you harm her at all, I'll see you in hell before you ever lay your hands on it. You can tear this town apart and never find it."

Newkirk and Nance stopped. Both wanted Lainie, but they wanted the ten thousand dollars even more. "He's got a point, Mr. Lieght," Newkirk said.

"Do as you're told."

"And then he don't ever talk and we've gone through this for nothing?" Nance wasn't about to give up his dream of a perfect whore for each day in the week. "Shit on that. Do what he says. Them two can't harm us."

"Yeah," Newkirk chimed in. "We ain't here for the fun of it."

Quick anger, controlled only with great effort, surged through Lieght. Slowly, he supplanted it with cold logic. He'd been without sleep for two nights out of the last three, a minor factor if he hadn't been flat on his back in bed for over a week. Newkirk and Nance hadn't figured out that they possibly could take him if they wanted to. Giving in was an indication of weakness, to be sure, but far less dangerous than even hinting that the two ruffians wouldn't get the money. Step by step, each so concrete Lieght could almost see them, the next few hours unfolded in his mind. The girl and the old man leaving, Phillips telling him where the money was, Phillips dying, Newkirk and Nance preoccupied by the sight of the ten thousand dollars and dying, the fast trip to catch up to the girl and the old man . . .

"Very well," Lieght said finally with a show of reluctance. No more than a second had passed, but he was certain the quickly formulated improvisation would work. "You win the battle, Phillips, if it makes you feel any better. I'll take the war."

"Two horses," Roman said, vastly relieved. "One for each of them, and a two-hour head start."

"No!" Lainie cried. "I won't leave you."

Roman nudged Wind River with his right elbow. "Blast it, you old bastard, help me," he said.

Wind River leaned forward and talked across Roman. "He's made his choice, Denver Gal. I don't see any other way. You got no call to undercut him."

"Take them to the barn and see they get saddled up, Newkirk. The old man's horse and one of the mules Romeo here bought in town will do. See they don't try anything funny with our mounts."

Newkirk grabbed Lainie by the arm. "Come on, Dora. You too, Spook."

"Roman. No!"

"I'll want to see him back here," Roman warned.

"Please, Roman!" Lainie sobbed. "I don't want to — "

"Go on, Lainie, damn it!" Roman shouted, near tears himself. "And I'll want to see them ride out of town. Alone."

"You will." Lieght kept an eye on Wind River as the old man passed behind him. "You'll have a long, long time to regret it, too, if you fail to keep your end of the bargain."

"I won't, damn it!" Roman promised. "Just get her out of here!"

Newkirk shoved her toward the door. Sobbing, Lainie stumbled and would have fallen if it hadn't been for Wind River taking her arm. "Come on, Denver Gal," he said, wanting to get out before Lieght changed his mind and shot them all. "Your man's making one hell of a play. He don't want you to turn him down."

"But he . . . I . . . ."

"Shhh!"

"Keep it moving!" Newkirk ordered, prodding Wind River with his rifle.

Lainie glanced over her shoulder for one last look. Far, far away, a million miles away, framed by the double doors between the lobby and the dining room, Roman sat hunched over, the tommy gun pressed against the back of his neck.

And then they were outside and he was gone. The sunlight was brilliant, hurt the eyes as it reflected off the diamond-bright frozen snow. Wind River tried to pull Lainie along faster, as if the more quickly he was away from Elkhorn the more easily he could escape his own feelings of guilt. Lainie walked numbly, plodded up the street toward the barn. Newkirk followed them. Their footsteps crunched, sometimes squeaking on the hard, slippery crust. Lainie almost lost her footing when she turned to look back at the hotel.

"Ain't nothin' back there for you, sweetheart, so just keep on goin'." Newkirk leered at her. " 'Course if you want to slow up later . . . A man with five thousand dollars wouldn't be a bad start for a pretty little gal who's just lost her man."

Lainie caught her breath, turned around quickly. "Slow down," she whispered under her breath to Wind River.

"The hell you say," Wind River hissed back, tugging at her arm to hurry her along.

"Oh!" Lainie appeared to slip and fell to one knee before she could catch herself.

Newkirk stopped right behind her. "Get up," he growled, gesturing with the rifle. "You ain't hurt."

Feigning fear, Lainie looked up at him. "Don't hit me," she pleaded, hiding her elation.

"Jesus, Dora," Newkirk snorted impatiently. "I ain't gonna hit you, okay? Now let's go."

Lainie grabbed Wind River's hand for support, looked up apprehensively at Newkirk again, and struggled to her feet. She had been right! The tiny, circling dot she had seen high in the sky was actually there. They had a chance! An exaggerated limp slowed her as she let herself be led toward the barn. Hope grew with each second that passed. The shadow in the front of the barn was a deep purple in contrast to the blinding brilliance of the snow. It would be difficult for a man's eye to penetrate that darkness from the hotel. There it was she would have to find a reason to stop long enough and buy the time she so desperately needed.

Wind River lifted the plank bar from the doors, swung them open to form a short corridor leading into the black interior of the barn. Lainie let herself be led another two steps and then, hidden from the hotel by the open door as well as the heavy shadow, suddenly stopped and turned to face Newkirk.

"What the hell do you want now?" Newkirk snarled.

Lainie smiled seductively. "Just a little idea I had," she said.

"Jesus, Denver Gal, don't try nothing now," Wind River

pleaded, horrified. "They done give us our chance." He turned to Newkirk. "Look, mister, " he started to explain, and then stopped dead when he saw what Lainie had seen: a speck in the sky, a rapidly growing brown blur which meant they had been spied as well.

"Don't listen to him," Lainie said hurriedly. "Look, why don't the two of us take the money? It would be five thousand for each of us. I'd split it half and half with you."

Newkirk spat to one side. "Sorry, Dora. It's a little late to butter me up."

"No, it isn't!" She wanted desperately to look up but forced herself to keep her eyes on Newkirk's. "We have time. We could take the horses, go out the back way, and sneak behind the bank. By the time they figure out—"

"So that's where it's hid," Newkirk said, his eyes widening with greed. "The bank! That's rich, honey, but you just stepped in it for sure."

"You don't like my idea," Lainie asked, crestfallen.

"I like to eat my cake without worryin' about gettin' it all down my gullet. Lieght ain't a man to forgive and forget. Sorry."

"Well, I'm not," Lainie said. Newkirk looked at her, perplexed by her odd reply.

"Now!" Wind River yelled.

Lainie and Wind River dropped to the ground. Newkirk stared at them as if they had lost their minds. He had only a second to dwell on the matter, though, before a streaking bolt of taloned fury slammed into the back of his head.

Whap! A sound not unlike that of a melon dropped from a tree.

"Yeeaghh!" Newkirk squawked, flailing at the explosion of feathers atop his head. Like a skater out of control, his feet slipped out from under him and he lost his balance. The rifle flew from his hands and landed in front of Lainie, barrel pointed up, stock dug through the crusted snow

Lainie and Wind River scrambled to their feet. Newkirk landed with a thud. The falcon, screeching a cry of victory and revenge, took to the sky.

"Gahhh . . ." Newkirk groaned, and tried to rise.

"Gah, yourself," Lainie said coldly as she grabbed the rifle by the barrel, pulled it out of the snow, and swung it like a club.

Another melon. Newkirk's eyes rolled back in his head and he rolled over, unconscious.

"Good hit. Now, come on. Let's get out of here."

Lainie stared at Wind River in disbelief.

"Don't wrinkle your brows at me, girl. They called the game and dealt the cards. This ain't playtime. It's real. Here, give me the damn gun. I'll . . . Oh, for Chrissake! . . ." Frantic, he grabbed her coat and pulled her back behind the protection of the door. "Where the hell do you think you're goin'?"

"Back to the hotel," Lainie said, whirling and holding the gun ready to club him if necessary. "I'm going to free Roman."

"Oh, no," Wind River moaned. "You can't, girl. Little thing like you against those two? We got us a chance to skedaddle!"

"So what's stopping you?" Lainie asked, her eyes blazing with contempt.

Wind River's face flushed with embarrassment. Terrified, he peeked around the door to look at the hotel, then back to Lainie.

"Well?" Lainie said.

Fear turned to anger beneath her accusatory stare. "Nothing," Wind River spat at last, turning and stalking into the barn. "Nothing at all."

29

He had failed, Roman repeated to himself. He had done his best and failed. Lainie and Wind River had a chance, so it wasn't a total loss. Lieght would no doubt try to find them and quite possibly succeed, but that was a worry beyond his capacity to deal with. He had given them what he could. However sadly, the rest was up to them, unless . . .

The muscles in the back of his neck screamed with pain from the tension. There was one more thing, he thought, fighting his cramping neck. No matter what Lieght did to him, not telling where the money was meant Lainie had just that much more time. He wasn't sure how long he could hold out, but any delay would be worth it. The money wasn't all that well hidden, he knew, but finding it would take at least another hour or two. Two hours before Lieght started on him if he was lucky and Lieght kept his word, another one or two before the mobster gave up and pulled the trigger, another one or two to look for the money. Sweat trickled down the side of Roman's nose. He flexed his muscles and tried to find an easier way to sit. As few as two, as many as six. Christ! If only the damned Appaloosa wasn't so slow!

"Tie him up," Lieght suddenly said.

Roman almost jumped out of his skin. "I'm not going anywhere," he said, somehow managing to maintain his stoic façade. "You said I could watch them ride out," he added accusingly.

"You will. Tied." Lieght jerked his head toward Roman. "Hands behind his back, a separate knot for the thumbs. What the hell's keeping them?"

Nance stood, hitched up his trousers, and swaggered toward Roman. "Sim's probably gettin' himself a piece of that cake before he puts her on a horse. Be just like the son-of-a-bitch to—" He stopped dead in his tracks, and gulped.

Roman followed his line of vision, saw Lainie standing in the doorway to the kitchen. She held the rifle leveled at Nance. Lieght had just reached the window when some inner warning swung him around. Roman leaped upward as Nance looked back to Lieght for guidance, and slammed a fist into the side of the logger's head. In the same motion, he picked up his chair and hurled it at Lieght, just as the tommy gun swung into action.

The chair was heavy, made of wood and leather. Where he found the strength to throw it so far or hard, Roman would never know. The first burst of fire from the tommy gun caught it in midair, but only slowed it slightly. Splinters and ricocheting slugs whined through the air, but the chair had enough momentum to slam into Lieght, knock him off balance and the tommy gun out of his hands.

Roman hadn't waited to see what was happening. Ahead of him, Lainie was pointing the rifle at Lieght and squeezing the trigger, but the gun wouldn't fire. Roman leaped Nance just as Lieght recovered enough to unlimber his automatic. Bullets singing around him, Roman tackled Lainie and knocked her sprawling into the kitchen. Behind him, the last three rounds in the clip ripped the wooden sill, ricocheted over his head, and clanged into the cast-iron stove.

"Keep down!" Roman shouted, pushing Lainie farther to the side and rolling after her. "Out! Out" he screamed, dragging her to her feet and pushing her through the open back door.

The crust on the snow, strong enough to hold them if they had been walking, broke and slowed them down as they ran.

Roman grabbed the rifle with one hand and Lainie's wrist with the other, cut to the right, then to the left, and right again to take advantage of the cover offered by the broken wagons. Behind them, Lieght appeared in the doorway and cut loose with a new clip. All seven bullets chipped ice off the wagons and buried themselves in the snow before, its magazine emptied, the gun clicked on empty. "Now!" Roman ordered, already running up the rear slope toward the line of frozen aspens. They reached the trees and dove for cover just ahead of the first new rounds from the .45.

Lainie followed Roman deeper into the trees before she collapsed on a fallen tree. "It wouldn't fire," she panted, gasping for breath and shaking with fury. "The damn gun wouldn't fire!"

"Doesn't matter," Roman said, his voice still shaking. "Just being there was enough." He tried to work the pump, but the slide was clogged with soot and ashes. "The bastard never thought to clean his rifle. It's useless until I can take it apart, if I even can without any tools." His chest heaved as he tried to catch his breath. "Come on, " he said, pulling Lainie to her feet. "No time to rest. We've got to hide, find someplace to hole up until the sun sets."

"I know a place. The falls. There's a kind of cave behind the water."

Roman looked behind them. A line of craters in the snow delineated their path up to the point where they had walked the last few steps. "Let's go, then," he said, looking for their tracks on the glazed surface and having difficulty finding them. "We'll take a chance and walk. Make it harder for them to follow us." Gingerly, careful not to break the snow and holding on to tree trunks for support when they could, they started up the hill. "By the way," Roman said after they'd negotiated the first hundred yards successfully, "where's Wind River?"

"I tried to get him to come with me, but he wouldn't." Lainie's voice was heavy with disappointment, but she was too weary to be angry any longer. "He ran, I think. He's gone."

Newkirk staggered in through the front door. Nance was busy wiggling a broken tooth he'd knocked out on a chair when he fell. Lieght was inspecting the tommy gun and cursing under his breath. "You ain't gonna believe me when I tell you what happened," Newkirk said, rubbing a goose-egg-sized lump on his head.

"Fuck what happened," Lieght said, furious. "The past doesn't interest me. It's enough to know you somehow managed to let a helpless old man and a mere girl take your rifle. I should have sent a first-grader." The magazine had snapped off at its base and was beyond repair, under the circumstances. Lieght threw the tommy gun to one side, pulled a spare clip for the automatic out of his pocket, and started jamming cartridges in it. "Nance has an extra revolver. Take it and come on. We'll see if you can hunt any better than you can walk down a street."

Careful, mindful of the rifle Roman carried, they filed out the back door and ascended the slope. Lieght led the way for the first few, easy hundred yards, but stopped when the obvious tracks ended. "Which one of you is the best tracker?" he asked.

"Me, I guess," Nance allowed, moving up to take the lead.

"Then let's move out," Lieght said. "You," he added to Newkirk, "in front of me where I can keep an eye on you."

His face beet red with embarrassment, Newkirk scrambled after Nance. "It was the damnedest thing," he said, trying to explain, even though he knew no one would believe him. "This bird . . . I swear, this goddamn *bird* . . ."

30

Wind River counted to three as, one by one, Lieght and his men came into sight behind the hotel and trudged up the slope. Well concealed, he hunkered even farther behind the pile of hay he'd pushed to the front of the open loft and watched until they were well out of sight, then scrambled down the ladder and mounted the Appaloosa. The horse didn't like the crusted snow, but Wind River had wrapped his legs with rags so he wouldn't be cut, and walked him through the livery door and down the street.

The Great Northern Bank was hidden from any watching eyes on the opposite slope by the looming bulk of the hotel. Dismounting, Wind River walked quickly into the foyer, stopped, and looked around. An even film of dust covered everything. "Well now, let's see," he mumbled to himself. "If I wanted to hide ten thousand dollars where it would be safe . . . Hot damn!"

It was so obvious! Where did anybody put money when they left it in the bank? In the safe! And the safe, its pins rusty with long disuse, was set in the back wall. His heart beating wildly with excitement, Wind River hurried around the tellers' cages, grabbed the vault handle, and pulled with all his might. Slowly, groaning against its own great weight, the door swung open. "I knew it!" Wind River cackled, staring at the double set of footprints that, protected from the wind in the vault, led to a pile of old papers in the corner. A quick glance over his shoulder reassured him that he was still undiscovered. Ten thousand dollars! His! All his! Beside himself with unholy joy, Wind River kneeled by the papers and began to scatter them in every direction. "Oh, swee . . ."

The sentence trailed off in mid-word. Horrified, Wind River stared at the bag of money and the gun and belt that lay beside it.

"Pick it up," Creed said from the front of the vault.

Wind River leaped to his feet and spun around.

"Pick it up!"

"You did this," Wind River said, his voice hoarse.

Creed shrugged. "Maybe. Maybe not."

Wind River thought he might be going mad. "I don't believe that," he said with a nervous laugh.

"It's all the same to me," Creed said. "You believe what you want."

"You're damned right I will." Wind River backed up until his foot hit the valise of money. Creed wasn't doing anything, hadn't pulled open his shirt. He just stood there staring. Slowly, Wind River bent at the knees and groped for the handle. "I didn't ask them to come here," he said, rationalizing as much for himself as for Creed. "They got no claim on me. Fool kids, both of them. Should've known better. 'Sides, they got away. I seen 'em runnin' up the hill." His hand touched the gun instead of the valise, and he jerked it away as if the metal had burned him. "Had a gun, they did. Lieght won't catch 'em."

Creed puffed on his pipe. "Of course not."

"Of course not," Wind River mimicked angrily. "All these years, Creed. Why? Why now?" His voice rose to a shout that filled the vault. "What do you want from me, damn it? What do you want?"

"Nothing, you jug-headed, jackass-stubborn son-of-a-bitch!"

Wind River quailed. Creed never talked like that, never lost his temper.

"I *never* wanted anything. I just been hangin' around all these years until the time was ripe. Now it is, but seein' as you're too damn donkey dumb to see it, I'm callin' your attention to it."

"And what's that?"

Creed's eyes burned in the shadow cast by the cowl of his capote. "A chance, Wind River. *The* chance. Maybe the last one you'll get."

"I don't need your chance," Wind River said defiantly. "I got a whole bagful of my own right here at my feet."

"The chance I'm talkin' about is worth a hundred of them bags, younker," Creed said, his temper once more in check. "You know that same as I do."

Wind River's face turned as white as the snow. When he spoke, his voice was so weak it could barely be heard. "You don't know what you're askin', Creed. You don't know . . ."

Creed shook his head. "I'm not askin'. You are, Wind River. You are." He pushed back his cowl. His bald scalp shone in the dim light. "You've been askin' for thirty-five years, only you're too damn deaf to hear."

"No," Wind River whispered with every ounce of his being. "That ain't true."

"Listen, younker. If you've never listened in your life, listen now."

Wind River's lips were dry. He tried to wet them, but his tongue was like parchment. His eyes wide, he stared at Creed, then down at the gun and back to Creed. "I'm afraid, Aden," he finally said. "I'm afraid."

Creed nodded, understanding. "You're also the Wind River Kid."

31

Roman pressed a hand over his chest, as if in some fashion to muffle the resounding thudding sound his heart made. He was certain it echoed off the rocks. Behind him, Lainie trembled. They were both shivering from the drenching they'd received walking into the tiny grotto behind the falls. Roman stared at the outside world as one might when surfacing from the deepest sleep. Water shielded them and blinded them. The world, as seen through water, became a confusion of colors. Suddenly he tensed. Lainie, her arms around him, felt him stiffen, and only then heard the voice of Harry Lieght.

"I don't give a damn," he was saying. "They can't go too far. They're not dressed for the weather."

They were barely visible from inside the grotto. Nance was kneeling by the stream where it spilled out of the pond. Newkirk and Lieght were crossing the stream to approach the pond and the falls from the west. "They came this way," Nance said. "I'd bet on it." He rose and walked out onto the small, windowlike drifts. "Could have gone across the ice, I suppose."

"You could have missed where they turned off, too."

"Not hardly. You may not have much opinion of me, Mr. Lieght, but when it comes to huntin', I'm a natural-born tracker. I ain't missed nothing, I guarantee."

Newkirk hung back nervously, kept a jaundiced eye on the surrounding trees. Lieght had told him the girl had tried to fire his gun and it wouldn't work, but he still didn't like the idea of them having it. Who knew? Maybe she just didn't know how to take it off safety. What it added up to was stupidity. Lieght was crazy to find the money and was taking unnecessary chances. A light breeze drifted across the clearing, set the aspens chattering. Newkirk watched Lieght carefully. If there was some way he could sort of fade back and slip downslope before the others missed him, he might still have a chance. Moving fast, he might get to the money and the horses and mules and make a clean getaway. If the girl hadn't been lying, that was. The notion filled him with dismay: he couldn't leave. He had to stay. Softly, trying to minimize the squeak of his boots on the crusted snow, he moved a little farther along the edge of the pond.

Lieght was almost halfway to the falls before he stopped to search the silence. It didn't make sense. If they were running, he ought to be able to hear them; if walking, to have caught up with them. Which meant they were hiding. He looked back over his shoulder at Nance, who had worked his way around the bottom of the pond on the opposite side and had stopped to kneel again.

"I told you," Nance called softly, pointing to the ground. "They came this way. Headed straight for the falls, looks like." The trees were flocked with whiteness. All the world lay draped in pure vestments of snow. A new breeze stirred the aspens and pines. Clumps of frozen beauty dropped from wearying branches and made skittering sounds on the frozen snow. Lieght saw without seeing. His attention riveted on the falls, beauty passed him by. "Credit where credit is due, Nance," he said, peering at a shadow behind the falling water. "Let's see just how much." Smiling, he raised the Browning and pointed toward the falls.

"Pepperdine!"

Harry Lieght lowered the automatic and turned toward the eastern edge of the clearing. Behind the curtain of water, Roman recognized Wind River's voice. "Oh, my God!" Lainie whispered behind him.

Wind River stepped out of the trees and walked toward

the pond. He wore his overalls and plaid shirt and battered cap and new ostrich boots, of which he was proud. His gun was belted in place, high on his waist, and hung for a cross draw. "You been lookin' for me, Pepperdine?" he asked in a harshly resonant voice.

Lieght stared in amazement. The old man appeared not to notice Nance, standing to his left and on the same side of the pond, or Newkirk across the way, yet Lieght had the strangest sensation that the codger was aware of everything that lived or moved in the clearing. While Lieght watched, Wind River stopped at the edge of the pond. His hand hovered near the worn and polished bone grip of his navy Colt. Lieght slowly raised his automatic. "You *are* a crazy old fart," he said.

"No!" Roman stepped from behind the falls. Lainie emerged to stand beside him. Distracted for the merest fraction of a second, Lieght glanced to his left. Nance and Newkirk had no such excuse.

And the Wind River Kid slapped leather.

32

Years later, in describing it to his and Lainie's children, Roman was able to slow down the fight and expand the seconds into minutes and the minutes into lifetimes.

One second.

Wind River's hand blurred in a never-forgotten motion of deadly economy. The Colt was holstered, then filled his hand. Smoothly, the gun rose and bucked, and Harry Lieght staggered. Astonished, the pain as yet unfelt, he sank to one knee. To his right, Newkirk was in the process of raising his revolver when Wind River pivoted and fired again.

Two seconds.

A red mist blossomed from his face, and Newkirk arched backward through the air. Wind River was already spinning to his left, feeling but not caring as hot lead seared the side of his cheek. One shot was the extent of Nance's stomach for the fight, and he turned to run. Wind River's gun spat flame for the third time.

Three seconds.

His spine smashed, Nance tripped and dove over a log. His head broke through the crusted snow. The softer stuff beneath the surface filled his mouth and stifled his scream. At the same time, Newkirk landed in a clump of bushes. Blood masked the remains of his face, and snow from the branches above settled on him and turned crimson as it soaked up the discharge of his mortal wound. A cursing Lieght rose from the ground and charged toward Wind River.

Four seconds.

Lieght fired as he ran. Gun blazing, he crashed through the ice and roared through the shallows like a colossus. Wind River did not move, did not flinch as bullets furrowed the air around him. Unperturbed, he aimed and squeezed off a round. Firing but no longer aiming, Lieght stumbled.

Five, six, seven seconds.

Wind River fired again. Lieght doubled over in the middle of the pond. Wind River thumbed back the hammer and watched while Lieght collapsed beneath the water and then, water streaming from his overcoat and spewing from his lips, struggled back to his feet. The water came to just below his knees. Water ran from his head, drip drip dripped from his jaw. There was a hole in the side of his coat, another in the middle of his vest. His left arm hung useless. His fedora was gone, floating upside down. He held his right hand palm upward. It was empty. "I dropped my gun," he said.

The eighth and last second.

"That's too damn bad," said the Wind River Kid, and he fired and shot Harry Lieght in the heart. The gangster was slammed backward by the force of the bullet and sat in water that came up to his chest. Then, his overcoat weighing him down, he settled over onto his side.

Quiet.

The sulphurous smell of gunsmoke.

Together, Roman and Lainie stared at the carnage, at dead men blasted to bloody ruin, and at the harmless old spook who lived alone in Elkhorn and talked of ghosts and bears and times past, never to come again.

The Wind River Kid.

Blue lightning with a gun.

HARRY LIEGHT
BORN??? DIED OCT. 8, 1927
HE DROPPED HIS GUN

There were three new graves on the hill above Elkhorn.
Wind River stood back and admired his handiwork; uneven
printing was the best that could be done with hard wood and
a dull blade. The day before had been a burying day, the
night one for carving proper markers. Now another clear
morning and bright sun attacked the thick layer of new
snow. All three were officially buried. His task completed,
Wind River wiped the sweat off his forehead.

Down in Elkhorn, Nance's jenny and the three mules
Roman had bought were tethered in front of the hotel. A few
yards downslope, Roman and Lainie, mounted and ready to
ride, waited for Wind River to finish.

"Glad you're takin' that white mule," Wind River said
gruffly, letting the shovel down gently so he wouldn't startle
the horses.

"He didn't want to stay." Roman grinned. "Told me old
gunfighters are the spirits of white mules, and he won't feel
safe until he's shaken the dust of Elkhorn from his hooves."

Wind River had to smile at that. There was hope for the

boy yet. "Remember to muffle their hooves the way I showed you," he warned. "And walk 'em through town after one in the morning. Don't sell 'em, now, until you get to Idaho Springs. Don't nobody need to know who they belonged to. That bill of sale I doctored up for you should do the trick."

"I'll remember," Roman said. He leaned from the saddle and stuck out his hand. Wind River took it, shook it solemnly. "Thank you, Wind River."

There was nothing else to say. You either owe a man your life or you don't, Roman would tell his children, years later.

"Ride on the dry side, younker. Take care."

Roman wheeled his horse and, without waiting for Lainie, trotted down the slope. Wind River kept his eyes on Lainie. Tears streamed down her cheeks. When she started to dismount, he held up one hand. "Hold on, Denver Gal. Leave that hurricane deck and it'll be rough goin' for us both. You got your man waitin'."

"But . . ."

Wind River grabbed his cap by the brim and slapped it across her horse's rump. The animal whinnied and leaped away. "Christmas and the Fourth of July, Denver Gal," Wind River shouted over the pounding of the mare's hooves. "Don't forget!"

Lainie held on to the saddle horn for dear life. "I love you, Wind River," she called, trying to look over her shoulder. "I love you!"

Alone again, Wind River raised his hand and waved farewell.

34

The sky, an inverted blue glazed bowl marred by nothing more than a circling, jealous dot.

Mountains of seamed granite.

A valley of winter awaiting spring.

A sleeping bear hidden in a deep cave until the warmth comes back to wake it.

A spotted horse slow of hoof and set of mind.

A town checkered with frost.

Echoes intangible.

And two old men sitting on a porch.

Aden Creed, ancient mountain man, puffs on his long-stemmed clay pipe. Wind River, rocking next to him, enjoys the sun and the Chinook winds that quickly carry off the snow.

"Chinooks'll trick you," Creed says. "Get the blood runnin'. A man leaves his cold-weather gear on the back of his mule, and then behind the Chinook, a norther. Many a man been found frozen in the act of reachin' for his mule."

Wind River continues cleaning his six-gun.

"Where you gonna put it?" Creed asks.

"Over the hearth next to the Hawken. Unless you got a mind to object."

"Naw. Sounds good to me."

"Heard the bear again last night."

"Some things don't change," Creed opines.

"Yeah. Let him come." Wind River rocks for a moment. "Is it gonna hurt when it does happen?"

The question takes Creed by surprise. "What?" he asks. "Oh! That. No. Easy as eatin' sugared peaches. Don't worry. I'll be there to help."

"Thanks."

"What are friends for?"

Wind River looks sideways at the mountain man. "Creed? I never had much tongue oil when it come to . . . Well, that is . . . About Angelina. It never amounted to anything. It was only once, and my first time at that. I wasn't really so all fired hot at . . ." Bumble-tongued, he pauses, searches for the right words. "What I'm tryin' to say . . ."

"Forget it," Creed says. "What is a petal plucked from the flower of womanhood among friends?"

"But . . ."

"You talk too much." Creed pulls the cowl of his capote forward. Only his nose and the bowl of his pipe stick out. As far as he is concerned, the conversation is ended.

"Me?" Wind River blurts. "Me! Why, after all the dadblamed stories you been fillin' my ears with for all these years, and I talk too much? Well, let me tell you a thing or two, Mr. High and Mighty   "